After Innocence

BRENDA JOYCE

After Innocence

AVON BOOKS NEW YORK

AFTER INNOCENCE is an original publication of Avon Books. This work has never before appeared in book form. This work is a novel. Any similarity to actual persons or events is purely coincidental.

AVON BOOKS
A division of
The Hearst Corporation
1350 Avenue of the Americas
New York, New York 10019

Copyright © 1994 by Brenda Joyce Senior
Back cover photo by Volkmann © 1994
Published by arrangement with the author
Library of Congress Catalog Card Number: 94-94086
ISBN: 0-380-77572-7

Printed in the U.S.A.

This one's for Marjorie Braman, my editor and my friend.

Not only because of her enthusiasm, her energy,
her loyalty and support,
but because she understands my need to be challenged,
because she encourages me to take risks,
because she pushes me to be
the best that I can be—
and because she is one great editor!
Thank you, Marjorie.

Prologue

New York City, 1890

"Sofie, where are you?"

The little girl cringed. She set her mouth stubbornly and did not move from the small corner in her bedroom, trapped between the cheerfully papered wall and the adult-sized bed.

Footsteps sounded, approaching. "Sofie?" Her mother's tone was sharp, annoyed. "Sofie! Where are you?"

Sofie inhaled hard, tears filling her eyes, as the door banged open and Suzanne appeared in the doorway. *If only Papa were here. If only he hadn't gone away. If only he would come home.*

"Sofie! When I call, you come! What are you doing? I have something important to tell you!" Suzanne said in a strident voice.

Sofie reluctantly met her mother's gaze, which quickly turned furious, spotting the paper at her feet.

"What is this?" Suzanne cried, bending. She snatched the sheet of paper, brilliantly, boldly colored, from her. Still, even to an adult, there was no mistaking the figures in the drawing, which, while childish, were surprisingly vivid and real. The picture was composed of a man, whose proportions were gigantic, heroic, and a very small blond child. Both characters were running, the child after the adult.

"Look at you—you're a mess!" Suzanne cried, tearing the pastel painting in two. "Stop drawing your father—do you hear me? Stop it!"

Sofie dug her back more deeply into the corner. She said nothing. She wanted her papa. How she wanted him. How she missed him.

Her big, handsome papa, always laughing, always hugging her, always telling her how much he loved her and how good and smart and beautiful she was.

Please come home, Papa, Sofie thought.

1

Suzanne made an effort to relax. She held out her hand. "Come here, dear," she said, softly now.

Sofie didn't hesitate. She gave her palm to her mother, who pulled her to her feet. "Sofie," Suzanne began, then hesitated. "You must know. I have bad news. Jake is not coming back."

Sofie recoiled, jerking free of her mother. "No! He promised! He promised me!"

Suzanne's beautiful jaw flexed. Her eyes were hard. "He is not coming back. He cannot. Sofie—your father is dead."

Sofie stared. She understood death. A few months ago her cat had died and Sofie had found it, stiff and unmoving, its eyes open but unseeing. But her papa, Papa could not be like that!

"He is not coming back," Suzanne repeated firmly. "He is dead." Suzanne grimaced. "Just what he deserved, if you ask me," she muttered to no one in particular.

"No!" Sofie shrieked. "No, I do not believe you!"

"Sofie!"

But it was too late. Sofie flew from the room, as fast as her gangly legs would carry her. She raced down the corridor of the huge, frightening home her father had built so proudly for them, a home they had moved into only a few months before he had left. He could not be dead! He had promised to come home!

"Sofie, come back!" Suzanne was shouting.

Sofie ignored her. The marble stairs were ahead of her. She did not care, did not slow. Sofie hit the first step, the second. It was only when she lost her balance that she realized she should have slowed much sooner. With a cry she fell, tumbling down one step after another, like a Raggedy Ann doll, limbs sprawling, hair flying, around and around, down and down, until she landed with a final thump on the floor below.

And there she lay, unmoving.

Sofie was stunned. But whether from the fall or the news of her father's death, she hardly knew. Slowly her head stopped spinning and her vision cleared. She did not move. *Papa was dead. Oh, Papa*, she wept.

She became aware of an excruciating pain shooting through her ankle, and when she sat up, it was so intense that white light blinded her. She panted and the light disappeared, but the pain did not. Still, instead of holding her leg, she held her chest with both hands, curling into a ball, weeping.

"Miss Sofie, Miss Sofie, are you all right?" The housekeeper came rushing to her.

Sofie looked up the stairs at her mother, who stood silent and frozen on the landing two floors above, her face white, her eyes wide. Sofie looked at the ground. "I am fine, Mrs. Murdock," she lied. Her mother didn't love her, and Papa was dead—how could she survive? "You are hurt," Mrs. Murdock cried, bending to help her up.

"If she is hurt, it is her own fault," Suzanne said coldly from above. Glaring at Sofie, she turned away.

Sofie gazed after her mother, starting to cry again. *I am hurt, Mama. Please come back!* But she did not call after her.

Mrs. Murdock lifted her to her feet after Suzanne was gone. Sofie could not stand on her right foot and leaned heavily against the kind housekeeper. She had to bite her lip to keep from screaming now.

"I'll see you to bed and get the doctor," Mrs. Murdock said.

"No!" Sofie cried, panicked. Tears started to stream down her cheeks again. She knew Suzanne would be furious if she was really hurt, and she was sure that if she rested, it would go away. And maybe, maybe if she was good, if she was very good, if she stopped drawing and did as she was told, Suzanne would love her more. "No, no, I am fine!"

But she was not fine. She would never be fine again.

Part One

The Prodigal
Daughter

1

Newport Beach, 1901

$\mathcal{J}$t was a glorious day. Sofie no longer regretted leaving the city in order to attend her mother's weekend beach party.

A large sketchbook in one hand, charcoal in the other, Sofie paused on the crest of a dune to take in the view. The Atlantic Ocean lapped the shore, dappled from the sun. Above, gulls wheeled. The sky was a nearly blinding shade of blue. Sofie smiled, lifting her face, shadowed by a straw hat, towards the sunlight. It was moments like these that made Sofie realize that there was life outside of her studio's four walls.

Then the throbbing of her ankle brought her back to her senses. She should not linger. Coming down to the beach could still prove to be a mistake. She did have a wonderful preliminary rendering of Newport's shore, which she would begin in oils as soon as she returned to the city, but an entire evening awaited her, and it would be even less pleasant for her if she was limping more than was usual. Suzanne had a houseful of weekend guests, and Sofie could not help but feel some dread. In truth, if she had her choice, she would lock herself in her room and paint. But she did not have her choice, she had promised Suzanne to be her most sociable self, and Sofie intended to try her best to please her mother.

Sighing, Sofie imagined the long evening ahead as she began to descend the dune. She wondered if she would know any of her mother's guests. She hoped so. As immersed in her world of art as she was, Sofie rarely ventured out into society, and could not converse with strangers and mere acquaintances with the casual ease that seemed to be second nature to everyone else. Her younger sister, Lisa, had once told her that one conversed upon whatever topic was at hand or in sight—such as the beautiful porcelain vase one stood near. It sounded much easier than it actually was. Sofie decided not to worry about the impending evening. No one expected her to be the belle of the ball.

Sofie moved awkwardly down the scrub-covered dune in her uneven gait, and after several feet, paused to rest. Trying to catch her breath, she glanced about and her eye caught a flash of bright white. Sofie looked again. She glimpsed a man strolling down another path in the dunes just below her. Like herself, he was leaving the beach, but he had not seen her.

The sight of him was so arresting that Sofie froze, completely forgetting herself and the rest of her surroundings. He was bareheaded, his thick black hair a startling contrast to the stark white of his finely tailored linen sack jacket. He wore it casually open, its sides billowing in the breeze, and his hands were shoved deep into the pockets of his pale cream-hued trousers. He was a large man, Sofie could see that, for he was tall and broad-shouldered, but he moved with the grace of someone much smaller, somehow as lithe and sleek as a black panther she had once seen in the Bronx Zoo. Sofie was captivated. From this distance she could just make out his tanned features, which seemed to be extraordinarily handsome. She had to paint him. Abruptly she sat down, flipping open her notebook. Her heart thundering in excitement, she began to draw.

"Edward! Wait!"

Sofie's hand froze as, startled, she watched a woman flying up the path after the stranger. Sofie recognized her neighbor, Mrs. Hilary Stewart. Why on earth would Hilary be running after this man in such a fashion, with her skirts lifted high in one hand, shamelessly revealing long, white-stockinged legs? Then it dawned on Sofie what Hilary might be about, and she blanched, shocked.

Sofie sternly told herself that it was not her affair and that she should go. Quickly she tried to finish the study of the stranger, adding a few last strokes. Then the sound of his voice, male and low, silken and baritone, made her hand still. Sofie lifted her head, finding herself helplessly ensnared by the masculine sound, involuntarily straining to hear.

Hilary was clutching his shoulders. She swayed a little, as if pushed by the breeze—or as if waiting for his kiss.

Sofie's heart beat double time. It was as she had thought—as she had feared. She dug her fingers into the warm sand, her sketch forgotten, knowing she must go before she saw something she had no right to see—but she was unable to move, absurdly paralyzed.

Hilary's throaty laughter sounded. Sofie's eyes widened. Hilary slowly unbuttoned her pin-striped jacket.

* * *

He wondered if he was growing old before his time—he was certainly too old for this. Africa had not solely been responsible for jading him, but it had certainly convinced him that life's comforts were worth waiting for. He had no intention of fornicating in the sand when cool, clean sheets would be available later. Besides, Hilary Stewart had only left his bed a few hours ago.

His smile was wry. He had met Hilary at a party a few weeks ago almost immediately upon his return to the city. He learned that she had married a much older man just a few years ago and was now newly widowed. Edward preferred widows; they tended to enjoy sinning without feeling guilt or making demands. The attraction between them had been mutual, and they had been carrying on ever since.

Now they were both guests at the Ralstons' summer home. Hilary was undoubtedly responsible for his invitation, but Edward did not mind. He liked her outside of bed as well as inside it, and the city was hell in the summertime. Suzanne Ralston, their hostess, had kindly given them adjoining rooms, and last night Hilary had preoccupied him from midnight until dawn. Yet apparently Hilary was far less sated than he was.

He wondered when his enthusiasm, once boundless when it came to pretty, available women, had begun to die.

Still, he was a man, and his gaze flitted from her brown bedroom eyes to her pale, white hands as they worked the buttons of her jacket free. Hilary was ravishing and voluptuous; despite his better intentions, knowing her as he did, his loins stirred.

"Darling, this might be indiscreet," Edward drawled.

Hilary's only answer was a coy smile as she pulled open her fitted jacket. She wore nothing underneath, not even a corset. Her breasts were large and milk white, the nipples ruby red.

Edward's mouth twisted and he sighed. Still, he slipped one hand around her waist as his other palm cupped her weight. "I'll meet you later tonight," he told her in a low, somewhat husky voice.

She moaned, arching her neck back. His thumb moved over her nipple, methodical and skilled. She moaned. "Edward, I am so mad about you, I simply cannot wait."

Her skin was silk, and for another moment he fondled her, too much of a hedonist not to enjoy what he was doing, his trousers becoming painfully tight. For a moment he was quite tempted and he debated; then he flashed his dimples. "We're both old enough to understand anticipation, darling," he said, kissing one nipple lightly, then pulling her jacket closed. Quickly and efficiently he slipped each black button into its frog.

She gripped his wrists. "Edward—I don't want to wait. I'm not sure I *can* wait."

"Of course you can wait," he murmured, his smile quick. "We both know it will be better if you do."

Her hand snaked out and she gripped his steel-hard erection. "How can *you* wait?" she whispered.

"Honey, rolling in the sand is *uncomfortable*."

She sighed with frustration, with resignation. "I'm afraid you'll go back to southern Africa and I'll lose you."

He laughed, prying her hand free—with more than a little reluctance. "Not a chance in hell," he said, meaning it. Edward put his arm around her shoulders to pull her forward for a quick, good-natured kiss. Instead a flash of movement caught his attention and he started.

His gaze swiftly sifted through the scrub-covered dunes just above and beyond Hilary. His eyes widened. Crouched in the dunes above them was a voyeur.

He swallowed his surprise, quickly looking away. But the sight of a pair of wide, avid eyes in a pretty oval face remained in his mind. The voyeur was a young lady with a blue-ribboned straw hat, apparently fascinated with them.

Hilary now gripped his wrists, he still had one arm around her, and his erection was suddenly the size of a cannon.

Edward was swept with a rush of excitement. He pulled Hilary close, wondering how much the voyeur had already seen and if she would go away now, and kissed her. It struck him that he was truly depraved. For he was far more excited by the thought of some young lady watching him making love than he was by the prospect of the actual act itself. Fornicating in a bed of sand no longer daunted him.

He kissed Hilary, acutely aware of being watched. He kissed her deep and openmouthed, stroking her tongue with his, pressing her up against his rock-hard cock, until she was moaning loudly and clinging to him, her knees so weak, he had to hold her up. When he broke away he saw that the intruder was frozen and mesmerized. She had not moved from her crouched position behind the scrubby bush, but her hat had blown off and tawny golden hair blew around her face. Even from the distance separating them, he could feel *her* excitement, too. She hadn't realized that he had seen her.

His hand flicked down and quickly he worked the buttons of his trousers open, his breathing coming harsh and fast. His mind was disapproving even as his manhood sprang free. He heard a gasp and knew damn well that it had not come from Hilary, whose eyes were closed.

"C'mon, sweet," he whispered, nipping her neck even as his conscience sternly berated him for his appalling behavior. But he couldn't stop seeing the voyeur with his mind's eye, couldn't stop seeing what she must be witnessing. He closed Hilary's hand around him. He found her mouth again. He rained kisses down her throat to her collarbone and lower, working the frogs free as he did so, finally taking one large red nipple deep into his mouth. Hilary collapsed, but Edward was prepared and he caught her, slowly sliding her down to the sand.

A moment later he dropped down to his knees, lifting Hilary's skirts and sliding deeply into her in one smooth, practiced thrust. As he moved inside her, fighting for self-control that should have been second nature after the previous night's excess, he was aware of the blood boiling inside his veins, expanding there. He felt as if there were two women lying beneath him. Suddenly he wanted to know who the tawny-haired stranger was. And then he could take it no more, and even as he was undone, he glanced up and glimpsed a wide-eyed face framed by golden hair. When he looked up again, sometime later, the voyeur was gone.

Edward closed his eyes. What had become of him? Suddenly he was ashamed, and worse, he was frightened. It occurred to him that his black reputation was not as exaggerated as he liked to think.

Sofie tripped many times in her haste to get back to the house. There was a croquet game being played on the back lawn, but she did not want to be seen. She must not be seen. Not now, not like this, not after what *she* had seen. Her face was hot and flushed, she could not breathe normally, and everyone, especially Suzanne, would instantly comprehend that something was wrong and demand to know just what.

Sofie avoided the back lawn even though it meant a much longer walk to the house. Instead she hugged the dunes until she came to the tennis court, which was, thankfully, empty. She could no longer stand the pain in her right ankle, which had grown worse with every step. With a small cry, she collapsed in the sand just behind the court, covering her face with her hands.

She did not know how she could have done such a thing? When she realized that she had stumbled across two lovers—one of them her lifelong neighbor, dear God— she should have turned and fled. But she hadn't. She had lost all control of her body and her mind. She had stayed. She had stayed until the very end.

Sofie trembled wildly, reaching for her leg. *What was it like, to be kissed like that? What was it like, to be in the arms of such a man?*

Sofie shut off her wayward thoughts, gripping her ankle. That she had stayed to watch was horrible enough, but to be thinking in such terms was even worse. She had never indulged in such speculation before—now was not the time to start. She would never know what it was like, and that was that.

Sofie held her ankle, moaning, as tears filled her eyes, but whether from the anguish afflicting her lower leg or from something far more wrenching, she did not wish to know.

Sofie blinked back her tears resolutely. They hadn't seen her, so her terrible secret was safe. At least, Hilary hadn't seen her. For one brief instant she had thought the man had glimpsed her, at the end, but she knew that she must have imagined it in her distress, otherwise he would have cried out in shock instead of passion and stopped what he was doing.

Sofie began to massage her aching ankle. She must not think about what he had been doing, or how he had looked while doing it. In truth, that stranger had been a glorious sight. Now Sofie understood why women were forbidden to attend classes using nude male models at the Academy.

She grimaced and slowly got to her feet. Pain shot through her ankle right up her thigh to her hip, finally distracting her. She bit her lip, refusing to cry out. Suzanne would say it was her own fault for going down to the beach unaided in the first place.

But sometimes Sofie grew so tired of being confined, of not being able to do what everyone else took for granted. And when she worked, she could not bear company, outside that of a model, if she was using one, or an instructor. And Sofie had spent the past two and a half months in the city, a fact that had made this day at the shore even more inviting, enough so that she had relinquished all of her customary caution and common sense. So rarely did she find the opportunity to work *en plein air*, and so rarely at the beach. Foolishly she had thought she might make such a journey without mishap— how wrong she had been!

Sofie shook the sand from the ruffled cuffs of her white shirtwaist. At least she was breathing evenly now, and her hands no longer trembled quite so much. She wondered who the stranger on the beach was. His first name was Edward, which meant nothing to her. Sofie closed her eyes. "You fool," she whispered aloud. A man like that would never look twice at a woman both lame and eccentric like herself.

* * *

"Mrs. Ralston?"

Suzanne's pleasant smile was automatic and she turned, poised before wide, open French doors. Behind her was a brick patio, below that the sweeping lawns, where some of her guests played croquet. The mid-sized salon she had paused in now was shady and cool. Sofie's mother watched the slightly chubby young man approach, trying to recall his name.

She did remember that he was a poor distant cousin of Annette Marten's, recently graduated from Harvard law school and about to open a private practice in New York. Annette was abroad, so she had asked Suzanne if she would invite her cousin to one of her weekend house parties, in order to introduce him to her society guests. Bachelors were always welcome, even if impoverished and especially if blue-blooded. "Hullo, Mr. Marten. Are you enjoying yourself?"

His smile was engaging, making Suzanne realize that if he lost some weight, he would be attractive. "Very much, Mrs. Ralston. I could never thank you enough for inviting me. And your home is stunning." He was wide-eyed.

Suzanne winced inwardly—he was definitely *gauche*. "My home is hardly as grand as those of my neighbors, Henry." She had finally recalled his name. "But thank you for your kindness." Her veiled warning to be less enthusiastic and more sophisticated was the least she could do for Annette.

"Mrs. Ralston, I do believe I saw your daughter going to the beach." He flushed.

Suzanne was not surprised that he would be interested in Lisa, who, although only seventeen, already had many admirers, all lined up to court her next year in earnest. Her dark beauty was compounded by her large trust. "Lisa was at the beach? I thought she was playing tennis this afternoon." How to tell this young man that he was reaching above himself? He was either dim-witted or ambitious, Suzanne had yet to decide.

But then Henry startled her. "No, Mrs. Ralston, it was your daughter Sofie I saw, not your stepdaughter."

Suzanne started.

"I mean," he fumbled, "I thought it was Sofie. After all, we have yet to be introduced. She has blondish hair and she is of medium height and stature." He was anxious. "I was hoping for a proper introduction."

Suzanne still stared, knowing she had been set up by her friend Annette. While Henry Marten undoubtedly needed introductions for his new law practice, he had come here to sniff after her daughter. Not only was Sofie of a marriageable age, having turned twenty in May, it was well known that her father's estate, left in trust for her, was adequate. Indeed, after his death, the exact size of Jake O'Neil's estate had shocked everyone, not least of all Suzanne.

She still could not figure out how a common Irish laborer-turned-builder had managed to amass assets of close to a million dollars in the short six years they were together.

"Mrs. Ralston?"

Suzanne recovered, trying not to tremble, but whether she was angry because she could not think of Jake without becoming furious, especially in regard to his estate, or because this upstart had come to court her daughter, she did not know. Suzanne plastered a smile on her face. "You must be mistaken. Sofie would not go to the beach."

Henry stared. "B—But I am certain it was her."

"Was she limping?"

Henry started. "I beg your pardon?"

"Surely you know that she has a dreadful limp."

"I was told she has a slightly uneven gait, the result of an unfortunate childhood accident."

Suzanne knew why Annette had been so charitable when discussing Sofie with her cousin, when she had never been charitable towards her and her limp before. Suzanne managed a smile. "Her limp *is* the result of a terrible childhood accident. When she was nine years old she fell down a flight of stairs. Her ankle was broken and never healed correctly; it is quite twisted. Annette did not tell you that my daughter is a cripple?"

Henry had become increasingly ashen as Suzanne spoke. "No."

Suzanne said, her smile more genuine now, "Of course, I am pleased to introduce you to her. Although she is twenty, she has never had a suitor."

"I . . . I see."

"Come—let us find her, shall we?" Suzanne touched his arm lightly.

By the time Sofie arrived at the kitchen entrance of the house, she was not just exhausted from the painful aching of her ankle, she was distraught. She had left her sketchbook at the beach.

Sofie's work was the most important facet of her life, her *raison d'être*, and she had never carelessly left her notebook behind before. That she had done so now was just another indication of how agitated she was by having seen the two lovers together.

She paused inside the narrow hall, thankful for the coolness inside. One of the servants passed her and paused to ask her if she was all right. And to tell her that Suzanne was looking for her.

Sofie was certain that she looked a sight, and knew that her mother would remark it, as well as her distress. Of course, Suzanne would never guess at the cause of her upset.

Her limp much more pronounced than usual, Sofie followed the hall to where it entered the house's central foyer and found her mother standing in the green and white salon, conversing with a young man.

"Sofie! There you are! We have been looking for you everywhere. Henry said you were at the beach. Is that true?" Suzanne's brows were raised as she took in her daughter's disheveled appearance.

Sofie paused as her mother moved towards her, the young man following closely behind. Suzanne was both an elegant and beautiful woman, her figure willowy and perfect, her hair dark, her skin as pale as ivory, and she was only thirty-six. Sofie had realized some time ago that she had been conceived when her mother was only sixteen. Often she had imagined how her beautiful mother had been swept off her feet by her handsome, charismatic father, Jake O'Neil. As often, she had imagined what their life would have been like if Jake had not been forced to flee New York fourteen years ago. How she missed him, and loved him, even to this day.

Sofie hoped her smile appeared genuine. "I am sorry, Mother. I was at the beach sketching."

Suzanne blinked. "Alone?"

Sofie nodded.

Suzanne turned towards the man, who seemed quite nervous. "Did I tell you that my daughter is also an artist? She studies by day at the Academy and often paints all night in her studio at home. She is pursuing a career in art."

Sofie blinked at her mother, who never spoke about her professional intentions publicly. While almost a quarter of her class at the Academy were other young women, equally as dedicated as Sofie, it was still considered very odd for a woman to be pursuing art instead of a husband. She glanced at the young man, who had managed to shake his head no. She realized why he was dismayed.

"Sofie is very talented," Suzanne said, smiling. "Dear, show us what you have done today."

Sofie froze, recalling her sketchbook, left at the beach, and why it had been left there, and her heart skidded uncontrollably. "My notebook is in my room," she managed. "I would be glad to show it to you another time." But she stared at Suzanne, wondering what she was about. Her mother did not approve at all of her art, especially recently, and would not normally suggest showing it to her guests.

"I want you to meet Henry Marten, dear," Suzanne said, guiding him forward. "He is a cousin of Annette's. He has just graduated from law school and he will soon be opening up his own law practice."

Sofie smiled, forcing her attention to the young man, who appeared uncomfortable and ill at ease. She extended her hand, guessing at the source of his discomfort. He probably thought that Suzanne was matchmaking, which she was not. Sofie had not even debuted. How could she when she could not even dance?

Not that it mattered. Sofie had always aspired to being a professional artist. She had never been so naive as to think that a man might want to take a cripple for a wife, especially an art-mad one. She and Suzanne had agreed years ago that Suzanne would not push her onto the marriage mart, that they would not seek a husband for her. It would be too humiliating, and as success was obviously impossible, Sofie would devote herself to her real love, instead.

And it was for the best. When Sofie turned twenty-one, she would go to Paris. There she would continue her studies of art, perhaps even study with someone as great as Paul Cézanne or Mary Cassatt, two great artists whom she vastly admired.

Sofie looked at Henry Marten, who could not know that she was not interested in marriage, who was pale facing her, thinking himself a prospective beau. Sofie wished she were in her room, painting. But she took a deep breath and smiled too brightly and said, "How do you do, Mr. Marten. And congratulations. Where did you graduate from?"

Henry took her hand, dropped it immediately. "Nice to meet you, Miss O'Neil. I . . . er . . . Harvard."

Suzanne excused herself with a smile, and Henry Marten appeared even more distraught once they were alone. Sofie felt her cheeks heating, wishing her mother had not put her in this awkward spot. "That is a grand achievement, sir."

He stared at her, wet his lips. "Yes, thank you."

Sofie forced a smile again. "It is no easy feat to be accepted there, is it?"

Still he stared. "No, it isn't."

"How proud you must be." She shifted her weight again to relieve her aching ankle. She did not suggest that they sit, because she wanted to leave, to find Lisa. Her notebook would still be at the beach, and she *must* recover her study of the dashing, dark stranger named Edward.

"Shall we . . . er . . . walk, Miss O'Neil?"

Sofie took a deep breath and smiled again, bravely. "Oh, ordinarily I would love to, but I am afraid that I must leave you to rest in my room if I am to regain my appearance for this evening."

He hesitated, clearly relieved. "Of course, Miss O'Neil."

Sofie smiled, as relieved, then quickly they separated, rushing off in opposite directions.

"Sofie—it is not there!" Lisa cried, closing Sofie's bedroom door behind her.

Sofie jerked. She was soaking her ankle in a salted footbath, clad only in a cotton wrapper. "But it must be! You did not look in the right place!"

Lisa, small and dark-haired and exquisitely beautiful, exclaimed, "I did! I took the path that starts near the tennis court, and I went all the way to where you can see the ocean from the crest of the last dune, as you instructed— where you can see another path below. It was not there. I found your hat, though."

"Oh, dear," Sofie cried, dismayed and gripping her chair. "Someone has taken my study? But who? And why?"

"I really did look everywhere," Lisa said.

Sofie barely heard her. "How will I paint him now?"

Lisa touched Sofie's hand. "Paint him? Paint who?"

Sofie stared at her stepsister, at a loss.

Lisa gazed at her inquiringly.

Sofie realized what she had said. She took a deep, calming breath. "I saw this very debonair man walking on the lower path while I was on the dune sketching, and I did a rendering of him. He did not see me, of course." She knew she was blushing. The skin on her face was warm. She felt as if omitting the entire truth was akin to lying, which it was not. But she could never tell her younger sister what she had really seen.

And what had happened earlier that day on the beach still refused to quit her memory. She could not stop herself from remembering him, nor could she cease thinking about what he had been doing with lovely Hilary. Even now, shamelessly, she could see his expression of rapture at the very end. Her thoughts were so thoroughly indecent, so thoroughly wicked, so unnerving . . . Sofie could not believe she was so consumed with them— with him. And all afternoon since she had finally retired to her room, she had planned her painting of him, debating composition and coloring. She intended to change what she had seen just slightly for dramatic purposes.

"Who was he?" Lisa asked with real interest.

"I do not know. She called him Edward."

"She? He was not alone?"

Sofie wished she could take back her words. "No," she said, not looking at Lisa. How could she have let that fact slip?

But Lisa had sat down hard on the edge of Sofie's chair, crowding her. "You must mean Edward Delanza," she cried in excitement.

Lisa's words stirred up a spark of both horror and anticipation. "Who is Edward Delanza?"

"I met him last night before supper—oh, how I wish you had been there! If only you had arrived yesterday instead of today!"

Sofie fervently hoped that the man she had seen on the beach that afternoon was not a weekend guest at the house. Hopefully she would never see him again. She would certainly never be able to look that man in the eye.

Sofie's insides began to curdle. "He is dark and handsome?"

Lisa gave her a look. "Far more than handsome. He is devastating! Dashing!" She lowered her voice and leaned towards Sofie. "*He is dangerous.*"

Sofie was ashen. No—Lisa could not be talking about the man she had seen on the beach. Surely he was not their houseguest this weekend. Surely not!

"He has the women in the house in an uproar," Lisa chattered on. "Every woman found him fascinating last night—our guests, the maids. Even your mother looked at him more than once."

Sofie had a very bad feeling, and she clenched her fists—afraid they were speaking of the same man, afraid he was there in her own house.

"His reputation is blacker than the night, Sofie." Lisa was now whispering, her tone conspiratorial. "They say he carries a small gun at all times, that he is a diamond smuggler—of stolen gems—*and he is a rake.*"

Sofie could not help gasping, her heart palpitating wildly. She closed her eyes, remembering in complete detail what she had seen that afternoon. Even though he had been the very picture of casual elegance, how easily she could imagine him smuggling diamonds . . . or seducing a young innocent. She picked up a novel she was partially through and vigorously began to fan herself with it. "I am certain the rumors are quite exaggerated. After all, why would Suzanne invite him if he were so despicable?" But she already half believed the gossip, oh, she did.

Lisa smiled. "Because he is hardly despicable, Sofie, despite what he does. They say he was wounded in Africa, and that makes him something of a hero! Several of the ladies here have set their caps for him, too; after all, he must be as rich as Croesus. I cannot wait for you to meet him, Sofie. This once, even *you* shall be smitten!"

"You're the one who sounds smitten," Sofie said, surprised that her tone was so calm.

"I am smitten, but he is definitely not for me. Papa would never allow such a man to court me—and we both know it." But Lisa's dark eyes glowed. "Last night after everyone retired, he was with one of the women outside on the terrace. I saw them—it was shocking the way he held her. He was kissing her, Sofie!"

Sofie was frozen. "Who?" She croaked. "Who was he with?"

"You won't believe me—I didn't believe it either. It was Hilary Stewart." Lisa leaned close. "I have heard that she wishes to marry him, too!"

Sofie could not respond. It had finally dawned on her that the man she had spied on at the beach *was* Edward Delanza, and that in a very short time she would come face-to-face with him. Dear God, how could she possibly face him after what she had seen?

2

Standing on the balcony outside his bedroom, Edward Delanza lit a cigarette. He inhaled deeply, then settled his hip on the banister of the wrought-iron railing.

He glanced down at the perfectly groomed lawns. To his left were brilliantly colored formal gardens; far to the right he could just make out the edge of the tennis court. Directly ahead of him the cream and green dunes slid away from the lawns, and a lazy steel blue ocean swept in upon the beachfront in playful white-capped waves. In the west, unseen by him, the sun was setting on the other side of the house, turning the sky a dull, softly glowing pink.

Edward enjoyed the view. It was peaceful. He had lived so precariously this past year that he appreciated even life's quietest—dullest—moments. But not for long. It never lasted for long. In a few days, a few weeks, a few months, he would get that unquenchable restlessness again, a restlessness that had its roots deep in his past, and in his very soul. Sometimes he thought of it as an octopus, whose tentacles he could not shake, and stricken with his burden, he would move on.

But right now he was happy to be just where he was, thank you very much. There was a helluva lot to be said for a peaceful smoke on a summer evening like this. He lifted his face to the still evening air, which was thick and humid and warm but nothing like a south African summer's eve.

Too well, as if it were yesterday, he recalled his last night in southern Africa, crouching down behind a mountain of crates in Hopeville not far from the rail depot, which was on fire, bullets banging and ricocheting all around him, explosions sounding not too far in the distance. The British and the Afrikaners had been going at it all night, and he had been caught in the middle. It had been endless. Edward vividly remembered craving a cigarette, but when he'd dug deep into his pockets, he'd only come up with two handfuls of diamonds.

Right then, he'd have tossed every rock aside for a single drag, if he could have.

The train from Kimberley had arrived two and a half hours late. Edward had gotten himself badly cut up getting through the barbed wire, and he'd suffered a flesh wound in his shoulder, too, shot by some soldier who'd seen him at the last moment as he dashed for the train. But he had made it. He'd leapt aboard the last coach, and when he'd arrived in Cape Town, greeted by a blood red dawn, he'd made the merchant vessel, too, just as she was slipping free of her moorings. He'd been bloody, hurting, and exhausted, but he had made it. With both pockets full of diamonds.

He was *never* going back.

Remembering, Edward smoked the cigarette right down to the end, until he'd burned his fingertips. He forced himself back to the present, and realized that he'd grown rigid with tension and was starting to sweat, a reaction he always seemed to have in response to the unpleasant memories. There was no hope for southern Africa; he'd realized that many months ago. The hatreds ran too deep and were far too complex. He was going to sell out just as soon as he could. There was no way he could enjoy being rich if he was dead.

His gaze soaked up the pretty, peaceful lawn scene below him. Several guests had strolled outside, drinks in hand, in their black dinner jackets and jewel-toned evening gowns. Not for the first time, his regard wandered back to the balcony's single chair, which was poised by the door to the bedroom. On it was an open notebook. Its pages fluttered slightly in the breeze.

He was quite certain that the notebook belonged to the voyeur. When he and Hilary had returned to the house separately, taking different paths, Edward had found it lying abandoned in the sand in the exact place where she had crouched, watching him perform for her. His interest had been surprisingly acute. But that emotion could not compete with his surprise when he saw the rough sketch she'd made of him. He couldn't help being somewhat flattered that she had drawn him, but there'd been a couple of other sketches in her book, too, of the Newport beach. The little voyeur was talented, he could see that.

Not quite calm, Edward lit another cigarette, wondering about her. He had thought about her quite a bit since the incident earlier that day on the beach. *The incident.* He was still somewhat dismayed with his own behavior, which was thoroughly reprehensible. Of course, he hadn't forced her to stay and watch. Now he realized she'd been drawing, her reason for being there in the first place.

Still, most young ladies would have run away instantly. *Not her.* She had stayed, right until the end. Just thinking about it, he could feel his damn cock stiffen. Edward realized that, despite his many hair-raising escapades—

and near brushes with death—he had become far more jaded and dissolute than he had guessed. The incident was proof. How else could he explain his own behavior? How to explain hers? They hadn't even met, and yet, he was intrigued.

He assumed that she was a guest of the Ralstons'; he hoped so. He found himself anticipating their next, real meeting with a mixture of both amusement and excitement. Surely he would find her downstairs with the other guests.

Edward stood, aware of the fluttering in his chest, amused with himself. Goddamn, his blasted heart was beating twice as fast as usual. He couldn't remember when the last time was that he had felt his pulse accelerate in response to the mere thought of a woman.

Edward moved back into his bedroom, paused briefly to check his necktie and slip on a white evening jacket, then he hurried down the stairs.

On the ground floor he slowed and entered the formal salon. The guests were clustered in groups of twos and threes, chatting amiably as they sipped before-dinner drinks passed about by servants in uniform. At least two dozen people were present; apparently neighbors had been invited to supper that evening as well. His glance skidded past everyone—including Hilary Stewart—and slammed to a halt. The voyeur stood alone in front of the French doors on the other side of the room.

His heart seemed to slam, too. But his first thought was, no, this is impossible!

She made a thoroughly nondescript figure of a woman, one he would not normally ever look at twice. Except he was more than looking twice at her now—he was mesmerized. He could not look away.

She had a god-awful style. Her hair was drawn into a severe chignon, she wore no jewelry, not even earbobs, and the gray gown she was wearing was absolutely the worst color she could choose. In his imagination, Edward stripped her naked, fantasized alluring curves, saw her with her hair down. He imagined her wearing nothing but an oversized necklace made with his glittering diamonds while he made love to her, repeatedly.

Rigid with new tension, Edward stepped into the room to take advantage of the salon's electric lighting, certain that her appearance was deceiving. He could see her better now—and it was deceiving. She had no style, that was true, but she wasn't homely, far from it. True, she was not his type— he preferred women who were obviously lush and startlingly attractive, not ones who hid behind ugly gowns and uglier hairstyles. But he was fascinated nevertheless.

And she was staring back at him, too. Edward wondered how she had felt earlier that day, watching him with Hilary. He wondered how she was feeling now. What she was thinking. She had turned crimson. His heart beat harder, faster. Their gazes held. An eternity seemed to unfold before he could look away.

Christ! He reminded himself that she was young. *Very young.* Far too young for him. He doubted she was more than eighteen. Undoubtedly she had only just made her debut that year. Undoubtedly she was a very proper, very young, very innocent lady—except that he had just destroyed her innocence that day. Oh, God!

Edward stood rooted near the doorway, flushing with sudden, real mortification as he finally comprehended the full extent of what he had done— and what he was thinking of doing now. He had purposefully made love to his mistress in front of a young lady just out of the schoolroom. And he was aching to make love to that very same young lady right now—to show her the glory of carnal passion, to introduce her to the pleasure, the agony, the rapture. In fact, he was anticipating it, not just with his body, but with his mind.

Edward forced himself to look away from her. He was shocked with himself, shocked with what he had already done and what he wanted to do now. His heart was pounding so hard, he could hear it in his ears. What was wrong with him? Not only wasn't she the kind of woman he dallied with, his interest was founded upon all the wrong reasons.

His glance crept back to her, of its own volition. She was staring at him, still flushing right down to the high, tight collar of her horrendous gown, and she turned abruptly away when their gazes collided again. He was more than fascinated. He had a terrible inkling that he was out of control.

But why? This woman was not and never would be appropriate for him. She was undoubtedly seeking a proper husband, would one day have a few children in her very proper home. His interest was futile, for Edward was a determined bachelor. He knew, firsthand, how rotten marriage could be. Lust could not hold a couple together, and Edward did not believe in love. His separated parents were living proof of that. As were the hundreds of married women who sought his bed.

Hilary appeared at Edward's side with another woman. "Hello, Mr. Delanza," she said politely, as if they hardly knew each other.

Edward forced a smile onto his face and bowed, taking her hand and kissing it. He spoke automatically, unable to rid his mind of the image of the proper young lady across the room. Or of other images of her, ones that were far from proper. "Mrs. Stewart, have you enjoyed your day in the sun?"

Her long lashes fell. "Very much. And you?"

"Mmm, of course."

"Do you know Miss Vanderbilt?"

"How could I forget?" Edward said with a smile, also bowing over her hand and lifting it to his lips.

Carmine Vanderbilt laughed nervously, but she was smiling widely, reluctant to drop her hand.

As Hilary chatted, Edward responded when he sensed it was up to him, yet he kept one eye on the young woman on the other side of the room. After a few short moments he realized that something was wrong.

She stood alone, completely alone, as if a pariah. But that, of course, was impossible.

"Who is that young lady?" he asked the two women abruptly.

Immediately Hilary and Carmine followed his gaze, and when they saw whom he had asked about, they were both wide-eyed with surprise. "That's Sofie O'Neil," Hilary said easily. "She is Suzanne Ralston's daughter from her first marriage. But why do you ask?"

"Because she's standing alone, and obviously distressed because of it." Edward's dimples flashed. "I think I shall rescue her," he stated, and with a nod, he left both women gawking after him.

Edward crossed the room.

He nodded at those he passed but did not pause to converse. He told himself that he was acting honorably, and managed to believe it. He failed to understand why no one had gone to Miss O'Neil's rescue as of yet. Was he the only gentleman present? He was irritated with the assembly for their universal indifference. And he ignored the partly tumescent presence between his thighs.

As he approached his quarry he began to assimilate many interesting details. She was of medium stature, but he suspected that her proportions were perfectly suited to her moderate build. He glimpsed traces of gold in her brownish hair, recalled how golden it had been in the sunlight, and saw that her skin had a warm tone not unlike that of apricots, which made her really quite remarkable. He wondered who had done her hair in such a severe and spinsterish style, wondered who had picked the awful gown, and found himself annoyed. She was not going to find herself a husband if she presented herself this way.

Then he imagined her with another man, and his annoyance grew.

She had seen him. He watched as her eyes grew wide. He had approached her in an unwavering, direct line. How he regretted his horrendous performance of the afternoon. But it was too late for regrets. She knew who he was—she had looked right at him. But she need never know that he was so unconscionable as to have been aware of her watching him. She would never know. And once the first tense moment of meeting face-to-face had passed, they would converse as if nothing untoward had ever happened. Maybe one day she *would* forget.

She had eyes only for him. She seemed to understand his intentions. Her mouth formed an O. Her cheeks mottled red. She took a deep, desperate gulp of air. But she did not break and run.

Edward paused in front of her, taking her tense hand in his, his smile warm. He was well aware that women found him irresistible—and he saw her eyes widen even more. "Miss O'Neil. I am delighted to make your acquaintance. I understand that your mother is my hostess. Edward Delanza, at your service."

She stared in disbelief.

Edward raised her hand and kissed it. There was no question that, despite her spinsterish disguise, she was pretty enough. Her nose was small and straight, her cheekbones high, her eyes wide, long-lashed, and the shape of almonds. Her face was a perfect oval, and her coloring was frankly exotic. Her eyes, he saw now, were an amazing shade of amber, like the best French sherry. He stared into them and she stared back, unblinking and mesmerized. For a moment he could not look away.

She could even be a beauty if she really wanted to be, he thought. A golden beauty, not too flashy or too obvious but enticing nevertheless, a woman who would turn more than a few heads.

"Mr. D-Delanza," she said huskily.

Edward regained his composure and cleared his throat. "Did you just arrive in Newport?" He had not seen her last night when he had arrived, for if he had, he would certainly remember.

She nodded, her eyes still upon his.

"It is wonderful to escape the city, is it not? The heat is unbearable just now."

"Yes," she whispered. Her breasts were heaving while her chin lifted a notch.

Edward wondered if she was shy, in awe of him—or perhaps still shocked by the incident. Inwardly he grimaced, imagining that the last was probably true. Outwardly he dazzled her with another smile. "Will you stay the rest of the summer, then?"

"I beg your pardon?" Her tongue flicked over her lips.

Edward repeated his question, trying not to think nasty thoughts.

She swallowed. "I don't think so."

He was surprised. "Why not?"

"I have classes. At the Academy." She flushed and lifted her chin higher, proudly. "I am studying art."

He recalled her sketches, which were certainly talented, and had an inkling then, a sense that there was far more here than met the eye. "You speak with passion."

"I am passionate about my work."

He lifted a brow, genuinely curious. "Yes, I am beginning to see that. Are there many young ladies at the Academy?"

"Perhaps a quarter of the class," she said, and suddenly she smiled. "We are all devoted to art."

For a moment he stood very still, staring at her. He reassessed. Sofie O'Neil was beautiful, for when she smiled she lit up and glowed from deep within herself. Something stirred, and it wasn't just his groin. For a moment he wished he were younger, more idealistic, and interested in a wife. It was a ridiculous notion.

"That is admirable, Miss O'Neil," he said, meaning it. He couldn't help taking stock of her ugly gray gown again. He had never before met a woman who was not devoted to pretty gowns, jewelry and handsome beaux. She should be dressed in white silk, sporting pearls and diamonds, surrounded by eager young men. Why was he the only gentleman in attendance? He shoved the rude thought aside and smiled. "Soon, though, I suspect some handsome gallant will chase you down and earn some of that devotion."

She stiffened.

"Have I said something wrong?"

"Yes," she murmured, glancing away.

He could not fathom what it could be. Because soon some young gentleman would see past the old-lady hairdo and the awful clothing and win her heart; it was inevitable. Edward ignored a small but very real pang of regret.

But the analogy was clear. She reminded him of the uncut diamonds he had carried back to New York from Africa, appearing dull and lackluster— but it was an illusion. Once cut and polished, even the most flawed became brilliant.

She faced him again. "I intend to be a professional artist," she said.

"A professional artist?"

"Yes." Her gaze was unwavering. "I intend to earn my living by selling my art."

He could not help staring. Well-bred ladies did not earn livings, it was as simple as that.

She wet her lips again. "Have I shocked you?"

"I'm not quite sure," he said honestly. "But I am rather liberal. Perhaps your husband will not be of the same mind."

She clenched the folds of her skirt. "Undoubtedly, should I wed, my husband would not allow me to earn my living from anything, much less the sale of my art."

Edward could hardly believe his ears. "You do not mean to tell me, do you, that you will not wed?"

She nodded.

It was one of the rare moments in his life when he was genuinely shocked. As he stared at her, seeing her classic beauty despite the absurd clothes and horrid hairstyle, he recalled that she had chosen to stay and watch him make love to Hilary. Then he thought about her excellent sketches. It struck Edward that he had never met a woman like this before. That she was hardly as she appeared. A keen interest seemed to creep over him and he trembled ever so slightly.

"You . . ." she licked her lips nervously yet again. "You, sir, are staring at me as if I have two heads."

Edward inhaled. He was staring, and her artlessly sensual action did not help. "Surely you are accustomed to amazing society with your avowals to live from the sale of your art instead of as a man's wife?"

"No, I am not." Her dark lashes lowered. "I rarely attend social events. And I never profess my intentions."

Edward almost took her hand. As she would not look up at him now, his whisper-soft words fell on the top of her tawny-haired head. "Then I am flattered by your confidence."

She jerked up.

Edward smiled gently. "Is that why you dress as you do? Do you deliberately attempt to hide your beauty to fend off unwanted admirers?"

She gasped. Her jaw tightened. "You think me a fool?" She was terse now, and pale.

"Miss O'Neil—"

She inhaled hard and held up a hand. "Why would you say such a thing? We both know I have no beauty to hide."

She did not know. She did not even guess her own charm. And suddenly Edward was determined to shake her up until she saw herself as she should. "But it needs to be said."

She crossed her arms. "You are toying with me," she whispered uneasily.

"I am not toying with you. I don't play with people or their feelings— not ever."

She gazed at him as if torn between hope and disbelief.

"Accept the truth, Miss O'Neil. For soon your other admirers will come forth with the exact same claims, despite your professional aspirations."

Her breath escaped. "I do not think so."

"No?"

"There are no admirers." She started to move away from him, but he caught her arm. "My mother is signaling everyone that it is time to go in to dinner," she cried.

"You're afraid of me." He turned the full force of his blue gaze upon her— a look no woman had ever resisted with any degree of success. "Don't be."

"No, I am not." She shrugged free of him. Her gaze was direct. "For there is no valid reason for me to be afraid of you, is there?"

Edward actually flushed, ashamed. Their gazes locked. "Miss O'Neil, don't believe all that you hear."

She stiffened, biting her lower lip, which he now realized was full and provocative. "I do not condemn others, Mr. Delanza, based on hearsay or gossip."

"I am relieved to hear that." His smile flashed, but his cheeks were still uncomfortably warm. "Perhaps you will not condemn me, either, for any other happenstance?"

She blinked and became very still, a fawn poised to take flight.

He hoped he had not given himself away. She would never speak to him again if she knew he had been aware of her presence in the dunes, not that he would blame her. She must not find out. "I really am not a hopeless cad," he cajoled.

After a long pause she finally said, "I never thought you were."

He was truly startled—and ridiculously, he was hopeful. "Then you are far more charitable than I would have ever thought possible," he murmured. He extended his arm. "Shall we go in to supper together?"

"No! I don't think so!" Her gaze swept the salon with some degree of panic, as if looking for rescue from *him*.

Edward glanced up and saw that they were almost the last ones left in the salon, and that Suzanne Ralston regarded them intently from the doorway across the room. Of course, Suzanne would be worried about his interest in her daughter, not knowing that she had nothing to fear. He sighed. "Until we next meet," he bowed, smiling at Sofie.

She merely stared up at him.

A woman touched his arm briefly from behind. "Edward?"

"Mrs. Stewart," he murmured, turning to face her, hiding his reluctance to leave Sofie.

Hilary was smiling, but her eyes were darker than he remembered, darker and far more inquisitive. "You can escort me, if you wish," she said lightly.

"Gladly." And when he turned around, Hilary on his arm, Sofie O'Neil was gone.

Sofie spent the next two hours avoiding Edward Delanza's intense blue gaze.

Hilary had been seated on his left. They were seated across the table and far to the front by Benjamin Ralston at the table's head. Sofie had gladly obeyed Suzanne's instructions to sit at the other end with her. She wished to be as far away from him as possible.

She was distressed, far more than she should be. Sofie prided herself upon her level headed composure, but tonight it seemed to have escaped her. It was hard to be dignified when confronted with a man whom she had seen in the throes of passion with another woman; indeed, it was impossible for Sofie not to burn with heat every time his questing stare wandered over to her—which it did repeatedly.

Why had he singled her out for his attentions? He was Edward Delanza, dashing and dangerous, persona non grata, seducer of women, diamond smuggler *extraordinaire*—if all was to be believed—and he had singled her out the moment he entered the salon.

Sofie did not understand it for a second. He could not find her interesting or attractive; the very idea was absurd. *Why* had he singled her out?

She glanced down to the other end of the table where Edward sat. He was leaning towards Hilary, his head cocked, his black hair shining in the light cast by the chandeliers overhead. His profile was breathtaking and nearly perfect—his nose strong and straight but a bit large. His mouth had formed into a soft smile as he listened to something Hilary said.

Finally he grinned. Then his grin died and he straightened, quickly looking up to find Sofie staring. Their gazes clashed. Sofie quickly dropped her glance—for the hundredth time that night, she blushed. But now he stared. She could feel it.

Cautiously yet unable to prevent herself, Sofie lifted her gaze. Edward Delanza was far more than handsome, just as Lisa had said; there was something infinitely compelling about him. He and Hilary were so beautiful together. They made the perfect couple. And although Hilary was behaving with absolute propriety now, Sofie imagined that beneath the table her thigh pressed his, perhaps even her hand. Every time Hilary smiled at Edward, Sofie thought about what they had shared—what they would undoubtedly share again that night—and she was distraught.

Was she jealous? She had her art to consume her; she had decided against marriage. She was happy with her decision. If she had any doubts, she had only to think of Mary Cassatt, a renowned artist who had remained single in order to devote herself to her work.

Edward caught her regard, and this time his glance turned to smoke.

Immediately Sofie's insides melted.

"Sofie, you are staring, and it is most unbecoming," Suzanne whispered.

Sofie jerked. She could feel her face burning. She thought that there had been a message in Edward Delanza's blue eyes, but surely she was wrong. Surely he was not looking at her with such alarming intensity and such predatory interest.

Suzanne had turned to her guests, making a witty comment that caused them to laugh, but not before giving Sofie another concerned glance.

Sofie had had enough. She could not imagine how she would survive another day and night until the weekend was over and she returned to New York City. Perhaps she would plead an illness and remain in her room abed.

His incomprehensible flirtation with her before dinner was still fresh in her mind. He was the very first man who had ever evinced the slightest interest in her, the first to ever flirt with her, to smile and flatter her. Had he seen her crude gait, he would not have been charming—he would have ignored her like everyone else.

Suzanne had stood, signaling that dinner was over and they might all now adjourn to the drawing room. Sofie had been lost in the fantasy of another flirtation with Edward when she heard the scraping back of chairs as the guests stood also. Sternly she told herself that it would never be. Once Edward remarked her as she limped from the room, he would lose interest. Even had he really found her attractive before, he would not find her pretty once he saw her ungainly, clumsy gait.

Sofie refused to budge from her seat. She was aware of his glance lingering upon her, openly curious, but she avoided returning his gaze. Finally he sauntered out with the other men to take brandies and cigars in the smoking room. Sofie rose to her feet slowly and trailed after the other women. She was torn.

On the one hand, she wanted to flee up the stairs to her room. He would not realize that she was a cripple. And then she could give in to the urge to draw, which was overpowering. *The urge to draw him.*

On the other hand, she did not want to go at all.

Lisa fell into step beside her, shortening her stride to Sofie's. "Was it him?"

Sofie's smile was wan. "Yes."

Lisa's cry was excited. "Oh, you could paint him, Sofie, and how stunning the portrait would be."

Sofie said nothing—what was there to say? She intended to paint him, and it would be an extraordinary work. Sofie had no doubt.

"What do you think of him?" Lisa paused outside the salon, the other women going in ahead of them.

"I think he is everything you have described, Lisa." Devastating, dashing . . . dangerous.

"You are smitten, too!"

Sofie swallowed. "Of course I'm not."

Lisa was openly curious. "What did the two of you talk about before dinner? Is he not horribly charming? Do you think—do you think there is anything between him and Hilary?"

"Lisa!" Sofie was scandalized that she would mention the affair now, when they might be overheard.

"Well? She is so beautiful, he *is* a rake and she's a widow, and I *did* see them together," Lisa whispered.

"How—how on earth would you know anything about rakes and their . . . pursuits?" Sofie sputtered.

Lisa smiled, serene. "I do not lock myself away at the Academy, or in a room, painting day in and day out, as you do, Sofie. I have friends. I go out. Everyone talks. Widows have *experience*, and they are far safer than married women."

Sofie could only stare.

"Well, Newport has never been so interesting, I can certainly admit to that." Lisa laughed and hurried away after the other women, into the parlor for sweets and sherries.

Sofie gripped the banister, relieved that Lisa was gone, wondering what was going to happen now. In another twenty minutes or so the men would rejoin the ladies. It was not long to wait—if she dared.

And if she remained seated, he might never learn of her limp tonight. Sofie knew she was being irrational but found her usual common sense dissipated by the day's events and her unholy desire to be in Edward Delanza's presence just one more time. To be the recipient of his electrifying charm.

"Where are you going?" Suzanne paused beside her.

"I was thinking of going to bed."

Suzanne gripped the railing. "I don't think you should retire just now, Sofie."

Sofie looked at her mother, saw the tension in her. "I do not mean to be rude."

"Retiring so early would be rude. Just as it was rude to go off alone today, ignoring all of my guests."

Sofie paled. "Mother, I am sorry."

"Of course you are. I know it was not intentional. But, Sofie—" Suzanne took her hand "—just the other day I heard someone mention you. She called you a recluse! It is difficult enough that you are considered eccentric."

Sofie was wounded, but tried not to let it show. "Mother, what would you have me do? How can I paint *and* go to parties and races and teas? If your friends choose to think of me as eccentric, perhaps they are right. To them I am odd."

"You can be as eccentric as you want, dear, as long as you keep up certain pretenses. You have been alone in New York for two entire months, devoting yourself to your art. This weekend you must devote yourself to my guests. Really, Sofie, is it too much to ask?"

Sofie shook her head. "Of course, you are right, and it is not too much to ask."

"Perhaps I should not have allowed you to remain in the city by yourself, perhaps I should have insisted you summer in Newport with your family."

Sofie grew alarmed. "That will not make my art go away, Mother."

Suzanne grimaced. "Unfortunately, it won't, and I realize that." She hesitated, holding her daughter's gaze. "I watched you with Edward Delanza tonight, Sofie. And I do not think tonight was the first time you have been with him."

Sofie gasped, flushing dully. Of course, that evening had not been their first encounter—not for her, at least—but she could not tell her mother that she had been so immoral and depraved as to spy upon him while he made love to their neighbor.

"I'm right!" Suzanne cried. She was incredulous.

"Not exactly," Sofie said. "Not really. I saw him earlier, that's all, but we never spoke."

Suzanne raised her finger. "I want you to stay away from him—do you understand me? If for some incredible reason he pursues you, stay away!"

Sofie sucked in her breath. "I have every intention of staying away from him. I am not a fool."

"But a man like that is adept at turning a green girl's head."

"Not mine. And I am hardly a girl anymore, Mother. Twenty is quite long in the tooth." Sofie gazed at Suzanne. "Does he really smuggle diamonds?"

"Yes, he does, and if that is not enough to forewarn you, he is an accomplished, unrepentant rake."

Sofie was not as ready as her mother to condemn Edward to the pits of irredeemable impropriety, no matter what she had seen. She recalled his earlier words, how he'd asked her not to believe everything she'd heard about him. "If he is so horrible, then why is he here?"

Suzanne sighed. "He rounds out the party. A handsome bachelor always does. And Mr. Delanza in particular is popular precisely because his background is so suspect—not to mention the fact of his astounding looks and charm. Who do you think the ladies are talking about now? He has already made my house party a big success." Then Suzanne came closer, lowering her voice. "You are far past the age of innocence, Sofie, so listen well. If Hilary or anyone else decides to avail themselves of his virility—and his fondness for rich, beautiful, experienced ladies is undisputed—that is their affair. They know what they are doing. You do not. You are neither rich nor beautiful, and despite your age, you are far too innocent. You were very foolish tonight, allowing him to carry on with you, encouraging him. I am telling you to stay away from him for your own good."

Sofie was hurt. She should not have been; she knew she was a plain, lame woman and could never be considered even remotely beautiful, and she had always known that. But it was a moment before she could speak. "I am not as foolish as you think. I did not entice him, or encourage him, and I never will."

Suzanne suddenly smiled, reaching out to hug her daughter. "I do not want to see you hurt, Sofie, dear; surely you know that. I, more than anyone, know what it's like to love that kind of man. I am trying to protect you."

"I know, Mother," Sofie said quietly. She had understood the reference to her father, but would not dispute it tonight. "You know I am not interested in men."

Suzanne looked at her. "All women find a man like that interesting, Sofie. You could not possibly be an exception."

3

There was not a chair to be had in the salon, but Hilary Stewart stood when Sofie came in, giving her a soft smile. Sofie sat down promptly. Hilary's kind gesture was not a surprise; Hilary had always been warm and friendly to her, and Sofie had always liked her. Most of Suzanne's friends actually pitied Sofie, and did not quite hide it. Sofie in turn ignored their condescension, carrying on as if all were as it should be. But Hilary did not pity her. Nor did she pretend that Sofie's limp did not exist. Hilary's manner was breezy and warm in general, and it did not change when Sofie was present. Still, Sofie could not get over the fact that her elegant neighbor was a seductress in disguise. She did not feel quite as friendly towards Hilary as she once had, and she was dismayed to realize that.

Sofie became aware of the other women in the parlor, whose glances kept straying in her direction. She grew uncomfortable. She recalled what Suzanne had just said to her. Did everyone think she had been encouraging Edward Delanza as Suzanne did?

Everyone had seen him flirting with her; how could they not? Now the ladies kept looking at her with real curiosity, hardly hidden, and the attention she received had nothing to do with her limp. She was certain of that. Even Hilary cast a few speculative glances her way.

Suddenly Sofie felt very angry. Nothing had gone as it should that day. She was inordinately tired, inordinately distressed. She had seen things she shouldn't, felt things she shouldn't, glimpsed possibilities that were impossible for her. Edward Delanza had so casually upset her carefully balanced world, without his even knowing it.

Yet there she was, lame, eccentric, and plain, waiting for him to return to the salon, hoping he would flirt with her again. She should be upstairs, working. Her life was her art, and it was a serious, dedicated life. And it wasn't fair that today Edward Delanza had entered her world, making her aware of him in a way she had never been aware of any man, making her aware of herself as a woman. No, it wasn't fair at all.

"Sofie, dear, what do you think?"

Sofie had just decided that she must leave the gathering, as soon as possible, before Edward Delanza returned, before she made a fool of herself publicly, or worse, before her feelings exploded into some immense emotion that might never go away, but Carmine's words jerked her to attention.

Carmine Vanderbilt was plain and thin—Sofie saw that with her artist's eye—but one hardly noticed because she dressed in the most exquisite and flattering custom creations from France, because she dripped the most expensive, stunning jewels, and because she had a hairdresser who worked wonders with her only real physical asset, her heavy blue-black hair. Most important, she was the greatest heiress in New York, if not the land. Everyone knew she would marry an impoverished British nobleman. It had become the fad for great heiresses these past two decades, and Carmine had been courted for some time now by one of these aristocrats, in her case, an elderly duke.

Carmine was smiling, but her black eyes were malicious.

"I am afraid I did not hear the question," Sofie said uneasily. She rarely crossed paths with Carmine, but now she felt the woman's seething hostility.

"What do you think of Mr. Delanza? The two of you had such a long conversation before dinner—surely you have an opinion?"

Sudden silence filled the salon as more than a dozen ladies, all magnificently dressed and heavily jeweled, turned to stare at Sofie. She could feel the stinging heat on her face. "We—we barely talked," she croaked, suddenly losing her voice. "He—he seems . . . quite nice."

Carmine laughed. Everyone else tittered. Carmine turned to Hilary. "I think Mr. Delanza has made another conquest," she all but snickered.

Sofie gripped the arms of her chair. She was ready to respond in kind, but held herself back. For it struck her that Carmine was jealous.

Obviously Carmine wished it had been herself who had the pleasure of Edward Delanza's attentions. Sofie gazed at her, imagining her stripped of her gowns and jewels and money, leaving nothing but a skinny, mean-spirited spinster. But Sofie suddenly understood. How pleasant could it be, waiting for the duke to offer marriage while knowing that the only reason he was doing so was because of her father's money?

Sofie knew that had she decided to marry, that would be akin to her fate, too. Her stepfather would have had to pay handsomely in order to find her a husband.

"I think we are all smitten with Mr. Delanza," Sofie heard Hilary say in her defense.

Sofie was about to speak up, for Hilary hardly had to defend her. Then Carmine snickered and said, "But we are not all cripples, dear Hilary. Mr. Delanza might find any one of us attractive, don't you think? But not poor Sofie."

"That is beyond the pale, Carmine," Hilary snapped as she immediately came over to Sofie, patting her shoulder reassuringly.

"Sofie knows her own limitations, Carmine, dear," Suzanne stated coolly, striding over. "Don't you, dear?"

"Indeed I do," Sofie said, managing a show of outward calm. "I know my own limitations very well. I have no interest in Mr. Delanza or any other man. Or did you forget that I never made my debut?"

"Oh yes, you are studying art," Carmine said. "How convenient for you."

Sofie stiffened her shoulders, her eyes blazing, trying to control the sudden temper she found herself in. But she failed. "I think my art is as convenient for me as your duke is for you."

Carmine gasped at the insult, but before anyone could respond, the men returned, distracting everyone. Sofie sat as stiffly as a board, hardly able to believe she had been so rude, even if it had been deserved. And then she saw him and she forgot all about Carmine Vanderbilt.

She watched him as he entered the room, his strides long and lithe, a glass of brandy in one hand. He was smiling, and his teeth were stunningly white in his tanned face, his two dimples endearingly deep. His wandering, nonchalant gaze connected with hers for an instant. Sofie's heart was already in the midst of a somersault. She became frozen and heated, all at once.

Then Lisa rushed to Edward's side, laughing. Conversation resumed in the room, picking up in tempo and amplitude. Sofie could not take her eyes off her sister and Edward.

Lisa had her arm looped in his, swayed gracefully as they walked together, and she laughed again and again, at everything he said. She was animated, breathless, beautiful.

Sofie loved her stepsister. She had liked her from the day they had first met as little girls, soon after Jake's disappearance, when Suzanne began her acquaintance with Benjamin Ralston. Shortly after Jake's death, which they'd heard had occurred during his escape from prison in London, Suzanne had married Lisa's father. The friendship between the two girls, only three years apart in age, had been immediate, and had blossomed into the kind of love that close siblings might share. Lisa was effervescent, generous, and kindhearted, not to mention beautiful. Sofie had used her numerous times as a model for her art.

But now Sofie looked at her and felt quite ill. She had to face a brutal and ugly truth. Just as she was envious of Hilary, she was envious of her own sister, and it was horrible.

Sofie had never envied Lisa before. But now she watched her flirt so effortlessly with Edward Delanza and knew that he must find her as beautiful in spirit as she was in appearance, so beautiful and so perfect, and Sofie wished that she were different.

What would it be like, to move so easily, as Lisa did? To be hanging on the arm of a handsome man, holding his attention so completely? To be attractive and graceful, to take life and all it offered for granted? What would it be like to walk over to Edward Delanza while laughing, without an awkward gait, without feeling gauche, different, pitiable?

It was too much. The day had already taken its toll of her, but this was the last straw. Her jealousy of Lisa was intolerable, her wild daydreams were dangerous. Abruptly Sofie stood, and just as abruptly she gasped, unable to bite off her cry of pain.

It was enough. Instantly those standing near her turned to look; as quickly, they turned away, awkward and embarrassed. But not Edward Delanza, who had also whirled at her cry of distress. Even though he stood on the other side of the room, immediately he started towards her, his smile gone, his face concerned.

Sofie fled. It seemed that her limp had never been as heavy as she rushed from the room.

Outside on the veranda she collapsed into an oversized rattan chair, half-hidden beneath the fronds of a royal palm, refusing to cry. He had seen. Edward Delanza had finally seen her awful limp.

Sofie closed her eyes, trying to will away the tears. It was no easy task. Tonight she was far more than hurt or distressed. She was perilously close to falling in love with a complete stranger, and it was more than absurd, it was infinitely dangerous.

Sofie leaned down to massage her foot, fighting to regain her composure, wondering what Edward Delanza was thinking now that he knew the truth about her.

If only today had been different, she thought abjectly. Normally her limp was hardly noticeable, but she had abused her bad ankle so thoroughly, and now she was paying the piper. Rising from her chair too quickly, thoughtlessly, had added to the aggravation caused by the day's adventures. In another day or two her leg would be as fine as ever, as long as she was careful to rest. Sofie sighed. She must heal herself quickly for another reason as well, the most important reason of all—when she returned to the city she must be able to stand at her easel. Her work could not wait. Edward Delanza's elegant yet rawly masculine image as he had been at the beach that day flitted through her mind. She had decided upon the work's composition and planned to proceed without the rough study she'd lost.

"Are you all right, Miss O'Neil?"

Sofie gasped as Edward Delanza—the very last person she wanted to see—materialized from the night shadows and knelt in front of her chair.

"Can I help?" he asked, unsmiling. His blue eyes were filled with concern. Sofie started when she realized he had gripped her hands.

He did not know. Still he did not know. Sofie was sure of it, because there was no pity or revulsion in his steady gaze. And for just an instant, with him kneeling there in front of her, she felt like a beautiful damsel in distress, and he seemed like a knight in shining armor.

She took a breath. "I . . . I am afraid not." She turned her face away, grinding down her jaw, wanting to scream at him to go away. His kindness was unbearable. Especially when she knew without a doubt that it would metamorphose into ugly pity or uglier revulsion soon.

"You have hurt yourself," he said, his voice husky with worry. "Did you twist your ankle? How will you get upstairs to your room? Surely I can be of help."

Sofie inhaled hard again, about to become seriously undone. Obviously no one had thought to tell him the truth. If only someone had! Maybe it would be better if she did herself. But God, was she brave enough? "I am fine."

Abruptly he released one of her hands—only one—but only so he could grasp her chin very gently yet firmly and turn her to face him. "You're not fine. You've hurt yourself. I heard your cry of pain—I saw you limping."

"You do not understand," she said through stiff lips. His blue, intense gaze was riveting. No man had ever looked at her with such concern—except for her father, who had died eleven years ago.

If only it could be as it seemed.

"I don't? Then explain, so I can understand," he insisted gently. His fingers tightened around her palms.

"I . . . I did not sprain my ankle, Mr. Delanza." Sofie took a deep breath and tried to extricate her hands from his, which was impossible. His hands were large, hard, warm. Her next words took more bravery than she had known she had. "You . . . you see, I am a cripple."

He did not see. He stared. Then his eyes gradually widened as he finally comprehended her words.

Sofie gave a superhuman effort and jerked her hands free. She looked anywhere but at him, her face hot and red. "Normally I am not so gauche." Her voice sounded husky with tears, even to herself. "It seems that I have been far too candid with you already today."

She faltered, thinking of his surprise when she had told him, quite deliberately, of her professional aspirations—and still she could not understand why she had revealed herself in such a manner to a complete stranger. Then she thought of him as he had been with Hilary, and she trembled. Her ankle still ached horribly, and despite her resolve, a tear finally slid down her cheek. "But this day has been quite unusual." Finally she managed to smile overbrightly. "So there is nothing you can do. Would you mind excusing me?" She finally met his gaze.

Her eyes widened. There was still no hint of pity or revulsion in his eyes, which were intent, studying her so closely, she felt him trying to pierce through her every shield and defense, trying to break down the barricades to breach her very soul.

Softly he said, "What happened?"

She could not move or breathe.

"Why are you telling me that you're a cripple?" he asked in the same tone.

"Because it is true," she said in an unnatural voice.

His smile was soft, but strange. "Is it? I find your declaration interesting, Miss O'Neil, because I've always found appearances to be deceiving, and truths to be hidden where one least expects them to be. What happened?"

She had no time to ponder his statement. "There . . . was an accident."

"What kind of accident?" He was calm, still unbearably kind. And he still held her hands, but now Sofie realized his thumbs fluttered over her palms. Her pulse was skittering wildly.

"I . . . I do not wish to discuss it," she managed.

"I'm your friend," he murmured.

Sudden warmth unfurled inside Sofie at his suggestive tone. "My father had . . . left home, some years ago. I loved him so. Then I learned of his death. I was just a small child and I was so afraid, so upset. I fell down the stairs, breaking my ankle." She was caught up in the power of his gaze.

Edward's expression had not changed. "Broken ankles heal."

Sofie flushed. "This one did not heal correctly. It was my own fault. I did not want to make Suzanne angry—she was already angry with my father, with me. I did not tell her I was hurt. I was a very foolish child."

Edward stared at her, eyes wide, his expression drawn, pained. "Or a very brave one," he finally said.

Sofie started.

"Why are you crying?" he asked gently.

Sofie realized that tears were trickling down her cheeks. She was mortified. And she could not wipe them away, for he held her hands. She shook her head, unable to speak, having no intention of explaining the precise cause of her grief. In truth, she did not understand it herself.

"Is the pain in your leg so bad? Or is it something else?"

"You go too far!" she cried, panicked. "Now, if you would . . ." She rose, a mistake. She whimpered. And collapsed into Edward's powerful arms.

For just an instant, as he had risen simultaneously with her, she was in his embrace, every inch of her body pressed against his, her cheek against his chest, her thighs glued to his. And he held her for a single heartbeat, and in that heartbeat, Sofie knew she would never be the same again.

So this was what it was like to be held by a man!

How right he felt—how strong—how right!

Sofie pulled away from him, and instantly Edward helped her back down into the chair. His gaze met hers and she could not look away, her body tingling from the heat and power of him, her heart dancing from the comfort he afforded her even now. "I have overdone it," she whispered, an understatement.

"Yes, you have," he agreed. He knelt before her, and his hands found her right foot.

Sofie cried out, not in pain, but horror. "What are you doing?"

His tone was spun silk. "When I found you out here, you were massaging your leg. My hands are much stronger than yours." In the blink of an eye he unlaced her special shoe, as ugly as sin, slid it off her foot, and tossed it aside.

Sofie was aghast. "You must not." Her protest died. She was achingly aware of his hands enclosing her small stockinged foot.

He looked up at her as he knelt in front of her. "Why not?" His grin flashed, boyish, playful, sexy.

She was frozen. He held the foot of her bad leg and already his thumbs moved, kneading the inner arch. All the pleasure she might have felt gave way to panic, to terror. But she must not let him even glimpse her twisted ankle. He would be repulsed—and now Sofie knew she must not repulse him; at all costs, she must not.

"Relax, Miss O'Neil," he murmured. It was the exact tone of voice he had used while making love to Hilary. Sofie whimpered, this time real pleasure mingling with the desperation. "Please," she whispered, aware of more stinging tears, threatening to fall, "please stop!"

He paused. "What are you afraid of?"

"This—is unseemly."

He made a disparaging sound. "What are you really afraid of?"

She was too choked up to answer, not that she ever would.

His keenly intelligent eyes held hers, and she knew he understood. But suddenly his dimples deepened and then he winked. "All right," he said, resuming the massage, which both soothed and distressed her at the same time, "I'll admit it even at the price of shocking you, Miss O'Neil. I have seen more than a few female feet in my short lifetime; I've even held them in my hands. There, what do you think of that?"

Despite the cloying fear, Sofie did think him funny—but she could in no way laugh. Instead, she pursed her lips hard together, trying to control her rioting emotions.

"Your foot feels no different from any other," he continued, giving her a scandalously bold and sensual glance from under his lashes, which, she now realized, were longer than her own. "In fact, it feels exceedingly, boringly normal."

Sofie whimpered. They both knew she was not normal. "Why are you doing this?" she whispered.

He paused, staring into her eyes. "I don't like your demons."

"I do not know what you speak of!" she cried.

"Don't lie to me, Sofie."

Sofie tried to jerk her foot free, but he would not let her. In fact, his hands closed around her ankle, and she froze, horrified. How could he do this? Why was he torturing her like this? Why?

Gravely he looked up at her. "Your ankle is swollen."

"Please, do not do this."

His jaw flexed. He would not let her gaze wander from his. Finally he said grimly, "Your ankle feels like any other, except for the fact that it is swollen."

She whimpered. He was wrong, wrong, so very wrong.

Suddenly he smiled, very gently moving his thumb across her ankle, the massage turning into a caress. "All right, I'll admit the entire truth at the risk of shocking you senseless. I lied. I am the horrible cad everyone accuses me of being. There is nothing under your skirts, I'm certain, that I haven't seen before."

Sofie sputtered, truly shocked.

Edward grinned, looking anything but repentant—looking exactly like a devilishly handsome and self-satisfied rogue.

"I can't deny it. I've seen more than my share of ankles. Fat ones, skinny ones, young ones, old ones, white ones—yes, don't be shocked—even brown ones and black ones."

Sofie stared. She did not know whether to laugh or cry. She heard herself say, "Black ones?"

He winked. "There are a lot of black ankles in Africa. Hell, that was nothing. I've even seen red and purple ones—at the Carnivale, of course."

She made a strange hiccuping sound. He smiled and stroked her again.

Sofie swiped at the tears, which just kept flowing. "Why are you doing this?"

"Because I haven't seen you laugh yet."

Finally the smallest, strangest sound sputtered from her pursed lips. It was unquestionably hysterical, but it might have qualified as laughter, too.

Edward smiled at her, a smile so warm, it went arrow-straight to the center of her heart, and he placed her foot on his hard thigh, covering it with one palm. "I know when to declare victory—even if it's a toss-up."

Sofie had stopped crying. She looked from his handsome, smiling face, from his blue, tender eyes, to his lap, where her foot nestled not far from his groin. He looked, too. In that instant, everything changed. He was no longer smiling. The light in his eyes became brighter, his expression grew strained. When his thumb paused over her instep, she felt it all the way up to her loins.

But all he said, his tone suddenly raw, was, "Miss O'Neil . . ."

Sofie said nothing. She did not know what to say. He had held her foot, had touched it, and now the atmosphere was so charged around them that Sofie felt the heat and thought she was about to explode.

"Sofie, dear, don't you think you have caused enough talk tonight?" Suzanne said.

Sofie jerked her foot off his lap at the exact instant she realized her mother stood behind Edward on the veranda. She flushed, sitting up straighter, gripping the thick arms of the chair. Her mother's expression was carefully controlled. Edward slowly rose to his full height, as graceful and sleek as an oversized panther, and before he turned to face Suzanne, he gave Sofie a smile that might have been meant as encouragement, but that was so warm, it would have melted a frozen stick of butter. Sofie's heart beat double time.

Sofie closed her eyes in despair, praying for guidance, praying for help before it was too late—before she took an irrevocable plunge into the deep, still waters of love.

"Sofie, put your shoe on," Suzanne said.

Sofie did not move. Her shoe was out of reach.

Edward moved with the speed of a striking cobra, retrieving the unfashionable shoe and sliding it onto her foot. Sofie glimpsed his face, which had tightened with anger. As he laced it up, she dared to look at her mother, who was just as displeased.

"Mr. Delanza, would you excuse us?" Suzanne asked, her tone clipped.

Edward placed himself squarely between mother and daughter. "Your daughter, Mrs. Ralston, is in some pain. I would like to help her upstairs." His tone was cool. "With your permission, of course."

Suzanne's voice was sugar-coated. "That will not be necessary, sir. I shall have one of the servants aid her. However, might I have a word with you on the morrow—say, after breakfast?" She smiled with vinegary sweetness.

He bowed. "Of course. Good night, madam." He turned, giving Sofie a look filled with dark concern, and with something more, something conspiratorial and intimate that made Sofie's pulse race. "Good night, Miss O'Neil."

She managed a wan smile. Edward left. Suzanne stared after him, waiting until he was gone. Then she turned to her daughter. Her hand swung out. Sofie cried out in surprise and pain as Suzanne's palm cracked across her face. It had been many years since her mother had slapped her. She drew back against the chair, holding her stinging cheek, stunned.

"I told you to stay away from him!" Suzanne cried. "Don't you understand? He is exactly like your father, your goddamned, rotten father, that miserable Irish bastard—and he'll use you just like your father did me!"

Sofie did not sleep. She did not dare think, either, or try to analyze what had happened. She would never be able to understand the events that had passed this day.

She sketched. Sofie preferred color, oils being her favorite medium, but she knew that her mother would have never allowed her to bring her paints to Newport for the weekend, and in truth, a short trip hardly justified lugging all of her equipment such a distance. And she had come to the beach house with the honorable intention of being sociable, which was not possible if she locked herself in her room painting all day, nor was it easily accomplished if she spent all night with her work, either. But she was helpless to fight the urge to draw, an urge she had fought all day, and now she gave in with single-minded frenzy. Sleep was the very last thing on her mind.

She drew with abandon. Her strokes were mostly hard and bold. One sketch rapidly followed another. The subject never changed. The portraits were all of the same man; only the poses were different. They were all of Edward Delanza.

She drew Edward kneeling, standing, sitting, sauntering, she drew him holding her ugly shoe. In every portrait she drew him fully clothed but in his shirtsleeves, so she could hint at the powerful musculature she had felt against her body but had not seen. How she wished she had seen him fully unclothed—for then she would draw him nude.

His body, she defined in a few powerful, simple strokes, unable to do more. But in every portrait she detailed his face with great care. In every portrait, his expression was the same. As she had last seen it, tender, concerned, yet somehow wicked with promise, too.

4

Suzanne paced. She had spent a sleepless night. And of course, when Benjamin had asked her what was wrong, she could not tell him.

She was in the music room, alone. She paused to look in the Venetian mirror on the wall above a small marble-topped Louis XIV table. She wore her dark, shoulder-length hair swept up loosely, for it was the perfect foil for her flawless ivory complexion and her classic features. Her morning dress was simple, a fine peach-hued cotton with a deeply veed neckline and a fitted bodice despite the fact that fashion tended towards high necklines and loose, billowy tops. Suzanne knew her figure was superb, and since her remarriage, she had always flaunted it. Now, self-consciously, she smoothed down her skirt, which clung to her hips before flaring out in the customary trumpet shape. She could find no flaw with her appearance, except for the faint circles beneath her eyes.

She was sorry about last night. God, she was. But she had told her daughter to stay away from Edward Delanza, and Sofie had not listened. If only she hadn't lost her temper. But perhaps Sofie had learned her lesson.

If only he did not remind her so damn much of Jake.

Suzanne inhaled hard. Jake had died eleven years ago, and she still felt that horrible gut-wrenching emptiness whenever she thought of him—which was often. Yes, she missed the miserable bastard, she always would—but she also hated him. He had come so close to destroying her!

Suzanne just could not forgive Jake any of it, not his taking her away from society, from her possessions and her wealth, not the other women, not his intention to separate from her when she flatly denied him a divorce. And when Jake had been forced to flee the country, she had been branded the wife of a murderer, of a traitor. Had Benjamin Ralston not married her upon Jake's death, giving her back her place in society and her respectability, she would still carry Jake's heinous brands.

Most important of all, she could not forgive Jake for leaving his entire estate—comprised of a million dollars in assets and cash—to their daughter. That had been the greatest blow of all. Sofie would receive it immediately should she marry, or begin receiving installments at twenty-one, the final sum to be received on her twenty-fifth birthday if she was still unwed. After all Suzanne had suffered, after all she had endured and given up, he had not left her a single red cent. Not one.

She knew that it was his way of getting back at her as he had threatened to do the last time they had seen each other, even though he had been behind bars then. Neither one of them had ever thought he would be dead two years later, and Suzanne had also thought the threat idle, for how could he strike at her while incarcerated? But it had not been idle. Despite his incarceration, despite his death, Jake had carried out his threat—even now, he was carrying on their passionate love-and-hate war from the very grave.

But it was Suzanne's turn to hold the upper hand. Seven years ago the executor of Jake's estate had died, and Suzanne had been appointed executrix of Sofie's trust. Suzanne imagined that Jake was spinning in his grave right now, for Suzanne was administering the trust in a manner that benefited not just her daughter, but herself.

Abruptly, despite the fact that she was expecting Edward Delanza at any moment and was prepared to do battle with him over her daughter if she must, Suzanne sank down into a plush brocade chair, stabbed with sudden anguish. It wasn't fair. Not any of it. Not his death, and not the fact that, when it had all begun, she had been far too young and too spoiled to appreciate what they had had—and what could have been theirs if only they had tried.

Suzanne closed her eyes, her anguish turned to an intense longing. How well she remembered what it was to be fifteen and obsessed with Jake O'Neil. She smiled, and allowed herself to be swept back into the past.

New York City, 1880

Suzanne dashed from the house, her black riding skirts flaring around her, a jaunty hat with a half veil set at an angle on her head. Her magnificent bay hunter was waiting for her. Suzanne allowed the groom to help her mount. Excitement rippled in her, hardly containable. The groom mounted another horse and followed at a discreet distance behind her.

Suzanne spurred her hunter forward. She was not going riding in Central Park, nor was she meeting friends, as she had let her parents believe. Her heart beat wildly now; she was perspiring. She was acutely aware of the feel of the saddle leather between her thighs.

Would he be there? Would he be there today, as he had been yesterday and the day before and the day before that—ever since she had first laid her eyes on him?

The week before, Suzanne had gone riding with a group of friends. It had been a large, raucous group of young ladies and eligible bachelors. There had been much ado in the papers recently about all the building on the city's west side, a direct response to the opening of the Ninth Avenue El the year before. Suzanne and her friends had never been farther west than Central Park, except for occasional shopping excursions to the boulevard farther downtown. The entire group had enthusiastically decided to visit the newly opened Riverside Park.

Crossing town, one and all scoffed at the idea that one day the West Side would be fit for habitation—much less a rival for the East Side's residents. For they rode through open dirt streets, past small farms with cows and dogs, past shabby, lonely shacks. Gas and water lines were few, barren fields everywhere.

On Riverside Avenue they paused before one development. Some fifty laborers were hard at work, banging nails, lifting posts, laying bricks. Below the site of this dwelling's foundation, everyone agreed that the view was spectacular. There the Hudson River churned, framed by striking cliff palisades.

Suzanne did not hear. She sat her bay at the edge of the group—closest to the building activity. One of the laborers was shirtless, bronzed from the sun. His tawny hair was thick and wild and streaked heavily with gold. She watched him bending over. Watched the tight fit of his denims over high, hard buttocks, watched him straighten, saw the play of muscle in his broad back. When he turned, not yet aware of her, she continued to watch. He was superbly built, all lean, exquisitely defined muscle, and when she glimpsed his face, she gasped. He was as handsome as the gods of classical Greek mythology.

Suzanne was no stranger to lust. She had been flirting with the opposite sex since she was thirteen, had been mildly attracted to many young men, and even some older ones. But more important, at night she was restless and unable to sleep. At night she burned with forbidden heat, dreaming of a handsome, faceless stranger, and she yearned to explore herself, to discover the extent of her own passion.

That day, sitting on her hunter, she had begun to throb heavily, watching the stranger—who was no longer faceless.

He paused, stood, turned. Instantly his restless gaze found hers. He did not move, staring back at her as openly as she stared at him.

It sizzled between them, like a jagged, white-hot streak of lightning, the current of animal desire. He did not smile, but his lips curled slightly and something unspoken seemed to pass between them.

Suzanne could not stay away. Now she was stricken with burning restlessness at night, the fever of her body a conflagration that had gone out of control. She no longer rode with her friends. She took the old groom, instructing him to stay far behind her. Every day she ventured across town to Riverside Avenue. Every day he was there, and she watched him. Every day he watched her.

Today Suzanne pressed some coins into the groom's hand and told him that she did not feel well, to get her some lemonade from the fruit stand she had seen a few blocks away. When he had left, she turned, meeting his tawny gaze.

Suzanne licked her lips.

He dropped the hammer and moved towards her. As always, he was shirtless. A faint sheen glimmered on his golden skin. He moved with predatory grace. When he paused before the hunter, Suzanne started when she realized he was hardly older than herself.

"I was wonderin' when you'd get rid o' him," he said, his glance skewering her. It was bold and sexual. His tone was dry and rough.

"I—I don't feel well," Suzanne said, her voice sounding strange to her own ears. Staring at him, she realized that he might be a year or two older than she, but he was hardly a boy. He exuded a dangerous male vitality, something ineffable, powerful.

"Can I help?" His eyes gleamed.

Suzanne slid off the hunter. He steadied her. Suzanne couldn't help herself, she glanced down between them, at his thick, denim-constrained groin. "Only if you have some water." She lifted her chin, regaining some of her composure. Some of her imperiousness. After all, he was only a laborer, an Irish one at that. There had been the faintest hint of a brogue in his tone.

"Water?" He released her, folded his arms. He was amused. "That's all you want from me, Miss . . . er . . .?"

"Miss Vanderkemp," she said softly.

"Of the Fifth Avenue Vanderkemps?"

She was proud. She nodded.

He laughed. "Jake O'Neil, Miss Vanderkemp. Of the Ballymena O'Neils."

His long, dark lashes lowered, and when he looked up from under them, his gaze was potently seductive. "Are you goin' to meet me, Miss Vanderkemp?"

Suzanne did not have to think about it. It was all she had thought of for the past week. Soon she would marry some pale, boring Knickerbocker, or maybe some moneyed newcomer. She could imagine herself in bed with Peter Kerenson, or with Richard Astor. It wouldn't be horrid, but it would hardly be exciting. She wanted Jake O'Neil more than she had ever wanted anything, and she would have him, too, while she could. She nodded.

He sucked in his breath, the wry amusement gone now, the bulge in his denims far more pronounced. "Let's go."

"Now?" She gasped.

"Now," he said, low and rough. "Right now. Right goddamn now. You've been teasin' me all week, Miss Vanderkemp—and now it's my turn."

Suzanne did not make him wait. She remounted with his help, acutely aware of his hands on her waist, careless of what the groom would think when he returned and found her gone. He slid the key to his flat into her palm, giving her directions. Alone, Suzanne galloped off.

She did not notice the squalor of the shack he rented two blocks north of Ninth Avenue. She paced the main room, kept staring at the rumpled bed. She prayed for him to hurry. Her heart was in her throat. Her blood churned hot and wild. She thought that if he did not appear in another moment, she would scream with agony, with rage, and claw her own clothes from her body.

"Sorry, ma'am, to keep you waitin'," he said from the doorway.

Suzanne whirled. "I did not hear you come in!"

He gave her a mock bow. "Learned how to move real silent, I did, when I was a boy pickin' pockets in Dublin."

Suzanne didn't know whether to believe him or not. She couldn't care. He stared at her, but he was unbuttoning his cotton shirt, slowly, leisurely, provocatively. Inch by inch he revealed more of his hard, tanned chest, his torso, his flat, hard belly. He finally pulled it open. Suzanne was aware of how brazenly he was behaving, but she was mesmerized by his performance, and hurting now more than ever, the muscles in her inner thighs bunched into tight knots.

He shrugged off his shirt, tossing it to the floor. "Do I get paid for this?"

"What?"

"I don't come cheap."

"I . . . I don't understand . . ." Suzanne couldn't continue.

He had yanked off his shoes; now he was unbuttoning the fly of his Levi's.

He did not rush, seemed to enjoy the way his fingers brushed over the hard bulge there, seemed to enjoy her wide-eyed, speechless stare.

His grin came, wicked and wry. An instant later he had slid his faded trousers down his lean hips, freeing his erection.

Suzanne whimpered.

"Like what you see, darlin'?" he asked.

Suzanne had never dreamed that a man would look like he did. She wrenched her gaze away, to his beautiful amber eyes. He was stalking her.

"Like what you're gonna get?" he whispered, pausing in front of her. The ripe tip of his phallus brushed her skirts. Suzanne whimpered again.

He laughed once more before pulling her into his arms and seizing her mouth with his.

Suzanne came alive. She opened for him hungrily, clinging. He made a harsh sound as her tongue rushed into his mouth, deep. They sparred, quickly becoming frantic. The kiss took on its own wild, desperate life, tongues entwining. Jake began to rock his hips against hers with insistence.

He clutched handfuls of her buttocks, coming up for air, gasping. "Jesus," he whispered, his gaze wide and surprised.

"Don't stop," Suzanne begged, digging her gloved fingertips into his back. She undulated shamelessly against him.

"Words I love to hear," Jake muttered, abruptly lifting her in his arms. He tipped her onto the bed, sinking down beside her, claiming her mouth again. While he kissed her, he flipped up her skirts, cupped her sex. Suzanne gasped, arching up hard beneath his hand as he stroked her through her soft, white pantalets.

"God!" Suzanne screamed. "God, God, God!" She shattered. She shattered into a million tiny, shardlike pieces in the most brilliant, fantastic, all-consuming explosion. Her abandoned cries filled the shack.

Jake came down on top of her, ripping apart her underwear. He tossed shreds of the flimsy fabric aside, his big, naked body shaking. He thrust hard against her, did not penetrate, thrust again. He paused, panting.

"Relax, darlin'," he crooned against her ear. "This is gonna be so good, like you've never had before—I guarantee it, darlin'."

Suzanne was shaking with excitement, but also with some real fear. Her gloved hands gripped his shoulders, she wriggled her wet flesh against him, moaning with irrepressible need. But when he pressed forward, she stiffened in spite of herself. "I c-can't re-relax," she gasped.

"Shh, shh," he hushed, nibbling her ear.

"J-Jake," Suzanne said hoarsely, "please, be gentle, please."

"You don't want gentle, darlin', believe me, I know what you want—what you need." He licked her ear for emphasis, and Suzanne whimpered. But when he rocked against her again, she stiffened like a board.

"I don't think you can fit," Suzanne cried, tears of frustration filling her eyes.

Jake was frozen. "Darlin', you're not a virgin, I hope?"

Suzanne's grip tightened. She moaned again, long and low, desperate. The feel of his huge penis against her sex was making her feel close to exploding again. "Of course I am," she finally gasped.

He cursed. He cursed again, rolling off of her, flipping onto his back. He cursed her, he cursed himself, he cursed New York and Ireland, then her again. Finally he grew still, panting harshly. He threw one arm over his eyes.

"What is it?" she cried, leaning over him on one elbow.

He stared up at her. "Damn it, Miss Vanderkemp, but I do not fuck virgins!"

She whimpered. "But I want you to. Oh, God, Jake, I want you to!"

His jaw flexed. He looked at her closely. "How old are you?"

She hesitated. "Sixteen." Seeing his grim expression, she amended, "Almost."

Jake screwed his eyes shut, moaning. "Go away!"

Suzanne sat up. Her hat had come askew and she took it off. She looked down the length of his magnificent, quivering body. She looked down at her own legs, pale and naked, her skirts twisted up around her waist, her underwear in tatters on the bed. She stared at him longingly. Abruptly she reached out. She had forgotten to take off her butter-soft gloves, could not care. When her palm lay low on his belly, his breath hissed, his huge phallus jerked.

Their gazes met. "Please," Suzanne said very low.

Jake's hand covered hers; he sat up. "No." His tone was firm, final, absolute.

She whimpered. Holding his gaze, she slid her palm lower, then closed her fingers around him.

Jake gasped. Eyes wide, dark, dangerous, Jake threw his arm around her, pulling her close. "The answer's still no," he said, their mouths almost touching, their breaths mingling.

Suzanne began to cry with real dismay.

Jake kissed her, hot and openmouthed, tongue to tongue, wet and deep. And while he kissed her, his hand slid down her velvet-clad hip, over her soft, naked belly, through the nest of damp curls, between her glistening pink lips. "But you don't have to leave, not just yet," he said.

5

"You wish to speak to me?"

Suzanne started. She glanced up to see Edward Delanza lounging in the doorway, but for a moment she was still lost in the past, and despite the fact that he did not really look like Jake, it was Jake she saw standing there, tall, sexy, arrogant, golden-haired and golden-eyed. She stared as the past receded painfully, as she realized that she faced an entirely different man from her long-dead husband.

Slowly Suzanne got to her feet. It was very hard to smile at him. He emanated the same kind of negligent power that had so characterized Jake. Like Jake, he reeked of sexuality. But he was not Jake. He was a black-haired, blue-eyed rogue, and unlike everyone else of her acquaintance, Suzanne was not charmed senseless by his dark good looks and obvious virility. "Please, Mr. Delanza, come in."

His smile as patently false as hers, Edward strolled into the room. Suzanne quickly shut the heavy mahogany door behind them and leaned against it. Facing him warily, she wondered what it was he found attractive about her plain, eccentric daughter—if he did really find Sofie attractive at all. And if he did, she was more determined than ever to keep them apart—to spare her daughter from the kind of suffering Suzanne still understood far too intimately. "Good morning. I trust you had a good night's sleep?"

Edward eyed her. But his tone was equally polite. "Good enough. How is your daughter today? Is she feeling better?"

Suzanne's heart sank like a rock, making her feel quite ill. "Sofie is just fine." She forced a smile and walked to him, touching his arm lightly, flirtatiously. It was a gesture she used often with men. "You need not worry about my daughter, Mr. Delanza. I can assure you of that. Sofie overdid it yesterday, that is all. I am sure she will be fine today."

His smile pasted in place, he said, "Then you haven't seen her yet."

She shook her head. "She has not come downstairs."

His nostrils flared, his eyes darkened. "Perhaps she does not feel any better this morning. Perhaps you should check on her, Mrs. Ralston."

She laughed softly, but the sick feeling in her chest ballooned. "I know my daughter, sir. I really do. Nothing is wrong with Sofie, but if it soothes you, why, I will check on her in a few minutes."

"It would soothe me enormously," he said, a muscle in his cheek ticking.

"Mr. Delanza, you are overly concerned about my daughter!" Suzanne exclaimed.

"Your daughter was not feeling well last night; need I remind you of that?"

Suzanne summoned up another smile. "Mr. Delanza, might we be frank?"

"By all means."

"Your concern for Sofie . . . You are not really interested in my daughter, are you?"

He stared. His blue gaze was chilling, and she felt a frisson of fear. Like Jake, this man was far more than a rogue—he was dangerous if provoked. "I am very interested in your daughter, Mrs. Ralston, but not in the manner you suggest."

She was not relieved. "In what manner, then?"

"In the manner of any worthy gentleman towards any proper young lady."

Suzanne picked over his words.

"Contrary to public gossip, I do not pursue eighteen-year-old debs." He was grim. "Have I set your mind at rest?"

He had not, not at all. He was angry and unable to hide it. She decided against correcting the error he'd made regarding Sofie's age; if he thought her so young, maybe it would protect her from him regardless of what he avowed. "I was hardly disturbed," she lied.

He raised a brow.

Removing his gaze from her, he strolled about the room, inspecting bric-a-brac. He turned, flashed a seductive grin. "Now I'll be frank, Mrs. Ralston."

Suzanne tensed.

"I'm having a lot of trouble understanding why no one made any effort on behalf of your daughter last night when she got up from her chair and cried out in such pain."

Suzanne drew herself up straighter. "What?"

"Why was I the only gentleman to come to Sofie's aid?"

Suzanne drew her shoulders back. "Perhaps you have erroneously judged us, Mr. Delanza, as well as the situation. Everyone in our circle is quite aware that Sofie is a cripple, so no one was taken by surprise by her infirmity—

unlike yourself. Obviously you reacted instinctively, thoughtlessly, while the rest of us chose *not* to humiliate Sofie, by *ignoring* the fact that she is a cripple."

His smile was twisted and brief. "That's such an ugly word—*cripple*. Can't you find a better one?"

"But she *is* a cripple, Mr. Delanza."

His eyes blazed. "That's the third time in the space of as many seconds that you've cast that particular stone," he said, his smile hard and forced.

But Suzanne was afraid and angry—and tired of pretense. "I do not cast stones at my own daughter, sir."

"Then call her anything but a cripple."

Suzanne took a breath, reminding herself that he was not Jake and that he was a guest and that so far, nothing untoward had happened. *Yet.* "She has a deformed ankle, Mr. Delanza."

Edward paused, too. His left brow cocked up high. "Really? I massaged it last night and didn't find it deformed. Unless you call a small bump on the bone deformed?"

Suzanne's eyes widened. "Surely you jest! Are you making some kind of game out of my daughter, Mr. Delanza? Or of me? Are you amusing yourself at our expense?"

Edward stared, his eyes narrowed. "No, but I see that I'm going up against a brick wall."

"I beg your pardon?"

Abruptly he said, "She told me some of what happened. Why would a little girl with a broken ankle suffer rather than go to her mother for help?"

Suzanne paled and stiffened. "It is not your affair!"

His voice dropped low, became distinctly dangerous. "But I made it my affair last night—when no one else did."

Despite the fact that she knew him for what he was—another Jake—or maybe because of it, Suzanne felt her own heart flutter wildly in her breast in response to his soft, menacing words. More than that, she felt the blood in her loins, pumping more insistently now. She did not want to feel desire, and she stood very still, willing this feeling to leave her body. And because he was only a very attractive, younger man, because he was not Jake and never would be, the moment passed, her blood slowed and subsided.

Suzanne found her voice. "What is going on here?"

"I would like to ask that question myself," Edward said grimly.

"I have every right to know your intentions, sir."

"And I have every right to show compassion to another human being."

Suzanne gave up any further attempt at politeness. "Hah!" Her gaze flayed his groin. "I know exactly the kind of compassion you would like to show my daughter, Mr. Delanza! Your compassion was evident last night!"

He was still, his eyes blazingly blue, but a faint pink color tinged his cheeks, giving him away.

"You cannot possibly tell me your motivation is compassion. You think to seduce my daughter, do you not?" Suzanne heard the high, slightly hysterical pitch of her own voice.

He inhaled loudly. "No, I do not. I take offense at the mere suggestion. Jesus! I would not seduce an innocent."

"No?" She laughed, incredulous.

"No." He was firm, his jaw flexed. "I do not destroy innocence, Mrs. Ralston, despite what you may have heard."

Unfortunately, Suzanne was struck by an image of him embracing Sofie, and it felt like a premonition, seemed like a harbinger of doom. "So you wish to court her and one day propose matrimony, then?" she mocked.

His eyes widened. "No."

"I didn't think so!" she cried.

"You are overwrought without cause," he said flatly.

"No! I am not! You have gall—utter gall!" Suzanne had lost control, something she rarely did—except with Jake. "I know you, Mr. Delanza; do not fool yourself for an instant. You see, you are exactly like my first husband, who was nothing but an oversexed, philandering adventurer, and a Johnny-come-lately, too. So divert your charm elsewhere. Divert your lust elsewhere. I am warning you!"

"You are so fiercely maternal, Mrs. Ralston. Yet somehow I question the nature of your concerns."

"She *is* an innocent, Mr. Delanza. I do not wish to see her hurt." Suzanne trembled, thinking of Jake. "A man like you could only hurt her."

"I am not going to hurt your daughter, Mrs. Ralston, and that is a promise."

Suzanne laughed. "Men like you make promises only to break them. Listen closely, Mr. Delanza. Sofie has been unaware of men until now, and you are going to awaken urges in her that are better left dead. I forbid it."

"What has you so scared?" he demanded sharply. His gaze was hard as the diamonds his reputation was based upon. "If Sofie hasn't noticed men, then she should damn well start. Maybe she'd give up her ridiculous notions to remain unwed. I'd think you'd *want* her interested in marriage. If she's not interested, how are you going to find her a husband and convince her to wed?"

"That is not your affair." Suzanne was furious—and even more frightened of his interest in Sofie than before. But she added tersely, "For your information, sir, I support Sofie's decision to remain a spinster."

He started. "What?!"

"Sofie's only passion is art. She has no wish to marry—not ever—thank God. It is for the best, all things considered."

He was incredulous. "That is certainly very caring and maternal of you, Mrs. Ralston!"

Suzanne had had enough. She marched forward. "I am protecting her from bounders like yourself, and from far worse—from facing the fact that no man is prepared to take a cripple to wife. So leave her alone, Mr. Delanza, before you put impossible dreams in her head." Suzanne added, mockingly, "Unless you wish to marry her yourself?"

Edward continued to stare at her as if she were a two- headed monster.

Suzanne continued harshly, "I think it would be best for everyone if you left. You are interfering in Sofie's affairs, and I do not like it. I am sorry, Mr. Delanza—but I am asking you to leave."

A long pause ensued, Suzanne hard and determined, Edward expressionless. Finally he said, "If you really don't wish to see her hurt, stop calling her a cripple—stop treating her as one."

Suzanne gasped.

Edward's smile was cold. He bowed. "As you have not been reassured, Mrs. Ralston, I will leave immediately." With that, he made his exit, his strides long and hard and angry.

Edward waited for the carriage to come round to the front of the house to pick him up and take him to the depot in town. He leaned one shoulder against the white clapboard wall of the house, smoking. The starkly white driveway, composed of crushed seashells, stretched ahead of him, winding past the carriage house, stables, and servants' quarters, to finally reach the eight-foot-tall wrought-iron gates, now open. On the main road beyond, Edward watched several pairs of bicyclists go by, a half dozen horses and carriages, and finally a gleaming black "bubble," driven by a grinning young man in a duster, cap, and goggles. There were three young ladies in the backseat, similarly clad, screeching in both fright and laughter.

Edward smiled slightly, the sight of the automobile momentarily diverting him from his feelings of guilt. He had not seen Sofie as he'd hoped to, he had not said good-bye to her. She had not been at breakfast that morning, nor had she taken a morning perambulation with the other guests. He recalled her terrible limp last night, remembered how swollen her ankle had been, and guessed that she was still abed. He told himself it hardly mattered that he was leaving without a proper good-bye now; he would see her again in the city. He would make a point of it.

Edward was giving in to the strangest compulsion—to champion her. For it was abundantly clear to him that Sofie needed a champion.

He winced, thinking of Suzanne Ralston. There was nothing unusual in her desire to protect her daughter from hurt; indeed, Edward would have been appalled had she not rushed forward to intervene once she saw his concern for Sofie. But there was far more to Suzanne Ralston than the maternal instinct of protectiveness. Edward could not decide if she was aware of the extent of her own cruelty. He hoped it was not deliberate. Yet how could she flagellate Sofie so callously with the epithet of cripple? Did she really believe that? Did she have something to gain from that? And how could she agree with Sofie's decision not to marry? It was absurd. Every mother hoped to see her daughter safely and securely wed.

Edward inhaled hard. Despite himself, he was swept back to southern Africa. The plain shimmered in front of him, glowing from the unworldly heat. An acrid stench bit into his nostrils—the stench of burned flesh, both human and animal, of charred wood and crops.

The scorched-earth policy had been begun by the British, but it had quickly been copied by the Boers. And its victims were the innocent. Edward had seen bodies burned to death of both sexes, all ages, all sizes. He knew firsthand that life was both fragile and precious.

And he had seen cripples. Real cripples. He had seen men blinded from the battlefield, men missing arms or legs. He had even seen one shockingly pitiful wreck who had lost all four limbs. It was one of the most horrid sights Edward had ever seen. It was a sight that he would never forget.

Sofie was not a cripple. Edward remembered how she had felt in his arms last night for that one single heartbeat of time. Warm, womanly, wonderful. He recalled her pronounced limp. She was not perfect, but then, no one he knew was. She was young, lovely, very talented, and preciously alive. But she had yet to really live.

She might think she was devoted to her art—and he sensed that was true—but he also sensed it was partly a way to avoid what she feared—the kind of rejection he had witnessed last night in the salon. How stupid everyone was.

So it seemed that Edward was going to rescue Sofie from herself. And why shouldn't he? Wasn't it time for him to atone for some of his own sins? His whole life had been nothing but self-serving; he was a hedonist through and through. Wasn't it time to take on someone else's cause? To do something noble and worthy for a change? Edward wouldn't mind proving, even if only to himself, that his reputation was half-wrong. Perhaps he might even redeem himself as a man.

And in the process, he would set Sofie free. He would liberate her from her own inaccurate self-perceptions, fostered by her mother, perhaps even encouraged by Suzanne for her own selfish ends. When the day came that Sofie realized just how whole she was, he would walk away, satisfied. Or would he?

Last night he had hardly slept. Concern for Sofie had consumed him. There were so many questions he wished to ask about her, each and every one far too intimate for a stranger to pose.

Hilary had tried to pry, but he was not about to share his thoughts of Sofie with his mistress. She had finally given up and left his room sometime before dawn.

Edward grew uneasy, recalling how soundly and heatedly he had taken Hilary last night. While he was making love to his mistress, he'd had images of Sofie filling his mind, images that were thoroughly erotic and vastly carnal.

Very firmly, Edward shoved his darkest thoughts aside. Sofie needed a friend, or an older brother, and it was going to be him. He would champion her and he would ignore the more depraved wanderings of his mind—and his libido. After all, self-control was what separated mankind from base bestiality. If he could not control himself, he was no better than his reputation claimed.

Two riders on horseback veered off the road and came down the driveway at a slow trot, interrupting Edward's thoughts. He was relieved when he saw Hilary. Not only was she the diversion he now needed, he had left a sealed note for her, one that barely explained his hasty departure. He much preferred explaining his precipitous exit to her himself.

Hilary slid down from her mount, giving him a bright but inquiring smile. He saw that the pudgy young lawyer from Boston was her companion.

"Mr. Delanza!" Hilary carelessly handed the reins to a groom who had come running and approached Edward with a long, breezy stride. "Are you leaving us?"

"Unfortunately," he said. "Good morning, Mrs. Stewart, Mr. Marten."

"How very unfortunate," Hilary murmured, no longer smiling. Her gaze was piercing. "Is there a problem?"

"Not at all. Just some business that I must take care of immediately."

"Perhaps we will meet in the city after the summer," she finally said. "In another two weeks' time."

"I count on it," Edward returned, letting her know that he was not abandoning her.

Her smile flashed; she had understood. "Perhaps it will be even sooner," she said, and after a few more polite words, free of innuendo, she took her leave of the two men.

Henry Marten had been silent the entire time, and now he stared after her wistfully. "She is very beautiful."

"She is indeed."

Henry turned to him, blushing slightly and frankly curious. "She likes you, you know."

Edward shrugged.

"Do you think—I've heard—that she's not quite, er—" Henry was beet red. "Is there something between the two of you?" he said in a rush.

Edward almost groaned. "I never kiss and tell," he said truthfully, "and take my advice—neither should you." Edward reached into the breast pocket of his off-white sack jacket and offered a smoke to Henry, who declined. "We should all be so wise," he said, deciding not to light up again. Then he saw the carriage finally coming round, and his chest tightened. He did not want to leave, if the truth be known. And he was not thinking of Hilary Stewart.

"I suppose it doesn't really matter, if she likes you."

Edward raised a brow.

"I mean—you have so many women running after you, don't you?" Henry flushed. "I've heard all the stories, the diamonds, the women—you are a dashing rogue! Everyone knows."

Henry was so obviously admiring that Edward could not take offense. Edward said nothing—what could he say? Undoubtedly the tales were exaggerated, but he was hardly averse to the secret envy of the men and the open yearning of the women.

Henry sighed. "My cousin thinks I should marry Miss O'Neil."

Edward jerked.

Henry appeared somewhat downcast. "I am not like you, if you take my meaning. I do not have any woman running after me. I would be lucky to wed an heiress, even one with a small trust like Miss O'Neil."

Edward was seized with anger, so much so that he did not pause to think of how irrational he was being. "So you will marry her for her money?"

"Doesn't almost everyone marry for money? But I don't know," Henry said, gazing at his jodhpur boots, which were obviously brand-new. "I can't decide what to do."

"Why not?"

Henry met his gaze. "That dreadful limp—and she's odd, too."

Edward stared, his lips curling down. "So you find her distasteful, do you? But you might marry her anyway?"

Henry hesitated. Seeing Edward's chilling gaze, he realized he'd made some faux pas, but could not fathom what.

"But you will marry her even though you find her repulsive?" Edward said dangerously.

Henry blanched. "Have I offended you, sir?" he squeaked.

"Answer my question and we shall see."

"I do not know. I have no wish to marry a cripple. I was told she had the slightest problem, not a serious deformity. But even so, she is quite nice; she's even pretty, don't you think? But she is a recluse as well, and an eccentric, did you know? But I'll probably never find another heiress. Damn! What a coil!"

Edward ground his jaw down. "I dislike the term 'cripple,' Mr. Marten. In fact, she is not crippled at all."

"What?!"

"You heard me." Edward stared down the young lawyer. "Her right ankle was set improperly when it was broken many years ago—that is all. She is talented and pretty and as normal in every way as you and I—but a far nicer person, it seems."

"You—you like her?" Henry's eyes bulged.

"Very much," Edward said flatly. Then, softly, he said, "She shall be a most intriguing woman, I have no doubt."

Henry Marten gaped for the second time that morning. When he realized that Edward had picked up his valise, he recovered. "I am sorry! I did not mean to offend you. I wish to be your friend."

"Do not apologize to me," Edward said, striding to the carriage. He ignored the coachman and tossed the bag into the backseat himself as if it were a weightless toy. "You owe Miss O'Neil the apology, Mr. Marten. I hope you are man enough to see that she gets it."

He leapt in and paused. "And for God's sake, don't marry her. She doesn't need your pity—she's got enough of that as it is. She needs something far different than pity."

Henry stared after the carriage and Edward Delanza's linen-clad back as it drove away. He was reeling. Was it possible? Could it be? Edward Delanza, lady-killer without peer, diamond smuggler *extraordinaire*, a present-day pirate and a living legend if the gossip was true, was interested in Miss Sofie O'Neil?

Henry would swear that he was.

6

Sofie felt much better the following morning, and her limp was far less obvious. She had slept deeply despite the madness of the day before. Now she found herself dressing with care. Instead of donning her habitual shirtwaist and navy blue skirt, she slid on a white cotton dress, the high neck trimmed with frothy lace, the billowy bodice ruffled, as was the hem of the flared skirt. As she put on her shoes, she strained to hear Edward's voice from the many raised in conversation and laughter on the lawn just below her open terrace doors. Surely she would recognize his slightly sandy baritone the moment that she heard it.

She moved to the balcony, not venturing out on it. Below her a cricket game was in play. The women were so pretty in their pastel frocks, the men in pale linen jackets and trousers or knee breeches. Her smile faded. Edward was not a member of the group.

Then Sofie realized exactly what she was doing and she sat down hard on the closest chair. What was wrong with her?! She was acting very much like some young and green love-struck fool!

Sofie felt herself flushing. She was hardly love-struck. She was too sensible and too serious to be love-struck. Tomorrow morning she was returning to New York City, to her daily classes at the Academy, to the nightly solitude of her studio. After this day, she was not going to ever lay eyes on Edward Delanza again.

Still, she recalled the madness of yesterday and was amazed that any of it had actually happened. Sofie's crimson color increased as she remembered the intimacy they had shared. Dear God, not only had he touched her weak ankle, exposing it, he had so casually discussed it as if nothing were wrong. And in turn, she had almost told him her most private and most guarded thoughts, had almost shared her greatest fears. And he was a complete stranger.

Sofie reminded herself that last night had only been a flirtation for him, one of hundreds, no, thousands, in which he must have participated in the course of his life. Of course, for her, it would seem much more significant, as it was her very first encounter of such a nature. Still, she could not forget his kindness, his concern—or his so very devastating charm. He had not seemed insincere. To the contrary; he had seemed earnest and genuine.

Sofie dared not speculate any further. It was almost noon, and by now the guests were being summoned to the spectacular luncheon Suzanne always had at these weekend house parties. Sofie could hear them gathering inside the house on the floor below. As she crossed her bedroom, she avoided glancing at her reflection in the mirror, as was her habit. Then her feet grew leaden. Sofie paused. Last night Edward Delanza had asked her if she hid her beauty to avoid unwanted suitors.

Slowly, with some dread, Sofie turned to face the mirror, knowing full well that she was not beautiful and his words had only been another form of flirtation. Yet in her fancy summer dress she felt quite pretty, and last night she had almost felt beautiful. Sofie gazed at herself, trying to glimpse a trace of beauty in her appearance, but she was disappointed.

A pretty summer dress did not change the fact that she was prim and plain and that her face was only ordinary. She was not ever going to be a flamboyant beauty like Hilary or Lisa—and no amount of flirtation was going to ever change that fact.

She hurried from her room and down the stairs, almost tripping in her haste. She paused in the salon as pairs and groups of guests trooped in, laughing and chatting, progressing towards the dining room. Edward still did not appear. She wished her pulse would slow down from its rapid, staccato beat.

"Good day, Miss O'Neil."

Sofie started. Henry Marten stood behind her, blushing slightly. Sofie managed a smile. "Good morning, Mr. Marten. Did you enjoy your ride?"

"Yes, I did, thank you, Miss O'Neil. Might I escort you in to eat?"

Sofie lifted a brow in surprise. Last night Henry had not said a word to her, either before or after supper. She wondered at his change of heart, but smiled. "Of course."

Inside the dining room all the guests were assembled, awaiting their turn at the buffet Suzanne offered. Sofie was touched with dismay. "I wonder," she said softly, her cheeks growing warm, "where Mr. Delanza is?"

Henry stared at her. "You did not know that he has departed? He did not tell you?"

Sofie thought that she had misheard—surely she had misheard. "I beg your pardon?"

"He has left Newport for the city. Miss O'Neil, are you all right?"

She could not respond. She was stunned.

"Miss O'Neil?"

Sofie inhaled hard, shocked. Her disappointment was vast. No matter how she had tried to dissemble to herself, she had looked forward to another shared flirtation with Edward Delanza. In truth, this time she had hoped to be more demure and less frank, more ladylike and less eccentric.

And she had secretly hoped that Edward would find her somewhat intriguing, and see her not as an object for his kindness but as a flesh-and-blood woman like any other.

"Miss O'Neil?" Henry gripped her arm, real concern in his tone.

Sofie realized just what a fool she was. Hadn't she known all along that theirs had been an insignificant meeting for him, one single and casual flirtation? Sofie pulled herself together with great effort. She realized she was close to shedding tears. That was ridiculous, and instead, she smiled at Henry, hoping her dismay was not too obvious. She held out her arm. "If you would, Mr. Marten," she murmured.

Luncheon proved to be endless.

Sofie sat upstairs on her bed, hands clasped, wondering at herself for her wild emotionalism.

She had learned, at a tender age, to hold in her feelings. At least outwardly and publicly. Shortly after her father left, Sofie became fixated with painting. Her childhood art had been a wild and shocking explosion of color and line. She had missed her father tremendously and didn't understand then why he had left her. In the beginning, she knew now, much of her art had been angry.

Sofie smiled slightly. When she had begun to study art in earnest, at the age of thirteen, she had been forced into the carefully circumscribed mold of classicism, of precise linear drawing and absolute adherence to realistic detail. It had not escaped her that recently her art was unraveling in a regression back to her early childhood years, that her use of line and color was rapidly becoming explosive again, although hardly primitive.

Sofie reached for the new sketchbook she had been working on last night. She flipped it open, staring at Edward Delanza's portrait. Her use of line was so bold that his cheekbones and jaw stood out like slashes, yet the portrayal was astoundingly accurate. She gazed at his eyes, lit up as they were with suggestions she dared not even guess at.

It hurt. Sofie had to face it. He was gone and their social flirtation had meant nothing to him—unlike what it had meant to her.

Lisa barged into her room.

"What is wrong? God, you were as white as a sheet during the luncheon!" Lisa hurried to her, sitting down beside Sofie on the bed, putting her arm around her.

"I am fine."

"You did not eat. Are you sick?"

Sofie sighed. "No, of course not." And even if she could find the words to express her confusion and her disappointment to her stepsister, Lisa was the one who cried on *her* shoulder—not the other way around.

"Are your sure?"

She smiled at Lisa. "I am sure." What had happened was for the best, she told herself. She had been very close to taking wing on hopeful fantasy into a world that was closed to her. It was a good thing that Edward had left now, before she had lost her heart to him, perhaps even making a spectacle of herself as well. His precipitous departure was conclusive proof of just how insincere his charm and gallantry were.

"Come downstairs and walk with me and the others," Lisa urged. "That lawyer is quite interested in you, you know."

Sofie waved at her. "Mr. Marten was only being polite."

"Sofie, must you be a recluse, always?"

Sofie blinked. She recalled Suzanne's small lecture last night. "Do I really appear such a misfit?"

"Not a misfit, just reclusive. Sofie, I wish you would get out more. Gatherings are fun. When I debut, I hope you are going to come."

"Of course I shall," Sofie said firmly. Perhaps she should get out just a little bit more. Yet how could she complete her studies and her works in progress if she did? And she had never liked "gatherings"—that is, not until last night. Was she making a mistake in concentrating so wholly upon her art, to the exclusion of all else?

Lisa sighed and stood. "Are you going to draw?" She eyed the page in Sofie's hand.

"Not today," Sofie said, putting the sheet aside, making her decision.

"Oh, Sofie, you've crumpled your art." Lisa knew how important her art was to her and she quickly smoothed it out. Her hands stilled. Lisa stared. "Sofie, you've been drawing *him*!"

Sofie did not respond.

But Lisa was frozen. "You are in love with him!" she finally cried.

"No!" Sofie cried back.

Lisa stared breathlessly at the portrait. "I can see it, Sofie—it's right there on the page."

Sofie was rigid. "I do not even know Mr. Delanza, Lisa. It is ludicrous to claim that I am in love with him."

"Ludicrous? Hardly! Half the women in town are in love with Edward Delanza!" Lisa embraced her. "Oh, you poor dear. I never thought that you would fall in love with him when I said you'd be smitten. I just meant you'd find him as exciting as we all do."

"I am *not* in love with him," Sofie said tersely, but her heart was palpitating. "He is just . . . terribly attractive." She envisioned him with Hilary, recalled his glorious virility.

"Dear, he is utterly attractive, of course he is, but he is utterly unacceptable—and utterly dangerous." Lisa bent to hug her once again. "You could not be safe with a man like that. He might very well decide to seduce you, Sofie," Lisa warned.

Sofie gasped. Her cheeks flamed. "Now you are speaking utter nonsense," Sofie cried. "He would never try to seduce *me*!"

Lisa gazed at her for a moment. "Sometimes you are a complete ninny," she said. "Obviously you did not notice how he was looking at you last night—but I did. I think it is for the best that he left today, Sofie, when all is said and done."

Sofie could only gape at her stepsister. While images of Edward embracing her danced in her mind.

"Mother, you wished to speak with me?" Sofie asked.

Suzanne sat at her small French escritoire and did not look up until she finished penning the guest list for the last weekend of the summer. She studied her daughter's somber countenance. Like Lisa, she had noticed that Sofie was unusually pale and withdrawn during the luncheon. "I think you should stay here, Sofie, for the remainder of the summer."

Sofie stiffened in surprise. "I must go back!"

Suzanne laid aside her pen. "I've thought about it since you arrived yesterday. Really, you *are* becoming a recluse. Reputations are easily made but impossible to unmake, Sofie. I am worried about you." It was the truth.

"I thought I was only coming for the weekend," Sofie cried, pale. "What about my art classes?"

Suzanne sighed. "The Academy will still be there when you return, Sofie. If you miss a few weeks, it will not be such a tragedy."

"Mother, I must go home. I cannot miss my classes."

Suzanne stood, gripping her pen. She thought of Edward Delanza, who was involved with the very beautiful Hilary. Yet he had flirted with Sofie, and Suzanne recalled just how he had looked at her. She thought about the young lawyer, Annette Marten's cousin, who had made an about-face since the other day and now appeared interested in Sofie. Suzanne knew she could not let Sofie go back to the city alone. Just thinking about it panicked her. At least here Suzanne could keep a sharp eye on her and control any more surprising situations. "Sofie, dear. I miss your company, and as always, I have your best interest in mind. I would like you to stay with me for the rest of the summer. You would disobey me?"

For a moment Sofie, pale and drawn, did not answer. "I prefer not to disobey you, Mother. But I am not a child anymore. I am a grown woman; my twentieth birthday was just last May. I cannot leave my classes for an entire month."

Suzanne was unsmiling. "I know when you were born, Sofie. And you may be twenty, but you are hardly a grown woman. Or has Edward Delanza convinced you of that with his kisses?"

Sofie started, flushing. "He never kissed me."

"Well, that's a relief!" Suzanne paced to Sofie and put her hands on her shoulders. "It's best if you stay here for a few more weeks. You must learn to be more sociable, Sofie." *And I can watch over you, protect you,* Suzanne thought. She forced a smile. "I will send for all of your supplies. We can even turn one of the guest rooms into a temporary studio. I do not expect you to give up your work, you see."

"Mother, if only I could make you understand how important my studies are!" Sofie cried.

"I do understand. I've understood ever since you were a withdrawn child who refused to attend birthday parties and other amusements, a child who could stare at a painting for hours and hours and who always had her hands in a pot of paint. I understand, Sofie."

"If you really understood," Sofie said tersely, "we would not be having this discussion."

Suzanne flinched. She decided to change the subject, to another topic that was bothering her as much as anything else. "You did not look well at lunch today. Is something wrong?"

Sofie looked at her mother, hesitating.

Suzanne's heart lurched. "It's him, isn't it? You know you can confide in me, dear."

Sofie trembled. "I find him terribly attractive, Mother," she finally said, low.

Very carefully, Suzanne returned, "All women find that type of man enticing, darling. You are one of hundreds, I promise you that."

"I realize that. It's just—" she flushed "—I am a social disaster, and the only man who has ever been kind to me is Edward Delanza—and he was only that, kind."

Suzanne guided her to the sofa, where they sat down. She studied her for a moment. "He was toying with you, dear. I know his type. He is exactly like your father, ruled by whim and lust, so that nothing else matters, not even if it means destroying innocence."

"Mother!" Sofie gasped. "You are wrong about Mr. Delanza, for he does not find me attractive—and you are wrong about my father."

Suzanne's face hardened. "Let me be blunt. Jake O'Neil was a rotten philanderer, and so is Edward Delanza."

Sofie's shoulders squared. "Mother, please. That's not fair. Jake is dead. He can't defend himself."

Suzanne smiled bitterly. "Even were he still alive, he could not defend himself on that account."

Sofie hesitated, then slid closer to her mother, to put her arm around her. "He loved you, Mother, I know it."

But Suzanne slipped away and stood. "As if I care whether Jake O'Neil loved me or not." But even as she spoke, she knew it was an absolute lie.

"Sometimes people hurt one another without intending to," Sofie said slowly.

"He wanted to hurt me," Suzanne said emphatically, facing her daughter. "That is why he left everything to you, and not a penny to me."

"No," Sofie said, "you are wrong. That was a mistake, I am certain of it." She smiled brightly. "Besides, it doesn't matter. I don't need those kinds of funds. There is plenty for the both of us."

Suzanne stared, feeling a stabbing of guilt. "That is not the point, Sofie. There is a principle here."

Sofie was silent, clearly sympathetic. Finally she said softly, "I'm sorry Jake hurt you."

"He didn't hurt me." Suzanne was cool and she shrugged. Appearances were everything—she had learned that the hard way when she was young and thought herself above social ostracism and reproach. How quickly she had learned that no one was immune from society's cold, unforgiving shoulder. Long ago, at the age of twenty-five, she had finally grown up and married

Benjamin, not for love, but to regain acceptance and respectability from the society that had both spawned and rejected her.

Suzanne paced, wishing she could fling aside her memories. But she knew she needed to cling to them, needed them to remind her that once she had been a woman, one very much alive. "Enough of your damned father. What did Edward Delanza say, Sofie, when the two of you were alone on the veranda?"

Sofie stared. "He was merely being kind. I explained about my limp—and he was unbelievably kind."

"His kindness is a disguise for one thing—his intention to seduce you and ruin you," Suzanne snapped.

"No," Sofie said firmly. "No, you are wrong. Edward has no interest in seducing me. He was only being gallant. He was being a gentleman."

Suzanne stared. "Sofie—you sound dismayed! If he truly is not intent upon seduction, then you are very fortunate. I hope to God that you are right and you shall be spared the kind of grief a man like that leaves in his wake. And how gallant is it, my dear, to smuggle diamonds or carry on with Hilary Stewart out of wedlock? He *is* having an affair with Hilary Stewart. Why do you think I gave them adjoining rooms?"

Sofie stood, her hands raised. "I realize that he is fond of Hilary," she said hoarsely.

Suzanne was staring at Sofie, comprehension searing her. Her daughter was enamored of Edward, she could see that, and distraught over his relationship with their neighbor. Suzanne was horrified. Tragedy flashed through her mind. Jake had nearly destroyed her, and she could envision Edward destroying her daughter. "Hilary was not in her room last night—you realize that."

Sofie blanched. "How would you know?"

"Her bed wasn't slept in. I saw that myself when I stopped by her room on my way to breakfast—and the maids do not get into the guest rooms that early, Sofie." Seeing Sofie's dismay, she said softly, "I make it my business to know what goes on in my own home, Sofie."

"I don't want to hear any more."

"I'm sorry that you must learn about life so abruptly," Suzanne said. "But it's for your own good. If your paths should ever cross again, steer clear of him."

Sofie nodded stiffly. "I have learned my lesson, Mother," she finally said. "I enjoyed flirting with him, but no more. Have no fear." She took a deep breath. "If I do not return to the city, Mother, I will not be able to finish Miss

Ames's portrait in time for her birthday. Or have you forgotten despite your having arranged it, insisted upon it?"

Suzanne studied her, hardly hearing what she said. If Sofie was so enamored of Edward Delanza, then she herself must change tactics immediately. Hilary had a summer home not far from the Ralstons' beachfront retreat, and Suzanne imagined that Edward would be spending a lot of time in Newport Beach, warming Hilary's bed. When he was not with Hilary, what if he was sniffing around Sofie? "I have changed my mind," Suzanne said abruptly, perspiring. The very idea of Edward being so close to Sofie made her heart pound with fear. "You may leave Monday morning as we planned."

Sofie's eyes widened. "Thank you, Mother." She embraced her, but she looked at her queerly, and then she hurried from the room.

Suzanne stared after her daughter, prickling with unease. Sofie had never been interested in a man before, Suzanne was certain of that, and now she was far more than interested, despite her denials to the contrary.

Suzanne crossed the floor and watched from the doorway as Sofie hurried awkwardly up the stairs. She frowned. It did not make sense. Edward Delanza could have any woman he chose. Why had he pursued Sofie while at their beachfront home? Had his interest grown out of boredom, or perhaps out of some bizarre sense of empathy? Surely he would not extend himself to chase her, not now that it was hardly convenient. Not a man like that.

Suzanne's palms were sweating just the same. She decided that she would not take any chances. She made a mental note to send word to Mrs. Murdock to see that Sofie was chaperoned at all times. If for some incredible reason Edward Delanza chose to pursue Sofie in Manhattan, Suzanne would learn of it immediately.

7

*T*he roaring increased until it was deafening. The ground beneath Sofie's feet actually vibrated, as did the wall of the brick building behind her, and its glass windowpanes. The canvas on her easel seemed to quiver beneath her hand. Sofie did not notice.

Standing there on the sidewalk of Third Avenue, she worked with single-mindedness intensity, her strokes sure and short and swift. Finally the elevated train above the broad thoroughfare passed and the normal sounds of the streets came to the fore again—the competing cries of the strolling vendors, the animated Yiddish of the East European neighbors, the shouts and laughter of small children playing in the tenement-lined street below the El. Horses clip-clopped by on the cobblestones, carriages, carts, and lorries rumbled loudly, a trolley went clanging by. A policeman's whistle blew in short warning spurts a few blocks away. Gangling boys played a game with a stick and ball there. Drovers and carters yelled at them for blocking the traffic. And a fat German grocer stood in the doorway of his shop, just across the street, watching the passersby and Sofie while guarding his stand of fruit from thieves. She had been coming to this spot to paint since June, and while at first, people had been curious, they now seemed to accept her presence readily. Sofie sighed, staring now at the heavily shadowed canvas, and finally she put her brush down.

Sofie knew it was time to leave and that she was late. She checked the man's pocket watch she had left open on a small folding table behind her back, where her other art supplies lay in apparent disorder. Miss Ames would be at the house at any moment to inspect and pick up her portrait. Still, Sofie was reluctant to leave.

Sofie stared at the genre painting, scowling. Her impressions were exact; she'd captured the two heavyset women on the stoop of the tenement in front of her just as they were, tired yet animated, clothes worn but colorful. Mrs. Guttenberg wore a red dress, a brilliant splash of color in the otherwise dark painting. But despite her surprising use of red and the way the sunlight danced off the pavement at their feet, the work was missing something.

Sofie knew what one of her problems was. She was not enamored of her subject anymore. The subject she was enamored of, she refused to paint. That subject was Edward Delanza.

She was not going to paint him.

Sofie sighed. She had returned to the city more than a week ago, and she had spent that entire time working on this canvas and finishing the portrait of Miss Ames, yet she could not shake him from her mind. Sofie estimated that the amount of time they had conversed that weekend at the beach did not even total fifteen full minutes. Nevertheless, he lurked about in her thoughts constantly.

Sofie grimaced. Regardless of all else, Edward Delanza was the most splendid specimen of a man, and as a model, he would be glorious. Sofie put down her brush. How could she resist the temptation of painting him? How?

Especially when the very idea made Sofie breathless with anticipation, with excitement.

Sofie forced her attention back to her "genre" painting, which she was determined to complete before the end of the summer. It was a setting she had never done before and would most likely not do again for some time, at least, not until she reached twenty-one and was living on her own. Suzanne would never allow her to frequent this kind of neighborhood in order to paint real-life scenes of working-class people and immigrants; had she ever tried to gain permission for such an endeavor, she would be denied. Sofie did not have permission now. She did feel guilty, but her art came first.

Sofie was doing the canvas on the sly. It was no coincidence that she had taken up this project in the summer while Suzanne was ensconced in Newport. With Suzanne away, the odds of getting caught were very low indeed.

Of course, she was supposed to be at class at the Academy. But it was a class that was of little interest to Sofie; she was not interested in engraving, and she had been cutting it for the past six weeks in order to do this oil.

The coachman stood some distance away. Sofie had convinced Billings that this was an assignment she must complete for one of her classes. She did not think he believed her, but he was so loyal that he had come, afraid she would go without him, afraid to let her out of his sight. The Ralston servants had known Sofie since she was nine years old, and everyone was well aware of Sofie's passion for art.

   That passion had been evident from the very first day that Sofie had arrived at the Ralston mansion to take up residence there as Benjamin's stepdaughter. Benjamin was a collector of art. Like many of his peers, his interest was primarily in American art, but like some of the more discerning American collectors, he had attained a dozen works of the early nineteenth-century French Barbizon artists, including some rural and peasant landscapes by Millet and Rousseau, as well as the flashier, more erotic works of the Salon artists Couture and Cabanel. More important, Benjamin had been favorably impressed by the first full-scale exhibition in New York in 1886 of the French artists labeled *les impressionnistes* by the press and critics alike. Immediately afterwards, he had acquired both a Pissarro and a Degas, and in the four years since, he had bought another Degas and a still life by Manet. Sofie had been dazzled when she discovered his gallery. She had spent hours and hours there every day.

   Sofie had begun to dabble in art before coming to the Ralston mansion to live, as most young children do. At the Ralstons', her education included art, and her first governess began to seriously encourage her sketches and watercolors. By the time Sofie was twelve, she had surpassed her teacher, and realizing this, Miss Holden had brought the matter to Suzanne's attention. Suzanne had not been interested in the fact that her daughter possessed an unnatural aptitude for art and had no intention of finding Sofie a genuine art instructor.

   Sofie had begged, insisted, fought. She had been a quiet child ever since her father's death, unassuming, uncomplaining, undemanding. But not now. In real annoyance, Suzanne had threatened to take away her paints and brushes, forbidding her to ever draw or paint again. Fortunately, due to the unusual uproar in his home, Benjamin Ralston was alerted to what was occurring, and he had intervened.

   Because Benjamin rarely interfered in matters affecting his wife's daughter—or his own daughter, for that matter—Suzanne could not defy him. She found Sofie an instructor. Paul Verault taught at the Academy of Fine Arts and also gave private lessons on the side if he deemed the student worthy enough.

   And Verault instantly found Sofie worthy of his time and attention. Sofie began her studies with Verault at the age of thirteen and continued for three years. He was demanding and exacting, frequently given to criticism, all of it just, and very rarely given to praise. Verault insisted Sofie begin with the basics—with the study of linear shapes and form. That first year Sofie drew only with charcoal and she sketched some five hundred still lifes depicting almost every object imaginable, until a simple juxtaposition of fruit done in pencil had exploded with life.

A year later Verault pronounced her done with studies of shape and form; it was time to move on to color and light. Sofie was jubilant—for she loved color, she always had. And Verault no longer minded teaching privately at all. He was wide-eyed when he realized that his young student was far from ordinary, that her feeling for color bordered on brilliant. Sofie wanted to use color and shading boldly, in an unorthodox manner, but Verault would not allow it. "One day you may be original, *ma petite*, but only after you have mastered what I must teach you," he told her, and it was a refrain he often repeated in the next few years when Sofie grumbled about copying one master after another at the city's different museums. Sofie wanted to create, but Verault demanded she re-create.

Finally Sofie turned sixteen. She had already applied to and been accepted at the Academy, where she would soon continue to study with Verault as well as with many other teachers. But one day he came to her with tears glinting in his dark eyes. "I am going home, *ma petite*," he said.

Sofie was stunned. "Home? To France?"

"*Oui.* To Paris. My family is there, and my wife is not well."

Sofie wrung her hands, trying not to cry. She had not even known that this moody, untalkative man had a family anywhere, much less in Paris. How she would miss her teacher, her mentor, her friend. "You must go, of course," she whispered. "I pray that Madame Verault will regain her health."

"Do not look so crestfallen, little one." Verault took her hand. "You have learned all that you can from me, *ma chère*," he said, kissing her hand. "Indeed, in my last letter home to my old friend André Vollard, I said as much."

Vollard was an art dealer in Paris whom Verault had mentioned to Sofie from time to time. "Now you must learn from the other fine teachers at the Academy," Verault continued, "and from those around you, and then from yourself—and from life." He finally smiled. "But have patience, *ma petite*. Have patience. One day you will be free to use those oils as you long to do. You are young, there is time. Study hard with your new teachers. And when you are in Paris, come visit me."

After he had left, Sofie wept, feeling as if she had lost her dearest friend— her only real friend. For several days she had been unable to paint or even think of it, missing Verault terribly. He was the only one who had ever truly understood her in the years since her father's death.

When she returned to her studio, she disobeyed his last directive. She had been working on a pastoral scene, the canvas simply titled *Central Park*. Model boats sailed on a small lake, the little boys in knickers and the grown men in their shirtsleeves watching their toys, excited and laughing, cheering. She stared at the oil, angry her teacher was gone, feeling young, wild, and rebellious. In another week she would begin her first classes at the Academy. To Sofie, it felt as if time was *not* on her side—it felt as if it were now or never.

Her heart began to pump more vigorously as she picked up a medium-sized brush, suddenly afraid. Then she dabbed it feverishly in bright yellow. Soon the placid water had become more blue and green than brown, flecked with yellow, and the once white sails billowed multihued. The pretty lake scene exploded with hot color and vibrant movement. Sofie had been thinking of Monet as she worked, whose works she often saw in the exclusive Gallery Durand-Ruel downtown.

She had been so proud of her first foray into the modern, proud but doubtful and desperately needing encouragement and reassurance. Had she been crude and obvious where Monet was subtle and extraordinary? Shyly she told Lisa what she had done, daring to reveal her hopes that her art had taken a new direction and that she had discovered her true style. Lisa had been thrilled for her and had told Suzanne, who insisted upon seeing her work. Sofie had invited her mother and sister into her studio to view her art, trying to ignore her fear and anxiety. Sofie's art had shocked them.

"You're crazy!" Suzanne had cried. "And everyone will say you're crazy! They'll say you're a crazy cripple! You are not allowed to paint in such a manner, Sofie. I forbid it. Do you hear me? What's happened to your fine portraits and sweet landscapes? Why don't you do a new portrait of Lisa?"

Sofie could not hide her anguish. She had wondered if they were right, if her attempt to emulate the great Monet was so monstrous, if it was so shocking, if it was as ugly as they said. She had thrown the painting away, but Lisa had rescued it and put it in the attic. And Sofie had gone to the Academy and continued to study the traditional use of line and form, shading and color, spending three or four hours every day after class at the Metropolitan Museum of Art copying one renowned artist after another.

But she was no longer so alone. Midway into her first semester, Sofie made two friends for the first time in her life. Jane Chandler and Eliza Reed-Wharing were both young society women like herself, and they were both as fervently devoted to art as Sofie. Together the trio haunted museums and art galleries when they were not at class or at work. They took all the same classes, sitting together whenever they could, studying together for examinations. The next few years were the happiest and most exciting of Sofie's life.

But eventually she began to feel as if she had had enough. She was tired of copying the old masters. She had mastered female anatomy. The study of male anatomy was not allowed. Drypoint and etching did not really interest her. Sofie wanted to try her hand at something new and different. She wanted to explore color and light.

It had begun as a dare. Sofie had voiced aloud her yearnings to her friends. But Jane was happy with the curriculum, for she planned to work for her father, an engraver, and so was Eliza, who intended to become a portrait artist; both girls attended all their classes dutifully without complaint. Indeed, they both planned to marry and have families as well. Recently both girls had become engaged to fine young men from socially prominent families. They never said anything, but Sofie knew they wondered why she did not become engaged, as well. Sadly Sofie realized that they did not really understand her after all.

"If you want to do your own work so much, Sofie," Eliza had said, "just do it. Or are you afraid?"

Sofie was afraid; how could she not be? But she was burning with need, too. Her search for a suitable subject had finally led her to Third Avenue in lieu of her third-period class.

So she had decided to do a genre work, but not as Millet might, nor as Rousseau or Díaz, but as she, Sofie O'Neil, preferred.

"Miss Sofie, ma'am," the coachman said gruffly, interrupting her thoughts. "It's half past three."

Sofie sighed. "Thank you, Billings. I'll pack up." It was time to go and greet the crusty Miss Ames.

Sofie froze on the threshold of her mother's salon.

Edward Delanza stood on the other side of the room. His smile was warm.

Eyes wide, Sofie could not look away. Finally she realized that Miss Ames was also in the room, seated on the sofa by the marble-manteled hearth. The old spinster was greedily observing both Sofie and Edward with her darting black gaze.

Sofie felt a momentary panic. *What was he doing here?*

Edward strolled towards her, his gaze taking in every inch of her appearance with unnerving intensity. "Good afternoon, Miss O'Neil. I happened to be driving by, and I thought to leave my card. When I realized you were due home at any moment—" he grinned, his blue eyes holding hers "—I knew I had to wait."

Sofie had yet to move. When his glance slipped over her clothing, she realized just what she must look like. Sofie was horrified. How different she must seem now than she had that night on the veranda, when she was carefully coiffed and clad in an evening gown. Far more eccentric than he had ever dreamed, and far more eccentric than she had ever wished to appear.

For she was a mess. Her hair was escaping its thick, loose braid, a braid that was no longer coiled around her head. She could feel the heavy mass on her neck, and knew she was within a moment of having the plait burst free, allowing the unwieldy tresses to cascade down her back. Worse, her blouse and skirt were covered with paint, and she knew she smelled of turpentine. She had been more careless than usual with her appearance because she knew Suzanne was in Newport and that the house was empty—she had not been expecting a caller other than Miss Ames.

A caller? Was Edward Delanza calling on her?

"Cat got your tongue, gel?" Miss Ames stood. "Don't you care to say good day to the handsome gentleman?"

Sofie went red. "Mr. Delanza," she croaked. It was dawning on her that he had come to call on her. Then Suzanne's words suddenly echoed in her mind: *His kindness is a disguise for one thing, his intention to seduce and ruin you.*

"Where's my painting?" Miss Ames approached, her cane thumping.

Sofie was jerked to the present, paler now, her heart pounding. "Miss Ames," she managed, acutely aware of Edward. "How do you do?"

"My painting, gel!"

Sofie took a calming breath. She did not dare look at Edward, who was smiling at her. *He was toying with you, dear.* "It's here, Miss Ames. Jenson, do bring it in, please."

The butler entered, lugging the large canvas with him. He set it down facing the trio, huffing. And suddenly Sofie was anxious. Not because of Miss Ames, who would undoubtedly like it, but because of Edward Delanza.

It was competent, but it was hardly exciting. It was run-of-the-mill. She had forced herself to do it. She found herself looking at Edward, not Miss Ames, awaiting *his* reaction. That was ridiculous, because she should not care what he thought of her work. Then she wondered what he would think of her genre painting of the two immigrant women.

She shouldn't care. She *didn't* care, she corrected herself. He had no right even being there in her home. Why had he come? To toy with her, to seduce her? Was he tired of Hilary? Did he think her easy fodder for his mill? *Why had he come!*

"That does look like me," Miss Ames said grudgingly. She stared at herself on canvas. "A bit too real, don't you think? Couldn't you have prettied it up a bit, gel?"

Sofie didn't respond. Edward was gazing at the portrait, his brow furrowed, then he turned to look sharply at her. "You are very talented, Miss O'Neil."

Sofie's jaw was tight. If she ground down any harder, she might crack a tooth. "Thank you, Mr. Delanza," she said stiffly.

"You claimed that you were passionate about your art," Edward said, gazing at her as if perplexed. His glance went back to the portrait. "You have captured Miss Ames exactly."

Sofie felt herself flushing, because this portrait was devoid of passion, and she knew it. Did he? Was his comment a veiled criticism? "With photography one can do the same thing—even better," Sofie said tartly.

Edward started.

"There, there, he's complimented you, gel," Miss Ames said suddenly, but Sofie could not regret her candor, even though it had been nothing short of rude. "You are a talent, that you are. Come, Jenson, bring it out to my carriage." She looked at Edward. "I see you've got one of them damn fool motorcars, but as far as I can see, a horse and buggy was good enough for my parents and it's good enough for me."

Edward smiled at the old lady. "I went to an automobile show in London last November. I've been hooked like a mountain trout ever since."

"Humph," Miss Ames said. Then she winked. "Take her driving. All the young gels quite like it, it seems to me."

Sofie's pulses rioted as she walked Miss Ames to the door. Whatever was the old lady thinking? Still, she had the unwanted image of herself in the front seat of some fancy black roadster, with Edward in cap and goggles beside her. She had never set foot in an automobile before, probably would die without ever doing so. To imagine herself in one, with Edward Delanza, no less, was romantic nonsense.

But when she returned, she was terribly aware of being alone with Edward, and her pulse had yet to quiet down. He had left the salon, and she found him studying a painting in the corridor, which she had done some years ago. He turned. "You did this one, too."

It was a portrait of Lisa as a child. Sofie had painted it from memory, with the aid of a photograph. "You are a connoisseur of art, Mr. Delanza?" She was uneasy with the thought, just as she was uneasy with him.

"Hardly." His smile flashed.

"You have a good eye, then, Mr. Delanza." She smoothed nonexistent wrinkles from her skirt. To her dismay, her hand came away streaked red. "I am afraid you have caught me somewhat *en déshabillé.*"

His grin turned rakish, secrets sparked in his eyes. "Not precisely, Miss O'Neil."

His words stirred up fantasies she had thought securely shoved aside. Her body seemed to tighten. Defensively she folded her arms across her breasts. "Why are you here?" she asked hoarsely.

"Why do you think I'm here, Sofie?" he returned softly.

Sofie felt a rush of unwanted longing, felt the blood heat in her veins. She reminded herself that he was a rake, an unprincipled one. Did he really think to seduce her? It hardly seemed possible.

Yet why else would he be there—why else would he call her by her given name in such a seductive manner? Sofie stiffened her spine, and with it, her resolve. She had almost fallen for his looks and charm once before; she would not be so foolish this time. He could do what he wanted, say what he wanted, but she would remain rational and in full control of any unwanted desire. "I cannot fathom why you are here, Mr. Delanza," she heard herself say briskly.

"I'm calling on you, of course." His dimples were deep, his teeth very white and bright. His bold blue eyes locked with hers.

Despite her determination, Sofie felt herself begin to fall inexorably under his spell. His magnetism was overpowering. "Mr. Delanza, I do not understand," she said stiffly. "Why are you calling on me?"

"Do you ask the other gentlemen why they call upon you?"

She flushed with genuine embarrassment. "I believe I told you that I do not have admirers."

He stared, his smile gone. "You do not have callers?"

Her chin lifted. "Not gentlemen callers, no."

His gaze was wide, incredulous. Then his dimples reappeared. "Well, now you have one—me."

She inhaled. Her pulse still pounded recklessly. "You are a man of the world," Sofie said, choosing her words carefully. She was determined to learn his intentions. Determined to end this hopeless charade once and for all.

His left brow rose in a high, inquiring arch.

"And I am, as you can see, a dedicated but eccentric artist. And . . ." She couldn't say it. She couldn't bring up the real reason he could not find her interesting.

His eyes had darkened. "And what?"

"Why would you call on me?" she cried, losing her precarious control, and with it, her temper.

He loomed over her. "So you're eccentric, are you? That's funny, because I don't find you eccentric. Original, talented, intriguing, yes. Eccentric? No. Whose words are those, Sofie? Yours or your mother's?"

Sofie gasped.

He moved towards her—Sofie backed away. "Aren't you forgetting something?"

Sofie licked her lips. He had backed her into the wall. She was shaking and afraid—she stared at him, stubbornly mute. She wondered if he might take thorough advantage of her now and kiss her. Then what would she do?

It flashed through her mind that, as she had never been kissed before, she could enjoy it.

His eyes had turned storm blue. "I don't give a damn that you've got a bad ankle, Sofie."

Sofie did not believe him. "Then you are the only one."

"Then everyone else is a pack of damn fools."

Sofie stared, acutely aware of the fact that mere inches separated their bodies. She could feel his heat. Worse, she could feel herself heating up, too, in ways she had never felt before. "What are you saying, precisely?"

He lifted one hand. For a heart-stopping moment, Sofie thought he was going to touch her. His hand seemed to linger near her shoulder, and then he placed his palm against the wall, just to the side and over her head, and leaned his weight on it. "I'm saying that I've come to call on you like any other man might. All nice and proper-like. Because I find you intriguing. Yet you, you act as if I'm a leper."

"I did not mean to give you that impression," Sofie said thickly. The sleeve of his jacket was so close that she could feel the soft fibers of fine blue wool against her cheek.

Edward stared at her. "Why are you afraid of me?"

"I'm not." But she was—oh, she was. *What on earth would she do if he kissed her?*

His smile was twisted. His blue eyes held a bitter light. "I guess I don't blame you. But I promise, Sofie, I wouldn't hurt you. I want to be your friend."

He had spoken that last sentence in a soft, seductive murmur. Sofie's response was immediate. Her heart rate tripled. She could not breathe, could not even swallow. What kind of friendship, she wondered, did he have in mind?

Sofie looked into his brilliant blue eyes. And an image leaped into her head, of a man and woman entwined. The man was Edward, the woman was herself. Surely there was another, deeper, more sophisticated meaning to his words; Suzanne would insist that it was so. But Sofie could not decide. For she recalled how protective of her he had been on the veranda in Newport that night. And she did not know if she would be relieved or disappointed if he was speaking with utter sincerity now.

He commanded her gaze with his own. "Are we friends, Sofie?"

Sofie trembled. She knew he could feel it, because her cheek brushed his arm. And if he leaned just a bit more on his hand, their knees would brush, too.

"Sofie?"

She tried to think of how to answer him. There was no way to avoid the trap of a double meaning. "Of course we are friends, if that is what you wish." She knew she was blushing.

He appeared pleased. And then his next words truly undid her. "Would you paint something for me?"

"*What?*"

"Would you paint something for me, Sofie?" he repeated.

She stared, unmoving. Inside her chest, her heart thundered anew.

"Paint something for me," he cajoled. "Anything. Whatever strikes your fancy." He spoke in a tone and manner that Sofie imagined he had used many times before, to many women, when he was intent on coaxing his prey into his arms and his bed.

Sofie pressed her back into the wall. "No. I don't think so. No."

His smile faded. "Why not?"

"It's not a good idea."

"Why?"

Sofie wasn't sure herself. Instinct warned her against yielding to his request. Perhaps it was because she found him so irresistible, and because she wanted his approval even though it was irrelevant to her work and her success. Somehow she sensed that to bring Edward into her world of art was a very dangerous thing—far more dangerous than being alone with him right now, or than agreeing to be friends. "It's a great deal to ask."

"Is it? You painted the portrait for Miss Ames."

"That's not the same."

"Why not?"

Sofie could not answer. She was not about to tell him that Miss Ames was an old but likable crone, while he was every woman's prince of dreams. That her own mother had insisted on the one commission, not a gorgeous, threatening male stranger. "I am very busy," she finally said, her tongue tripping on the truth that was, as an excuse, a lie. "My classes and my studies take up almost all of my time."

"I see." He appeared hurt. He dropped his arm from the wall. "I thought, being as we are new friends, you might make the time—for me."

Sofie was frozen. What if he really was gallant? What if he really wanted to be her friend? What if they succeeded in forming a platonic yet warm bond? Sofie's heart twisted with yearning. With a start, she realized that she was loath to see him exit her life. That already he had become a part of her world, despite his having hardly entered it. "Why are you doing this?" she whispered.

"Because it needs to be done," he returned as softly. His gaze was bold. "You need me, Sofie. You need shaking up."

Sofie could only stare.

Suddenly both of his hands were on the wall, just above either side of her head. "You need shaking up," he said again, this time roughly, and suddenly his thighs closed in on hers. "Badly."

Sofie was frozen, agonizingly aware of the weight of his muscular thighs against her own soft ones, and of the heat that his flesh engendered in her own. She was lost in the brilliant, gleaming depths of his eyes, which had begun to glitter wildly in a manner that Sofie had never witnessed before, not in man or woman. She licked her lips. Her heart beat wildly. It did not seem possible, but . . . Sofie had the absurd idea that he was going to kiss her. And if her instincts were right, then she should send him away, in no uncertain manner. Sofie tried to summon up the words to do so, and failed.

"I'm going to shake you up, Sofie," he murmured, eyes blazing, and he leaned even closer until his chest was just grazing her breasts.

Their glances locked and something sizzled between them, something so strong and so bright that Sofie forgot propriety and all of Suzanne's warnings and every decent inclination that she had. She thought "yes" with all her heart. He knew and his lips curved slightly and he bent his head. Waiting for his kiss was the most wonderful, and the most painful, moment of her life.

Sofie forgot everything then. Fire rushed along her veins, burning up her skin, swelling the softness at the apex of her thighs, making her ache with a strange and new sexual awareness. She heard a small, breathy sound escape her own lips, just before his full weight touched her. Sofie gasped as the entire length of his swollen, steel-hard manhood was pressed against her belly, and she was paralyzed.

His mouth touched hers. Sofie made a sound, a soft whimper of desire. His lips brushed hers again. Sofie curled her hands into fists to prevent herself from gripping his broad shoulders. Her body throbbed wildly in response to the delicate and feather light touch of his lips, to the massive and heated weight of his groin. She was astounded with the blazing need she felt for him, a need to melt into his arms, touching him everywhere, yes, *everywhere*, a need to sink to the floor, her soft naked flesh against his pulsating hardness. She wanted to weep with it, she wanted to moan and groan and shriek with it, she wanted to shout "Yes!" She wanted to shout "Now!" And she wanted him to kiss her the way she had seen him kiss Hilary. Deep and open mouthed, as if he were drinking from the chalice of her lips, in a prelude to the way he would claim her with his magnificent and virile body.

But none of that happened. Instead, after the briefest moment, after the gentlest brush of his mouth upon hers, he froze.

Sofie's eyes were closed. But she was breathing hard, as if she'd run an entire marathon. Her own nails dug into her palms. Her body quivered like a finely strung bow.

"Jesus," he whispered roughly.

Sofie dared to open her eyes, dared to look into his. And she was scalded by the male lust she saw there.

"Jesus!" he exclaimed, and he moved away from her, nearly shoving her against the wall.

Sofie could not believe it. She leaned against the wall, desperate for air, her heart beating madly and so loudly, she thought he could hear it. Realization dawned slowly. He had kissed her, but so briefly, it could not have lasted for more than a handful of seconds. And she had been complacent.

No, not complacent. She had not even been remotely complacent. She had been wanton and wild and mindless, and on the verge of acting out the most shocking fantasies.

Sofie covered her mouth with her hands, unwanted tears rushing to fill her eyes. Dear, sweet God!

"Dammit," he said. He had stridden across the room, away from her, and now he stood with his back to her, raking his hair with one hand repeatedly.

Finally he turned. The entire room separated them; he flashed a smile. It seemed less cocky, more uncertain. "I guess I really want that painting," he joked.

Sofie did not answer because she could not speak. But if a painting would make him go away, forever, leaving her with her virginity and her sanity intact, why, then, he could have one. Or could he?

"Sofie? Are you all right?" He wasn't smiling anymore.

She wondered if he could see just how distressed she was. Sofie forced herself to stand straight and smile brightly—hoping against hope that he would not remark the wetness of her eyes, and that he had not remarked the insanely frantic response of her eager and yielding body to his hard, aggressive one. "Of course."

His smile seemed forced. "I'm sorry." He hesitated. "You're very pretty, Sofie, and I . . . forgot myself. Will you accept my apology?"

"There is nothing to apologize for," Sofie said, trying to decipher his meaning. She was aware of her mouth trembling. And she was amazed despite her aching distress. Did he really find her pretty? Why else would he have kissed her? But she was plain—and she was lame. "Really, Mr. Delanza," Sofie added, swallowing hard.

"Once again, you are far too charitable," he murmured, his eyes locked on hers.

Sofie could not bear the intimate joining of their gazes, and she glanced down at the floor. Every muscle froze as she heard him coming towards her. When she looked up, he had stopped, apparently careful to leave a good distance between them. "Have I endangered our friendship?"

She hesitated, then decided to be bold. "I don't know. Have you?"

"If I have, I will make it up to you," he vowed instantly, his jaw hard. "I promise you that, Sofie O'Neil."

He could not be insincere. Sofie spoke from the heart. "We are still friends."

He smiled, relieved. "Does that mean I get my painting?"

She ignored the warning voice inside her. "Yes."

"What will you paint?"

"I don't know."

He said, "I know what I want."

"You . . . do?" Her voice had become husky. For she imagined herself in his arms again, and she was feeling every inch of his intriguingly masculine body as if she really were in his embrace.

"I want a portrait of you."

Sofie gave a nervous little laugh. "You are still trying to shake me up, I see."

"A self-portrait would shake you up?"

"I don't do self-portraits."

He stared. "Then do one for me."

"No." She crossed her arms, almost hugging herself. "That is impossible."

"Why? Why don't you do self-portraits?"

Sofie stared, at a loss. "You can have something else—but not a self-portrait."

He nodded after a pause. "I know when to admit defeat." Then he came forward briskly and took her hand, lifting it but not kissing it. "I am late." He smiled. "I hope to see you again, soon."

Sofie extricated her hand, aware of being breathless and hoping he did not notice. "It will take me some time to complete an oil, if it is an oil you prefer."

"You are the artist; you may chose the medium as well as the subject."

Sofie nodded, clasping her hands as she walked him to the door. It wasn't until he had left that she realized she should have made a bargain with him. In return for a painting, she should have asked him to model for her.

He stood with his back to Central Park, facing the five-story, fifty-eight-room mansion across the street, his hands deep in the pockets of his beige trousers, a rakish straw hat shielding his tan weathered face from the glare of the summer sun. And from the curious stares of any passersby who just might happen to glance at him. It was unlikely anyone would recognize him, but he couldn't take the chance.

It was time to go. Very reluctantly, he turned away and began to walk slowly down Fifth Avenue. He'd gotten what he'd come for, even though he'd waited all day for it.

He'd waited all day for a glimpse of her. Just a glimpse of his dear daughter. It had been manna for his starved soul.

8

*E*dward cruised his gleaming black Packard to a stop in front of the Savoy Hotel on the southeast corner of Fifty-ninth Street and Fifth Avenue. A hansom and a carriage were ahead of him, discharging their passengers, and at the sound of the Packard's engine, the carriage horses began to prance wildly. Edward shifted into idle, awaiting his turn to pull up in front of the hotel's granite steps. The matched bays harnessed to the open coach finally quieted.

He clenched the braided leather steering wheel, staring straight ahead without really seeing anything. He could not believe himself. More precisely, he could not believe what he had done—and what he had wanted to do.

For a moment he had forgotten every notion of decency he had. He had forgotten his intentions. He had forgotten that Sofie was too young and too innocent for him. All he could think about was kissing her, and now, however briefly, he supposed that he had. How had it happened?

It was true that Sofie had been enchanting with her thick, mussed braid and her paint-splattered clothes. There was no question that she was pretty enough to kindle a man's interest. But surely not a man like himself, one used to far more beautiful and far more flamboyant women, a man whose only real interest in women was based on mutual carnal pleasure.

Yet the attraction was there. It made no sense. Or did it? He had never come across a woman quite like her before. She was so refreshingly original and so startlingly unique. Unquestionably she was talented and dedicated to her art. Her talent was enough to pique a man's curiosity, yet somehow her art perplexed him, too. She had told him that she was passionate about her work, yet he had not seen any passion in the portraits of Miss Ames and Lisa. He did not believe her incapable of passion. Any woman whose declared ambition was to live off the sale of her work and to remain unwed was capable of more than the circumscribed propriety he had so far seen. Yes, Edward was intrigued by her originality and her independence and by the contradictions he felt rather than saw within her. He was certain that beneath the calm surface she liked to present, there was so much more to Sofie O'Neil than anyone would ever guess.

There was no question that Sofie needed shaking up, Edward thought very seriously. But could he really rescue her from herself? Could he set off a volcano in her private little world, could he make her forget that she had ever labeled herself an eccentric or a cripple? Could he make her realize just how extraordinary she was? Could he show her all that life had to offer, drag the passion out of her, make her want to live the way a woman should—without ruining her?

It was a startling thought. Until now, Edward's intentions had not included any form of lovemaking. He imagined kissing her the way a man was meant to kiss a woman. If he could kiss her and then walk away, why, there would be nothing wrong with that. In fact, a few red-hot kisses were just what was missing from Sofie O'Neil's life. That would shake her up, all right, make her want to live the way every woman should.

Did he dare? Edward was an experienced hand when it came to seduction, but he had never before indulged in the kind of games that did not provide a satisfactory conclusion for both parties involved. He wondered if he could exercise the kind of self-control that would be necessary to play in such a game. He wondered if he could follow his own rules, rules he had never had to follow before.

As the carriage ahead of him drove off, Edward shifted into gear and moved forward. The liveried doorman came down the steps to direct him to a parking place. He drove the Packard ahead into the allotted space and slid out and locked the door, aware of his enthusiasm for his next meeting with Sofie. If he did not know better, he might think himself somewhat infatuated with her. But the very idea, for a man such as himself, was ridiculous.

Edward bounded up the red-carpeted steps of the Savoy, while the doorman in his red livery opened the glass door, saluting him. Edward nodded, thoroughly preoccupied. If he was going to see to it that Sofie began to enjoy life, why, there were many amusements for them to experience together. He crossed the voluptuous, marble-floored lobby briskly. Perhaps they would start with a drive and lunch at Delmonico's.

As he stopped at the front desk for his mail, he glimpsed a tall, bronzed man turning to stare after him. Edward thought perhaps he should know him, but one glance assured him the man was a stranger. As he turned, sorting through envelopes the clerk had handed him, he was bumped by someone standing near him. His mail scattered to the floor.

"Sorry, pal," the man drawled in a husky, lazy tone. "Here, let me help you."

Edward stared as the tall, tanned man whom he had just seen staring at him now stooped down to gather up his letters. The man stood, as tall as Edward but some fifteen years older, handing him his mail. His mouth formed a smile, but his very unusual eyes were piercing.

For an instant Edward stared. He knew those eyes. Those eyes were unforgettable. "Do I know you?"

The man's mouth formed a smile. "I don't think so."

Edward felt sure, now that he had seen the man's eyes, that they had met somewhere before. He also knew a hustle when he'd been the victim of one. His own grin flashed. "Thank you, sir." He wondered if the man had stolen one of his letters, and not having had the chance to glimpse them all, he could not know. He wondered what this man would want with his mail. He was expecting a communication from the DeBeers company, the great mining consortium in southern Africa, but all else was irrelevant. Perhaps this man wanted his mine as DeBeers did.

"Hope I haven't disturbed anything," the man drawled, his gaze cool, his tone wry. A very engaging smile flashed, one Edward was certain was false. Then the stranger turned and strode away.

Edward stared after him, wondering who the hell he was and what the hell he wanted—and where he knew him from. He was very disturbed.

Jake O'Neil walked through one room, and then another, and then another and another. He walked through the entire spanking new mansion. His footsteps echoed on the marble floors and in the high-ceilinged hall. After he had toured the first floor, he went to the second, the third, and finally the fourth. There in the servants' quarters he paused to gaze out the window. The Hudson River gleamed like a slippery black snake in the whitewashed moonlit night far below him.

The only room he did not enter was the nursery.

In the course of his tour, he remarked every piece of furniture, every single rug, every painting. He noted the colors of the walls, the fabrics on the chairs and sofas and beds, the draperies and wall-mounted lights and chandeliers. He eyed each cornice and every molding.

If he was pleased, no one would know from his impassive expression. If he was pleased, no one *could* know. For he was alone.

Jake moved downstairs at the same steady pace, his strides carefully controlled. Still no emotion showed on his darkly tanned, weather-beaten face. Again his footsteps echoed as he crossed the foyer. He moved into the room he had appointed his library. It was dark with wood paneling, made darker still by the burgundy hues of the Turkish rug underfoot, two walls filled with shelves of books, the mantel over the fireplace green granite. No fire burned there. The room was unlit, with the exception of the small lamp on his large Chippendale desk, and somehow it was cold, sterile.

He crossed without pause. He stopped only to pour himself a glass of the finest scotch whiskey his money could buy, and he downed it in a single gulp, then poured himself another. Now he moved to the green leather sofa, sinking down upon it. The fiery feel of the whiskey in his gut did not, could not, alleviate his misery. His chest was constricted with it.

He closed his eyes, his long, muscular legs stretched out, his expression strained with pain that was not physical.

Jake made a sound, half sigh, half sob.

He was alone in his huge three-million-dollar home, alone, without even a single servant—but he wanted it that way. He had been alone for a very long time, and it was the only existence he knew.

Of course, now that he was back, now that this house was finally finished, he would need an army of servants to run it. He supposed he would have his secretary begin to hire tomorrow.

Wouldn't servants be some comfort?

He heard it then. Sweet, childish laughter. Echoing in the hall outside.

Jake stiffened, not daring to open his eyes, listening acutely for a sound so dear to him—a sound he hadn't heard in fourteen years—a sound he would never hear again. But he had only imagined it, lost as he was in this mausoleum he now called home; he had only imagined it in his never-ending grief. It wasn't the first time he had listened for and been rewarded by her sweet laughter, and he knew it wouldn't be the last. For Jake allowed himself fantasies—because that was all that was left to him.

And for just an instant, Jake wondered if he was succumbing to madness. He'd had that horrendous notion before, too—while rotting in prison.

But if he was, he could not deny himself his memories, he could not. It was those very same memories that had kept him alive and somewhat sane during the two years of his incarceration, before his successful escape.

Eyes closed, he listened for her laughter and heard it again. It was hard to breathe. He heard her footsteps as she came racing though the door. Her blond braids were flying, her cheeks rosy and flushed as she came galloping to him. How beautiful, how dear, how perfect she was. "Papa, Papa!" she cried, arms outstretched.

He almost smiled—except that long ago he had forgotten how.

Besides, there was nothing to smile about, certainly not about a thirty-eight-year-old man on the verge of insanity, whose only gratification came from his imagination, from heartbreaking memories of the past.

Sofie. God, how he missed her. Sometimes, on days like today, he could hardly stand it. He wasn't sure that coming back to New York with the intention of residing there after all these years was a good idea after all, and his doubt had nothing to do with fear of discovery by the authorities. Jake O'Neil was dead and buried, the victim of a shootout with the police that had turned a small warehouse into a blazing inferno. His partner in escape had been shot to death, and Jake barely remembered changing name tags with him while the flaming walls began to cave in. But he did remember the London newspaper accounts the next day. He had even gone to his own short, unattended funeral, both to grieve for the young man who had died in his place and to grimly salute himself—for Jake O'Neil would never be resurrected again.

He was Jake Ryan now, a respectable international businessman. He'd made his first fortune in construction in New York City, made his second in Ireland in construction and other, more dangerous, endeavors. It was highly ironic to credit Ireland with any of his success at all. When he had fled his country as a young, suddenly homeless boy, running from the British authorities and the crimes he had committed in outraged grief and vengeance, he had never dreamed he would ever be able to return.

Then he had been grief-stricken with the thought of leaving the Emerald Isle forever. He could not realize that one day he would return, and be even more grief-stricken, forced to leave his daughter and wife behind in America.

Sofie. God. How he loved his dear daughter. How hard it was to be so close to her, to actually see her, yet be incapable of coming forth to speak with her, touch her, hold her.

Jake's hard jaw flexed. He stood and walked to his desk, where an empty silver frame from Tiffany's stood. One day, somehow, he'd get her photograph and place it in its frame, keep it with him always.

Jake rubbed at his damp cheeks, picking up the telephone. The operator answered immediately. Jake gave him the number he was calling. A moment later he heard Lou Anne's breathy, childish voice as she answered, and he almost hung up without a word. But he could not face another night alone.

After Lou Anne had agreed to come, he hung up, staring blindly at the dark brown walls surrounding him. If only he could come forward, if only he could reveal himself—just to Sofie.

Of course, he could not. Sofie would not want to meet her father, a man officially condemned as a murderer and a traitor. If he ever approached her, she would run the other way, screaming, as any refined young lady would. Maybe the shock of learning he was alive would be too much for her. He didn't give a damn about Suzanne, hardly gave a damn about himself, but the last thing he would ever do was hurt Sofie. She had the best of all worlds now, she had wealth *and* respectability, and she didn't need a pariah in her life.

Sofie backed up as far as she could go until her back hit the wall of her studio. Across the dimly lit room, Edward stared back at her, smiling that slight smile of his, his gaze suggestive, seductive, sexual—wicked. From a canvas.

Sofie realized that she was hugging herself. Through her studio's two large windows, she saw that the sky outside was turning gray as dawn tiptoed over the city, and more specifically, over the lush garden outside. She had not slept a wink all night. She had painted in a frenzy. She had painted and painted, not stopping to sleep or eat or drink. Now he stared at her from across her small studio, bold and vibrant and somehow alive. Sofie abruptly collapsed to the floor.

She was exhausted. She lifted her trembling hands to her mouth, knowing that this was the best work she had ever done. Edward moved with negligent grace against a backdrop of sand and sky, the picture of casual elegance, his hands in the pockets of his pale trousers, his white sack jacket open, necktie askew, glancing ever so slightly over his shoulder at her. Unlike the genre painting of the two immigrant women, she had chosen a light but surprising palette, in which lavender and pale yellow abounded. Like the genre canvas, she had kept the background unfocused and imprecise; Edward's form was far more detailed, and his face was haunting in its clarity.

She drew her knees up to her breasts, staring. He was the epitome of dashing elegance, of confident masculinity, of nonchalance and intelligence, of male sensuality. She had captured him perfectly and she knew it.

His gaze stared back at her, filled with a promise she did not comprehend fully. Dear God, how she wanted to understand that promise completely! His pull had never been stronger, his lure was now irresistible.

Sofie sighed, the sound loud and shaky. Surely she was still in the throes of madness to be thinking as she was. When the day grew brighter, as the sun moved higher, surely her own sanity would return. The promise Edward offered her or any other woman was utter ruination, nothing more. But

Sofie trembled, imagining too well just how pleasurable that fall from grace would be.

Sofie thought about how wickedly carnal he had been with Hilary, she thought about how hot and demanding his open mouthed kisses had been. Hot color stained her cheeks, making them burn, as she recalled the way he had driven himself into Hilary, but she could no more stop her mind now than she could have stopped herself from painting him earlier. If only she could forget what she had seen that day at the beach.

And if only she could forget the touch of his mouth on hers, and the hot, electric feel of his heavy erection thrusting against her skirts.

Sofie hugged herself. Although she was exhausted from working all night in feverish excitement, sleep would be impossible. Never had her body felt more stingingly alive. Every nerve she had seemed to be quivering and strained, on the brink of Sofie knew not what. But she was woman enough to know that she was ensnared in the web of desire—a desire she would undoubtedly never see fulfilled.

Oh, God. Sofie felt close to weeping. How had she come to this horrendous circumstance? Not so long ago she had been oblivious to men, to passion, to the world that existed outside of her work. Not so long ago she had never even known that Edward Delanza existed. Yet yesterday he had kissed her; tonight she had stayed up in order to paint him. And she had little doubt that this canvas would only be the first of many.

Sofie thought about his claim that they were friends. She was not so unsophisticated that she did not know that sometimes a man might call his paramour his friend. And he had kissed her. Was Suzanne right? Was he preying on her with the intention of seducing her—of taking her as a lover?

She closed her eyes, releasing her breath harshly. The question she had avoided all night finally loomed before her, impossible to turn aside. If that was what he wanted, did she dare become his lover?

Sofie sat on the front stoop with Mrs. Guttenberg, her back slumped. She was too tired to do any more work that day. She had not slept at all. But after finishing Edward's painting at dawn, she had been so elated that she had decided to go across town to work on her genre painting—much to Billings's chagrin. She had one week in which to finish the canvas before her family returned from Newport for the start of the fall season, and she was very aware of the clock ticking.

Sofie stiffened. She heard the motorcar first. She heard the roar of its engine and the screech of its tires. Her eyes widened. Careening around the corner was a gleaming black automobile. Its horn was blowing—pedestrians leapt out of the mad driver's way. Horses bolted from its path. Brakes screeched as the motorcar skidded to a halt behind the Ralston carriage, just missing it. Its front tires jumped the sidewalk.

Sofie did not move as Edward catapulted out of the car without deigning to use the door. He had not dressed for the drive; he wore no duster, no cap, no goggles. He paused when he saw her sitting on the stoop, his expression drawn and severe. Then he stalked towards her. "I cannot believe you would come here to paint."

Sofie inhaled, not so much in response to his anger—for he was tight-lipped with it—as in response to *him*. He was dressed as he had been that day at the beach—as she had just painted him—in a pale, rumpled linen jacket and slightly darker, equally rumpled linen trousers. His necktie was askew, his thick, dark hair windblown. He was so utterly male that Sofie could not look at him without feeling a deep, dark response in her own body.

Beside her, she heard Mrs. Guttenberg breathe, "Who is zat?"

Edward crooked one finger at her. "Come here, Sofie."

His anger made him compelling, exciting. Sofie had never been faced with a man's anger before. Her eyes wide, she stood up as if a puppet on his string. He crooked his finger at her again, and Sofie found herself walking towards him, her heart pounding very hard.

She paused in front of him. "What are you doing here?"

"Shouldn't I be asking you that?"

And that was when Sofie realized that she had been caught, discovered, found out. "I am painting," she said, imagining the worst. Edward would tell Suzanne about her defiance, and Suzanne would be furious. "How did you find me?"

"There is a whole city out there where you can paint," Edward said, avoiding her question, his blue gaze holding hers. "But Jesus, Sofie, you had to pick a place like this?"

Her spine stiffened automatically. "There is nothing wrong with this place." By now his automobile had drawn a crowd, including most of the neighbors in the tenement and all the vendors on the street. Small boys raced around it, oohing, aahing, gawking.

"No?" His tone was rough. "This is a tenement neighborhood, Sofie, and I know you know it."

"Of course I know it. That is why I am here." She smiled at him too sweetly. "I do not believe that this is your affair, Mr. Delanza."

His eyes widened. Sofie was a bit surprised with herself as well. She had never argued with a man before—much less such a devilishly handsome one.

"I've made you my affair, my dear," he said, staring her down.

Sofie could not look away. His choice of words, his bedroom tone, his bold, blue gaze, all had quite the effect upon her. Sofie flushed scarlet, finding it difficult to breathe. And she knew Suzanne was right. He wanted to make her his lover. He wanted to take her to his bed. His intention was seduction.

Knowing that, Sofie could not respond. Mutely she stared.

Edward finally sighed. His gaze found her easel, which faced away from them. He cast a long, enigmatic look at Sofie, and started towards it.

Sofie did not like that. She tensed as he went around it to view her work. She gripped her hands, her heart suddenly in her throat. No matter what she might say to herself, it did matter what he thought of not just her, but her work. Sofie was suddenly terrified that he would burst into laughter—and tell her that she was a crazy cripple.

He glanced up at her from where he stood in front of the canvas, the easel between them. "This is very different from Miss Ames's portrait."

"Yes."

His gaze dropped as he studied the oil.

Sofie clasped her hands to her pounding heart. "Do you . . . like it?"

He looked up. "Yes, I do. I like it a lot." But his stare was somewhat puzzled, somewhat perplexed. There was a slight furrow on his brow.

"What is it?" she asked, unable to believe that he really liked it.

"I've misjudged you," he said.

Sofie was frozen, not sure if his words were a compliment or a criticism.

He moved away from the canvas and came to face her. "Yesterday I thought your work talented, adequate. But I thought that there was something missing."

Sofie did not reply, her eyes glued to his.

"Now I know exactly what was missing." His gaze flared. He jabbed his finger towards the easel. "Because it's there."

Sofie whispered, "What?"

His smile was hard. "Power. Passion. That is powerful, Sofie. I look at those women on the stoop and it brings tears to my eyes."

Sofie was speechless.

"Don't you ever tell me you are eccentric again," he said harshly, "because you're not. You're extraordinary."

Sofie's heart began to beat very hard. Tears rushed to her eyes. "No. I'm not. You exaggerate," she whispered. Her life was beginning to feel as if it belonged to someone else, or as if it were all a wonderful dream.

He gave her a warning look, then ignored her denial. "Does Suzanne know you do work like this?" Edward asked suddenly.

Sofie began to recover some of her composure. "No. She wouldn't like it. She wouldn't understand it."

"You're right," he said. "To hell with her."

Sofie bit her lip. That was going too far.

Then Edward's eyes widened with sudden comprehension. "You don't have permission to come here—do you?"

Sofie did not hesitate. "Of course not." She searched his gaze. "Are you going to tell her?"

"No."

She was flooded with relief. "I'm appreciative," she said softly.

Suddenly his head came up and his gaze pinned her hard. His blue eyes blazed. "Good. You owe me—and I'm calling in my marker."

Sofie froze, choking on her understanding. Dear God, he was going to make his move now! He moved very close to her, and her eyes widened when he tilted up her face, holding her chin in his long fingers. She was in disbelief and close to swooning. He was going to kiss her now, in public, on the street, in broad daylight. Would he kiss her with the same heated abandon with which he had kissed Hilary?

And then Sofie realized that she had mistaken him completely.

Because he did not kiss her. Seduction was not his intention, not then, not there. He only held her chin and said very softly, his blue gaze determined and bright, "I want to see the rest of your work, Sofie. Will you show me?"

9

*E*dward followed Sofie through the house. She said nothing. Her shoulders were squared, her head held high. He could hear her slightly uneven breathing. He suspected she was afraid.

He wanted to reassure her, but was afraid himself that she'd back down on her invitation into her studio if they began a discussion about it, so he did not. Instead of following her, he quickened his pace and drew abreast of her so he could glance at her tightly drawn face.

They paused at the end of the corridor. She opened the door but did not step inside. Pale and tense, she met his gaze steadily. Edward smiled at her reassuringly. She did not smile back.

"Go in," she said. "If that is what you still wish to do."

Edward entered the large, airy room. There were oversize double windows on the far side, and an open doorway directly ahead, leading to another part of the studio. Several canvases were lined up on the walls.

Quickly he moved forward, his gaze roaming over the paintings. In particular, he found himself drawn to a beautiful portrait of Lisa in a frothy, full-skirted ball gown, the rendering soft and romantic, the colors pastel and light. The tulle skirt, similar to that a ballerina might wear, had been portrayed with such interesting effect that Edward almost expected it to froth up out of the canvas at him.

He paused before a still life of brilliant red and purple flowers. The floral was as different from Lisa's portrait as night from day. Sofie had used a dramatic, almost harsh palette that was mostly red and very dark, and her brushwork was frenzied and obvious, while the background remained in unfocused shadow. Edward was impressed. These canvases were not tragic like the oil of the immigrant women, but they had been rendered in passion, and they were somehow as powerful. All of her work was extraordinarily different from the usual drawing room fare, and the effect far more powerful, far more beautiful, than anything she might have labored over with the kind of precision she was capable of.

He had known from the first that beneath her serious exterior, there was so much more. Any lingering doubts he might have had were gone. Sofie was capable of boldness and brilliance, of daring and originality, of power and passion—and she must not hide her art or herself from the world any longer. Edward had never been more sure of anything.

He turned to stare at her, deep in thought. What other secrets lurked behind her facade of commonplace propriety? For there was nothing, he saw now, that was commonplace or average about her. His pulse quickened at the very intriguing thought that she might be as powerfully passionate in the bedroom as she was in an art studio.

"What are you thinking?" she whispered, her cheeks stained with a delicate pink color.

"You amaze me, Sofie." He knew he still stared but could not help himself. Nor could he seem to smile.

She was unsmiling and tense, too, her gaze riveted on him. "You do not like my work." She spoke hoarsely, but matter-of-factly.

Edward realized that she did not understand. He tried to choose his words with care, his gaze skidding over all the canvases again. Edward froze, riveted now by one of her other paintings, a smaller one he hadn't paid any attention to before. It was a portrait of a young man, and she had painted it with classical precision. It might have been a photograph, except that it was in color. The tawny-haired man was sitting in a chair, gazing directly at the viewer. Edward grew uneasy. He knew this man. "Sofie—who is that?"

"My father, as I remember him before he died many years ago."

Edward walked closer and stared at the handsome, golden-eyed man. His heart suddenly skipped. Jesus! He would swear that this man was the same one who had run into him yesterday in the Savoy while he was retrieving his mail—the very same man, just a dozen or so years younger!

But that was impossible, wasn't it? "Sofie, how did your father die?"

She started. "He died in a fire."

"Was positive identification made?"

She didn't blink. "You mean, of his body?"

"I'm sorry," he said gently. "Yes."

She nodded. "He was . . . unrecognizable, but . . . he had been in prison. He wore a special name tag. It was . . .intact."

"I see." A new thought occurred to Edward. "He was caught in the fire alone?"

Sofie shook her head. "I guess you've heard the rumors. Don't believe them, Edward. My father was a great man. He lost his mother and sister in a village fire set by British soldiers when he was just a boy—and boys don't think clearly. He sought revenge. He blew up an army camp. Unfortunately, a soldier was killed and Jake had to flee his homeland." Her jaw flexed. Her nose had reddened slightly. "Of course, he came to New York City. Where he met my mother and married her." Sofie halted, clenching folds of her skirt.

As she did not seem intent on finishing the story, Edward prodded gently, "What happened?"

"He was successful here. He began as a common laborer, but soon acquired his own building contracts. Suzanne, of course, was from society. He built her—us—a beautiful home on Riverside Drive. Soon they moved in high circles. It was a fluke, an ugly fluke, but one day a visiting Englishman, who just happened to be a retired military officer, one who had been at that army camp that day, recognized him at a social affair they were both attending. Not only did he recognize him, Lord Carrington recalled his name. Foolishly my father had not changed his name, never dreaming the past might catch up with him in New York City."

"That was an incredible coincidence," Edward agreed, reaching out to touch her arm lightly, comfortingly. "Your father must have looked so much different, an older man by then."

"He was twenty-four and I was almost six. You see, he was really only a boy when he met and married Suzanne."

"I'm sorry, Sofie," Edward said softly, taking her hand.

For a moment she allowed him to hold it, before pulling her palm away. "I was six years old, but I'll never forget the day he said good-bye." Sofie forced a smile. "I was devastated. I cannot remember what he said, and surely he would not have told me that he might never return, but somehow I knew. Children, I think, are astoundingly astute."

Edward nodded gravely, aching for her.

"Less than a year later, he was captured, and shortly after, he was extradited to Great Britain and imprisoned there—for that single crime of passion. After two years of incarceration, he escaped, with another man—only to die in a fire himself."

"I'm sorry," Edward said again. "What happened to the other man?"

"He was never found."

And then Edward knew. *He knew.* He turned to stare at Jake O'Neil's portrait. *You son of a bitch*, he was thinking, torn between admiration and anger. *You're alive, aren't you? Alive and hiding? But don't you want to see your daughter again? How could you stay away from her like this? And why were you stalking me the other day?!*

Jake O'Neil stared back at him, his golden eyes arrogant and mocking. "Edward?"

He turned and saw that Sofie's amber eyes were huge, her face pale. "Are you all right?" he asked. "I didn't mean to bring up a painful topic."

"I will always miss him," she said simply.

Instantly Edward knew that he was going to find Jake O'Neil and make the bastard come forward to a reunion with his daughter. Suddenly that seemed as important as anything else. Then he was struck by a thought. Jake O'Neil was alive—but Suzanne had remarried. He turned to look at Sofie, who was watching him, trying to imagine the scandal should Jake's public resurrection ever occur. He flinched, because he did not have to be a wizard to know that a lot of people would be hurt. Was that why Jake had remained dead and buried all these years? Perhaps he did not give a damn about his wife or his daughter. Perhaps he cared too much. In any case, Edward intended to find out.

"Edward?" she said, her voice low and hesitant. "What, exactly, do you think of my work?"

Edward took her arm, moving her with him to stand in front of the floral. He looked at the vibrant still life. "This is my favorite. I don't know how anyone could make a few simple flowers so exciting."

"Suzanne saw this in May," Sofie said slowly, her cheeks coloring slightly. "She said they don't even remotely resemble flowers. She said a five-year-old could paint flowers like that."

Edward jerked. "I can't believe she said that."

Sofie's gaze was intense. "You don't agree?"

"Hell, no! I like this painting *best*."

"You like my work?"

He turned to her. Very softly, he said, "Very much. You are brilliant, Sofie."

She ducked her head. He realized that she must seldom hear praise for her work from her own family. Edward turned to stroll around the room, glancing out the windows into the garden. But as he approached the open doorway, only slightly curious about the rest of her studio, Sofie's head jerked up. Harshly she cried, "Edward!" It was a warning.

He halted. She had turned ashen. "I am not allowed to go into the rest of your studio?"

She seemed incapable of speech.

Now Edward was very curious, because he knew that, once again, Sofie was hiding from him. "What is in the other room, Sofie?"

She opened her mouth, but no words came out. Finally she croaked, "Something I have only just finished."

Edward could not resist. He heard her moan as he moved decisively forward. But on the threshold of the second room, he froze, reeling with absolute shock.

This, apparently, was where she worked. The room was smaller but very light and bright, one entire wall consisting of floor-to-ceiling windows. The room was completely empty except for a large portrait, which stood on an easel in its center, and one small stool and table, the latter cluttered with tubes of paints and palettes and all size and manner of brushes. The smell within was strong, of oil paint and turpentine.

"Jesus," he whispered, mesmerized. *She had painted him.*

And what a work it was. The canvas vibrated with tension and color, and Edward expected to see his image walk out of the painting and into the room at any moment. "Do I actually look like that?" he heard himself ask.

Sofie did not answer.

He stepped closer and paused again. There was such power and passion in this portrait that he was still stunned. He was also exultant. He turned to look at her, but she refused now to meet his gaze. She was blushing furiously.

Edward studied the portrait. Although his image leapt out of the canvas with lifelike clarity, it was as if Sofie had painted in a mad frenzy, her strokes shorter and more insistent, colors more vividly displayed, the background far less concise, almost a collage of rainbow colors, with soft shades of purple and yellow predominant. The work was light, bright, and exuberant. It was joyous and hopeful. And she had portrayed him as a hero, not as the flawed man he knew himself to be.

"Say something," Sofie said.

He turned to look at her, at a loss for words. "I am not a godamned hero," he finally said.

She lifted her gaze. "I portrayed you as I recalled you."

He turned back to the canvas and studied the image he saw there, and he wondered if there was really such a roguish, amused, and knowing sparkle in his eyes. He was hardly as handsome, as rakish, as disturbingly powerful, as she had portrayed him.

It finally dawned on him; in order for her to portray him as she had, she might very well be in love with him.

He froze, turned slowly, stared at her, his blood heating now dangerously. How could he direct her passion so that it never became anything more than a schoolgirl crush? And did he even want to?

"You are staring at me," she said stiffly. "Are you shocked?"

At first he could not speak. He was appalled with his wayward thought. Shocked not with her, but with himself. "Yes."

She turned away. "I thought so."

He reached for her. "Sofie—I am shocked, but not the way you're thinking." Their gazes locked. He was aware of her arm beneath his hand, of the proximity of their bodies, of her slightly parted lips. Of the now insistent and heavy pulsing between his thighs. "I'm honored, Sofie," he said low.

She stared, unblinking.

He had already realized that she had worked on his portrait with great stamina and great passion. He now wondered what it would be like to receive that passion directly from her, as a lover would. "I'm shocked because I never expected to find my own portrait here. I'm shocked because, although I am no connoisseur, this is so damn good."

Sofie inhaled hard, holding his gaze.

Edward felt the heat flare between them, wondered if he had even seen a jagged line of white light, akin to a bolt of lightning. "You just completed this?"

"I finished it this morning."

"You worked on my portrait last night?"

"Yes." She was strained, her voice low, husky. "Usually it takes me several days or even several weeks to complete an oil, but I began your portrait last night—and finished it at dawn."

His jaw flexed. His body blazed to life. Edward forgot his image on the canvas behind him. His hands touched her shoulders. Sofie shuddered visibly, but made no attempt to resist or move away.

"Sofie," he said huskily, "I am more than honored."

Her lips parted as he pulled her slowly forward and into his arms. "Edward," she began hoarsely.

He smiled down at her, his pulses rioting, sliding his hands down her slim but strong back. She inhaled as he pressed her against the full length of his hard, aroused body. His hands slid lower, gripping her hips just above the tempting curve of her buttocks. "Relax," he whispered, lowering his head. "I'm going to kiss you, Sofie, and I want you to relax and enjoy it."

She made a sound very much like a whimper, looking into his eyes with both desire and despair. "I'm not sure," she said, anguished. "I haven't made up my mind."

Edward did not really understand her remark, and did not care to, not now. Not when he had just realized that Sofie had melted against him, despite her words, and that her hands gripped the lapels of his jacket. He was instantly aware of the softness of her breasts crushed against his chest, of his phallus lengthening even more in eager response, and straining high against her soft, warm belly. The heat between them coursed electric and red-hot.

"For you, Sofie, just for you," he murmured, rubbing his mouth against her cheek. And then his lips brushed hers, soft and gentle, and then tenderness was lost to lust.

The passion exploded in him so quickly that Edward was helpless to defy it. His mouth took hers, Sofie's gasp was smothered by the invasion of his tongue. And Edward felt as if he had finally reached heaven as he sucked her mouth with his the way he had been dreaming of doing for days.

For a long time they kissed, tongue to tongue, his huge, hardened loins burning against hers. Edward scraped the wetness of her mouth dry, invaded as deeply as he knew how, wanting to show her with his tongue what he could do to her with his manhood. Sofie's tongue flicked ever so lightly against his. Edward made a sound, half gasp, half growl, and found himself gripping her buttocks now, and pressing her up against his erection. He expected her to reject this overt intimacy, but Sofie did not stiffen. Instead, her mouth opened wider for him and she began to spar with him. He heard her whimper.

Edward began to rock himself against her very intently, perilously close to losing control. His hands slid lower on Sofie's bottom, indecently so. A remnant of sanity returned to him, warningly.

He closed his eyes hard and succumbed just for another instant to the illicit pleasure of the wet and thrusting kiss and to the raw agony of holding her in his arms while he throbbed and pulsed against her. She was panting. He derived immense satisfaction from the fact and was aroused impossibly more. Yet he wished to hear her moan in need, in ecstasy. With complete abandon. But he dared not prolong the encounter, dared not go any further, for if he did, he was afraid there would be no turning back.

And if he seduced Sofie, he could not live with himself.

Groaning, Edward tore his mouth from hers, forcing his eyes open. Her thighs still pressed against his, and he was very reluctant to move away, but finally he did, putting a few inches between their straining, overheated bodies. Startled, Sofie lifted her lids, and he saw that her gaze was glazed and unfocused and that she was flushed with genuine desire.

He was more tempted than he had ever been. He'd never had to fight the urges of his body before. Not like this. But of course, he'd never played this kind of game before, had never kissed a woman only to teach her to live and not to teach her to love. He swallowed hard and shifted away from her completely, pressing his cheek into the wall beside her, ignoring her small, raw cry, which only increased his excitement.

It was many minutes before he could move, and by then, she had slipped away from her position next to him. Edward straightened, inhaled deeply, turned. Sofie stood with her back to him, hugging herself tightly.

"Sofie?"

She stiffened, then slowly faced him.

He had been afraid she would be furious, but there was no trace of anger in her expression. Indeed, she was remarkably composed, far more so than he. But by now he knew that she wore her dignity about her as one would a big, hooded cloak—the better to hide behind. He smiled. "If you tell me I am a cad, Sofie, I will not blame you."

She searched his gaze. Her lips were very swollen. "Are you a cad, Edward?"

His smile disappeared. "To steal that kind of kiss? Yes. Unquestionably."

She wet her lips, and he realized that she was still every bit as hot as he, and far more nervous. "I . . . I don't mind."

He was stunned. "Does that mean I may take such liberties again?"

She hesitated, still hugging herself. "Yes."

"Sofie." He paced forward, screeched to a stop. "Sofie—you must never allow *any* man to kiss you in such an intimate manner! Not even me!"

She said nothing, staring, unblinking.

He fought for calm, could not find it. "I did not mean to go so far," he said truthfully, now rueful as well.

"What did you mean, then?"

"Just a kiss, a small, sweet kiss."

Her breasts heaved.

"Sofie?"

"Edward, I think that now is as good a time as any to ask." Color crept up her face in waves. "What are your intentions?"

The truth would never do! She was proud and she would be furious—she would kick him out immediately. So he smiled and pried one of her arms free and tucked it in his. "My intention is to be a good friend, Sofie. A true friend—one you will not forget."

10

*L*adies did not drink, except for the occasional glass of wine at supper and perhaps a sherry afterwards. They certainly did not sip delicious French wine at noon. Sofie watched the white-coated waiter hover over her, about to pour the pale golden Chablis into her wineglass. And she declined. "I cannot."

Edward smiled at her from across the small table. His expression was both bold and intimate. "You can't say no," he said. "Not to me."

Sofie looked at him, then dropped her eyes and turned to look around them. She felt as if she were moving in a dream, she was in such a state of disbelief. The most beautiful ladies she had ever seen, it seemed, were present that day in their brightly colored tea gowns and prettily matching hats. Their escorts were the most handsome, dapper men, some in dark business suits, others in more casual yet elegant sack jackets. Yet no gentleman present was as handsome or as dashing as her own escort.

Sofie trembled slightly. It hardly seemed possible that she was sitting right now in the oh-so-famous Delmonico's with such a man. But she was. Nor did the events of that day seem even remotely possible, but they were. Edward had seen all of her work, had not just admired it, he thought it brilliant—he thought her brilliant. He had said so.

She shook yet again. And he had kissed her, the way he had kissed Hilary, with raw and scorching and sublime passion. He had kissed her deep and openmouthed the way she had secretly dreamed of being kissed by him, and more thoroughly than she had even thought possible.

Unquestionably he was a cad. Suzanne was right. He intended seduction. And Sofie intended to be his very willing victim.

Sofie nodded wordlessly at Edward, accepting the glass of white wine. She watched the waiter pour.

Edward grinned, both dimples blossoming. "That's my Sofie."

Sofie looked up, shuddering with the force of her emotions, with fear, with excitement, with passion—but she must not fall in love with him, she must not. Sofie was no fool. Their affair was going to be glorious, or so she prayed, despite the fact that she was far less perfect than the other women he had known, and far less experienced. Their affair would be wonderful. She—plain, lame, eccentric Sofie O'Neil—would finally learn something of love and passion and life, it seemed. Who would have ever thought she would have such a chance—and with such a man? But it would inevitably end, perhaps sooner than later. She must not allow herself to ever lose sight of that fact, she must prepare herself for it even before they had begun. She must not allow herself to fall in love with him, no matter what happened.

Quickly Sofie reached for her wineglass, taking a sip of the almost sweet liquid, which seemed to float over her tongue as smoothly as silk.

"Good?" Edward queried, watching her closely.

"Delicious," Sofie said truthfully. "I've never had better."

While Edward ordered them a meal that they could never in a hundred years finish, Sofie took the opportunity to glance around yet again. They had a window table. The main dining room overlooked Fifth Avenue and the lush green park of Madison Square. Couples strolled on the paths below, ladies with their parasols to shield their complexions from the blazing summer sun, the men in jaunty straw hats or conservative felts. The sky was an extraordinary blue, and big, puffy clouds floated by.

And the restaurant itself was a sea of contrasts, of the ladies' bold jewel-toned gowns, of the gentlemen's gray wools and nearly white linens. The tables were all clothed in startling white, sparkling with crystal and silver, and each was brightly festive with a centerpiece of fresh-cut rainbow-hued flowers.

"Who is going to eat all that?" Sofie asked after the waiter had left them. "And more importantly, who is going to drink all this wine?"

"We don't have to finish anything," Edward said. His tone dropped. "I want everything to be perfect for you, Sofie."

She paused, playing nervously with her fork. Then her gaze met his. "It is perfect already, Edward," she whispered. His stare was so intense, she looked away, taking another sip of wine. Her pulse was pounding. Clearly the seduction he had begun in earnest in her studio was continuing now. Sofie knew she should not be nervous, for Edward was undoubtedly a gentle and skillful lover. Would he want to take her somewhere private later, after lunch? Her wits seemed to scatter at the notion, her pulses soared.

"Why are you against marriage?" Edward asked.

Sofie almost lost her napkin. "What?"

He repeated the question.

Sofie stared. "That is the strangest thing to ask me just now."

"Why? The moment we met, you declared that you never intended to marry." Edward's eyes were warm and amused. "*That* was strange."

Sofie stared into his sparkling eyes, relaxing slightly. She *had* avowed her intention to remain unwed—she recalled it clearly. For the life of her, she could not fathom why she had said such a thing to a stranger, but she could guess why he was bringing up the subject now. He was not thoroughly dishonorable—Sofie had never thought that. He wanted to make sure she was not sacrificing her precious virginity to him when it should be guarded for her future husband. Sofie managed a smile. "Edward, need I remind you that I do not have suitors banging down my door?"

He was serious now, leaning forward. "So you intend to remain a spinster only because you think you cannot attract a suitor?"

Sofie flushed, eyes sparking. "There is more to it than that."

"Is there?"

"Yes. I am completely devoted to my work. No man would be pleased to have his wife in her studio all day—and maybe all night—and you know that. Wives are supposed to run households and raise children, Edward."

"So you are not interested in children?"

She froze. "I am not going to have children, Edward, because I am not going to marry."

"And you have no doubt that this is the course your life should take?"

She lifted her chin, refusing to admit that of course she had doubts. There were many times that she had longed to have what seemed to come so easily to other women—a home and family. But she refused to dwell on it. "No."

He stared at her, and she saw that he did not believe her and it frightened her. She could not tell him that she would throw her shocking avowals aside if she might ever find love and be loved in return. But she knew enough to understand that men did not find her attractive because she walked with a limp, never mind that she was also an artist. Nothing could change that fact, no amount of secret yearning, nothing.

"Perhaps one day you will change your mind," Edward finally said, slowly. His gaze still probed hers. "When you meet the right man."

Sofie forced herself not to flinch and look away. Her thoughts rang loud and clear, unbidden. *But I have met the right man.* And Sofie was shocked and dismayed. She was afraid she had already fallen in love with him, and that must not happen, it must not.

"Why are there tears in your eyes?" Edward asked softly, covering her hand with his.

Sofie jerked her hand away. "There is dust in the air. Edward, this topic is ridiculous. I have no suitors and I never will. No man wants to marry me, and we both know why. Let us leave it at that."

"No, Sofie," Edward said, "you may think you know why, but I am hardly convinced."

And Sofie was angry. Now she leaned forward. "Are you encouraging me to go on the marriage mart?"

He met her gaze. "I think that one day you should. When you are ready."

Sofie smiled, throwing down her gauntlet. "I will seek marriage, Edward, when you do."

He stiffened.

Sofie felt a moment's savage satisfaction. "Well, you have made my private goals your affair—so you cannot tell me I am intruding."

His smile was reluctant, tugging at the corners of his mouth. "Touché."

Her eyes widened with mock innocence. "Oh, come, Edward. Confess. We both know you are a rogue right now, but surely you will one day seek to wed? All men want a woman to run their homes and raise their children."

Edward's smiled faded. "Not this one."

Sofie stared, uneasy and genuinely surprised. "Are you serious?"

He nodded darkly.

"Why?"

His long fingers caressed the stem of his glass. "I have seen it all, Sofie. And life is not a garden of roses. It is rarely roses."

"What a jaded thing to say."

His gaze met hers, dark and somber as she had never before seen it. "You would be shocked if you knew how many married ladies flirt with me, attempting to entice me into their beds."

"Of course, there are married women without morals. There are husbands equally unfaithful."

"Yes. But I have found that fidelity is almost nonexistent in this world."

Sofie almost gaped. "Surely you exaggerate. And are you saying that you will not wed because you could not bear it if your wife was unfaithful to you?"

His smile was a shadow. "I do not exaggerate, unfortunately. And I do not believe in love, having only witnessed lust. And yes, I could not bear it if my wife was unfaithful. You see, deep down, my values are somewhat old-fashioned. As importantly, I could not bear my own lapse into infidelity—which, should I marry, would undoubtedly occur."

Sofie was silent. Edward was either a very romantic man or a very disillusioned one. Or maybe a combination of both.

They lingered over coffee. The restaurant was mostly empty now, and they were the last to leave . . . and in no hurry ,to do so.

"This was wonderful, Edward," Sofie said. She had consumed more wine than she should have, and it had diminished the nervousness she had felt earlier. In truth, there was only sweet, tingling anticipation now.

"I'm glad." He looked at her with a gentle gaze. "Sofie, have you ever tried to sell any of your work?"

Sofie started, eyes wide, instantly alert. "No."

"Why not?" Edward's tone was casual, but his piercing look was not. "You haven't thought of it?"

"Of course I have thought of it. I have intended to be a professional artist for years. But—I am not ready."

"I think you are more than ready."

Sofie stared across the table into his brilliantly blue eyes. Her hands, in her lap, were clenched together. She said nothing.

"Shall I ask around—find out who the reputable art dealers are? Perhaps make an appointment?"

Sofie was trembling. She was not ready, she knew it. "I know who the best dealers are," she heard herself say.

"You are afraid."

"Yes."

"Don't be. Rejection will undoubtedly be a part of your life. Even great artists suffered a lot of rejection in their early years."

He was right. But Sofie was still afraid—and torn. It would be so easy to trust Edward and allow him to guide her as he willed. "I don't know."

"Let's call in a dealer," Edward said.

Sofie looked at him, as fearful as she was growing excited. "I don't know," she repeated.

"I think you should come out of hiding, Sofie," Edward said abruptly. "Paint what you want. Openly. Sell your paintings. Risk rejection. Wear beautiful gowns, change your hair, go to society balls and teas and the races. Let men see you as you really are."

Sofie gaped.

He smiled, staring.

"What do my clothing and men have to do with the subject of my art?" she asked, trembling with anger.

"Everything, I think," he said flatly.

"No." She was firm, but she was shaking, because there was temptation in the concept he had offered her. In truth, she didn't feel very much like herself anymore. She didn't feel like a plain, crippled eccentric; today she had actually felt young and perfect and beautiful. She did feel like parading around in a bright and festive gown, with her hair piled loose and high. She could almost see herself at a ball, surrounded by admirers—and Edward.

Sofie forced her absurd thoughts aside. She swallowed and said, "I am not hiding, not from anything."

"No?" he asked, obviously not believing her.

Sofie dared to stare him in the eye, refusing to even think that he might be right. For he was not right—he was not. "If I were hiding, Edward, then I would have turned away from you long ago."

Edward met the challenge, leaning across the table, his eyes dark and intense. "You couldn't hide from me, Sofie, no matter how you might try."

His tone was as primitive as it was male, and Sofie shivered in sudden awareness. "You . . . threaten me?"

"No. I am your champion, Sofie. Never forget it."

A thrill swept through her, raising goose bumps all over her flesh.

Edward added, "If you do not take risks, you will never succeed."

She stared. She thought about the risk she intended to take by becoming his lover. It would change her as a woman, and undoubtedly it would change her life forever.

His hand tightened on hers. "You've already taken risks, lots of them—and you don't even know it. You're an adventurer, Sofie, a daring adventurer, and this will only be one more adventure for you in a lifetime of adventures. I am sure of it. I have never been more sure of anything."

Tears filled her eyes. No one had ever praised her like this before. "All right."

He leaned back now in his chair, smiling, satisfied, masculinity in repose.

It flashed through Sofie's mind that she would paint him this way, immediately, relaxing in a chair in fabulous Delmonico's. Her heart tripped hard in new excitement as she forgot her fears. "Edward," she blurted, shamelessly bold. "Will you do me a great favor?"

He eyed her. "Of course. Anything. Anytime. Name it."

Her heart beat harder. "Will you model for me?" she asked.

11

Newport Beach

Suzanne paced her bedroom, pausing to stare across her terrace at the starlit ocean. She was familiar with the view and hardly saw the silver caps on the slick, roiling black water. She was so absorbed in her thoughts that she did not hear the knock on her door. When Benjamin called her name softly from the threshold, she started.

He, too, was clad in his bedclothes, in a velvet-trimmed paisley silk robe and pajamas. "Suzanne?"

Suzanne knew why he had come. She had not married Benjamin for either love or passion, and therefore had not expected a passionate relationship from him. In the ten and a half years since their wedding, she had few regrets, and the fact that he came to her bed at all, much less frequently, was not one of them. She would never turn him away or allow even a hint of her indifference to show. She smiled. "Come in, Benjamin."

He smiled, too, slipping inside. "You are worried, my dear. What about?"

Suzanne sighed, sinking down on the foot of her bed, a canopied affair done up in multiple shades of gold and yellow with accents of red. "I'm not at all sure Sofie should be alone in the city."

He sat down beside her, his knee brushing hers. "Whyever not? Sofie is mature and capable. Has something happened that I do not know about?"

Suzanne smiled at Benjamin. He was not the kind of man to elicit passion in a woman, but he was a dear man, kind and caring, although not demonstrative. One had to know him in order to comprehend his steadfast concern. "No," she said, thinking of Edward Delanza. She had seen Hilary the other day. Hilary had been openly restless, and soon Suzanne had learned why. Edward was not at her summer cottage with her. He was in the city. Suzanne hated the idea, and was frightened by it. "I think we should send for her again. Really, there is so much to enjoy here at the shore."

"Darling, Sofie is twenty years old, an intelligent and sensible young woman, devoted to her art. Leave her be. In another few weeks we will be returning to New York anyway."

Suzanne managed a smile. "Of course, you are right," she said, but she was still worried, because she had a sixth sense and did not like what it was telling her. She had not heard from Mrs. Murdock, who'd received explicit instructions several weeks ago to notify her should Edward Delanza call on Sofie. That should have been all the reassurance Suzanne needed, but it was not.

Benjamin patted her hand and got up to turn off the lights. Suzanne shed her silk robe and slipped under the covers, clad in a turquoise satin nightgown. Benjamin reached for her. Suzanne closed her eyes as his hand slid over her breast. Quickly he thumbed her nipple until it had peaked.

Suzanne let him fondle her, barely aroused. As always, she began to think of Jake. She saw him as vividly as if he were present in the room, tall, broad-shouldered, lean-hipped and golden and so unbearably sexy. God. Goddamn him. If only he hadn't been forced to flee. He would still be alive. Incarcerated, but alive. Suzanne imagined what it would be like to visit him in prison, imagined herself all dressed up in her couture finery, being escorted by prison guards to his cell, walking down endless dimly lit corridors, past other prisoners, all of them hot and male.

And Jake would be waiting, ready. Jake had always been ready when it came to sex.

Suzanne whimpered, aroused now, seeing Jake behind the iron bars in his drab prison uniform, knowing his cock would be hard in anticipation of their fucking.

Benjamin slid on top of her, and Suzanne gripped him, spreading her legs wide, hot and wet and open.

The cell door was unlocked. The guard grinned, lewd and knowing. There were hoots from the other cells. Suzanne did not care. She entered the cell, mesmerized by Jake's glowing golden gaze. The door closed behind her, the lock clicked. Jake pushed himself off the opposite wall, his erection tenting the thin material of his cotton pants. The corners of his mouth lifted. He crooked a finger at her. Suzanne rushed forward. He forced her against the wall, ripped her skirts out of the way, and impaled her, hot and hard, almost hurtful.

Suzanne cried out. Benjamin was inside her now, and she was coming, lost in fire and light, and it was glorious.

Sometime later she opened her eyes to stare up at the ceiling. Benjamin kissed her cheek, said "thank you," and rolled over onto his stomach facing away from her. The nights he came to her, he always stayed until the morning, which Suzanne did not really mind. But he would sleep soundly, not touching her again.

And now Suzanne ached. Her sex still throbbed, but it was more than that. Tears glistened in her eyes. Her heart ached. She hated him, she missed him, she wanted him. Not a night went by that she did not want him, but the nights when Benjamin came to her were even worse.

It was impossible not to make the comparison between what she had once had and what she now had, and although logic reminded her that she had been unhappy then and was content now, logic was a cold, uncaring bedfellow. So was contentment. Benjamin's presence beside her always brought forth a yearning as hopeless as it was intense.

Suzanne finally rolled away from Benjamin, cuddling her pillow. It was not the first time that she had fantasized about making love to Jake while her husband made love to her. Jake always shared their bed. But the fantasies were not based on reality. The last time she had seen Jake alive, it had been in prison, but it had not been at all like her fantasy. He had not wanted anything to do with her. The tears fell now, inexorably, as she remembered.

New York City, 1888

"Come with me, ma'am." The guard was solemn-faced.

Suzanne wore a black suit that fit her dark, angry mood of mourning. She wore a black hat with a half veil and black gloves as well. She held a white handkerchief to her nose to ward off the prison's many offending odors, mostly of unwashed male bodies. She followed the guard, head high, nose tilted up in a show of real snobbery, inwardly fuming. Her high heels clicked loudly on the stone floors. The guard unlocked a door, and she entered a small room with a scarred wooden table and several chairs. Jake sat in one of the chairs, tense and drawn. Another prison guard stood behind him.

The first guard had allowed Suzanne to precede him in. Both he and his partner wore big black guns in holsters and carried big brown bats on chains hanging from their belts. Just in case, Suzanne knew, Jake might attempt to escape.

Jake regarded Suzanne with absolutely no expression. Suzanne glared at him, then turned to glower at the guard who had escorted her to her husband. "Do you mean to tell me that we will not have a single moment's privacy?"

The guard ignored her outburst, leaving, with his partner. Suzanne waited until they were gone, the door firmly locked behind them. She knew they watched them through the window on the wall. She whirled on Jake. "Tomorrow they are extraditing you," she cried. "I cannot believe it."

He stared, impassive. "Where's Sofie?"

She blanched, then strode forward, fist in the air. "Sofie! Sofie is at home, where little girls belong. Damn you!"

He stood, towering over her, finally angry, too. "I wanted to see Sofie, Suzanne, to say good-bye. Why didn't you bring her?"

"What about me?!" she screamed, and she began to beat him with her fists. "What about me, you bastard? What about me! You are locked up, but I am free—but now it is worse than ever! When I walk down the street, my friends run the other way!"

Jake made no move to duck her blows, aimed at his chest and face, and she soon grew tired of hitting him. Suzanne was crying, but she regained some control and said, "They are deporting you, and I will be alone! Damn you, Jake."

His mouth tightened, his eyes darkened, but he did not respond.

Suzanne had stopped weeping now and she stared at his handsome face. "Do you even care what will happen to me?"

His jaw flexed, as if he refused to answer.

"It was bad enough when we married. But with your success in business, we got past that. Not completely, all doors did not open, but many did. And now they are all closed again—every single last one of them!" She started to cry again.

Finally he said, "I'm sure you'll survive, Suzanne. And well. You're very good at that."

She uncovered her eyes, no longer crying, furious. "Like I survived the first miserable years of our marriage in that shack you dared to call our home?"

"Yeah. The way you survived then." His eyes were hot and furious.

She thought of being pregnant and alone in that shack while Jake worked day in and day out as if she did not exist. She thought about the few hours they shared together each day, hours of mindless, animal passion. She thought about her first affair, her second, her third. "Everything was your fault. Don't you dare blame me."

"I guess I've heard that before." His mouth was an arrow-straight line. "Maybe you're right. I am sorry. I'm sorry you got pregnant, sorry I was stupid enough to insist we marry, sorry I was stupid enough to want to marry you." His tone dropped. "I'm sorry I kept on caring, long past the time any other man would."

She was stunned. He had never apologized to her before, not for anything. And this was the first time he had openly admitted any of his feelings—feelings that thrilled her and gave her hope. "Jake." Swiftly she approached again. "I can't bear it." She wrapped her arms around him tightly. "God, I can't bear it! They could put you away for life!"

He quickly untangled her body from his and pushed her away. "Nothing has changed," he said stiffly.

Suzanne looked up at him, stunned. "I love you. And—you love me. Why—you just said as much!"

His smile was twisted, but he did not refute the last statement. "If you love me, Suzanne, you have a great way of showing it. Tell me, who warmed your bed last night, while I rotted in this cell? And who's going to warm it tonight—and tomorrow and the next night?"

Suzanne stiffened. "No one," she said. And it was true that last night she had been alone, and she would probably be alone tonight, too. But if he thought she would let her body wither up and die while he was in prison, why, he was wrong.

He laughed harshly. "Do you expect me to believe that you're going to be faithful to me now, when you've never been faithful to me before? Do you expect me to believe that no man's going to stroke that hot little body of yours while I guard my ass and rot in jail for the next ten or fifteen years until I get paroled—if I do?" He was shouting now.

And Suzanne was as angry. "How could you even expect that of me now!" she cried. "When this is all your fault to begin with?"

As quickly as the anger had erupted, it was gone. Something dark and sad flitted in Jake's gaze. "Right. Of course. All my fault. As always." His expression hardened as they stared at each other. "Bring Sofie to me, Suzanne. Now."

Suzanne tensed. If Jake were not leaving tomorrow, she would turn on her heel and walk out on him for his obvious preference for their daughter now, when he should be thinking only of her, his wife, when he should be begging *her* for forgiveness and declaring his undying love. Damn him! But he was leaving, and he would be convicted for his crime and imprisoned in England, and Suzanne did not know how long it might be before she would be able to visit him again. Or if he would ever be paroled—if he would ever come home at all. And suddenly she was frightened, some of her anger draining away. What if she never saw him again?

It was a terrifying thought.

If only the past could be changed.

Resolutely Suzanne stepped forward, intending to use her sexual allure to soften him, to tame him. It always worked.

She stalked forward, purring, "Jake. I'll bring Sofie. Later. I promise."

He stared at her, unmoving and skeptical.

She paused before him and touched his chest very lightly. "I love you. You know it. I know you know it, because of what I do to you when we're alone, when we're in bed." Her tone had dropped, low and sultry. "Do you think I do those things to other men?"

Jake made a sound of bitter laughter. "I know you do."

Her heart thundered. "That's not fair. It's not true. And there wouldn't be anyone else, not if you would stop being so stubborn and so head-strong."

"Cut the crap, Suzanne," Jake warned.

The danger in his tone made her swell and grow slick. Suzanne smiled seductively and touched his shoulders. He flinched. She pressed her warm, pulsing sex against his groin. The guards were probably enjoying this, too.

"I love you. I always have," she whispered, rubbing against him. And she was rewarded, because he hardened instantly.

She was triumphant. "You still want me!"

"I've been behind bars and without a woman for a month, Suzanne; what other reaction would you expect?" He laughed in her face and pushed her away. "You love my cock, Suzanne, not me."

She paled.

"Get out." His eyes blazed, filled with fury. "But if you don't bring Sofie to me, today, I will get back at you—I swear it. I'll find a way, even from prison."

"Sofie!" she cried. "Always Sofie! I do hate you, Jake, I do!" With that, she turned, crying and humiliated and furious and suddenly glad he was being extradited, yes, glad, damn him, and she banged on the door, demanding to be let out.

And that night, while he rotted in his cell, she stayed at home, unable to sleep. But she was not alone.

Suzanne brushed the tears from her eyes, hating Jake all over again as she had that day for rejecting her. She had not brought Sofie back to visit him. Suzanne regretted her foolish pride and her childish desire to hurt Jake by denying him a last visit with their daughter. Two years later he had escaped prison in England and been killed in a fire, so neither she nor Sofie had ever seen him again.

She was older now, and wiser. There was so much she would do differently if she could. She knew now that she should have returned with Sofie. If she had been a mature adult instead of a selfish child, she and Jake might have parted as lovers should, instead of in anger, as enemies would.

She thought about the trust he had left for Sofie, a direct result of her behavior that day. Her anger swelled in spite of any and all logic. Jake had been the one imprisoned, he had been the one to die, but he had made good his threat. As he had promised, he had struck back at her, even from prison, getting far more than even with her.

Suzanne closed her eyes. Whenever she thought about Sofie's trust, which she frequently used to buy lavish clothing and gifts and even jewels for herself, she felt guilt as well as anger.

Suzanne had also embezzled several hundred thousand dollars from the estate, which was now in her own private banking account. Sofie still had plenty of funds left over, and would never know that anything was missing. Whenever her conscience intruded, reminding her that she had stolen from her own daughter, whom she loved, Suzanne would switch it off, reassuring herself that she was owed every single penny she had taken.

Suzanne sighed. She would do more than change that day at Randall's Island if she could. If she could, she would have changed it all. It was hard to remember, now, so many years later, why she had been so angry at Jake almost from the start of their marriage. It was that anger, and the neglect she felt from him, that had led her astray, and his apparent indifference to her behavior had only made her more flamboyant in her infidelity. If only she'd had a hair of the wisdom she had now.

But even if she'd been less wild and willful, Suzanne wasn't sure their relationship would have been any different. From the beginning, theirs had been a tempestuous and volatile, sometimes violent, union; Jake had been as arrogant and proud as she. But for every instance of hell, there had been at least one instance of heaven.

Suzanne did not want to remember any of it, not the good, not the bad. She lay beside her second husband, staring up at the ceiling, tears streaking her cheeks as she cried silently over the past.

She wiped her eyes with the backs of her hands, swallowing a ragged sigh. Suzanne could not let the same thing happen to Sofie. Surely a daughter should profit from the mother's mistakes. Motherhood had not come naturally to her as it did to some women. But after Jake had been incarcerated, she had become a capable and concerned parent, and over the years, Suzanne had realized just how much she loved her daughter. She loved Sofie more than anything or anyone, except perhaps Jake. She had been protecting her from life ever since the accident—ever since Jake had died. She could not cease her vigilance now, not when it was more crucial than ever.

Suzanne decided that this time she would ignore Benjamin's advice. This time she would reassure herself personally that all was as it should be in New York City.

12

S ofie had directed him to the best gallery in the city, which had recently moved uptown to Thirty-sixth Street on Fifth Avenue. Edward paused outside the Gallery Durand-Ruel, one of the world's most renowned dealers, with offices in New York, Paris, and London. His clients included some of the greatest collectors in the world.

Edward had learned that he had bought and sold a small number of Impressionist paintings over the past few years, mostly Monet, but also Degas, and mostly upon the request of his clients. Edward knew little about art, but had made it his business in the last two days to find out more. He had visited a number of gallerys and museums. His untrained eye, after much intense scrutiny of many different works of art, finally told him that Sofie's work was similar to that of the French Impressionists she so admired. Yet it was different, too; he could not easily look at a soft Degas rendering of ballet dancers and exclaim, "Ahh, Sofie paints just like that!" because she did not. Her style was unique and entirely her own.

The tricolored flag of France waved atop the store's temple-fronted entrance. Edward stepped inside. Pale carpeted floors stretched away. He was in a single, large showroom. Art of all sizes and subjects, mostly paintings, hung on the blue-gray walls and were stacked all around the gallery. A few sculptures stood on pedestals. Almost every inch of space was being used to show the art for sale. Edward paused to glance at one small sculpture, a beautiful figure of a nude woman in bronze, and he read the plate: Auguste Rodin.

"Can I help you, sir?"

Edward turned to see a nondescript young man in a dark gray suit and tie. "Mr. Durand-Ruel?"

The young man smiled. "Monsieur Durand-Ruel is out of town, sir, purchasing Manet's *La Buveur d'eau*." He smiled, as if expecting an eager response from Edward, who only smiled back. "But perhaps I can help you? I am his son."

"Perhaps you can. Monsieur, I am not a buyer; in fact, I am not very familiar with art. But I do think I know brilliant work when I see it, and I have stumbled upon a young artist whose work I would like you to see."

The younger Durand-Ruel's smile had faded. "Indeed? And who is the artist? Perhaps I know of him already."

"He is a she. Her name is Sofie O'Neil."

His brows lifted. "A woman? An Irishwoman?"

"She is an American."

"That is hardly better. Our clients favor the French artists; surely you know that."

"You do not sell the work of Americans?" Edward asked, surprised.

"We do fairly well with Thomas Eakins, and of course, Mary Cassatt. I have no Cassatts for sale at the moment, but I do have an Eakins. *Viéns avec moi*, I will show you."

Edward, somewhat dismayed, followed the now enthused young man across the room. His dismay grew when he was faced with a large portrait that was as different from Sofie's work as could be. It was painted very realistically, and it was very dark. "How much is this?" he asked, curious.

"We might be able to get a thousand for it, as Mr. Eakins has a reputation."

"He is the only American you sell here?"

"Once in a while we might sell something else, but usually from an expatriate living abroad, like Cassatt. We deal heavily in the French art of the eighteenth and early nineteenth centuries, and there is always a great demand for the seventeenth-century Dutch masters. And recently there has been some demand for Goya." Seeing Edward's confusion, he said patiently, "He is a Spanish painter of the early nineteenth century who would be unknown except that our greatest clients, Mr. and Mrs. Havemeyer, have discovered him and wish to buy much more of his work."

"A collector can do that? Create a demand for a previously unknown artist?" Edward was amazed—and hopeful.

"Only if they buy a good deal of that artist's work. That, of course, inflates the value of that art."

Edward felt certain that, should Sofie wind up in this exclusive gallery, she would be discovered quickly by some great collector. "Twice you've mentioned a woman artist. Who is Mary Cassatt?"

"She is another great artist, renowned for her treatment of the subject of mother and child. Sometimes she is mistakenly labeled one of the Impressionists, but in truth, her mature style is all her own. She is American, but she lives in France and has done so for many, many years."

"She sells a lot of her work?"

"Yes." Jacques smiled briefly. "But it was not always that way, monsieur. A few years ago she was struggling, as were many of today's successful artists."

"Will you come to see Miss O'Neil's work?"

The man hesitated. "Why do you not give me the address of her studio, and when I have some time—when my father returns—I will make an appointment."

Edward knew he did not intend to come. "She is extraordinary," he said softly.

The young man, who had been turning away, jerked to meet Edward's intense gaze.

"You lose nothing if you do come, except some time—and if I am right, you gain everything," Edward said.

"All right. We have a telephone. Let me give you our number. Speak with the artist and arrange for a showing. The mornings are most convenient for me."

Edward smiled and the two men shook hands firmly. But as he left the gallery, his smile faded. He glanced at his watch. In another hour he was due at the Ralston residence. He had promised Sofie he would model for her.

Sofie trembled in excitement, so anxious to begin her latest endeavor that she could not stand waiting for Edward to arrive. Her studio had been prepared hours ago; she had positioned a chair beside a small table draped in white linen in front of the garden window. A rainbow-hued centerpiece of wildflowers was upon it, as were beautiful gold-rimmed porcelain plates, crystal glasses, and gleaming silverware. She planned to go back to Delmonico's, of course, several times, so when she was done, the table and background would appear exactly as they should be.

Sofie started at the knock upon her door. Mrs. Murdock poked her white head in. "Sofie, you have a caller." She beamed.

Sofie was aware that the housekeeper and Jenson were erroneously assuming that Edward was her suitor, and that they were pleased as punch about it. She had tried to correct them, but stubbornly they disagreed, insisting that Edward did admire her. Sofie had given up her attempt to dissuade them.

Now Sofie's heart skipped a beat. Edward was not due for another hour; he was early. She wondered if he was as excited about working together as she was. Smoothing strands of hair back behind her ears, she said brightly, "Do send Mr. Delanza in, please."

"It isn't Mr. Delanza. You have another gentleman caller, Sofie." Mrs. Murdock was obviously delighted. "It's Mr. Henry Marten, and he's in the green salon," the housekeeper said. "I hope I should not tell him you are indisposed?" She scowled at that.

Sofie was surprised. Whatever was Henry Marten doing there? She did not have a clue as to what he should want. "No, I will see him," Sofie said, following Mrs. Murdock out of her studio and to the front of the house. She imagined that, whatever Henry's business was, he would be gone long before Edward arrived to model for her.

Henry Marten stood in the middle of the salon, hands in the pockets of his baggy trousers, looking somewhat ill at ease. His dark suit did not fit him well, being somewhat oversized. He blushed when he faced Sofie. "I hope this is not too much of an inconvenience," he said.

"Of course not," Sofie returned with a smile. "Good day, Mr. Marten. How are you?"

"Fine, thank you." His color deepened. "I must say, you are looking very well, Miss O'Neil."

Sofie nodded and smiled, doubting it all the same. Her hair was in one long, fat braid, and as usual, she wore a plain navy blue skirt and a white shirtwaist. She gestured to two chairs and they both sat. "I have asked Jenson for some refreshments," she said.

"Thank you." He fidgeted. "I have been in the city a few weeks now, and I intended to call upon you sooner, but I have had several clients and I have actually been up to my ears in work."

"That is wonderful," Sofie said sincerely. But she was amazed. He was actually calling on her?

He smiled, obviously pleased. "Yes, it is, but not as wonderful as it should be, because it has kept me from seeing you."

Sofie blinked and sat up straighter.

Henry was now beet red. He looked at his hands, clasped in his lap.

They sat in sudden silence, Sofie too stunned to think of making polite conversation, until Jenson appeared with a silver tray containing plates of pastries and a Wedgewood pitcher filled with steaming black coffee. Sofie assembled the cups and saucers and poured them both coffee, adding thick, fresh cream and sugar, taking the opportunity to recover her composure. As she handed him his cup, she said, "Where is your office?"

He answered quickly, relieved. "Downtown, not far from Union Square." He coughed. "Perhaps I might show it to you, sometime when you are free?"

Sofie stared yet again, then caught herself and hastily replied. "Of course."

Henry set his cup down, not having taken a single sip. "Actually, Miss O'Neil, I was hoping I might, er, I might take you for a ride in the park sometime."

Sofie also set her cup and saucer down, but more carefully. She regarded him with wide eyes. Henry was nice enough, of course, but she had no time in her life for rides in the park. Even though the idea was somehow enticing and romantic. It was finally sinking in, though. He *was* calling on her.

He took her wide-eyed silence for the answer he wanted. "Perhaps even this morning?"

Sofie found her tongue. "Mr. Marten, of course I would love to go riding with you in the park." She did not have the heart to say no. And there was that secret fantasy, in which she was laughing and beautiful and gay, on the arm of a gentleman admirer, just like all the other young ladies her own age. But now, of course, that fantasy admirer of her dreams was bearing a suspicious resemblance to Edward.

Sofie shoved all such nonsense aside. "But this morning is impossible. You see, I am expecting Edward Delanza."

Henry started, then stared, finally flushing yet again.

Immediately Sofie realized her mistake. Henry thought Edward was calling on her as well. She felt her cheeks begin to heat. "You do not understand. He is not a suitor. He has agreed to model for me."

"To model for you?"

"I am an artist, remember?"

"Yes, of course; for a moment I had forgotten." An awkward silence descended.

Jenson led Edward into the room a scant instant later. He *was* early. Sofie jumped to her feet, beaming at Edward. He smiled back at her, dimples digging into his cheeks, and his gaze slid over her as warmly as any lover's would.

"Good morning, Sofie," he said, his tone so intimate that it made the simple greeting seem to be so much more. His glance moved to Henry, his smile remaining firmly in place. "Hello, Henry. Am I interrupting?"

Henry had stood, too. "No, of course not. It appears that I am the one who is doing that."

"You are not intruding, I can assure you of that," Edward said, strolling to him and clasping his shoulder in a friendly manner. His gaze swept over the tray with the unconsumed pastries and coffee. "Finish your refreshments, please."

As Henry sat back down, somewhat hesitantly, Sofie asked, "Will you join us?" Her smile was far wider now and she realized that Henry stared at her—and how it must appear to him.

"Of course," Edward said.

When they were all seated, a moment of silence reigned. Edward studied first Henry, then her, as Henry sipped his coffee. Sofie sensed his curiosity. She wondered what he was thinking about her being present with Henry Marten. Edward finally spoke, addressing Henry. "What brings you to this side of town?"

"I was hoping to call on Miss O'Neil several weeks ago, but my practice has been keeping me far too busy. I had thought to entice her to a ride in Central Park today, but she was expecting you, as it turns out."

For a moment Edward said nothing, but then he grinned, teeth flashing white. "Perhaps she will be free on the morrow?" he suggested.

Sofie stiffened, incredulous.

Henry's brows drew together and he stared at Edward, who still smiled, now benignly, then he turned eagerly towards her. "Are you free tomorrow, Miss O'Neil?"

"I . . ." Sofie was at a loss. And she was not pleased with Edward for his interference. Tomorrow she had class, and afterwards she intended to work on Edward's new portrait. "I expect to be working tomorrow," she finally said.

"Surely you can spare Henry an hour," Edward interjected smoothly.

Sofie stared at him. Henry was waiting anxiously for her reply. She managed a smile. "Perhaps later in the day—at four o'clock?"

"That would be perfect," Henry said, pleased.

Sofie looked from him to Edward, who stared now at them both. His mouth had a peculiar curve to it. Sofie trembled, comprehension beginning to sink in. And with it came hurt.

He had just foisted her off on another man. Even though his plans for her had been thoroughly dishonorable to begin with, it hurt—how it hurt.

"I have news, Sofie," Edward said quietly.

She turned slightly.

"Jacques Durand-Ruel has agreed to see your work. Mornings are convenient for him. Would you be available tomorrow morning should he come to view your work?"

It was hard to speak. Nervousness assailed her, cutting into her wounded feelings. Of course she would skip class if he would come. "Yes," she whispered.

Edward nodded and turned to Henry. "Sofie will be entertaining one of the premier art dealers in the world. If he purchases some of her work, it will be quite an achievement."

"I see," Henry said, looking shocked.

Sofie spoke up then, aware of exactly what she was doing. "One day I hope to live exclusively from the sale of my work, as a professional artist," she said. She was aware of Edward's shooting her a dark look, but she ignored him. If Henry was really calling on her, such eccentricity would drive him away quickly enough. "I shall reside in Paris, of course, with other bohemian artists."

Henry was now speechless.

Edward glowered; clearly he comprehended her game. He said, "Of course, that is only if some dashing gentleman does not sweep you off your feet and to the altar first."

Sofie felt her face burning. And she felt her wounds bleed. She thought, *But that will not be you, will it, Edward*? "I do not think that is going to happen, Mr. Delanza."

He arched a brow, as stiff as she. "No, I don't think it will—not when you fling your odd ideas into the faces of your suitors."

The stinging of her cheeks increased. Sofie could not find a suitable reply.

Henry rose to his feet, looking from one to the other. He cleared his throat. "I think it is time for me to leave."

Edward was standing as well. "There is no rush."

Sofie rose. "We must begin our work, Edward."

He ignored her. "Perhaps you would like to see some of Sofie's art before you go?"

Sofie almost choked.

Henry's eyes widened. "You know, I would like that." He turned to Sofie, suddenly eager. "Miss O'Neil, if you don't mind, I would like to see the work which you are so devoted to."

Sofie had no choice but to agree. To deny him would be the height of discourtesy, especially when she had allowed Edward into her world of art, and Henry knew it. But Sofie felt like murdering Edward—for everything.

* * *

Sofie could tell from the expression on Henry's face that he was at a loss. He turned to face her, coughed to clear his throat. "You are indeed talented, Miss O'Neil," he said.

She knew he lied, he did not understand her art at all, did not feel it or admire it. Sofie managed a smile. "Thank you."

"Of course, I am quite the amateur." He cleared his throat again. "I have seen this kind of art once before, though. Italian, isn't it?"

"The impressionists are French," Sofie said softly.

"Yes, well, you are every bit as good as they are," Henry assured her. He was ill at ease, eager now to be gone. "I think I must leave. Tomorrow, then, at four?"

Sofie nodded, walking Henry to the door of her studio. "I will be right back," she told Edward, who only nodded at her.

Sofie saw Henry to the front door and through it. Once he was gone, she marched back to her studio. She faced Edward, hands on her hips. "Just what was all that about?"

Edward smiled as if innocent. "I beg your pardon?"

"I think you had very well beg my pardon!" Sofie cried. "You maneuvered Henry into my studio—and he does not appreciate my art at all—and you forced the issue of an outing between us!"

He touched the tip of her nose. "You are not eager about your date tomorrow?"

"I most certainly am not."

His forefinger skidded to her lip and then was gone. "You see," he said, low, "you have a suitor, Sofie, despite your attempts to chase him away."

She stared at him, hurt and angry and at a loss. Did Edward hope for a real engagement between her and Henry? Did he think to marry her off? Did that mean he no longer sought to seduce her—to have an affair with her? "I do not want a suitor, Edward." Her tone was strained. "And you are not my father, to arrange for men to call upon me!"

"No, I am not your father," he said somewhat grimly, no longer smiling at all. "But someone has to set you straight."

"How bold and . . . how presumptuous . . . you are!" Sofie cried.

"I am guilty as charged, Sofie," he whispered. "But someone has to take care of you."

"So you have appointed yourself my caretaker?"

"Yes."

She batted his hand away when it rose to touch her face again. "You are so arrogant, Edward."

"I am your friend."

Sofie turned her back to him. To her dismay he cupped her shoulders from behind. He pulled her backwards against his body. "Why are you so upset?"

She could not tell him the truth, not ever, so she shook her head and said nothing.

"I apologize. Maybe I made a mistake. Henry is a nice chap, but awfully rigid in his views. And he is not smitten with your art like I am."

"Oh, Edward," Sofie cried softly, gripping his strong arms. "In the end, do you ever *not* say the right thing?"

"God, Sofie, I mess up all the time." His mouth touched her cheek. Sofie froze, because his groin cupped her buttocks, and she thought she felt a movement there. But he released her and turned her to face him. "You flatter me, sweetheart, more than you can know."

"Everyone flatters you, I am sure." His endearment wrung a response in her she was determined to ignore. Edward was only a rogue, nothing more. Love was not the issue, it never had been—never would be. Her recent hysteria was as out of character as it was inexplicable. Sofie felt grim. She sighed and redirected herself. "Are we ready to begin?"

Edward's smile faded. "That's why I'm here."

Edward obeyed Sofie's instructions and took his seat at the table set for two. He was aware of sitting unnaturally and being tense. But as he watched Sofie flitting about her art supplies, preparing herself to begin working, he began to forget about being a model. He studied her, enjoying the way she moved, quick and graceful in spite of her small limp. He liked the swing of her round hips. Finally Sofie turned to face him. Aware that he must be a model now, he tensed. Instantly she frowned.

"Edward, you must relax."

"That's not as easy as it sounds."

"Whyever not?"

He could not think of an answer, so he shifted in his seat, trying to get comfortable, aware of Sofie watching him very closely. It was a bit unnerving, like being undressed by her with her eyes. God only knew, he had undressed thousands of women with his eyes, yet it was very different to be on the receiving end. His pulse raced a bit faster than normal, and there was an incipient fullness in his loins. He could think of things he would much rather do, right now, alone with Sofie.

He shoved his wandering thoughts aside very sternly. He had promised to model for her. As much as he wanted to kiss her, to pet her, to hold her, their last kiss the other day had taught him how dangerous that could be. Their next kiss must be more chaste. God. The very idea was laughable, but he could not give up on Sofie now, he could not.

Edward inhaled deeply. He must not think such thoughts. Not if he was really going to model for her.

Besides, there was nothing sexual about what she was doing—she was only painting him, for God's sake. He was the one with the lewd, wandering mind. When he had finally settled somewhat comfortably into his chair, he looked up at her for approval.

"Edward," she said, "can you not lounge?"

His smile faded. "Lounge?" The word conjured up images of being in bed.

"Yes. When we were dining that day, you were lounging in your chair, utterly relaxed and utterly confident, at once negligent but impossibly elegant and so . . . so male. I am determined to capture you in such a mood exactly."

"Christ," Edward muttered, his cock stretching and hardening instantly. He expelled his breath shakily, staring into her eyes, wondering how he was going to survive the next few hours. Her admiration did things to him that no woman had ever done to him before with either hands or mouth or any other tempting portion of nubile female anatomy. Unfortunately, if she ever put her hands—or her mouth—on any private part of his body . . . he imagined he would respond as he had never responded to any woman before.

He muttered a curse, reaching for the collar of his shirt and tugging at it, when he would have much preferred tugging at his trousers.

"Edward? *Whatever* is wrong?" She was perplexed—and growing exasperated.

He managed a phony smile. "I have a feeling you'll find out before too much longer," he muttered, having opened the collar on his shirt and loosened his necktie.

But Sofie did not guess at the source of his agitation. She smiled. "Yes, that is much better! See—you have an innate talent for modeling!"

Edward laughed, the sound rough and sharp.

Sofie began to work, talking as she did so. "I am not painting the both of us, of course—just you. You will be very close to the viewer. You will take up most of the canvas, now that I've actually got you as a model." Her voice was husky now, and it vibrated with eagerness. "It will be an unusual composition, making the viewer feel that he is facing you from a close distance, as if he is there in the painting with you." She beamed, peeking over her easel at him. "Indeed, I hope that the viewer will feel that he is standing right there in Delmonico's, perhaps even conversing with you!"

Edward felt her excitement as he might her touch. "That is quite a challenge you have taken up, is it not?" he murmured.

Her head was bobbing now as she worked, looking up repeatedly at him. "It is a *great* challenge, one I intend to meet." She was using her brush swiftly now, frowning, eyes lowered. "Your portrait . . . I intend for it to be like you . . .unusual . . . outstanding."

He took a deep breath. Her head was out of sight, and Edward took the opportunity to adjust one of his pants legs. She was only painting him, for God's sake, but he was as aroused as if they were naked and entwined in bed. He wasn't at all sure he could sit like this for many more minutes, much less a few hours. Why did she have to be so frank with her admiration? And why did it have to affect him like this? Undoubtedly she put this kind of energy into all of her subjects. He doubted she felt anything special just because she was painting him.

Yet logic could not change the fact that every stroke of her brush upon the canvas felt like a caress upon his skin.

She popped out from behind the easel, a becoming flush staining her cheeks and throat. "Edward—might you open your jacket, please?"

Edward was startled. And dismayed.

She met his gaze, her eyes quite bright. "You did not sit with your jacket buttoned that day, and there are funny wrinkles that will not look right in the portrait."

Edward took a deep breath. This session would soon end. He was not cut out to be a model. Sofie was about to realize that—and just what she did to him with her words, her excitement, and her totally unique self as well. He opened his jacket. His sexuality had never embarrassed him before, but he could feel his cheeks tingling with a warm flush.

But Sofie was immersed in her art. Before he knew it, she was at his side, tugging on his coat so it would drape as she pleased. Inadvertently her hands brushed his thighs; he wanted it to be purposeful. He held his breath, watching her face, and saw the moment she realized that his thoughts were not on modeling. Her cheeks colored, her hands stilled. She lifted her gaze to his, wide-eyed.

Edward held her gaze. "Sofie."

"I . . . I hope you do not mind," she said in a strangled tone, "that I . . . that I . . ." She trailed off.

Edward caught her hands so she could not flee. "You know I do not mind anything that you do," he said, low and rough.

Her startled gaze shot to his. Her bosom heaved. "Edward, we are *working*."

"I don't seem to be very good at it," he muttered, a hairsbreadth away from pulling her onto his lap. "Surely you can see that?"

Her gaze flicked downwards, her blush now a fiery shade of crimson. "I'm sure you could be an excellent model if you wanted to be," she said hoarsely.

Edward felt a surge of male triumph. "Come here, Sofie," he ordered. When she remained frozen and undecided, he smiled at her—then yanked once on her hands and she tumbled exactly where he wanted her to be. On his lap.

"Edward." It wasn't much of a protest.

"I cannot model for you, not like this," he murmured, scalded by the pressure of her hip against his pounding loins. She did not move, did not even breathe. What had happened the last time they had kissed flashed through his mind. He knew he must be careful not to go as far as they had then. The thought, as soon as it came, was dismissed. The blood had flowed too hot and too hard into his veins, expanding every inch of him. He cupped the back of her head with one hand. "Give me your mouth."

Sofie whimpered as he guided her face to his.

Edward touched the seam of her lips with his tongue. "Open up," he whispered hoarsely. "I want in, Sofie." The thought of another kind of entrance, one he must never make, seared his mind, and as he probed her lips again, he saw himself in bed with Sofie, driving every inch of his hardness into her.

"Open up," he whispered again, feeling too ripe, too ready to explode. His hand slid from her waist to her hip, and then lower, to the outer curve of her thigh.

She whimpered again, obeying. Immediately Edward thrust deep into her mouth with his tongue. She began to spar with him as instantly, until sparring became sucking. Edward realized that Sofie clenched his neck and sucked on his mouth as hard as he was trying to devour her. Impossibly, he swelled yet again, and he knew she felt it, for she moaned.

Edward forgot everything then but the urgency in his loins and the woman shuddering in his arms. Reflexively he shifted her so that she straddled his lap, and then, when that was not enough, he gripped her skirts and lifted them so that the hot, moist juncture between her thighs had settled upon his long, swollen loins. For Edward, the thin silk of her drawers and the fine linen of his trousers only enhanced the sensation of Sofie astride him.

He could not stand his need. She squirmed atop him, an invitation he understood instantly, but one she probably did not even know that she issued. Moving his mouth to the underside of her neck, one hand fluttering over her breasts and teasing her nipples, Edward reached between them and under her skirts and pressed his thumb against the apex of her cleft.

And Sofie tensed. "Edward?" she gasped, clinging, her face buried against his shoulder.

It was a question. There was trust in it, and surprise—and fear, too.

Edward froze, his hand wedged intimately between her thighs, his enormous erection straining against her, beneath her, robbing him of the will to seek self-discipline or to think.

"Edward," Sofie whimpered again. "Edward."

Edward did not welcome the return of sanity, he did not. He was too ripe, too ready. But his mind began to function furiously. As desperately aroused as he was, Edward was also appalled. This was hardly a kiss. This was far, far more. And far, far too dangerous.

It seemed Sofie was recovering, too. She hid her face in his neck, breathing hard, shaking, and he could feel her thoughts spinning. If only he could discern what they were.

But did he really have to read her mind? He could make a logical guess. Surely Sofie was as shocked with his behavior as he was dismayed. Abruptly he shifted her so that her skirts came down, so she no longer rode him as a lover would. He was stricken with disbelief.

Sofie was innocent and trusting, a lady and his friend. In another moment he would have been deep inside her. And she would have welcomed him. *He had almost seduced her.*

He had merely intended to give her the kind of kiss that would awaken her desire to live more fully as a woman should. He had broken every single rule he had laid out for himself. More important, he despised the game now, and the rules he had made, because he wanted her so badly—and could not stand the thought of someone like Henry Marten one day having her in his stead.

Christ, he had maneuvered himself into an impossible position.

Suddenly Sofie slid from his lap. She backed away from him, eyes wide, then turned and fled across the room. "I'm . . . It's rather warm in here . . . don't you think? Let me open the windows."

Edward stared after her. If he could not play by the rules, then the game had to be stopped. Before Sofie really suffered at his hands. Before he proved himself irredeemable and far worse than his reputation.

Sofie had turned on the ceiling fan, and it began to whir. From across the room, she faced him slowly, blushing like a schoolgirl.

"I am sorry, Sofie," Edward said harshly, standing. Staring.

"You do not have to apologize," Sofie said, appearing as strained. But then her next words came, completely unexpected, shocking him. "Because I am not sorry, Edward, not at all."

Edward started.

Sofie glanced away, her cheeks turning red.

He could not even guess her meaning. Or could he? Sofie looked up, and he was worldly enough to recognize the yearning in her eyes. He was wordly enough to fathom that the next time—if there was a next time—she would not resist him.

And Edward grimly realized that he had already gone too far. Sofie had her virtue, but she had been seduced.

13

Sofie was unable to move, speak, or smile. She gripped her hands so hard that she was hurting herself. Jacques Durand-Ruel, a small, dapper man in his thirties, stood staring at Edward's portrait, now titled *A Gentleman at Newport Beach*. He had shown up promptly at noon, and this was the first painting he looked at.

Beside her, Edward stood with his hands shoved casually in his pockets, also watching the young art dealer. Occasionally Sofie could feel his gaze slipping to her, but she could not look away from the Frenchman. If only she could be as calm and cool as Edward; but then, it was not his art that Jacques was about to pass judgment on, it was not his very soul, his very life.

Jacques moved on. He had studied Edward's portrait for a long time, perhaps five full minutes. He ignored the genre painting, eyed the still life of florals briefly, stared at Lisa's portrait for about half that long, then bypassed all the rest of her work, except for Jake's portrait. He studied that for about thirty seconds and turned. He was not smiling.

Sofie thought that she might die. She felt Edward grip her elbow.

"Mademoiselle O'Neil," Jacques said in his heavy accent, "you are very talented."

Sofie thought she would weep, right then and there, for his next word resounded, unspoken. *But . . .*

And then he said, "I can only buy what I think I can sell. All your work is interesting to me as a connoisseur. I am certain that I could sell *Portrait of Jake O'Neil* and *Lisa*."

Sofie nodded. At least he liked Jake's and Lisa's portraits, which she had painted with such love. She told herself that she was not going to cry, not in front of him. She was stronger than that.

"That's it?" Edward asked, incredulous.

"The tenement scene is excellent, I truly admire it, but my clients do not even buy Millet's genre scenes, so they will not be interested in Mademoiselle's. Regrettably, I cannot take it."

Sofie swallowed hard.

"What about the floral?" Edward demanded. "It's fantastic."

"I agree. But I will never sell it."

Sofie blinked.

"But you like it?" Edward pursued.

"I like it very much. It is extraordinary. Powerful. It reminds me a bit of Cézanne. Have you heard of him? But we rarely buy him, either. He is very difficult to sell, if not impossible. Generally speaking, still lifes are a far more difficult market."

The urge to weep had vanished. Sofie could not believe what she had heard. "I have seen his work," she whispered, "just once. He is very, very good."

"And so are you," Jacques said, smiling. "You must not be discouraged. Perhaps this will help. I also wish to purchase Monsieur Delanza's portrait."

Sofie went utterly still, then her heart began to race. "You do?"

"I do not know if I can sell it. I have several clients who might be interested. Clearly your forte, mademoiselle, is figural painting. This work is beautiful. It is astounding. I will take a chance on it because I am so enamored of it."

Sofie's despair had become ecstasy. "Edward! He wants your portrait!"

"I heard," Edward said, grinning at her.

"You know," Jacques said, smiling back at Sofie, "I am a businessman. It is very unusual for me to buy so many works of an unknown, untried artist." His brown eyes were warm.

"It is?" Sofie squeaked.

"*Oui*," he said emphatically. "*Vraiment*. When I say you have talent and I purchase three canvases, you can know I mean my every word."

Sofie had to anchor herself to the floor so she would not begin to float upwards like a hot-air balloon. She did so by holding tightly on to Edward's hand. "I have just started another canvas, monsieur."

"If I can sell what I am buying now, I shall purchase more," Jacques said, and Sofie beamed. "But let me advise you—if you wish to sell your work, mademoiselle, stay away from the still lifes and genres, only because they are so difficult to find buyers for. Remain with the figural studies."

Sofie nodded, rapt. "The new work is similar to *A Gentleman at Newport Beach*."

"Good," Jacques said. "Now, to business?"

Sofie's eyes widened as Jacques withdrew his billfold from his jacket. He pulled out a number of bills. "I am prepared to give you two hundred dollars," he said. "For the three portraits."

"Two hundred dollars!" she echoed. It was not much, but she had never really believed she would sell anything at all, and she was thrilled to be making a genuine financial transaction.

But Edward stepped forward before Jacques could hand her the money. "Pardon me," he said, his smile dry. "Two hundred dollars is not acceptable."

"Edward!" Sofie gasped.

Jacques cocked his head. "Are you Mademoiselle's agent, monsieur?"

"Evidently. A hundred dollars for each of the smaller portraits—a thousand for mine."

Sofie gasped again.

"Fifty for each small portrait, three hundred for yours," Jacques countered without missing a beat.

"Seventy-five for each small portrait—five hundred for mine."

"Done." Both men smiled, satisfied, Sofie gaping, and then Jacques Durand-Ruel handed her six hundred fifty dollars in cash. "If I have success with your work, I will be back," he promised her.

Sofie was speechless. She managed to nod, somewhat dazed now.

"I will send someone for the paintings tomorrow afternoon." Jacques murmured, *"Au revoir,"* and left.

"Sofie?" Edward asked, grinning.

"Oh!" Sofie cried. Arms outstretched, she whirled in joy. She whirled and whirled, forgetting all about her weak ankle, until she stumbled ever so slightly, only to fall instantly into Edward's arms.

"Happy?" he asked, smiling down at her.

Sofie gripped the lapels of his jacket. "Ecstatic. Oh, Edward, I owe all of this to you! This is the greatest day of my life!"

His hands had moved to the small of her back, splaying out there. They tightened on her fractionally. "You do not owe me, sweetheart," he said. "You owe yourself, Sofie. You are extraordinarily talented, my dear."

Sofie threw back her head and laughed, exhilarated with her success.

And Edward laughed, too, his deep, masculine rumble blending with her feminine alto. And then she was airborne. Sofie laughed again as he swung her around and around and around in a moment of joyous celebration. When her feet finally touched the ground again, she needed no encouragement. Sofie hugged him hard. He hugged her back. In that single heartbeat of time, Sofie felt love rush with dizzying speed and overpowering force through every one of her veins. She did not care. She had finally succumbed, and it was glorious.

"I'm so happy for you, Sofie," he whispered in her ear. "And I like seeing you happy like this," he added, low.

Sofie lifted her cheek from his chest and met his gaze. She had to let him know. "You have made me happy, Edward," she heard herself say.

He stared, his smile fading, his blue eyes wide and dark and piercing.

Sofie felt the tremor in his body—and the answering shudder in her own. "Thank you," she said softly. Their union was inevitable. She recognized it then.

His expression became strangely intense. "You're welcome."

Sofie felt wild and reckless, bold and unconquerable, knowing he desired her in that moment as much as she did him. She reached up and laid her palm against his cheek, aching with the love that ran so hot and turbulent in her breast. Edward did not move. He was frozen, his gaze brilliant upon hers, and Sofie allowed her fingers to slide over his jaw, thrilled with the feel of his rough skin, wishing she could caress him openly, everywhere.

Unsmiling, Edward caught her hand, removed it, stepping slightly away from her. His expression was unreadable. And Sofie realized the liberties she had just taken, beginning to flush with embarrassment. Did she seem wanton now? Did it even matter, considering that she was wanton? For she was intending an illicit relationship with him. She knew she must apologize, but could not seem to find the right words. How did one say one was sorry for loving another person? Apologizing seemed absurd.

Edward had moved a few more steps from her, staring at her, arms folded across his chest.

"Sofie?"

Sofie jerked at the sound of Suzanne's voice. The sound of briskly clicking heels coming to a halt caused Sofie to face the door. Tension stiffened her shoulders, her spine.

Suzanne stood in the doorway, eyes dark with anger. "I was just told that *he* was here!" she cried.

It was then that Sofie recalled that Suzanne had warned her to stay away from Edward, and that she had promised to do so. "Hello, Mother."

Suzanne trembled, her gaze locking with Edward's. "I was right."

Edward stepped forward, standing slightly in front of Sofie as if protecting her. "Good morning, Mrs. Ralston."

"Oh—I do not think it is a good morning," Suzanne said.

"Mother," Sofie protested, genuinely embarrassed by her display of animosity. She had never seen her mother with such a vicious look in her eyes before.

Suzanne ignored her. "Did I not make myself clear?" She said to Edward. "You are not a welcome caller for my daughter, Mr. Delanza—even if your intentions were honorable, which we both know they are not."

Sofie gasped in mortification, well aware that Suzanne had just spoken the truth. "Mother—" she was desperate to defuse the situation—"you misunderstand. Edward is not a caller. He has helped me sell my art."

Suzanne finally looked at her daughter. "What?"

Sofie came to life. "Mother," she said, moving to her and taking her hand, "Edward arranged for one of the foremost art dealers in the world to view my art." She smiled brightly. "And he has just purchased three of my canvases for his gallery."

Suzanne stared at Sofie as if she had spoken incomprehensible gibberish. "Mother?"

"You have sold your art?"

Sofie smiled again. "Yes. To Durand-Ruel. Surely you have heard of them. I know Benjamin has."

Suzanne was as pale now as she had been red-faced before. Her wide gaze swept around the studio. When she finally saw Edward's portrait, she froze, her regard riveted there.

No one moved. Suzanne was motionless, staring, incredulous. *"What is this?"*

"Edward at Newport Beach, of course," Sofie said, trying to breathe more evenly.

"I can see that," Suzanne almost snarled, whirling to face Sofie. "When did you do that, Sofie?"

Sofie wet her lips. "Recently." She hesitated. "Mother—you don't like it?"

Suzanne's bosom rose and fell. "No. No—I do not like it. I hate it!"

Sofie felt like a child again, a child who had been struck across the face. She blinked back sudden bitter, childish tears.

Suzanne whirled on Edward. "I can only assume you are responsible for this! I must ask you to leave—now."

"What's wrong, Mrs. Ralston?" An unpleasant smile twisted his features, and his eyes were diamond-bright. "Are you afraid to see your daughter succeed? Afraid to see her excel? Afraid to see her *fly?*"

"You speak nonsense! I don't want Sofie seeing you!" Suzanne cried. She faced him, unmoving, eyes wild. "How far has it gone?"

"Too far for your liking," Edward said flatly.

Suzanne jerked.

His tone was dangerous. "After all, Sofie doesn't quite think she's so awful and unlikable anymore. She starting to *live* like a woman should. She's even begun to realize her dream of being a professional artist. What's wrong, Mrs. Ralston? Why don't you like the fact that Sofie's sold her art?"

Suzanne sputtered before grinding out, "I want you gone, now. Or shall I have you thrown out?"

Listening to them, watching them, caused something to twist painfully inside Sofie. "Mother!" Sofie was aghast. "Edward has helped me to sell my work!" She hesitated, aware of her cheeks being damp. "And he is my friend."

"He is not your friend, Sofie," Suzanne said forcefully. "You may trust me on that account. Mr. Delanza?"

Edward gave her a dark look, as openly hateful as the one she was giving him, before he turned to Sofie. Instantly he softened. His tone was as warm as his gaze. "Remember the success you have had this day," he told her. "And remember what you have told me. Your mother does not understand modern art."

Sofie understood what he was trying to do, and she felt like crying in earnest then. He understood her completely. He knew that her mother's rejection hurt her and he was trying to soothe her wounds. Sofie managed a small, quivering smile. "I will."

Edward smiled back at her, ignored Suzanne, and strode from the room.

And Sofie was left alone to face her mother.

Suzanne managed to find a shred of self-control. But when she turned to look at Edward Delanza's portrait, she felt another surge of red-hot rage. God, she had sensed that something was going on, and she had been right. But the real question was, was it too late? "What has happened between the two of you?" Suzanne demanded.

Sofie did not move. "Mother, I know you disapprove of Edward, but I can assure you, nothing untoward has happened."

Suzanne swallowed. "So it is 'Edward' now, is it? And do not lie to me. I can see that you are lying, Sofie. What has he done?"

Sofie had paled and she did not speak.

"Are you still a virgin?"

Sofie did not move a muscle. When the seconds ticked by and she did not respond, Suzanne was sick at heart, and filled with disbelief. Surely her precious daughter had not been touched by that amoral rake—touched and defiled. Too well, Suzanne could recall how she herself had succumbed to Jake at the age of fifteen. But Sofie was not at all like herself, and Suzanne clung to that fact, hard.

But Sofie's next words were a bomb, blowing up in her face, destroying her hope, shocking her. "I am not a child. You cannot ask me those kinds of questions."

"Oh, God," Suzanne said, staring at her daughter, unable to comprehend her defiance, unwilling to comprehend it. And what was the significance of what she was saying? Was her virtue lost? Could this really be her daughter? "I am trying to protect you. I have always tried to protect you."

"Maybe I do not want to be protected anymore, Mother. Maybe—" Sofie trembled visibly "—maybe I want to live—just this once—even if it is wrong." She turned and walked away.

"Sofie!" Suzanne cried, chasing after her. "You do not mean it!"

Sofie paused at the door, turned slightly. She was trying not to cry. "But I do mean it. You see, Mother, I am tired of being a crazy cripple."

Suzanne gasped and stared in bewilderment as Sofie walked away.

Upstairs, Sofie hugged her pillow to her breast and refused to cry. It did not matter that Suzanne hated her art. She did not understand it, and Sofie knew that. What mattered, incomprehensibly, was that Suzanne was right about Edward. He was dishonorable. Suzanne, in fighting him tooth and nail, was only trying to protect her own daughter from destruction. But Sofie had meant what she had said, too. She was tired of being protected, and she wanted to live.

But did she really want to live as a wanton, shameless woman? Could she really be happy as a man's mistress?

Sofie looked up as Lisa slipped into her room, her small face tense with worry, her large eyes dark and concerned. She had accompanied Suzanne back to New York. "Sofie? Are you all right?"

Sofie shook her head. Tears filled her eyes.

"Oh, dear," Lisa said, sitting down beside her and prying the pillow away. She held her hands tightly. "Sofie, whatever is going on?"

"I don't know," Sofie cried. "I am so confused. Lisa, I am so very confused."

Lisa studied her face. "Have you been seeing Edward Delanza?"

Sofie blinked back tears, nodding.

"Oh, Sofie. Surely you realize the error you are making!"

Sofie gripped Lisa's hands tightly. "Mother is right, I realize that. I know Edward wants to seduce me, Lisa."

Lisa bit off a gasp, wide-eyed. "Has he tried anything?"

"Not really. Not yet."

"Sofie, Suzanne is right. You must not see him anymore."

Sofie stared sadly at Lisa. "That is easy for you to say."

"Sofie, you haven't fallen in love with him, have you?" Lisa cried.

"Of course I have," Sofie said, whisper-soft. "How could I not?"

Lisa stood up, dismayed. "You must obey your mother. You must not see him anymore. Before you allow him liberties you will regret for the rest of your life."

"You are probably right," Sofie said softly. "But I can not stay away from him."

"You must!"

"Lisa, he is more than just a dishonorable rake intent upon seduction. He is my friend. My very good friend. I cannot imagine life without him in it."

Lisa stared, her dark eyes wide with horror. Then she said, very tersely, "Sofie, you are wrong. Edward Delanza is not your friend. If he were your friend, his intentions would be honorable."

And Sofie flinched, faced with the truth of her words.

14

$\mathcal{E}$ dward lay on his back, fully dressed except for his jacket, which hung in disarray on the back of a chair. His hands were behind his head, and he stared at the slowly moving fan on the ceiling of his hotel room. His expression was strained.

No matter how hard he tried, he could not stop thinking about Sofie. He remembered her exhilaration when Jacques had told her that he was buying the Newport Beach portrait, just as he remembered her stunned hurt when Suzanne had so cruelly told her that she hated that very same work. He recalled her anger yesterday when he had dared to maneuver her into an outing with Henry, doing what he thought best for her even though he had been resentful of the mere concept of Sofie enjoying herself with another man. And he recalled the way she had kissed him in her studio after he had failed to deport himself as a gentleman should.

And every time he remembered the way she had touched his face after the Frenchman left, his heart did a funny hopscotch kind of jump. His jaw clenched and a muscle ticked there. He was experienced enough to recognize when a woman was in love with him, and he had understood that Sofie was in love with him the moment she had touched him today. Perhaps, heartless as he was, he had recognized the extent of her feelings sooner. That day in the studio, he had seen her longing for him and understood that her capitulation was complete, but not wanting to leave her yet, he'd ignored the possibility that she might be in love with him. Thinking back, there had been so many warning signs.

Of course, undoubtedly it was a love based on gratitude as well as desire, for Sofie was a woman of great common sense. But it didn't really matter. The damage was done. He had to stop it, now.

Edward hated himself. He had come into her life to teach her to live fully; he had never meant her to fall in love with him. He certainly was completely wrong for her. Even if he wanted to marry Sofie, which he did *not*, he would never do so, because he couldn't bear the idea of the shambles that their marriage would undoubtedly become.

Edward squeezed his eyes closed, as if to ward off painful memories. It did not work. His parents' marriage had been a farce; his own mother had betrayed his father in a shocking way, and tried to cover it up with lies and manipulations. That marriage was now over, but not before Edward had seen the horrendous results. He would never be able to forgive his mother for her selfish actions.

He swung his legs over the side of the bed, sitting up abruptly. When he had told Sofie that his values were old-fashioned, it had been the truth. It was because of his values that he lived his life as such a rake. Marriage was forever, vows were made to be kept, and Edward knew firsthand how impossible it was for most people to live up to their promises.

Sofie seemed to see him as some kind of goddamned hero, but soon she would know better. He made a lousy champion. He was not a knight in shining armor and he never would be one.

But, God, he did want to be one in Sofie's eyes. He realized that he had *needed* her to think the best of him, to believe in him, to see him as a gallant adventurer, a storybook hero, because nobody else did. He'd made rescuing Sofie his goal—and he'd even screwed up that one single, lousy ambition, because now Sofie was in love with him.

Edward was loath to leave her now, like this, when they'd only just begun. He wanted to see her realize her dreams—all of them. He wanted to share in all of her triumphs—one by one. Yet it was impossible. He had no choice. He had to get out now, before he did more than damage her heart, before he destroyed what was left of her innocence and all her hopes for the future.

Sofie refused to think. She had left home in a near panic, shoving aside Suzanne's warnings and Lisa's sisterly advice. But as she crossed the lavish lobby of the Savoy, she felt as if everyone were staring at her, as if everyone knew what she intended, where she was going, and to whom.

But she would not stop, not now. Even though she was sane enough to know that Lisa was right. Edward could not be her friend, for his intentions were not honorable. Yet she felt in her heart that he *was* her greatest ally, that he *was* a genuine friend, that she could trust him with her very life. And by agreeing to show her art to Jacques Durand-Ruel, hadn't she done precisely that?

But no sane person could reconcile Lisa's logic or Suzanne's warnings with her heartfelt emotions, and Sofie was running as fast as she could. To him. To her destiny—even though that destiny was to be his lover instead of his wife.

At the front desk, cheeks flaming, she learned his room number. She knew the clerk stared after her as she entered the brass-doored elevator. It moved very slowly to the fifth floor. Sofie clenched her fists and prayed for the elevator to move faster. It seemed as if the couple she shared it with were staring, too.

Outside his door she ignored any second thoughts she might have. She held on hard to the fantasy of being in his arms and in his bed. Vividly she imagined the splendor of being in his embrace, of being the recipient of his touches, his kisses, his love. Sofie was desperate. She had never been more desperate in her life. She knocked on the door.

He answered it a moment later, clad in his shirtsleeves. His eyes widened. "Sofie?"

Sofie stared at him, unable to think of a single thing to say.

"What's wrong?" he said abruptly, gripping her wrist.

"Oh, Edward," she cried, then choked on a sob that was wedged deep in her chest. "May I come in?"

His eyes widened. He did not answer at first, and Sofie was afraid he would refuse. He looked down the corridor to her right, then to her left. "Let me get my jacket and we can find a comfortable place to talk about what's bothering you." He did not smile as he closed the door and left her waiting in the hall.

Sofie stared, close to weeping. She wanted to be inside his room, in his arms. She stood still as a statue as she waited for Edward to reappear. She could not understand why he hadn't allowed her into his room.

In a moment the door opened and Edward emerged to lead her to the elevator. "It's not a good idea for you to be up here, much less in my room," he said somewhat brusquely. "Did anyone see you come upstairs?"

Suddenly she was angry. "I did not know you cared about your reputation."

He punched the elevator button. "I don't. But I care about yours."

Sofie melted. "I'm sorry," she whispered. "I am not myself."

"I can see that," he said more gently. Genuine concern was reflected in his eyes. "How about a drive in the country?"

And Sofie nodded, overwhelmed.

Edward crossed the Brooklyn Bridge and headed for Long Island. Sofie appeared immersed in her own thoughts, immune to the increasingly pastoral scenery. She did not speak. Edward wanted to know what was bothering her, but was gentleman enough to wait for her to bring it up first. Sometime later Edward saw that she had fallen asleep, obviously exhausted. Soon her head rolled to the side and she snuggled against his arm.

He wondered what had transpired between her and Suzanne after he had left, could only imagine the worst, knowing Suzanne as he now did. He had never quite hated anyone as he hated Sofie's mother. It seemed a real miracle that someone so selfish and unkind could have given birth to someone as lovely as Sofie.

Sofie began to stir. She had slept for almost an hour. She sighed, turning her face towards him. He glanced down at her, his heart tightening. Today was not a good day for him to tell her good-bye.

Her lashes fluttered and her eyes opened. She met his gaze and smiled sleepily. "Edward?"

"Hello," he murmured. "Feel better?"

"Yes," she said, sitting up straighter. But her smile had faded as sleepiness left her. She glanced at him, as tense as before. "Where are we?"

"We're not far from Oyster Bay," he said. "I happen to know a very quaint little restaurant there. I didn't want to wake you, but now that you're awake, why don't we stop there for something to eat?"

"Yes," Sofie said, her manner strange. "That's a good idea." Her cheeks had turned pink.

Edward wondered what was making her blush. He was beginning to feel uneasy. Surely she was not thinking about the fact that they were alone together, and a good fifty miles from her family and friends? Edward regretted driving so far. As soon as they had restored themselves with some food and refreshment, they would head back to the city. It was a promise he made to himself.

But he felt her gaze upon him, and when he turned, he caught her staring at his mouth. She looked away immediately, but his blood ran hot at the thought of what her look had implied.

It didn't matter. He was not going to kiss her, not even once. He did not dare.

The countryside alongside Long Island Sound was lush and green, the beaches pale, the color of rich cream. Above the Sound the sky was bright blue, but in the east it was nearly black. Edward didn't have to be a seaman to know that a squall was moving in from the Atlantic. "It looks like we're going to have to stop anyway," he muttered, dismayed. "We're in for a storm. But these squalls usually blow over fast." He said a prayer that it would.

Edward parked the Packard in front of an old, colonial-style inn, square and tall with white clapboards and a high, sloping slate roof and two brick chimneys. A cheerful white picket fence and lush green lawns and gardens surrounded it. He covered the motorcar with an oilskin tarp while Sofie watched from the slate steps leading to the inn's front door, which was painted emerald green. The charming inn was deserted, but that was no surprise. After the first weekend in September, everyone returned to the city. The proprietor seemed thrilled to see them and gave them what seemed to be the best table, by a window looking out over the bay. Sofie let Edward order a light fish dish for her, accepted a glass of wine. The sky grew quickly darker, and before long, it appeared to be nighttime outside. Edward leaned closer across the table.

"What happened? What brought you to my room?" he asked quietly. "You are distraught, Sofie."

Sofie avoided Edward's gaze. "I feel that you are my friend, Edward."

He grew uneasier. "Yes, I am." *Which is why we shouldn't be here. I don't want to hurt you, Sofie, God, I don't.*

Sofie's smile was brief and strained. "I'm glad."

Edward's gut tightened. "Did you and Suzanne fight after I left?"

Sofie's expression was tight. "Not exactly."

"Sofie?"

Sofie blinked at him. "It's not true. That she doesn't want me to sell my art."

Edward said nothing, hurting now for her, burning, in the vicinity of his chest.

Sofie forced a bright smile to her lips.

Edward stared. "What did she say, Sofie?"

Sofie looked at the table. "She is only trying to protect me," Sofie said softly without looking up.

"You don't need to be protected, Sofie."

Her gaze flew up, her amber eyes locked with his, bold and frank. "Not even from you."

He could barely speak. He stared. It was the saint in him who finally answered, not the demon who was so damn tempted. "Not even from me."

She looked away. Her hands, on the table, toying with her silver, trembled. Then she shocked him. Not looking up, her voice low and hoarse, she said, "Even if I needed protection from you, I would not want it."

Edward jerked. There was no way, after these past few days, that he could mistake her meaning.

Edward was grateful to see their food arrive. He was on alert now; he sensed danger, danger both from her and himself. As soon as the squall blew over, they would be on the road.

But within minutes of their food arriving, the wind was pummeling the trees and the rain had become torrential.

Together they watched the storm outside the window, barely eating. The bay was black, but whitecaps frothed in frenzy on the water's dark surface. Their gazes met and held.

It was as if the rest of the world had ceased to exist. As if it were just he and Sofie and the savage storm outside. The world had become raw and untamed and even frightening, but they had attained a solitary niche for themselves, one warm and intimate, a niche occupied by just the two of them. Edward was seized with a fierce longing that seemed to come from his heart and soul, as well as his loins. A longing he would fight with every ounce of willpower he owned. Because it was all an illusion. The world was not a black, frothing vacuum, and they were not the only two people in existence, man and woman, destined to come together for all eternity.

Sofie stole a glance at him. "This is very romantic," she said, her tone husky.

Edward looked at her in the dim dancing light cast by the candle on their table. He tried to ignore what he was feeling. "It will be over soon."

Her fine nostrils flared and tears seemed to glisten in her eyes. "I know." She turned to stare out into the utter blackness of the storm.

Edward could not keep his thoughts from acknowledging that there were rooms for rent upstairs. He had never wanted any woman as badly as he wanted Sofie, and he had never wanted her as badly as he wanted her right now. He shoved his plate aside and forced ugly black temptation aside as well. The wind suddenly roared so hard that the walls of the restaurant shook. Leaves flew from the trees and danced and swirled wildly in the air. As he looked outside, Edward thought about the fact that it did not look like they were going to be able to leave anytime soon—and shortly it would be nightfall.

As if on cue, the proprietor came over to their table. "Folks? I've got bad news."

"What's that?" Edward asked, already knowing, dismayed. But not nearly as dismayed as he should be. His heart had begun to sound as thunderous inside his ears as the storm outside.

"We just heard on the telegraph that this here storm is the edge of a hurricane that began down in the Caribbean. Already the eye's in Virginia, and while it's expected to hit Long Island only indirectly, that's sometime tonight. You folks sure can't leave now. But I've got plenty of rooms." He beamed. "They say by tomorrow afternoon we'll have plenty of sunshine."

Edward nodded and the man left. His insides were tight, sick, as he turned to Sofie. "He's right. There's no way we can drive back in the rain, Sofie. I'm sorry."

Sofie looked him in the eye. "I'm not."

Sofie stood at her window in the small, quaint room she had been given. Night had fallen and the rain had drenched it silver. She stood listening to the rain and watching the torrents streak the windowpanes. She stood there thinking about Edward. Did she dare?

She turned to stare at the door on the other side of the four-poster bed that adjoined their rooms. It did not seem possible, but he had not come to her room. He had not made any attempt to seduce her. She did not understand. For if seduction were not his game, then what was?

Had she, and everyone, misjudged him entirely? Was it possible that he was truly her friend—and an honorable one at that? If so, Sofie knew that she should be glad, but she wanted to weep, not with joy, but with despair and unfulfilled yearning.

She had come this far, she could not turn back.

Sofie moved halfway across the small room and stopped. Once, not so long ago, when Edward had encouraged her to show her art to a dealer, he had told her that as she was an artist, rejection would become a part of her life, a fact she would have to learn to deal with. She had not told him that, as a woman and a human being, it was already a fact of her life, an inescapable fact, and that she had dealt with rejection hundreds of times before. Now Sofie was frozen, tears in her eyes. Being rejected by the likes of her mother's peers, or by Henry Marten and Carmine Vanderbilt, or by art dealers like Jacques Durand-Ruel, would be nothing compared to rejection by the man she had fallen in love with.

Sofie turned away from the door and stared at herself in the mirror over the room's single bureau. The innkeeper had been so kind as to lend her his daughter's nightgown and wrapper. The ensemble was too large. Sofie pulled the robe off slowly, let it slide to the floor.

The sleeveless nightgown was sewn from thin white eyelet cotton. Two pink ribbons held up the bodice. It was too long, covering her feet right to the toes, covering her misshapen ankle. If she stared closely, the outline of her legs was visible through the fine material. Yet she did not look ugly; she looked like a wanton. Sofie closed her eyes. Did she dare?

Trembling, Sofie lifted her arms and removed the pins from her waist-long hair. She brushed it out with her fingers, until it was a wild mane. She pinched her cheeks. She was going to do it. She was going to go to him because, apparently, he was not such a black rogue after all and he was not going to come to her. She was going to go to him because she loved him, and just this once, she wanted to be loved in return.

Sofie moved quickly across the room, before sanity might reclaim her, or before her fear might stop her. She knocked on his door. Her heart threatened to beat its way out of her breast, and time seemed suspended, unreal.

The door swung open, revealing Edward in his trousers and bare feet, his powerful torso unclothed. His eyes were wide, his jaw tight, and he was not smiling—not at all. Sofie was careful to look only at his face.

His voice was a croak. An angry croak. "What in hell are you doing, Sofie?"

"Edward," Sofie whispered, her pulse racing faster while she prayed to God that Edward would not reject her, that he would love her, just this once, just for tonight. "I don't want to be alone."

He said nothing, but his temples throbbed and his eyes darkened.

Sofie wet her lips. "Won't . . . won't you come . . . in? Please?"

He stared. He stared into her eyes, then at her mouth, then at the halo of her long, wild hair. Sofie could feel herself begin to blush.

"Dammit," Edward said, but now his gaze raked her, and Sofie was woman enough to know that he was looking right through her nightgown. Her fear increased. Even though she had thought the nightgown concealing enough, and enticing, perhaps he could see that her ankle was twisted and ugly. But then she looked into his eyes and saw his hunger. The force of her feelings caused her to sway. He caught her. He gripped her elbows so hard, it hurt. "Don't do this," he whispered. It was a plea.

For the first time in her life Sofie felt a hint of the power a seductress might feel. Edward wanted her, she had glimpsed his hunger, felt it. It surged in him like a living, wild thing. Hot and coiled, ready to strike. He trembled with it.

Sofie was very tense and she leaned forward, shaking with the residue of her fear, until the fabric stretched over her breasts touched the hard wall of his bare chest. Edward inhaled, flinching. His skin was so hot, it seemed to burn her nipples right through the cotton nightgown.

"Edward?" She looked up at him. *"Please don't reject me."*

He stood motionless, staring into her eyes, shuddering. "Don't do this, Sofie," he finally whispered, wetting his lips. "I can't do this. I couldn't live with myself afterward," he said harshly.

He released her, and Sofie felt him begin to back away. She reached out, touched him. He froze and they both stared at her small, pale hand on his bare, bronzed skin. Sofie had never touched his naked flesh before. He was as smooth as velvet, but warm, hot. And hard. No one had ever told her a man's stomach could be so hard.

Sofie's glance strayed ever so slightly. There was a massive bulge in his trousers, the fine linen fabric delineating his engorged manhood as thoroughly as if he were naked. Sofie froze. She realized that the top buttons of his trousers were undone. Her behavior was far worse than shameless, and she knew she should remove her hand, and her gaze, but she did not. She could not.

"Oh, God," Edward said, choked. "Oh, dammit," he cried. And his arms closed around her.

The devil in him was elated, the saint all but gone.

Abruptly he had her in his arms, was carrying her to the bed. Edward had ceased thinking—did not want to think. If he did, the saint would come back, ruining it all.

And it was impossible to think now. Edward dipped Sofie onto the bed, her long golden hair flowing over his hands like rippling skeins of silk. Edward straddled her, for just a moment overwhelmed by her beauty, while painfully aware of the close-to-bursting pressure in his loins—and in his chest.

He moved his arms underneath her, lifting her slightly—their gazes met. "*Sofie.*"

Her lips parted, her eyes shone. "*Edward.*"

And Sofie smiled. Edward felt his heart twist hard. Something strong and bright and irrevocable rushed through him—like a new life force—an emotion he could not stop to identify. Not now.

A second later they were both frantically entwined. Edward parted her lips instantly, urgently, forcing his tongue deep into her warmth. He spread her legs, nested his huge phallus there. He sucked her lips, tangled with her tongue, probed deep. Helplessly he rocked his massive loins against her, again and again.

And Sofie responded immediately to him. The strokes of her tongue against his were timid and unsure at first, but swiftly she began to spar with him, adept and bold. Their mouths fused, tongues entwined. Edward had the wild urge to rise up over her, show her how to flick her tongue over the plum-like head of his manhood.

But this was Sofie, beautiful, sweet Sofie, and he would not use her like that. Burying his face in her hair, Edward froze, panting, cursing the saint that lived within him who still tried to interfere, to deny him this woman he loved. But his loins were the tool of the devil, not to be denied, not anymore. He could not bear the pressure there, made all the worse because Sofie's soft hips were undulating in a rhythm of seduction and desire as old as time.

Edward emitted one last soblike gasp, slid his hands under her nightgown, and clasped her bare buttocks, pulling her even more closely against his erection. Abruptly he yanked the nightgown out from between them, rubbing himself against her soft naked sex. His linen trousers were still a barrier between them, but the fabric was so fine, it was as if it were barely there.

Sofie whimpered in his ear, clutching his shoulders. She mewled again, and this time her nails were like a kitten's small, sharp claws, kneading his flesh without quite pricking it. The hot, soft center of her undulated more insistently against him, and she began to emit soft, breathy little sounds of urgency and distress.

Edward gripped her face between his large palms. Their gazes met, hers bright and feverish. "I can't stop," he whispered. "Oh, Sofie, how I want you! How I need you!"

She cried out and gripped his hands as he held her face, and strained to meet his lips.

Their mouths fused. This time Edward sucked her tongue into his mouth, deep. He could not stand it. Abruptly he tore himself free, then raised himself onto his knees, straddling her. He fumbled with the buttons to her bodice, exposed her soft, white breasts. Their gazes met again.

"Oh, Sofie," Edward groaned, "You are so beautiful!"

Sofie half laughed and half sobbed.

Edward touched her, held her, closed his eyes, groaned.

He bent and touched his tongue to her distended tips, one by one. Sofie began to squirm and gasp. Her nails dug into his shoulders again. Small cries of breathless excitement escaped her.

When he paused he was breathing hard, on the verge of exploding again. Edward sucked in air. Sweat poured down his face and chest.

"Edward," Sofie moaned.

He opened his eyes and saw that she was staring feverishly at him, gripping his wrists. Then he realized that she stared at the rigid line of his manhood, straining against his thin trousers. Edward was not wearing his drawers. He realized that, as wet as he was, she could see through his pants, and that because the top two buttons were undone, an inch of his heavy red flesh was exposed.

Their gazes met, Sofie whimpering and wetting her dry lips. Edward bit back his own harsh groan as he pressed her small, delicate palm against his thickly swollen penis. Sofie gasped and became utterly still.

Abruptly Edward lifted her hand to his mouth and kissed it hard. "Forgive me," he cried, and he slid down her body, running his hands up her soft thighs, pushing them wide apart. Sofie cried out, not in protest, but in sexual distress.

"You are so damn beautiful," Edward moaned, kissing her navel.

Sofie jerked, crying out. Edward heard himself laugh, shaky and exultant, the sound heavy with raw male excitement. His thumbs flicked over her honey-colored hair. Sofie gasped again.

"Sofie," he whispered harshly, sliding his hand fully over her. He touched the seam of the heavy, warm folds he was searching for. "Darling."

She froze, but only for a heartbeat. Then she began to undulate shamelessly. "Edward!"

"Yes, darling," he coaxed, parting those swollen lips. He watched her face intently as his thumb slid up against the swollen, nervelike center of her sex. She gasped, arching up beneath him.

"Yes," Edward murmured thickly, kissing the inside of her thigh, rubbing the small quivering organ of her sex.

"Edward!" Sofie thrashed.

He grunted, pressing a kiss to the cleft there, then slid his tongue along the throbbing seam. Sofie jerked beneath him. He tested that cleft again. Sofie moaned. He inserted his tongue into the small valley and was rewarded with her loud gasp of pleasure. Edward began to lave and suck her flesh, to circle the distended tip of her with his tongue. Sofie gripped his hair spasmodically, starting to gasp and shake, and then she began to keen in helpless abandon.

Edward cried out, moving over her, watching her exquisite face while tearing open his trousers. Through the thick haze of desire, it crossed his mind that it must not come to this. Too late, his mouth found hers while he pushed himself inside of her.

Sofie gasped.

Edward gasped too, shocked by the tight, heated, intensely exhilarating feel of her. He froze, panting hard, then raised himself up to gaze into her face. Her eyes were wide, still dazed with rapture, and so blindly trusting—so openly loving. "Edward," she gasped, gripping him tightly. "Oh, Edward—darling!"

He kissed her with all the explosive emotion he was feeling, swiftly finishing what he had begun and plunging through her virgin membrane. His kiss smothered her small cry of pain. Edward drove deep and deeper still, needing to be buried inside her as far as possible, forever. There he paused, for one instant, shuddering with profound pleasure and an awareness he had never had before in such a moment of total ecstasy—an acute awareness of every exquisite facet of the woman he was united with.

Edward began to peak. He ground his teeth, buried his face against her neck and wrapped his arms around her, and clamped down hard on his own need to ejaculate. He wanted to take her soaring to heaven with him. It was too late. He sobbed. He exploded.

For a while he drifted, far above the earth. When he came to his senses, he felt her hand stroking his hair at his nape. Their bodies were entwined. Sofie was soft and warm and silken against him. Pain stabbed so piercingly through his chest that for an instant he wondered if it was physical and he was having a heart attack.

Oh, God—what had he done?

He heaved himself off of her, rolling onto his back. *You bastard,* a voice inside him growled. *You lousy, no-good bastard!*

He felt her turn to face him. She touched his hair again, his back. He was rigid. He squeezed his eyes shut tightly. Sofie caressed his shoulder, and it was somehow far more exquisite than all that had passed before. He could feel how much she loved him. He was sick.

"Edward?"

Any and all sense of elation was gone. How could he face her? How could he face himself?

But he did turn to face her.

"I didn't know," she whispered, her eyes wide, glowing. She smiled a woman's smile of utter satisfaction and profound amazement. "I had no idea."

Somehow, he managed to smile back. But he knew he hadn't done a very good job of it, because her own smile died a little.

"Edward?" She leaned over him, some of her hair falling onto his chest. Her bodice was open, and her high, round breasts swung forward slightly. They were blotchy from where the day's growth of his beard had scratched them.

His mouth turned down, for his groin was thickening yet again. He looked at her face. Her mouth was red and swollen from his kisses. He finally met her gaze.

"Edward? Is something wrong?" She trembled, the question there in her eyes, and with it, the fear.

He was not going to hurt her. Edward knew it, then and there. That knowledge took away some of the brutal cutting edge of shame and disgust. Edward sat up and pulled her into his arms, holding her tight. It was difficult to speak naturally, to keep his feelings hidden. "No, Sofie. Everything's fine. Just fine."

He pressed her face to his chest, cupping the back of her head, his fingers tangled in her wavy gold-streaked hair. And Edward closed his own eyes in abject despair. He had betrayed her trust in him, betrayed her faith. Edward wondered how there could be so much pain where there had just been so much pleasure.

15

Sofie knew something was wrong and she clung to him, her face buried against his chest, already terrified of what might happen next. It had been clear to her almost immediately that Edward was upset, not at all as thrilled as she was with all that had just happened. Sofie reminded herself that she had forced the situation, that, in effect, she had seduced him.

Gently Edward moved her face from his shoulder, set her aside from him, and got up.

Sofie dared to turn and look at him, her heart sinking. His expression was so somber, so grim. Realizing her bodice was open, she fumbled with the small buttons. "Edward?"

His smile was clearly forced. "In a moment, Sofie." Edward disappeared into his own room, adjusting his trousers as he did so.

Sofie fought panic and the threat of tears. There was a huge bubble in her chest, trying to choke her, and she fought that, too. She checked to make sure her nightgown covered her legs, and more important, her ankle, which it did. She clasped her hands in her lap and waited for him to return.

It was astounding, she thought bleakly, that one partner could feel such love during lovemaking, and that the other partner did not. She hadn't considered it might be like that, and now it was too late. She quickly swiped at a tear.

Edward returned to stand in the doorway, wearing his shirt, which he had buttoned from top to bottom but left hanging over his trousers. It was a funny sight, but Sofie could not smile, because there was nothing at all humorous about his expression or about the very pregnant feeling of this moment. She met his gaze. "Edward? Is . . . is something wrong?"

This time he made no attempt to smile. His eyes were so grave that she was chilled with fear.

"I owe you an apology," he said slowly, as if choosing his words with care. "Sofie, this should not have happened."

154

Sofie stared. Was he telling her that he regretted their glorious lovemaking? But how could that be even remotely possible? Surely the desire that had raged between them was extraordinary? Or was it very ordinary, a desire he had experienced a thousand times before with other women, and would experience a thousand times again—with others?

He shifted. "An apology sounds trite, considering what we just did." He flushed then, to the roots of his dark hair. "What *I* just did."

Sofie shook her head in negation. "No," she whispered. "You do not need to apologize."

"Sofie, I'm sorry. I am very sorry. You did not deserve this."

Sofie's eyes filled with tears and she looked away so he would not see, fighting for control. When she had regained some small portion of it, she met his gaze. "I wanted this, Edward. Please, you need not castigate yourself so. I am a grown woman, capable of making my own decisions."

"Don't cry," he said harshly. "God, the last thing I want to do is make you cry." He forced a smile and swiftly approached, sitting beside her and taking her hand.

Sofie wanted to leap into his embrace and hold on to him for her dear life, but she held back. She did not want to make this moment worse than it already was.

Very gravely he asked, "Will you marry me, Sofie?"

Her eyes widened in shock.

He smiled, but it did not reach his eyes. "That didn't seem very romantic, did it?" His tone was light. He tipped up her chin and nudged her lips with his. When Sofie did not respond, he began to kiss her with real, persuasive power.

Sofie was stunned by his proposal, her heart skidding wildly. But as his expert kisses became deeper and more insistent, she felt herself responding as she had earlier. He had just asked her to marry him, but it was hard to think, because his hands stroked her back now, dipping low on her hips and then her buttocks, teasingly, and his tongue was testing the joining of her lips. Sofie opened. And as she did so, he pushed her down onto her back, groaning long and low and very male in the back of his throat. Desire, already kindled, sparked and flared red-hot and urgent. Sofie shook with new excitement. Flames licked her limbs, up her legs, between her thighs. Sofie tried to hang on to the comprehension that he was seducing her now with the intent of gaining his way, but it no longer seemed to matter. She gasped as the full and heavy weight of his groin settled against the swollen and clefted folds of her femininity.

"Sofie," Edward growled, his hands on her breasts, inside her cotton gown.

Sofie arched wildly against him. His fingers played her nipples, strumming them until she was panting his name. Edward murmured an endearment against her mouth, bent and suckled on her. Sofie thrashed and wept with pleasure, her nails clawing his back as his tongue raked over the tips again and again.

This time, when he entered her, she was ready and it was painless. Sofie held him tightly as he glided inside her repeatedly. "I want you to come with me," Edward told her hoarsely, his eyes bright and wild. "I want us to peak together."

Sofie had never imagined it possible to talk in such a graphic and explicit manner while making love, and his words sent her spiraling out of control. Edward gasped and thrust harder, and even through the haze of ecstasy, Sofie thought she could feel him spilling new life inside of her, and she wept with redoubled pleasure. She knew she wanted to have his baby.

Afterwards, he did not release her. Edward held Sofie tightly in his arms, stroking her hair, her back, the curve of her hips. Periodically he would kiss her temple or her jaw. And before Sofie could remember his shocking proposal, she had fallen asleep, nestled in his embrace. Nor did she remember it later that night, when they came together as naturally as lovers of long standing would.

Near dawn Sofie woke up, frightened. The wind was howling, the rain was a torrential downpour, and something was banging loudly against the side of the house. She was alone. For a moment she was confused, unsure of where she was.

And then it all came flooding back to her. She was in a small inn at Oyster Bay. She had seduced Edward—and he had made love to her twice more since then. The tip of a hurricane was raging outside the house. But where was Edward?

The heavy banging against the side of the house grew louder. Sofie's heart clenched and she sat up. The rafters on the roof seemed to shake, and the wind was piercing. The sky outside was just beginning to lighten, and she could see the shapes of trees bent over double in the gale. Sofie told herself it was only a storm, told herself not to be afraid.

Her door slammed open hard. Sofie screamed in fright, then realized that the shadowy figure who had rushed into her room, holding a candle, was Edward.

"Sofie, get up," he ordered, pulling the covers off her. "Half the roof on the house next door just blew off. It's not safe up here and we're going downstairs."

Sofie was fully alarmed despite his calm tone. Suddenly they heard the sound of glass breaking and objects crashing down. Edward moved to the window, holding up the flickering candle. "The electricity's out," he said grimly, "and it's hard to see, but a tree just blew down Main Street. Get dressed, Sofie."

Sofie hurried to obey, her heart racing with fear. The banging continued, louder now, and the sky outside had turned to a strange, opaque gray. She managed to get on her clothes, but could not button up her shirtwaist— Edward had to help her. She was trying to braid her hair when a knock sounded frantically on the door. "You folks!" shouted the proprietor over the deafening noise of the storm. "Got to go down to the cellar!"

"Forget your hair," Edward cried, grabbing Sofie. They ran across the room, but when they opened the door, it flew so hard against the wall that it broke off its hinges. The innkeeper was cowering there with an old-fashioned lantern, ashen. "All the windows on the other side of the house have blown out!" he shouted. And as he spoke, the sky appeared above their heads as a part of the inn's roof was sucked away, and rain poured down upon them with bruising force. Sofie screamed when a sudden gale slammed her backwards down the corridor towards the stairs.

Edward caught her before she was blown to the floor below. He lifted her in his arms and shouted for the innkeeper. They raced downstairs and outside. Through the torrents of rain Sofie saw Edward's beautiful Packard smashed beneath a huge, uprooted oak tree. "Oh, Edward!"

"Forget it!" The wind tried to push him backwards, but he forced his way on, following the similarly afflicted innkeeper. They turned the corner and came to the cellar doors. The innkeeper went down first. Edward pushed Sofie down before him, clambering down last himself and pulling the doors shut behind him.

The proprietor's wife and daughter sat in one corner of the cellar with a pile of blankets and another kerosene lamp. The girl, about Sofie's age, was sobbing. The innkeeper joined them, his wife gasping with relief, then he handed a blanket to Sofie and Edward. Edward spread it out near the earthen wall and sat down. Sofie sat next to him, huddling close. He put his arm around her.

They looked at each other. Suddenly Edward smiled, and so did Sofie. Suddenly they laughed, in utter, shaky relief. Across the cellar, the innkeeper began to chuckle, too, and so did his wife and daughter. It was good to be alive, and everyone knew it.

And then Sofie remembered. She stopped laughing, unable to even breathe. Last night Edward had asked her to marry him. For all the wrong reasons. As atonement for his sins. How could she possibly agree?

A few hours later, they left the cellar. The sky was a robin's-egg blue, with fat, puffy, pure white clouds drifting by. The sun was shining brightly, merrily. It was as if last night's storm had never happened, as if the hurricane had been a bad dream.

But standing outside the inn, they looked around. The picket fence had been blown away. The houses across the street had all suffered damage; many windows were blown out. One half of an entire roof was missing on one green house; on another, a second-story balcony had collapsed onto the front porch. A cedar-shingled shed had been crushed by a fallen elm tree, and telegraph poles and lines were down.

Edward held her hand. "Wow."

They turned back to the inn. The southeast corner of the roof was gone, and almost all of the windows on that side of the house were missing. Edward still held her hand, and Sofie thought about how easily they might have been hurt.

But they hadn't been hurt. They were both fine. Did he even remember proposing to her?

Sofie swallowed and gazed up at his handsome profile. Perhaps it was better if he did not remember, because if the topic was forgotten, she would not have to say no.

But it hurt. How it hurt. Loving him hurt enough as it was, without the added factor of his having asked her to marry him out of a sense of decency and duty, instead of out of love and need and a desire to remain together for all of eternity.

Upstairs, they gathered their few things among the mess made by the storm. Desolate now, Sofie found her fringed silk wrap and reticule. How she dreaded returning to the city—how she dreaded the future. Edward waited for her in the doorless doorway. "How will we get back to New York?" she asked, hoping he had not detected the quaver in her voice.

"We can rent a horse and buggy. I inquired and the trains aren't running yet. There are trees and debris on the tracks."

Sofie nodded.

Edward added, his gaze direct, "We could spend another night. The landlord told me that he has some rooms downstairs which are fine. But your family must be hysterical with worry by now."

Sofie did not say anything, because they were moving on to risky subject matter. Yet Edward would not let the topic go. "Of course, once we tell them our plans, I'm sure it will all blow over," he added.

Sofie froze in the center of the room, filled with dread and anguish. She had never dreamed a broken heart could hurt so much. "What plans, Edward?" Her tone was thick with tears.

He started, unsmiling. "Our plans to get married."

Sofie found her voice, one of the greatest efforts of her life. "I did not accept your proposal, Edward."

He stared.

She hugged her wrap and reticule to her chest. "It is very gallant of you to propose matrimony, of course," she said, trying to sound calm and composed and sensible, "but it was not necessary."

He stared at her in disbelief.

"I did not become your lover to force you to marry me," Sofie said, chin high. She knew if she cried now, he would guess how much she loved him and why she was refusing, and it would be a miserable, pathetic coil, to be avoided at all costs. It appeared that she had nothing in this life but her pride—and of course, her memories and her work.

"Sofie." Edward was pale beneath his rich tan. "You were a virgin."

"I am aware of that. But that is not a good reason to get married."

His blue eyes were wide and piercing. "Sofie—I made love to you three times."

She felt herself blushing in response to his bald statement of fact, remembering the passion they had shared, at moments wild and thoroughly carnal, and at other moments, achingly tender and gentle and so loving, it almost defied description and recollection. "What does that have to do with anything?"

His jaw clenched. His temple throbbed visibly. His mouth had turned into a hard, tight line. "What if you're pregnant? With my child?"

It was salt on her open wound. "It's not that time of month," she lied.

His mouth seemed to soften slightly. "Sofie, we should get married. It's the right thing to do."

She was so very close to weeping. It was not the right thing to do—not like this. Marrying for *love* was the right thing to do, but that was not going to ever be. Not for her, not with him. Sounding unnaturally calm and almost like a schoolteacher, Sofie said, "I have no desire to get married, Edward.

Have you forgotten? Next May I turn twenty-one and I am going to Paris to continue my studies of art. I am sorry." Her voice broke. It was so hard to continue. "I cannot marry without love, Edward."

He did not move. He looked as if he had been dealt a solid and painful blow in the region of his solar plexis. Then, abruptly, he turned on his heel and strode away. "I'll wait downstairs."

Sofie sank onto the bed, still redolent from their lovemaking, gripping the covers, crying. It was over, then, before it had even begun.

The house was in an uproar when they returned, but Sofie had known it would be.

She felt a moment of sickening dread when, as they alighted from the hired carriage, the front door flew open and they could hear Mrs. Murdock inside crying, "She's here! She's here! Sofie is back!"

Edward did not touch her. He had not touched her since she had refused his offer of wedlock six hours ago. Nor had he looked at her even once. And he had only spoken to her a few moments ago, to tell her that they would insist that nothing had happened. In other words, they would lie—since she did not want to marry him. Edward seemed to be angry, as if expecting her to change her mind before it was too late. But Sofie had agreed to participate in his plan.

Sofie had no choice but to allow Edward to help her down from the carriage. His touch was so impersonal now that she almost broke into tears on the spot. And she was so sick at heart that there was no room for shame or guilt. Everyone would be thinking the worst—and everyone was right—but Sofie did not give a damn.

As she and Edward walked up the steps, Lisa flew down them, in tears. "Sofie, thank God! Are you all right?" The sisters embraced on the front stoop.

"Yes, I'm fine," Sofie said, holding Lisa's glistening gaze. "I really am fine." Her own eyes had become moist.

Lisa stared, then turned to look at Edward, both accusing and incredulous.

Suzanne stood in the doorway, ashen. "I should have known," she said tersely. "Sofie, no one had any idea where you'd gone—dear God!" She started to cry.

Sofie left Edward and hurried to her mother, embracing her. "I'm sorry," she said tremulously while Suzanne shed harsh tears. In her mother's arms, it would be very easy to cry her heart out as she longed to do. "Edward took me for a drive and then the hurricane hit and we got stranded in Oyster Bay."

Suzanne broke the embrace, blinking her eyes and turning furiously towards Edward. "I should have known that you are at the bottom of this."

"Hold your horses, Mrs. Ralston," Edward said coldly. "We had no choice but to remain out on the island last night. Had we tried to return, we might have been killed. As it was, my automobile was smashed in two."

Suzanne started, her face draining of color.

"He is right," Sofie said, and this much, at least, was the truth.

Suzanne put her arm around Sofie's shoulders and pulled her close. Her face was twisted with revulsion. "What have you done to my daughter?"

Edward's expression was impossible to read. "Nothing. Your daughter is the same as ever."

"Mother," Sofie said, attracting her attention. "I am fine. Really. You need not worry on that account. Edward was . . . a perfect gentleman." She forced herself to smile. She knew that Suzanne had noticed the hesitation. She hated lying, but to marry under the circumstances would be far worse.

Sofie saw a hard and cynical look in Suzanne's eyes and knew that she did not believe them.

Benjamin suddenly appeared on the threshold, joining the gathering on the front step. He paused beside Suzanne, grim. "Sofie, are you all right?"

"Yes."

He looked at Edward. "Are you going to do the right thing, sir? Now that you have compromised her thoroughly?"

Edward stiffened.

But Suzanne broke in smoothly, touching her husband's sleeve. "Benjamin, nothing happened. I know my daughter, and she would not deceive us—just as she would never allow herself to be truly compromised." Suzanne smiled reassuringly.

Benjamin regarded his wife. "She has assured you of that?"

"Yes. And I am certain that we can weather this small scandal, if there even is any scandal at all." Suzanne smiled again, at Edward. "Mr. Delanza, you must be exhausted; why do you not come inside for some refreshment? And you must be tired, too, Sofie. Dear, why don't you go upstairs and have Clara draw a bath? I will have some hot food sent up to you. You need not come down to supper, not after such an ordeal."

Sofie knew her mother realized the truth. She could not fathom Suzanne's motivation in supporting her lie. It did not matter. She was relieved that Suzanne was taking charge of the affair, diverting Benjamin from the role he was ready to assume as an enraged stepfather. Sofie did not wait to hear Edward refuse Suzanne's offer of hospitality. "I am more than tired," she said. She nodded at Edward, knowing she must now act as if on the Shakespearean stage. "Thank you, Edward, for seeing me home safely. And I am sorry if I have inconvenienced you."

He bowed briefly. His words were mocking. "It was my pleasure."

Sofie fled.

Sofie lay in bed, wrapped in a thick cotton robe even though it was seventy-five degrees out, a perfect and balmy summer evening. But she was chilled through and through, to the very bone, to her very heart. It had occurred to her that she would never see Edward again.

She told herself that she would survive, but she did not believe it.

Sofie turned onto her side, cuddling her pillow. Perhaps she had been wrong to reject his proposal. Perhaps it would be better to be his wife even if he did not love her, than to lose him forever. Already Sofie missed him more than she would have ever thought it possible for her to miss anybody.

Had she not boldly seduced him, he would still be a part of her life. He would still be her friend, her champion. Tears filled Sofie's eyes, but she could not regret the night they had spent together. Unquestionably those memories would last a lifetime. But so would the terrible, aching yearning and the grief of his loss.

"Sofie?"

Sofie sat up to face Suzanne, whose gaze was piercing. She closed the bedroom door and came to sit down beside her daughter on the bed. Sofie was tense, knowing how easily her mother lost her temper. But Suzanne did not shriek or yell. She said, "Are you all right?"

Sofie meant to nod her head yes. Instead, she shook her head no and a big tear trickled down her cheek.

Suzanne embraced her. "I know you did not tell the truth."

Sofie clung. "I am sorry. We decided we must lie."

Suzanne stroked her back, then pulled away. Her own eyes were red. "I would like to kill him!"

Sofie dared to look her mother in the eye. "It was not his fault. I seduced him."

Suzanne started, appearing appalled.

"I love him," Sofie said, in self-defense.

Immediately Suzanne cried out, sweeping her into her arms, crushing her there. "I wanted to protect you from him! I wanted to spare you this! Oh, God, Sofie, I know how you must feel!"

Sofie wept yet again, in her mother's arms. When she had finished crying, Suzanne handed her a handkerchief. Sofie wiped her eyes, then saw that Suzanne had been crying, too. "Mother?"

"Your father broke my heart, too. Many, many times." Suzanne fought for composure. She sniffled. "I *knew* Edward was just like him."

"He asked me to marry him," Sofie said.

Suzanne froze.

Sofie's eyes filled with tears again. "Of course, I said no. But I am not sure I did the right thing. I miss him so. Perhaps I should—"

"No!"

Sofie started.

Suzanne gripped her shoulders and shook her hard, once, twice, three times. "You have already been a fool! Do not be a fool again!"

"I love him. I know he doesn't love me, but—"

"Sofie, no! He will destroy you if you marry him, exactly the way Jake destroyed me!" Suzanne shrieked.

"You are probably right," Sofie said, but in her heart, she did not quite believe it.

"I am right. There is no probably about it. You would not be able to stand the other women. To lie in bed alone, night after night, listening to the clock ticking, counting the minutes, waiting for him to come home, praying that he will? To finally confront him at dawn, when he is wearing another woman's scent? I will not let you do it, Sofie."

Sofie sucked in her breath. Vividly she recalled that day at Delmonico's when Edward had told her that he could not be faithful to a wife.

But Suzanne would not let the subject drop. Her eyes welled with tears. "You are so naive. So naive, so young. Even if he were faithful in the beginning—as Jake was—do you really think you can hold the interest— the desire—of a man like that for an entire lifetime? Do you think you can compete with the likes of Hilary Stewart and so many others like her?"

"No," Sofie whispered, paralyzed by the ugly scenario her mother had painted. Suzanne was right. Wasn't she? She was merely Sofie O'Neil, small and plain and lame. Somehow, she had forgotten that.

"What makes you think that he would have even bothered to end it with Hilary at all if you had accepted his suit?" Suzanne said very bluntly. "Could you marry him knowing he keeps a mistress? Could you?"

"I am not marrying him," Sofie said, her mouth trembling and turned down.

Somehow she had forgotten that, during their brief relationship, Hilary had still been in his life, she had still been there for him at night. Sofie could not help remembering the passion she had witnessed once between them. She was sick.

"Ending it like this is for the best," Suzanne said fiercely. "For the best! It should have never happened, but in time, you will forget."

Sofie knew she would never forget a single instance of her life since Edward Delanza had first sauntered into it, but she did not say so. And if she had conceived during their brief but glorious liaison, their lives would remain linked, no matter how much of the earth separated them physically. Sofie hugged her knees to her chest, suddenly wishing desperately for what could only be considered by society to be the worst fate to befall an unwed woman.

"What is wrong, darling?" Suzanne asked sharply.

Sofie lifted her gaze. "What if I am pregnant?"

Once again, Suzanne paled. "It is unlikely, after one time."

Sofie looked at her toes, curled under the sheets.

"It was just one time?"

"No." Her voice was almost inaudible. Sofie was not going to reveal to Suzanne that Edward had loved her three times in a single night. Then she choked back another sob, because it hadn't been love, not for him, it had been lust.

"When was your last monthly?" Suzanne asked, fear in her voice.

Sofie did not look up. "Less than two weeks ago."

Suzanne's jaw clenched and she lost the last of her color. Then she took her daughter's hand. "Do not be afraid. I am sure you did not conceive. And if you did—" she inhaled "—you can go away to have the child. There is always adoption. No one need ever know."

Sofie jerked. "Mother, if I am so lucky as to be pregnant, then I am having his baby. And I would *never* give the baby up."

Their gazes locked, Sofie fierce and furious, Suzanne wide-eyed with trepidation. Finally Suzanne smiled and patted her daughter's hand. "Let us worry about that when the time comes, dear," she said. "If it does come."

Sofie nodded, looking away. Her pulse was racing now. And she was praying to God, whom she had stopped praying to long ago, when he had not brought Jake back to her, alive and free. *Let me have his baby*, she begged. *Dear Lord, let me have his baby. Please.*

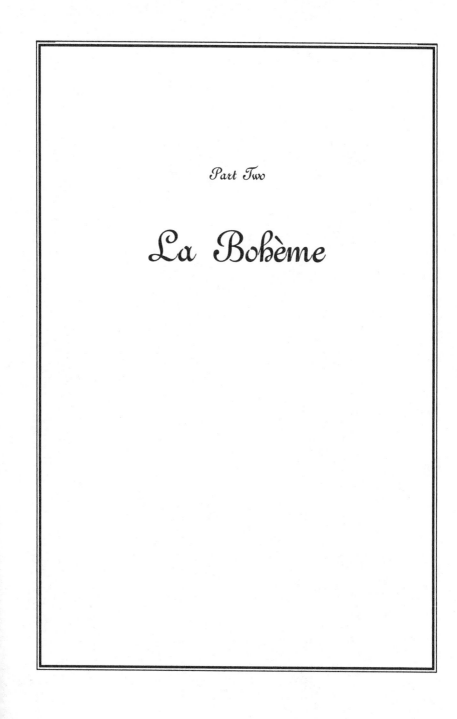

Part Two

La Bohème

16

*T*he diamond lay on the felt tabletop, as large as a man's fingernail, directly beneath the hanging lamp over the five card players' heads, sparking fire.

"Jesus, Delanza, are you out of your mind?" one of the players asked.

Edward lounged in his chair, a cigarette hanging from his mouth. His jacket had been discarded hours ago, as had his necktie and cuff links. His shirtsleeves were rolled up, his collar unbuttoned, his shirt wrinkled and barely tucked into his gray trousers. There was a heavy growth of beard on his face, and his eyes were rimmed red from either lack of sleep or the sting of too much smoke in the stuffy atmosphere. A voluptuous blonde, barely clad, hung on to his right arm, an equally well-endowed redhead was on his left. There were hundreds of private men's clubs in the city, many of them catering to the most elite clientele, many of them highly respectable. This was not one of those establishments.

La Boîte had a notorious reputation as being frequented by the fringe element of society, and its ladies were thoroughly acquainted with every type of pleasure—and perversion—a "gentleman" might require. Edward had entered this establishment for the first time only a few weeks ago, but in the time since, he had become one of La Boîte's best customers.

At the sight of the diamond, the women hanging on to him had gasped. The other players stared. Only Edward seemed indifferent to the glittering jewel winking amongst the scattered greenbacks. Edward drawled, "I'm out of cash." His words were slightly slurred.

"That gem is worth five times what's in the pot!" a bearded rake exclaimed.

Edward did not reply. He stared impassively at the speaker, then eyed the table at large with his bored gaze. "Are we playing or not? If not, I shall take myself elsewhere."

Quickly there were murmurs of assent and the play continued. Edward barely seemed to care as one player revealed a diamond flush, which beat out the previously shown two pair. Edward turned over his hand, three of a kind, without expression. The winner whooped and raked in the pot, the large diamond disappearing into his pocket immediately. "You are mad," he told Edward, grinning from ear to ear. "You have just lost a fortune."

Edward shrugged. "Really? I don't give a damn." He lurched to his feet, an arm around each woman. When he had regained his balance, he inclined his head to the table of players. Then, the women in tow, he strolled quite drunkenly from the smoky, crowded room.

Suzanne hurried downstairs, for she was late, not that it made too much difference when it came to the opera, for many other parties would also arrive late. She paused in the foyer to glance at herself, to admire her sleeveless evening gown. It was held up by two small beaded and fringed straps. The satin bodice was almost starkly bare in contrast, and just opaque, but the flared skirt was fringed and beaded at the hem. The ivory color set off her dark hair, which she wore pinned up in order to show off her fabulous dangling pearl and diamond earrings. She'd had to cajole and finally seduce her husband into buying them for her—but he'd balked at buying the matching necklace she also wore. She had purchased that for herself . . . with some of Sofie's money. She told herself that Sofie would not have minded if she had known.

Suzanne called, "Lisa? Where are you?"

Lisa appeared from within the salon, clad in a more modest evening gown of peach silk with small ruffled sleeves. Around her shoulders she wore a paler hued wrap. Eight-carat diamonds sat on her ears, her only adornment. "I've been ready for the past half hour."

Suzanne ignored that, pulling her own fringed shawl around her bare shoulders. "Let's go."

But Lisa did not move. "Don't you think we should ask Sofie to come with us?"

Suzanne flinched. "She is in her studio, working."

"She is always in her studio, working."

"She would refuse to come."

"Maybe not. Maybe not if I could speak with her." Lisa smiled, but it was strained. "She is crushed, Suzanne. Before, she was happy with her work. She is not happy anymore."

"She will get over it," Suzanne said tersely. "I do not wish to discuss this, Lisa. I know what is best for my own daughter."

Lisa's face tightened. Her voice quavered. "Suzanne, we both know the truth about what happened. This is not right. He should make amends and do what is proper."

Suzanne's pulse quickened. "You may not approve of how I handled Sofie's involvement with that man, but I did the right thing—and don't you dare interfere or even put any stupid ideas into her head!" Her fists found her hips. "Have you not heard the rumors? He is not even allowed in polite society anymore, his behavior is so reprehensible. Why, last week he showed up at a gala to raise funds to finish the new wing at the Metropolitan Museum with a *painted* woman—one who was *half*-clad!"

Lisa's shoulders were squared. "Perhaps he is unhappy, too."

Suzanne was furious. "I advise you to mind your own affairs, Lisa," she said coldly. "Sofie is my daughter. That man is out of her life, and I will not have him back in it."

"She is my sister."

"She is your stepsister, nothing more."

Lisa gasped. "Perhaps I had better stay home," she said, her bow-shaped mouth trembling. "I will not enjoy the opera knowing that Sofie is home alone and in such a state of mind." With that, she turned and fled, tripping on the hem of her gown.

Suzanne looked after her in frustration. She did not want to stay home. She thought about Benjamin, who even now was ensconced in his study with a lawyer and two bankers. When he concluded his business, they would smoke cigars and drink brandy, or they might adjourn to a private men's club. Perhaps, a few hours from now, he might seek her out in her bed for a brief interlude of restrained lovemaking, during which time she would fantasize about her dead first husband.

Suzanne regarded her reflection in the mirror, noticing with pleasure how lovely and desirable she looked. Suzanne had no intention of staying home, alone and bored, waiting for attention from her second husband, attention she did not really want. It was not really improper for married ladies to go to the opera or any other social event alone, not at her age. Suzanne decided that even if Lisa refused to accompany her, she would go anyway. Lisa was becoming far too impertinent for such a young miss, and the opera would be more enjoyable without her. Suzanne made a mental note to speak with Benjamin about arranging a suitable marriage for his daughter. Hadn't she recently heard that a very poor but very eligible British marquis was in town, looking for a wealthy bride?

Suzanne called for her carriage, thinking about Lisa while she waited, trying not to think about Sofie and her obvious unhappiness. After all, in time, it would become tolerable. Suzanne knew that firsthand.

Suzanne was having a wonderful time. The opera hardly interested her, but she was well aware that she was the focus of much attention, and that did interest her very much. Gentlemen in other boxes periodically turned to look at her, some daring to try to catch her eye and smile. Of course, her reputation was now spotless, and had been that way for years. After the horror of being a living scandal, she had no desire to ever repeat the event. The men might admire her from afar, but only from afar. She had been faithful to Benjamin for their entire marriage, no matter how she might yearn for something more. She was wise enough now, after the follies committed in her youth, to know that sex was not as important as respectability.

But she did crave the male attention she received, almost desperately, perhaps because Benjamin so rarely seemed to notice her as a woman. Suzanne pretended to ignore two keen admirers, but as she turned away, a strangely familiar figure was exiting a full box, a blond woman at his side. Suzanne's heart lurched.

When it began to pound again, now erratically, she was staring dry-mouthed and breathless after a tall, broad-shouldered man with thick, sun-streaked hair that brushed the collar of his tuxedo. She was mesmerized, helpless to look away.

No—she was going mad! It could not be Jake!

Jake was dead. He had died in 1890 in a horrible fire after escaping prison. He was dead and buried ignominiously in a London cemetery, a grave she had never yet visited, but one day would.

Suzanne calmed somewhat. Jake *was* dead, and although she knew that for a fact, having glimpsed a man so physically like him, even from behind, was terribly painful. Suzanne touched her hand briefly to her chest, but could not still her fluttering heart. Would the heartbreak of loss and disillusionment never fade? He had reminded her so of Jake.

Abruptly Suzanne stood. She was uneasy. She felt compelled, but to do what? Chase down this stranger and demand to see his face? And then what? Even if he resembled her dead husband, she was bound to be bitterly disappointed.

She bent and whispered to one of the women she knew that she would be right back, and slipped from the box.

*   *   *

Jake lengthened his strides. It had been a mistake. Coming tonight had been a big mistake.

But he was sick to death of remaining so anonymous that he never set foot out of his Riverside mansion. He worked there, he slept there. He took his meals there, had his mistress there. Lou Anne had become vocal in her complaints. She wanted to go out, wanted to have fun. Jake had not been insulted; she was still very young, and sex was just not enough of a substitute—not for anyone.

Not even for him.

"What are you afraid of?" she had asked.

Lou Anne certainly wasn't astute enough to guess the truth. But her innocent remark was accurate enough. Jake could not tell her that he was afraid that someone would recognize him again, in another act of sheer coincidence.

He could not tell her that he was more than afraid of being caught and sent back to prison.

He could not tell her that he was terrified.

He would die before ever being sent back.

So he hadn't answered her, had finally agreed to take her to the opera. And it had happened.

Of all the people to stumble across there at the crowded opera tonight, he had stumbled across his own wife. Thank God she hadn't seen him.

He hadn't been prepared for her, either. Hadn't been prepared for the surge of shock, followed swiftly by a flood of powerful and competing emotions, not least of which was anger and hatred.

Suzanne hurried down to the spacious, columned lobby where many operagoers mingled, sipping refreshments and chatting animatedly. She paused, scanning the crowd, clutching her beaded reticule. And she froze.

The man she was following stood with the blond woman, his back still to Suzanne. But she was closer to him now, and she would swear she was looking at Jake—or at his ghost.

The couple appeared to be arguing. Suzanne swallowed and stared at the man's broad back. He was leaning close, murmuring something in the woman's ear.

His posture was so familiar—she could almost hear his husky, seductive voice. Something rushed over Suzanne from her head to her toes. Something far headier and far more thrilling than anything she had felt in years. Every fiber of her being tightened.

It could not be Jake, but he was so like Jake—and Suzanne wanted him. She told herself that, because he was not Jake, she would be disappointed. And she reminded herself that she dared not sacrifice the reputation she had guarded so zealously for so many years.

The woman moved away, angry and sulking. She headed back in the direction of the opera seats, and as she passed Suzanne, Suzanne saw that she was not just very beautiful but very young—perhaps eighteen or nineteen. Her glance jerked back to the man. He had paused and turned to gaze after his ladyfriend, and their gazes met.

Suzanne cried out in shock and genuine disbelief. Then she realized the man was turning, rushing away out the heavy center doors and into the night.

She came to life. That *was* Jake! Jake *was* alive! Without stopping to wonder how that could be, Suzanne began to run in the direction he had taken. She was running after him, unaware that she was parting the crowd or that people were staring after her.

Suzanne rushed through the doors where he had just disappeared, panting wildly. She paused on the sidewalk beneath an electric streetlamp. The early fall air was warm and pleasant, but she did not notice. Where was Jake? She hadn't lost him, had she? She could not! She could feel hot tears coursing down her face.

Then she saw him striding down the block towards Sixth Avenue, nearly lost in shadows. "Jake!" Suzanne cried, lifting her skirts and running after him.

The man slowed and finally froze. He turned reluctantly and stared. His mouth curved into a hard, grim line. She came to a breathless stop in front of him. *He wasn't dead. He really wasn't dead.*

Ignoring everyone around them, Suzanne flung herself at him, throwing her arms around his shoulders, kissing his jaw feverishly—the only place she could reach. Instantly Jake jerked her off him.

Suzanne stumbled, standing a few feet away from him now. "You're not dead!" Some of the shock was beginning to wear off. It was beginning to sink in. All of these years she had grieved and mourned, missing him, thinking him dead.

"Really? And just think, I thought this *was* hell," Jake drawled, as insolent as ever.

"I could kill you myself!" Suzanne cried.

"If that was a murder attempt, I just learned something new." His gaze moved over her breasts and down her hips, lingering where her sex pulsed so strongly between her legs, with no small amount of contempt.

It clicked then. Fully. He wasn't dead—and for eleven years, she had suffered in anguish, in guilt, believing him dead. "You bastard!" she screamed, lifting her hand and swinging it with the force of a madwoman.

Jake caught her arm, staggered slightly, and then twisted hard once to subdue her. Suzanne obeyed, knowing the harder she pushed, the harder he would respond. For a moment her body was pressed against his, thigh to thigh and groin to groin, her arm pinned painfully against her back, and the blood rushed red-hot to her loins, pumping and swelling them immediately.

Jake eased the pressure on her arm. Suzanne looked up at him. His face was more weathered now, and there were crow's-feet around his eyes, but he was still the most handsome man she had ever seen. Suzanne inhaled, trembling with the lust that had seized her, and the love that had never died. "They said you died in a fire!"

"Apparently not." He moved away from her, regarding her impassively.

"You selfish bastard! All these years . . ." She broke off, choking on the old grief, the new anger, and the intense, frightening elation.

"All these years what?" Jake mocked. "Don't tell me that you've missed me?"

"I have!"

Jake laughed then, loudly. Suddenly he reached out, but lazily, caught her elbow, and reeled her slowly in. When she was in his arms, her throbbing sex pressed to his thigh, nearly riding him, he bent over her. "You didn't miss me. You missed this." He rotated his hips—and his huge erection—against her.

Suzanne felt a thrill go through her. It had been years since she had reached shattering ecstasy with a man without the aid of fantasies—fantasies in which Jake had starred. Jake was still the most devastating man she had ever seen, his body was still hard and strong, still utterly virile.

"Yes, Jake," Suzanne whispered, threading her fingers through the hair at his nape, "I missed this."

He was no longer smiling. Very coldly, he pushed her away. "And you're going to keep on missing it, darling wife of mine. Because that is dead and buried just like Jake O'Neil."

Suzanne froze.

"Oh, excuse me, how could I forget! You're not my wife—you're Ralston's now!" He was laughing at her.

Suzanne began to shake. "Oh, God."

"What's wrong—darling?"

"You know what's wrong! Oh, God! You're not dead—I'm married to two men!"

Jake laughed once, briefly, then his tone turned ugly. "Maybe you should have waited before you remarried. Or was there a reason for your haste at the time?"

Suzanne was filled with comprehension of her dilemma, and could not respond.

Jake stood over her now, his fury obvious. "When did you meet him, Suzanne? How soon after I was extradited were you in *his* bed?"

Suzanne jerked to attention. "I did not sleep with Benjamin until our wedding night."

Jake threw back his head and laughed loudly in absolute disbelief.

"It's true!"

He crossed his arms and stared at her, mouth turned down. "I was going to send for you."

"*What?*"

"I was going to send for you and Sofie. Have you meet me in Australia. But somehow the idea lost its appeal when you remarried. I never liked sharing, Suzanne."

Suzanne felt faint. "I thought you were dead! They said you were dead! There was evidence—"

He shoved his face close to hers. His breath was warm, clean. "You didn't even mourn my passing, you little bitch."

And Suzanne remembered now why she hated him. "I did! I've been mourning you for years!" She shook with her own fury—and her own fear. "Don't you dare blame me for this! This is all your fault! I remarried for Sofie's sake as much as for mine! You left us!"

"I was extradited, baby."

"You asked me for a divorce before that!"

"That's right." He stared at her, a bitter twist to his lips. "I guess prison does funny things to a man's mind. Makes a man think about family, makes him want to find the good and forget the bad. Makes him dream like a barnyard fool." He shoved his hands in the pockets of his black tuxedo trousers.

Suzanne inhaled. "I didn't know. I would have come."

"No, my dear. You would not have come to Australia to live like a pioneer with me. But I was too insane with loneliness at the time to realize it."

Although Suzanne could not imagine herself in a drab cotton dress, hanging laundry on a line stretched between trees out in the yard behind some wooden cabin somewhere out in the Australian wilderness, she could imagine having been with him these past fourteen years, as his wife, as the mother of his child. "I would have come," she insisted, even though she knew that the young, wild girl she had been would have refused him point-blank. Or would she?

Suzanne began to cry. Her tears were real, but she also remembered that, once upon a time, Jake could be seduced with tears when all else had failed. She cried harder. "I don't want to fight. You're alive, Jake. And I'm married to two men!" She didn't dare tell him, just yet, that in her mind she was first and foremost his wife, that she loved him, that she would leave Benjamin the moment he gave the word. And he would give the word—wouldn't he?

"Suzanne," Jake said, his voice heavy with warning, "Jake O'Neil is dead. Legally dead. You have one husband, not two. Benjamin Ralston."

She sucked in her breath. "You are not dead! We both know you're alive! Are you crazy, Jake? Is this some kind of mad scheme on your part? If so, why?"

"Why do you think I'd come back after all these years, risking my freedom?"

Suzanne froze. There was only one possible reason. No matter what he said, no matter how he acted, nothing had changed—not between them. Even when they had fought violently and viciously years ago, even when their marriage had been in dire jeopardy, the passion had been there, even stronger than when they had first met. For them, each and every crisis had resulted in an even greater eruption of desire. And hadn't the past fourteen years of separation been the greatest crisis of all? "To see me," she whispered, exhilarated. "You've come back to see me. You couldn't stay away. You never could."

Jake's expression changed. "No, Suzanne. I've come back because I could not stay away from Sofie."

Suzanne became utterly still. "Sofie?"

"Yes, Sofie. My daughter. How is she?" His voice was thick.

Suzanne reeled with hurt, even though she told herself that of course he would want to see Sofie, and that he was lying, too proud to admit how much he still wanted her. "Sofie is fine." She would not bother with the details of their daughter's life, not now.

"Why isn't she married?" Jake asked, more thickly than before. "When I last saw her, she was seventeen. I thought by now she would be wed."

Suzanne blinked. "You've been here before?"

"Yes."

"How many times before?"

"Many times. Every few years. I first came back in ninety-one."

Suzanne screamed and launched herself at him, trying to pummel his face, trying to kill him. Jake caught her wrists and held her while she struggled like a wild animal, both crying and cursing him. "I'd forgotten how much I really hate you!"

"That's odd. Because I haven't."

Suzanne was drained, as if he had physically sucked away all of her energy, and she slumped against him, exhausted.

Jake released her. "Why isn't Sofie married?" he asked again.

"She is in no rush," Suzanne said coldly. She was so angry, she would not tell him anything. After all, he had lied to them both, to her and Sofie. What right did he have to appear now, causing havoc? He had forfeited his rights as far as she and Sofie were concerned.

"She is almost twenty-one."

"She is studying art," Suzanne spat.

Jake suddenly smiled. "I know. Do you think I wouldn't know as much as I can about my own daughter? She is very talented, isn't she?" Pride made his voice rich and deep.

Suzanne backed away. "Her art is insane—like you are! How do you know about her? From all the times you have come here, lurking about, spying?"

"I've also hired investigators," Jake said flatly.

Suddenly Suzanne thought about the necklace she wore, paid for by funds she had taken from Sofie's trust. She deserved that money, but Jake would be furious if he knew she had taken some of what he'd given to their daughter. It was a risky topic, but Suzanne could not ignore it. "You didn't leave me a cent, you bastard."

"You didn't deserve a cent."

They stared at each other. It occurred to Suzanne that Jake was still a wanted man. That if he were caught, he would be returned to Great Britain—and to prison.

His golden eyes darkened. "Don't even think it," he warned.

She smiled. "Think what?"

"I've established a new identity for myself. One you will never learn of. And I'm now a successful businessman in Ireland and even in England, too. It is ironic, is it not? I have even moved in some higher circles here in the city—with care, of course. Don't even think of blowing the whistle, Suzanne. Because if you do, you will go down with me."

Suzanne was frozen, knowing he meant it.

Jake smiled; it was not pleasant. Suddenly his hand slid over her full, nearly bare breast. Suzanne gasped, with pleasure as well as outrage. He leaned close now, his magic fingers kneading. "Does he even satisfy you, Suzanne?" he mocked. They both knew he was referring to Benjamin. "I've seen him. I doubt you even think of him when you're in his bed."

Suzanne moaned, closing her eyes. "Oh God, you're right!"

Jake pushed up her breast, freeing it, bent, took the distended tip between his teeth and tugged. Suzanne cried out. He laved the nipple thoroughly, then began to suck. Suzanne felt her knees grow weak. Then Jake nipped her, just hard enough for a shaft of pain to mingle with the pleasure, heightening it. Suzanne gasped, clinging, her mind spinning.

But then Jake lifted his head, and their gazes met. He fingered her nipple. "You won't turn me in, Suzanne, and we both know it. Because if you do, you won't be able to hope that one night I'll slip into your bed with you and give you *exactly* what you need."

Suzanne whimpered, "I need you now."

He laughed. "Obviously." Suddenly he straightened, removing her hands from his person and setting her aside. "But I need to have all my strength when Lou Anne comes home tonight."

Suzanne screamed incoherently.

"And if that's not enough for you, then think on this," Jake said coldly. "If the truth comes out, you are going to be destroyed." He stared. "You and Sofie."

Suzanne stared, her breasts heaving.

His smile was twisted. "You'd be labeled a bigamist, dear, and upright Benjamin would throw you and our daughter out on your ass, right into the street. And we both know how much respectability means to you, don't we? Not to mention money." His white teeth flashed. "I'd take care of Sofie— but you won't get a penny from me. Not one goddamn penny. Good-bye, Suzanne." Suddenly he laughed, mocking her. "Sweet dreams, darling."

"Jake!" Suzanne screamed, but he was walking away. She gave in and wept, in fury and frustration and despair. "Damn you, Jake!"

But the night had enveloped him; he was gone.

17

Sofie stood on the sidewalk in front of the tall wrought-iron gates of the Gare St. Lazare, clutching Paul Verault's address in her gloved hand. Her heart was pounding in excitement. Not just at the prospect of seeing her art teacher again, but because, at last, she was in France. All around her was chaos of an infinitely interesting kind, taking her mind off her worries. Frenchmen and women and children from all stations of life were scurrying to and from the largest train depot in Paris. Beside her, a Negro porter was signaling a gleaming black hansom forward from a line of such waiting carriages. When she had given him Verault's address, he had tried to tell her that she did not have far to go, that she could take the Metro, but Sofie, dazed from the journey from Le Havre, much less from crossing the Atlantic, had politely declined.

Sofie's wide gaze as she stood on the Rue D'Amsterdam took in the heavy vehicular traffic of the tree-lined avenue, traffic that was hardly any different from any great city: the hansoms, the coaches and carriages, the lorries and drays and the cable cars. But the people were different. She thought that the slim Frenchwomen were very attractive and exceedingly stylish, the slender gentlemen dashing and debonair. The flurry of exotic French surrounding her was enticing as well.

Sofie knew, then, that she had done the right thing in coming to France. For the first time in three months, the anguish in her breast had dulled and become tolerable.

"Sofie, we really should check you directly into the pension first," Sofie's chaperon said tersely.

Sofie sighed, turning to face the ever dour Mrs. Crandal. Suzanne had hired the tall, middle-aged widow to accompany her across the Atlantic, and to stay with her until Sofie found her own companion. They had agreed that Sofie would choose as she saw fit, but that the servant must be a Frenchwoman. That she would be someone who would probably never go to New York, and if she did, she would never move in society, anyway—and thus would never be able to reveal Sofie's secrets. "Why don't you go ahead, and I'll meet you there after I've had a chance to speak with Monsieur Verault?" Sofie suggested.

Mrs. Crandal's eyes widened in shock. "I am your chaperon, miss!"

Sofie managed a polite smile. How could she forget?

In October Sofie had realized that she was pregnant. For the first time in her life, her prayers had been answered. It was strange how there could be so much joy and anticipation with so much grief and so much pain. Sofie had gone to Suzanne instantly, and her mother had insisted Sofie leave for Paris long before any sign of the pregnancy would be visible. Sofie had more than left New York—she had fled New York. She had fled *him*, and all the unsavory gossip associated with him.

Sofie wished she did not know any of it, but Suzanne had been oblivious to the fact that she was rubbing salt in Sofie's wounds every time she brought up Edward's name. Sofie had heard all about his scandalous social life—the women and drinking and all of it. She'd heard that he frequented the opera and he always had a female companion, usually a singer or actress and sometimes even a prostitute. She had heard that he had lost a small fortune gambling, as well. She knew he still escorted Hilary Stewart about from time to time. She knew he was no longer welcome in polite society, and knowing Edward as she did, she was certain he was not indifferent to the scorn and disapproval now heaped upon him by her class, who had once admired and envied him.

And, strangest of all, he had bought a large lot on the corner of Seventy-eighth street and Fifth Avenue and he had begun to build what appeared to be a huge mansion that might rival any one of the three grandiose Vanderbilt homes just twenty-odd blocks downtown.

Sofie wondered if he would live there alone, or if he had changed his mind—if he now wanted a wife and family. In the beginning, tears had poured down her cheeks every time she thought about it. No more. She was still sensible enough to know that even if she had accepted his proposal of marriage, she would never be happy because she would only represent *duty* to him—not love.

Sofie started when Mrs. Crandal jerked on her arm. "If you insist on seeing your art teacher before anything else, then let's go. The sooner we do, the sooner we can check into the pension and have a hot bath and a hot meal."

The porter was summoning them forward as he hefted their valises into the back of the hired cab, as well as a large trunk, filled with Sofie's precious art supplies. Sofie, regaining her composure, called out, "*S'il vous plaît, monsieur*. Take care of my trunk!"

Sofie climbed into the hansom, forcing thoughts of Edward aside. It was as impossible as forgetting him. The most she could do was gain a brief respite. Determined, Sofie leaned forward to look out the window and observe all that she could of the city she had dreamed of for years.

"*Monsieur, où est-il?*" Sofie asked, her French hardly fluent but certainly passable.

The driver glanced back at her from his seat above her. He was young and dark, in knee-high boots and a jaunty black cap and a dark wool jacket. "*Ce n'est pas loin mademoiselle*," he answered, assuring her that Verault's was not far. "The address you have given me is on the Butte."

"The Butte?" Sofie echoed.

"Montmartre," he explained. Then, swiveling to look at her again, he said, "*Pour vous?*" He shook his head. "*Beaucoup des bohèmes, mademoiselle. Pas du tout convenable.*"

Sofie's eyes widened and she stared at his slim back. He had just told her that Montmartre was bohemian and hardly suitable for her.

Unfortunately, Mrs. Crandal spoke French rather well, too—Suzanne had hired her for precisely that reason. "Bohemians! He lives among bohemians!" she cried, ashen. "We should turn around right this minute!"

"He is my friend," Sofie said softly but firmly. Since she had embarked on her journey, Paul had become more than just her friend, he had become a badly needed sanctuary. She knew she must immerse herself in her art in order to escape Edward. It was easier said than done. These past few months she had tried to work without any real passion, and her efforts had produced one disaster after another. Despite the fact that just before departing, she had learned that *A Gentleman at Newport Beach* had been sold. Not only should she have been far more thrilled, she should have been inspired, but she was not.

"You said he was your instructor!" Mrs. Crandal said sharply.

"Yes—and my friend." But Sofie felt some trepidation. She doubted her letter to Paul, informing him of her arrival, had reached him yet. It had been posted merely a week in advance of her own departure, due to the rush she had been in.

They entered the Place de Clichy, and Sofie made an effort to admire an old church on the southern corner as they passed it, turning right onto the Boulevard de Clichy. Her heart quickened. Small saloons and cafés lined the streets, and even though it was cool out, many small tables were outside, all occupied by boisterous patrons, and she could see that the establishments were crowded and busy both inside and out.

A theater advertised nightly performances by the incomparable Madame Coco. A group of shabbily dressed young men exited one café, their arms around one another, singing a rowdy French tune. A very pretty woman in short skirts lounged in a nearby doorway, and the men and woman exchanged greetings. Then one of the men pulled her close, and Sofie caught his words, which were quite suggestive and amorous, and knowing very well what he wanted now, she blushed.

What kind of place was this? she thought in alarm. Surely Paul Verault did not live here with his family! Montmartre seemed to be a thoroughly disreputable neighborhood.

Mrs. Crandal was voicing those very same thoughts aloud. "We can't be stopping here! Why, there's nothing but hooligans and shady ladies on the streets! Sofie?"

They turned the corner, passing a larger, very noisy saloon, one crammed inside to overflowing, the tunes of a piano and loud singing and laughter drifting onto the street. The red, oversize sign hanging in front was impossible to miss: Moulin Rouge. Sofie's heart skipped. She knew very well that when Toulouse-Lautrec was alive, he had frequented this very spot. She had seen one of his prints of this infamous cabaret, one she had very much admired.

Sofie began to tremble. Dear God, she was here, truly here, in Paris, where the greatest old masters had once lived, where David had been born, where Corot and Millet and the incredible Gustave Courbet had worked and struggled and lived, where even today she might glimpse her favorite living artists: men like Degas and Cézanne, or even the glorious expatriate American, Mary Cassatt.

"Mrs. Crandal," she said firmly, "this is a neighborhood of artists, and I intend to visit my friend Monsieur Verault. If you are afraid, you can wait in the hansom."

Mrs. Crandal's jaw tightened. "I am going to write your mother about this."

Sofie felt some dismay, but did not bother to respond. She wouldn't want her mother upset, but Suzanne could not rule Sofie's life now.

They turned another corner and the hansom came to a stop. "We have arrived, demoiselle, 13, Rue des Abbesses."

Excitement was rushing hotly through Sofie and she stumbled from the carriage in her eagerness. While the driver unloaded her bags, she found the francs necessary to pay him. The driver grinned at her, rakish and charming, then leaned close. "If you are ever lonely, *ma chère*, my name is Pierre Rochefort, and you can find me at the Café en Gris in the Latin Quarter." With another grin he bowed and vaulted onto his seat, leaving Sofie staring after him in surprise.

Whatever had elicited that? she wondered, bemused.

"Hooligans, every last French one of them!" Mrs. Crandal cried angrily. "How your mother could allow you to come here is beyond me!"

Sofie turned away and stared up at the brownstone building, number 13. She became nervous. Standing there on the narrow street in a strange and exotic neighborhood, one at once charming and suspect, the passersby somewhat disarming in their appearance (Sofie suspected a few might be actual criminals), alone in a foreign city with only Mrs. Crandal as an ally, alone and pregnant, Sofie could not help but be apprehensive and afraid. When Verault had left New York, his wife had been ill, and it was very possible she was arriving at a difficult time.

Male voices sounded, approaching. Sofie glanced up the street and saw three young men strolling towards them, immersed in a heated conversation. She sighed, facing the four-story building again. She could not stand on the street forever, and if worst came to worst, Paul would ask her to return at another time.

Then one of the men said, "But, *mon ami*, his palette is too light, and his talent is strictly for shading—he has no conception of form! Unlike you, *mon ami*."

Sofie whirled, her heart pounding; the young men were discussing art!

"He understands form very well, *cher Georges*," retorted the darkest man in the group, a man very close to Sofie in age. "Amigo mío, it is you who fails to truly understand form!"

Sofie wished that she knew who they spoke about—and how she wished to participate in their conversation. Suddenly her gaze collided with the first speaker, Georges, who stopped abruptly in his tracks. "Ah, *petite amie*, are you lost? Can I be of service?"

His grin was both bold and charming, his eyes blue, and with his dark hair, Sofie froze, reminded painfully of Edward. Before she could reply, Mrs. Crandal wedged herself between Sofie and the young men. "Miss O'Neil does not need your services, young man!"

The three young men looked at one another and broke into grins. "*Pardonnez-moi,*" Georges bowed, winking at Sofie.

But he was not Edward, and Sofie felt a wave of sadness engulfing her. He was a Parisian, and he and his friends were somehow connected to the art world, a world Sofie was here to become a part of. How she wanted to talk to them. She had dreamed of this for years. "I—I am looking for Monsieur Verault," she managed, her heart beating rapidly as she stepped past a furious Mrs. Crandal.

Georges's eyes widened. "Old man Verault? *Vraiment?*"

Sofie nodded, aware now that all three men stared at her with new interest.

"Come, *petite*, you are not French and you stand amidst your bags. *Vous êtes américaine?*"

Sofie nodded. "In New York Paul Verault was my instructor."

"*Ahh—la belle américaine est une artiste!*"

"*Bien sûr*," she whispered, while Mrs. Crandal gripped her elbow as if to jerk her away.

Georges grinned at her widely, then cupped his hands and startled Sofie by shouting loudly up at the building. "Monsieur Verault, Monsieur Verault, come out, monsieur—you have a charming guest!"

Sofie blanched, then met Georges's twinkling gaze and dimpled grin and had to smile. And suddenly she heard Paul exclaim from above, "Sofie?!"

Sofie looked up to see Paul staring down at her, incredulous, from an open window on the second floor. "Sofie!"

Sofie gripped her hands, worried now, as he disappeared from sight. "Oh, dear," she said to herself.

"Oh, *ma pauvre*, he does not know you are coming?" Georges grinned, unrepentant. "Forgive me, *ma petite*, my heart will be broken if I have gained your eternal disfavor," he cried, a hand splayed wide on his chest.

Sofie had to smile again. He was somewhat raggedly dressed, his tweed overcoat very worn, his knees patched, and he was certainly a tease, but his charm was irresistible—in a way, he still reminded her of Edward. As soon as she realized that, she froze, her smile gone, briefly stricken with anguish.

Would it always be that way? A brief reminder and she would be undone?

"Sofie," Paul cried from behind her.

Sofie whirled, saw his eager face, and flew into his arms. "*Bonjour*, Paul," she cried. And although she had never called him anything but Monsieur Verault before, suddenly it was appropriate.

He embraced her briefly, then kissed her on both cheeks. "Ahh, I knew you would come!" he cried. "Welcome to Paris!"

*   *   *

Upstairs, Paul had a two-room flat. Sofie quickly learned that he lived alone—that his wife had died several months ago. "I am sorry," she whispered, stricken.

They were seated at his small dining table, which was in the kitchen, the kitchen actually being a corner of the flat's largest room, which served as both a parlor and art studio. A single worn couch and low table were for guests, while a large easel dominated the room, a drawing table behind it. A small bedroom opened up on the room on the other side of it. The bedroom door was open, and Sofie saw that the chamber contained a small bed and a single bureau. However, above the bed was a large window, and the view of the tree-lined square below, filled with vendors, cafés and pedestrians, was charming.

Paul had served them steaming café au lait and a fresh pastry he had bought just that morning. "My dear Sofie, if you must know, I had not seen Michelle in nearly ten years, had not lived with her as a husband in twice as long as that. I am very sorry that she is gone, do not mistake me, but in truth, we were strangers, united only by the fact that we have one son, who is happily married with two children in Beauborg."

Sofie said nothing; what could she say? She was aware of Mrs. Crandal's stony silence. Her glance took in Paul's flat again. Although it was drably furnished, she understood why he had chosen this apartment, for the parlor windows had an incredible view of the windmills on the hill above, and the sunlight streaming into the apartment made it bright and airy. She wondered what he worked on at the easel. "I did not know you worked, Paul."

His smile was twisted. "The reason I left Paris in the first place, *ma petite*, was that I wished to teach students like yourself, but here the Academy controls art, or very nearly so, and they find my methods unacceptable. As I cannot teach officially, only privately when I am so fortunate, I find myself working again."

Sofie knew that art was strictly controlled in France. "But the independents have done well recently, have they not?"

"Ahh, yes, thanks to great dealers like Paul Durand-Ruel and my friend André Vollard, who dared to defy the Salon, to buy rejected artists like Degas and Cézanne before they became admired and known, giving them a livelihood and the means to continue their work."

Sofie leaned forward. "Paul, Durand-Ruel's son bought three of my canvases in New York just before I left." But the memory was tainted, for Edward Delanza was attached to it—and always would be.

Paul did not see her sudden spasm of grief; he was thrilled. "Oh, *ma petite*, how happy I am for you! Describe the works."

Sofie described the paintings and told him that *A Gentleman at Newport Beach* had already sold. "Monsieur Jacques is most interested in continuing to see all that I do," she told him. "He is very eager to acquire more figural studies in the same vein as *A Gentleman.*"

"I am overjoyed," Paul said, refilling her coffee cup, "but keep in mind that many great artists struggled for many years before becoming successful, and then they were in their middle age."

"I am very aware of that."

"And who is this Edward you have referred to—the one who brought Jacques Durand-Ruel to see your work?" Paul asked.

Sofie could not quite decide what to say, and a tense silence followed Paul's question. Both Mrs. Crandal and Paul were staring at her—she had to say something. Her mouth formed a smile. She hoped she would not cry. "Edward is—was—a friend."

"I see," Paul said, regarding her far too closely.

It was the pregnancy. Suzanne had told her that when she herself had carried Sofie, she had been an emotional wreck. Sofie wondered if she might discreetly dab at the corners of her eyes. Then Paul handed her a linen handkerchief, and it was no longer necessary to be discreet.

Sofie wiped her eyes and heard herself add, "He modeled for *A Gentleman.*"

Paul turned to Mrs. Crandal. "More coffee?"

The woman stood. "Sofie is overtired, as you can see. I am exhausted myself. It is time for us to leave. You may continue your visit another day."

Sofie found herself standing as well. "Mrs. Crandal is right. I have been selfish, dragging her all over Paris so we might see one another again." She smiled at Paul. "Besides, we have imposed long enough."

Paul took her arm and walked her to the door. "You are not an imposition and you never will be. You will come tomorrow," he said firmly. "I know everyone who is involved in art in any way here in Paris. You must begin to meet the artists, the students, the teachers, and 'the dealers. And of course, we must find you an atelier and a master."

Sofie felt a rush of warmth for this man who had been her teacher for three years and who was now her friend. "Perhaps you can help me in another way, as well. Mrs. Crandal must return to America, and I need a companion."

Paul nodded. "There are many young women who would be delighted to earn money in your employ, Sofie. I will think on it."

"She must be of high moral character," Mrs. Crandal interjected sharply. "No bohemian, sir. She must be a companion, a chaperon, and a lady's maid."

Paul nodded again, gravely.

Sofie stood on tiptoe and kissed his bearded cheek. Their gazes met in silent understanding. "Until tomorrow, Paul. *A demain.*"

The next few weeks flew by. Sofie took in the sights of Paris as any tourist would do while settling comfortably into her pension. Paul found Sofie an atelier. It was a large single room, airy and filled with light, perfect for an artist to work in, and of course, it was on the Butte. Mrs. Crandal disapproved. But then, she disapproved of everything, it seemed.

Women were not allowed to attend L'Ecole des Beaux-Arts, but many of the instructors there gave private lessons to females in their own ateliers. Paul recommended her to several masters. Sofie delayed making an appointment for an interview. She still had no desire to work. Every day she went to her studio, but could do no more than stare at her canvas.

Sofie woke up one morning, both surprised and relieved because she had no morning sickness for the first time in months. Thankfully it had never been severe, anyway, and during the transatlantic crossing, Mrs. Crandal had thought her illness to be seasickness. Sofie slipped from the quilts piled up on the bed—the old Parisian buildings had poor heating and were freezing cold at night. She started when she realized that the first snow of the year had fallen and that the narrow cobbled street outside her bedroom window was blanketed in white. So were the gabled rooftops across the street, and the awnings over the shops below. It was a beautiful, fairy-tale morning. The Ile-Saint-Louis had never been more picturesque.

But Sofie was not smiling as she got up and washed her face and hands, using a small porcelain bowl and a pitcher of frigid water left on her nightstand for just that purpose. Christmas was around the corner. The idea made her sad. And somehow it was even frightening. She had never spent Christmas alone before.

She wondered where Edward would be for the holiday, and whom he would share it with. She grew sadder. The raw stabbing of grief was sudden and intense.

Shaking off the despondency that was trying to settle like a heavy shroud upon her, Sofie braided her hair and dressed in her no-nonsense uniform of a white shirtwaist and a navy blue skirt. Both items of clothing were becoming tight. Sofie wrapped a large paisley shawl about herself, as much to hide the slight bulge of her tummy as to ward off the cold. As always, she joined Mrs. Crandal and several other pensioners downstairs for a light breakfast consisting of coffee and croissants. Then she told Mrs. Crandal that she was off to work. It was a fabrication, unless something had changed between last night and that morning.

As Sofie left the pension, Mrs. Crandal sharply reminded her that she must hire a companion soon. Mrs. Crandal was scheduled to leave for New York in another week. She wanted to be home for Christmas, and Sofie did not blame her. As important, Sofie's condition would soon become obvious to the other woman. She was three months pregnant. Suzanne had stressed many times that Mrs. Crandal had to leave before she guessed the truth.

Sofie walked two blocks to the Rue des Ponts, where she flagged down a hansom. Suzanne's desire to cloak her pregnancy in secrecy was understandable, but nonsensical. Eventually the world was going to find out. Before Sofie had left home, Suzanne had reiterated that she must give her baby up for adoption, and Sofie had again flatly refused. Suzanne had been adamant. Sofie could not return to New York with a child. Sofie had yet to think it out carefully, but she did intend to return to the city as an unwed mother, for she was not giving her child away, not ever. Suzanne might be afraid of scandal, but Sofie was not.

The hansom crossed the Seine. Sofie was now familiar with the pretty sight of the heart of Paris as she awoke in the mornings. Unlike New York, the pace was slower and more leisurely here. And now that she was there, the idea had been born that she did not have to return to New York at all. She could remain in Paris as so many American artists did. After all, there was nothing for her in New York except for her family, and surely they would come to visit her when the baby was due, perhaps even every year.

Sofie squeezed her eyes shut. She must not think about the father of her child, who was in New York—and who had no idea that he would soon become a father. She must not consider the question that kept trying to haunt her at steady intervals. She must not feel guilty for the fact that she was carrying his child without his knowledge.

Sofie was relieved when the hansom halted in front of Paul's apartment building. She had decided to skip going to her own atelier completely. She paid the driver and was surprised when Paul stepped out of the building and met her on the street. He was clad in a warm woolen coat and sturdy black boots. *"Bonjour, petite."* He beamed, kissing her cheek. "Where are your gloves?" he scolded, pulling off his own woolen mittens. "Put these on before your fingers turn blue."

Sofie accepted, secretly pleased to be fussed over. "Paul, you are going out?"

"Only with you. I have had an idea, and there is someone I want you to meet."

Sofie raised a brow as he took her arm to help her cross the frozen street. Above them on the hill the windmills stood as sentinels, their blades snow-encrusted and frozen. It was very cold out, and the Butte seemed deserted without its usual array of crowded tables and its heavy traffic of pedestrians. No shopkeepers stood in open doorways, no boys begged coins on the street.

"Rachelle is a model," Paul said. "She is in high demand, but she is not paid very much. I spoke with her about you. She would be very interested in being your companion. She would like to be able to continue modeling, of course, but if not, she would give it up while you are here in Paris."

"If you recommend her, I am sure I will like her," Sofie said.

Paul smiled and led her towards a doorway. A faded green sign hung over it, and as they approached, Sofie saw that the name of the establishment was Zut. The sound of conversation and laughter drifted to her. When Paul opened the door, she realized they were entering a saloon. Sofie froze.

Paul looked at her. "Rachelle said she would be here. She takes *le petit déjeuner* here most mornings."

"In a saloon?"

"We call it a bar. Many students, artists, models, and masters frequent Zut and the other bars around here, Sofie." He smiled. "This is not New York. It is a good gathering place."

Sofie stared past Paul, wide-eyed. The bar was a single room, wood-paneled and cozy, with a long counter on one side, behind which the saloonkeeper dispensed drinks. It was not crowded now, but Sofie saw that several tables were full. And that the patrons, most but not all of whom were men, were not all drinking coffee. Some were drinking wine, beer, or liquor. She glanced at Paul for reassurance. It was only eleven-thirty in the morning. She could not quite believe she stood in such a place, but as Paul had said, this was not New York. This was Montmartre.

"Rachelle is sitting by herself. Come, Sofie."

Her pulse racing, Sofie looked past a table where three young men sat, all looking bleary and tired, to a table where a lone woman sipped coffee and picked at a small baguette. No longer as reluctant as she was curious, Sofie trailed after Paul.

Rachelle stood up, smiling. She was tall and very beautiful despite the fact that she wore a nondescript black wool dress and boots very similar to Paul's. But she had wrapped a crimson scarf around her shoulders and she wore her long, curly auburn hair free. Her smile reached her eyes, which were so blue, they were almost turquoise. "*Bonjour*, Paul. *Bonjour*, mademoiselle. You must be Sofie. *Je suis enchantée.*"

Sofie liked her instantly. Her smile was genuine. One had only to look into her eyes to see a woman who was kind and good-natured and at ease with both herself and the world at large. Sofie looked again at her mannish boots. How could a woman be so lovely in such attire? "I am pleased to meet you, too," Sofie said.

"Please, *asseyez-vous.*" Rachelle gestured at the empty chairs.

Sofie sat. Paul ordered more coffee for the table. He and Rachelle began to discuss a recent canvas for which she had posed. They both agreed that the artist who had portrayed her, a man named Picasso, was quite brilliant but was holding something back. Sofie listened closely, studying the beautiful model. She had already decided that Rachelle would make a wonderful companion. For the first time in a long time, she began to feel a little bit excited about her life.

18

*H*e was drunk, but didn't really care. It was only noon, but it was also Christmas eve.

Edward told himself that was the reason he was sitting in his new motorcar, a long, black Daimler, on Fifth Avenue just across from the Ralston residence. It was Christmas eve, and everyone knew that Christmas was not a season to be jolly, but a season to be lonely and sad.

At least, Edward could not remember ever experiencing a joyful Christmas. He had only been eleven or twelve when his brother Slade, whom he had worshiped, had run away. Every Christmas thereafter had been a somber affair.

Edward gripped the steering wheel, feeling very much like that little, guilty boy of twelve who had felt responsible for his brother's running away. But he wasn't twelve anymore, he was a grown man, and now his guilt was festering from a different cause, and her name was Sofie.

Edward was usually successful in avoiding any and all thoughts of Sofie O'Neil. In the past four months since he had seduced her, he had become an expert at mental evasion. But it was Christmas eve. Today Edward did not want to be with some nameless woman with a painted face, his stomach rebelled at the thought of another drink, and he was broke, which ruled out gambling. He didn't think he could stand the conversation of his cronies at the moment, anyway. On second thought, they all had families to be with today. Only the loneliest wretch would be playing poker at La Boîte on Christmas eve.

Edward felt like he was a lonely wretch, too.

Edward stared at the Ralston mansion, wondering what she was doing at that very moment, if she ever thought of him, if she regretted what had happened—if she hated him as much as he hated himself when he happened to be lucid.

It was suddenly important that he know for sure.

Edward slid out of the Daimler. It was snowing lightly, and fat flakes melted on his nose. Edward had forgotten his overcoat, but he welcomed the bite of cold. If he was really going to see Sofie today, he needed to appear far more sober than he was.

But as he skidded across the deserted, frozen stretch of Fifth Avenue, he grew afraid. What in hell was he doing? Did he really need to confront Sofie to know that she despised him? Christ, she had refused his offer of marriage. It was still unbelievable. It still made him so angry that he wanted to put his fist through a wall. It still made him feel, inexplicably, as if she had used him.

The worst part was that he wouldn't have minded marrying her very much. If he had to marry a woman, then Sofie was his choice. It really was not an unpleasant prospect. Except—it was not a two-way street. Sofie was far more radical than he had dreamed. She preferred to live alone, forever, than to marry him.

He had thought her to be in love with him. How wrong he had been. How arrogant the assumption, how vain. "I cannot marry without love," she had said. Today her words were haunting. She had not loved him then. She did not love him now.

Edward passed the two sitting stone lions that guarded the entrance to the property and trod up the graveled driveway, past the huge evergreen in the middle of the lawn, which was draped with tinsel and crystal and crowned with a glittering star. He paused on the front steps of the house. He banged loudly on the brass knocker. It occurred to him that everyone was having dinner—he would be interrupting. He didn't care. He wanted to know if she was happy—if she had forgotten that single, incredible night.

Jenson opened the door. His eyes widened briefly before he resumed a butler's well-worn expression of implacability. "Sir?"

"Is Sofie in?"

"I'm afraid not."

"I don't believe you," Edward said, smiling unpleasantly. "Please tell her I am waiting to speak with her." His pulse had begun to race.

Jenson nodded and began to close the door. Afraid he would be locked out, Edward stuck his foot inside, blocking the door with his leg.

"Sir," Jenson protested.

Edward smiled again, as unpleasantly as before.

Jenson gave up, turning to go. But he had not quit the room when Suzanne called, "Jenson, who is it?," her heels clicking on the marble floors as she entered the foyer.

Edward tensed for the inevitable confrontation.

Suzanne halted, spotting him. Anger washed over her features, making her ugly. She rushed forward. "What are you doing here?" she hissed.

Edward had stepped completely inside the door, and now he closed it behind him. "I want to see Sofie."

Suzanne stared. "She's not here."

"I don't believe you."

"She's not here!" Suzanne was triumphant.

Edward's heart seemed to drop through the floor. "Where is she?" he asked sharply.

Suzanne hesitated.

"Where is she?"

"She is in Paris. Studying art—as she has always dreamed of doing."

Edward was stunned. Sofie had gone—gone to Paris. But hadn't she told him many times that it was her dream to study there with the great French artists? Something twisted inside him, like a knife. He was transported effortlessly into the past.

Sofie was rigid, unsmiling. "I did not become your lover to force you to marry me."

And Edward had a horrible inkling of what was about to occur. His heart seemed to stop. "You were a virgin."

"That is not a good reason to get married."

He could not believe what he was hearing. He had begun to argue with her. Sofie was unmoved by the facts, by what had occurred; it was like arguing with a sensible, composed stranger. "I have no desire to get married, Edward. Have you forgotten? Next May I turn twenty-one and I am going to Paris to continue my studies of art. I am sorry . . . I cannot marry without love."

"She is happy," Suzanne said, breaking into his thoughts. "She has written me recently. She has a lovely companion, she has her old friend Paul Verault, and she has been warmly welcomed by the Parisian art community. Stay away from her. She is happy despite all that you have done."

Edward blinked and faced Sofie's angry mother. "I am sure she is happy," he said, unable to disguise his bitterness. "Of course she is happy, in Paris with her art and artist friends. But you delude yourself if you think I would chase her down in Paris." He squared his shoulders, suddenly furious. "I merely stopped by to wish her a merry Christmas."

Suzanne watched him warily.

Edward bowed and strode to the door. He slammed it shut behind him, so hard that the festive fir and pinecone wreath almost fell off, and raced down the front steps. As if he would chase *her*. Christ! He was Edward Delanza, and he *never* chased women—women chased him. He especially didn't chase skinny, eccentric women who preferred studying art and pursuing a career to a lifetime shared with him. Oh no.

Edward decided to go back to La Boîte, where he would find a pretty woman to pass the afternoon and night with. Let Sofie share her bed with her art. Hah! What kind of bedfellow was that?

But as he climbed into his Daimler, he wondered if she had chosen her art because it was a far better mate than a man whose only genuine claim to fame was selfish hedonism and the destruction of innocence.

Sofie had never been more lonely. Paul had convinced her that she would be welcome for Christmas dinner at his son's home, so she had gone, but she was the outsider and acutely conscious of it. His son, Simon, seemed genuinely fond of Paul, despite the fact that Paul had lived apart from Michelle and abroad for so many years. Simon's wife was sweet and motherly to everyone, and their two small daughters were delightful. Sofie watched the affectionate and happy interchanges, unable to participate. She had never been more lonely, more miserable, more sad.

She wished she were in New York with her family. She missed her mother and Lisa terribly. She even missed Benjamin, whom she had never really been close to. But she would not think about Edward.

They had already eaten and left the dinner table. The girls were playing with their new toys. The diminutive Christmas tree took up a good portion of the small room. The girls had decorated it with popcorn and candy. Paul and Simon were drinking brandy and smoking cigars. Annette did not seem to mind. She was watching the children, slumped in a chair, smiling but obviously tired from having prepared and served a huge feast with only the aid of a single servant. Sofie had not been allowed to help, because she was a guest. Because she was an outsider. Because this was not her family, and no amount of kindness would make it so.

Oh, Edward. She could no longer resist him or her painful thoughts. *Will I be alone forever?*

Sofie was perilously close to losing control of herself, to succumbing to abject despair, when she reminded herself that she was not going to be alone forever, because in another five months or so she would have a beautiful baby. By the summer she would have her own family. And they *would* be a family, even though it was just the two of them. Sofie was resolved that her child would not even notice the lack of a father. Somehow she would be both mother and father to her child, even while pursuing her professional calling.

It seemed like a herculean task, but Sofie dared not contemplate the pitfalls that awaited an unwed mother bent on maintaining both a family and a profession.

A few hours later, she and Paul said *au revoir* and *merci beaucoup* and left. Simon lent them his horse and buggy. Sofie thought about going back to the pension. She dreaded the idea. It had been eerily deserted this past week as everyone had left to join their families for the holiday. Rachelle, who had become Sofie's companion several weeks ago and who had taken up residence with her at the pension, had gone home as well, to the small village where she had been born and raised in Bretagne. Sofie decided to go to her atelier instead. For the first time in months, she felt the creeping urge to draw. She wondered if it was genuine. If she put charcoal or ink to paper, could she once again create a work of art?

Paul had halted the buggy in front of the three-story brownstone where Sofie's studio was, and he swiveled to face her. "It is difficult to be alone right now. I remember too well how it was myself."

"I hope my behavior was discreet."

Paul smiled. "Sofie, one day you will learn to be less discreet—and you will be better off."

She did not smile, for Edward had said the exact same thing to her, only in different words. "Am I such a piece of deadwood?"

"No, *petite*. But life can be fun. *La vie, c'est belle.* Sofie—is there anything you wish to share with me?"

Sofie looked into Paul's kind brown eyes and saw worry reflected there as well. She wore an oversize wool coat, and an oversize wool sweater under that, hiding her growing body. Did he know? Soon he would have to know, soon everyone would have to know, but Sofie did not want to talk about it, not yet. If she began to speak about Edward and how she loved him, she was afraid she would not be able to stop. "No, Paul," she whispered. "No."

"Are you going to work tonight?"

Their gazes held. "Yes," Sofie said, her heart beginning to pound. "I think so."

Sofie rushed upstairs, unlocked the door to her atelier, lit the old-fashioned gas lamps. She did not waste a single heartbeat. Her excitement increasing, she hurried to her trunk and flung it open. She found the single preliminary sketch of Delmonico's that she had done before Edward had modeled so briefly for her; before the night of the hurricane. When she saw his roughly drawn face and form, saw how he lounged in such careless repose, she froze, remembering that wonderful afternoon as if it were only yesterday.

Sofie ignored the now steady drip of her tears. Because she knew what she must do—she was driven. She must finish this portrait immediately. Before she forgot that glorious day, before she forgot what it was like, exactly.

Sofie shed her sweater and donned an apron. She began to open tubes of paint, preparing her palette. Oh, God! Although she would use a light and airy color scheme as she had done with *A Gentleman*, she would also use shocking pinks and brilliant reds. In fact, to capture the moment exactly, to make the viewer feel a sense of immediacy, Sofie decided to place the waiter's hand and arm in the very front of the painting, as if he were serving Edward then and there.

For the first time in four months, Sofie put a brush to canvas. She was shaking with excitement. And she did not return to the pension for many days, losing all track of time and place.

"Sofie!"

Sofie stirred. She had fallen into a deep, dreamless sleep on the faded velvet sofa that she had acquired secondhand when she had first rented the atelier. It was the studio's only piece of real furniture outside of that necessary for her work.

"Sofie? Are you all right?" Rachelle shook her insistently.

Sofie blinked, very groggy, for a moment not sure where she was. It was so hard to wake up. But when she did focus, she met Rachelle's wide, worried turquoise eyes. Sofie levered herself into a sitting position with an effort.

"You have not been at the pension for days! When I returned this morning and found that out, I immediately went to Paul's. I was sure you would be there, but he said he had left you here on Christmas day and that he had not seen you since. Sofie—you have been here for almost an entire week!"

Sofie was fully awake. "I have been working."

Rachelle began to relax. "So I can see." She gave Sofie a long, speculative glance and walked away. As usual, she wore her heavy black boots and a plain wool dress, this one a dark green, with the same crimson scarf draped about her shoulders, her wild red hair unbound. As always, she was very beautiful. Rachelle stood in front of the canvas, hands on her hips.

Sofie could see the oil from where she sat on the sofa, and her pulse raced. From the center of the room Edward smiled at her from the canvas, the smile reaching his eyes, sexy and suggestive and warm and seductive. He was clad in near white. The table was draped in ivory linen as well. But behind him, the restaurant was a shocking red, pink, and purple sea of the women's vividly colored tea gowns. The waiter's black-jacketed arm and pale hand were in the bottom foreground of the work, jarring the viewer out of any complacency.

Rachelle turned toward Sofie. "Who is he?"

"His name is Edward Delanza."

Rachelle regarded her. "Is he really as handsome—as male?"

Sofie flushed. "Yes." But she had begun to become accustomed to Rachelle's frank bohemian manner and her sometimes shocking liberalism. Rachelle had a lover, a poet named Apollinaire, and he was not her first paramour.

Rachelle's glance strayed to Sofie's abdomen. "Is he the father?"

Sofie's heart skipped and she felt her face drain of blood.

"Come, *ma petite,* let us cease pretense." Rachelle walked to her and sat down beside her, clasping Sofie's hands in her own. "I am your friend, *non?* I was not fooled, not even from the start. You may have fooled Paul, but men can be so stupid at times. Especially when it comes to women."

Sofie stared at Rachelle. She had wept so much while painting Edward that she had no more tears to shed and she remained dry-eyed. That did not mean she did not hurt inside. "Yes. I am carrying his child," she whispered.

Rachelle pursed her mouth. "It is too late, you know, to do something about it. A few months ago I could have taken you to a doctor, a good one, and he could have removed the child from your womb."

"No! I want this baby, Rachelle, very much!"

Rachelle smiled gently. "Then it is a good thing."

"Yes," Sofie said, "it is a very good thing."

For a moment they did not talk. One by one, their gazes drifted towards the canvas facing them, towards the extraordinary man lounging there in his chair. "Does he know?" Rachelle asked.

Sofie froze. "I beg your pardon?"

"Does he know? Does he know that you are carrying his child?"

It was hard to speak. Sofie wet her lips. "No."

Rachelle gazed at her, patient and wise. "Do you not think it right for him to know?"

Sofie swallowed and glanced at the portrait again. Despite herself, her eyes grew moist. "I have been asking myself that very same question for a very long time," she finally said hoarsely.

"And what answer have you found?"

Sofie faced her beautiful, worldly friend. "Of course he must know. But for some reason, I am afraid to tell him. I am afraid he will not care. I am afraid he will care too much."

Rachelle patted her trembling hands. "I am confident you will do what is right."

"Yes," Sofie said. "I will do what is right. I must." She slipped her hands free of Rachelle's and hugged herself. "But the baby is not due until the end of June. There is time."

Rachelle's glance was sharp.

"Paul, I am tired, I really do not feel much like going to Zut today."

But Paul Verault ignored her, handing her a light shawl. "You have been driving yourself too hard, *petite*." He guided her out the front door. "For a woman in your condition."

Sofie sighed, resigned to joining him at the small bar down the street. "When I decided to do *Delmonico's*, I did not realize that, once I started to work again, I would not be able to stop."

"I know, *petite*," Paul said softly. He kept one hand on her bulky body as they went down the narrow, steep stairs. "I know how very hard you have been working. I know what the effort has cost you. But you have created some fabulous canvases."

Sofie swallowed, trembling slightly. Paul knew the toll her art had taken on her because he came to her atelier almost every day. He was not her only visitor. Sofie had many friends now, almost all of whom were artists or art students, except for Georges Fraggard and Guy Apollinaire, who were poets. They all dropped in periodically, except for Georges, who had become a visitor almost as frequent as Paul.

Sofie preferred not to think about why Georges came to her atelier so often. She told herself he was infatuated with Rachelle, who had broken off with Apollinaire in the early spring. There was no other explanation. And it was possible. Georges flirted with her, just as he flirted with every woman he met. Except for Sofie. He no longer teased or charmed her as he had done during her first few months in Paris, and had not done so once he had realized she was pregnant.

Ridiculously, Sofie missed his flirtation. She had not realized how very flattering it had been during the loneliest winter of her life. It had been somewhat like drinking sweet, warm wine on a bitterly cold day. Sometimes she wished he would see Rachelle elsewhere, and not in her atelier while she was working. Sometimes he still reminded her of Edward.

Working was her life now, as it had been before Edward Delanza had disrupted it so completely last year. And Sofie was glad.

Finishing *Delmonico's* had begun as an exorcism. But it had not worked. Instead of exorcising Edward from her life, instead of exorcising her grief, Sofie found herself more bound to him than before. Perhaps it was not just having completed *Delmonico's*, perhaps it was also the baby, who was growing so quickly and purposefully now inside Sofie's womb. When Sofie had felt her moving for the first time inside her belly, she had begun to feel fiercely like a mother, and the child had begun to take on a persona of her own. She was sweet and trusting and eager to be born. Somehow Sofie was certain that it was a girl. She would name her Jacqueline, after Jake, and Edana, after Edward.

Sofie had never been closer to Edward than she was now. She thought about him all the time, and if not consciously, he haunted the back of her mind. Deliberately she made sure that she had little time to herself. If she was not with her master, copying at the Louvre, or at her own easel in her own atelier, she was with her friends, in a café, or in one of their ateliers. When she did retire in exhaustion to her small flat in Montmartre, which she had rented after the New Year, she was not alone—for Rachelle lived with her. Still, when she finally fell asleep, it was Edward's dark, handsome image afflicting her.

She had painted other subjects since *Delmonico's*, genre works that were also figural studies of Rachelle and Paul in various aspects of bohemian living, but she had returned to Edward as subject matter again and again as well. She had even portrayed him nude, as she had always longed to do. And even Sofie knew that when he was the subject of her work, she produced her most exciting and powerful canvases.

André Vollard had snatched up *Delmonico's* as soon as he had seen it. Paul had insisted that his friend Vollard come to view the canvas the moment he had glimpsed it himself. Vollard had begun to beg for the opportunity to buy the work when he realized that Sofie had used Durand-Ruel previously in New York City. Sofie could not refuse, not his enthusiasm nor the one thousand francs he had offered her. Paul had assured her that, as she did not have an exclusive contract with Durand-Ruel, she could sell her work to whomever she chose.

Delmonico's had immediately caused quite a stir in the art world, even though it remained unsold. Rachelle was as proud as a mother hen. She told Sofie that every artist and amateur they knew had gone to see the brilliantly hued canvas, and that it had been a hot topic of conversation in many salons and ateliers during the first few months following Vollard's acquisition. In fact, Paul Durand-Ruel himself, whom Sofie had never met, had appeared one day on her doorstep, irate and intent on viewing the rest of her work. There was some rivalry between Vollard and Durand-Ruel, the latter being far more renowned and far more successful—but often more conservative in his acquisitions, as well.

Sofie had had several pastels of Rachelle and Paul ready and was finishing the nude oil of Edward. He bought the lot on the spot, including the sketches, for a significant sum of money and tried to convince her that she must show her work exclusively with him. Sofie promised to think about it, at once incredulous and torn. Before he left, to sweeten his offer, he hinted that he might see fit to hold an exhibition for her. Sofie had dreamed of having a successful solo exhibition for many nights afterwards. In her dreams, Edward was always standing at her side, beaming with pride.

"André tells me there has been much interest in *Delmonico's*," Paul said as they left the building.

Sofie's heart lifted. "Really?"

"In the past two weeks several of his clients have expressed interest in it."

Sofie tried not to feel too hopeful. *Delmonico's* had been on the market since January without selling, and the initial euphoria brought on by being sought after by two rival dealers had faded long ago. "Paul Durand-Ruel notified me the other day. The portraits of my father and Lisa finally sold in New York, to an anonymous buyer."

"That is welcome news," Paul said, smiling.

Outside, it was so warm that Sofie took off her shawl. It was a bright spring day, and wildflowers poked up beside the trees shading the street, pansies and geraniums in the pots on windowsills and doorsteps. They trudged across the Place des Abbesses, past the *bateau lavoir*, an old, crumbling building where many of Montmartre's poor artists lived, including some of Sofie's friends. Several vendors stood in their open doorways in their shirtsleeves and aprons: booksellers, an antiques dealer, an art supplier. As Sofie and

Paul passed, they were greeted with smiles and calls of *"Bonjour,* Verault, Sofie, *comment allez-vous?"*

Sofie smiled and waved back.

Paul looked at her soberly. "How is your family, Sofie?"

Sofie thought about her mother. "I think that Lisa is in love. Apparently she is being courted by the Marquis of Connaught, Julian St. Clare. From the tone of her letters, I think he has succeeded in turning her head."

Paul grunted. "And your mother?"

Sofie grew tense. "Well, she has given up demanding that I release Rachelle from my employ."

They turned the corner. A small boy ran up to them, begging for a coin, and Sofie gave him one. They ignored two shabby, unkempt women, undoubtedly prostitutes, who eyed them darkly from a door stoop.

Mrs. Crandal had not approved of Rachelle. She had not minced words, declaring that Rachelle was not just a model but a hussy through and through. And once in New York, she had gone directly to Suzanne, describing life in Montmartre and Rachelle. Suzanne had written to Sofie right away, demanding that Sofie dismiss Rachelle and forbidding her to carry on with hooligans and madmen posing as artists and poets in saloons disguised as cafés.

Sofie had come to love Rachelle and had no intention of severing their relationship. She had explained to her mother that Mrs. Crandal had exaggerated, but in truth, she had not. For there was no question that the residents of the small Parisian neighborhood were somewhat wild and quite unorthodox. But everyone shared a genuine enthusiasm for art in all its forms. There were very few pretenders in Montmartre. Sofie was not about to leave. She was happy—or as happy as it was possible for her to be.

They paused on the next street, waiting for an aggressive driver of a mule and cart full of sacks of meal and flour to go by. Paul held her arm. "Is she coming? You should not be alone now."

Sofie said, "I am not alone. I have you, and I have Rachelle." She and Paul crossed the street, arm in arm. "It is better if she doesn't come, anyway. She would be very upset if she saw where I live—and how Montmartre really is."

Paul only said, firmly, "You should not be alone."

Sofie refused to think about Edward, not now, not today.

They entered the small bar Zut on the Place Pigalle. It was early in the afternoon, but the single wood-paneled room was crowded and noisy; many patrons sat at small tables or stood at the long bar, and almost all turned to greet them jovially when they saw them. Paul enjoyed the camaraderie of the clientele there, and although at first Sofie had thought it quite daring for a proper woman like herself to join him in the evening for a glass of wine, she had quickly grown used to it. Zut was patronized by many young, fervent artists like herself, by poets as well as painters. Sofie had been immediately and warmly welcomed into their ranks.

"*Ah, c'est la bohème,*" someone cried, and several other men took up the cry, good-natured and teasing.

Sofie's smile was rueful in response. Georges had coined the nickname soon after they had met. She carefully avoided his eyes, but knew he watched her from where he sat beside Rachelle. It was a joke, and a funny one at that. She was hardly bohemian, and that had quickly become clear to everyone who knew her. Although her art was bold and unique and broke all of the Salon's rules, Sofie clung to the standards of propriety she had been raised with, regardless of her current situation.

Sometimes Sofie felt like a fraud. Sometimes she wished she could live as Rachelle and the others did, day by day, with great zest and intensity, without a real care, with that particularly French trait of *joie de vivre*. But she could not. No matter how she might try.

"You will join us, *non?*" Georges asked, unsmiling. With everyone else he was a charming rogue, but not with her. Still, Sofie admired him even though the tenor of their relationship had changed. He was a fine if not radical writer, often using his verse to defend the modern style of art.

Sofie allowed herself to be seated with him and Rachelle and his two closest friends, Picasso and Braque. Paul pulled up another chair. Charles Mauricier, David St. Jean, and Victoire Armande were also present.

Sofie had barely been seated when the men at her table began to sing at the top of their voices, even Braque, who tended to be aloof and melancholy. She went red as she realized that they were singing "Happy Birthday" and that the entire bar had just joined in. It was her birthday, but purposefully she had not mentioned it. However, Paul had taught her for too many years in New York not to have known the date. He squeezed her hand, singing with a foolish smile on his weathered face. Sofie saw the proprietor, Frede, bringing a small frosted cake with candles to their table, his rosy cheeks redder than usual. When the song was done, the cake deposited in front of her, everyone cheered. Rachelle came up behind her to hug her and kiss her, her eyes shining with affection.

Sofie told herself not to cry. This was so thoroughly thoughtful and kind and she had no right being sad, not anymore. She had a new life, new friends, she had her art, and soon she would have her beloved baby. Did she not have everything a woman could want? She blinked back her tears and smiled at everyone. *"Merci beaucoup, mes amis. Mes chers amis."*

Someone began to play the old beaten piano near the front window of the bar, a very tired instrument that was in use every single night of the week. Sofie saw that the player was Rachelle, and she was hammering out a lively tune, beating her booted feet to the rhythm. Some of the men stood up and began to dance, with each other or with the other women present in the bar. Georges leaned across the table, gripping Sofie's wrist.

She froze. His eyes were blue, like Edward's, but with an intensity she had never seen in them before.

"Dance with me."

Sofie's gaze widened; she did not move. Georges waited for her to respond. His regard was burning. Sofie shook her head, her pulse racing, shocked. What was happening? She did not understand! Georges was in love with Rachelle. "Thank you, but no, Georges." She had to wet her lips.

He was standing, leaning over her. "Why not?"

Sofie felt the heat of tears in her eyes. She shook her head. She could not use the excuse of being lame, because he would not care, no one in Montmartre cared about her limp. She could not tell him that she did not know how to dance, because he might offer to teach her—the way Edward had offered to teach her once, a lifetime ago. But he was not Edward, he would never be Edward.

"I will not hurt the child."

Sofie jerked her gaze to his. Around them, young men and women were dancing with increasing abandon and fervor. Rachelle had started to sing in her clear alto. Sofie turned to watch, to avoid his probing gaze. She was shaking now.

But Georges took her chin, forcing her gaze to his. "Do you want to take a walk, then?"

Sofie was beginning to comprehend what could not be. Surely Georges did not like her! Surely not! He was only being kind, because this was her birthday. But she did not see even a hint of kindness in his gaze. She saw anger, and it was utterly male. "I don't think so," Sofie said, a little desperately.

His eyes grew darker. "Why not?"

Sofie responded with a question of her own. "What are you doing?"

He pulled her to her feet. Sofie was as stiff as a board, but even so, he was a young man, not much older than she was, and there was something good about the feeling of his hard palms on her arms. "You pine for him, do you not? You pine for the famous model in your paintings! I am not stupid, nor am I naive. When I saw *Delmonico's* I understood exactly. He left you, did he not?" Georges asked furiously. "What promises did he make to you— what promises did he break?" Georges's eyes sparked. "He seduced you, got you pregnant, and left you. He is not a man. He is less than a man!"

Sofie stared, horrified. Did the whole world know that she and Edward had been lovers? Had they all seen *Delmonico's* and comprehended the truth instantly, as Georges had? Had she no secrets at all?

"Walk with me," he said again, low and insistent. "I will make you forget he ever existed."

Shocked by his words, his tone, and what he must be feeling for her, Sofie felt tears stinging her lids as she shook her head. "I cannot forget."

"Yes, you can. Let me help, *chérie*."

The timbre of his voice released her tears. He was so like Edward. "I do not want to forget."

He stared, his eyes softening with sadness. "When you change your mind," he said, "come to me then. I will never hurt you, *mon amour*." He turned and walked to the bar.

André Vollard's gallery was on the Rue St. Fauberg, in one of Paris's most exclusive and chic districts. He was about to leave, well aware that there was a small party in Montmartre at Frede's establishment for the talented American painter Sofie O'Neil. Vollard had no intention of missing the small *fête d'anniversaire*. He also hoped to acquire exclusive rights to her work.

But as he was about to leave, his assistant rushed into his office in the back. "André! Come quickly! Mademoiselle Cassatt is out front—she is asking about the new artist, *la belle américaine*."

Vollard actually knocked over his chair as he stood. While he had never handled Mary Cassatt himself, only discovering her work after it was too late, he knew her well. They moved in the same exclusive artistic circles, had the same friends, admired many of the same artists, and fought over those they did not. Mary Cassatt had become quite influential in the international art world, only partly because her own art had finally become renowned, admired, and much sought after—and therefore quite expensive as well. She also acted as a private agent for one of the greatest collectors in the world, H. O. Havemeyer and his wife, Louisine, which gave her an unusual amount of power. When Mary Cassatt convinced the Havemeyers to buy, not only did they do so, they usually pursued that artist with a vengeance, acquiring numerous works of his art and single-handedly creating a demand where previously there had been none. Less than a decade ago a Degas could be had for a few hundred dollars, but just the other day Durand-Ruel, Vollard's greatest rival, had purchased from a private collection Degas's *Dancers in the Rehearsal Room, with a Double Bass* for the Havemeyers for more than six thousand dollars.

Now Vollard rushed into the front of his gallery to find the middle-aged Cassatt studying the painting he had bought from Sofie O'Neil last January.

"*Bonsoir*, André," she said, smiling but only briefly. She was a distinguished, well-dressed woman in her middle years. Her gaze flew back to the work hanging on the wall. "Who is Sofie O'Neil? She is Irish?"

"She is American, Mary, but she is living in Paris right now. She is rather good, do you not think so?"

"Is she young?"

"Very. She is just twenty-one."

"Her talent is raw, but powerful. Her use of shading is formidable but untutored. She needs to study lighting intensively for a few years. The composition is bold and original. Her attention to detail in the young fellow's face is fantastic. If she wished, she could be a commercial success—if she returned to classicism."

Vollard's heart was pumping wildly. "Mary, she has studied since she was thirteen and has no desire to paint in the old tradition. She is desperate to study with someone like yourself."

Mary swiveled her head sharply to stare at Vollard. "Indeed?"

"So Paul Verault says."

"I wish to meet her," Cassatt said abruptly.

"I will arrange it. She will be thrilled."

Cassatt smiled. "She will be even more thrilled when you tell her I am buying this canvas of the handsome young fellow sitting in Delmonico's," Cassatt said.

DEAR LOUISINE,

Today I saw a work which moved me far more than anything has in a long while. The artist is a young American named Sofie O'Neil. I bought the work, titled Delmonico's. *The painting is in oil, of an extraordinary gent filled with masculine grace, superbly nonchalant, lounging in his chair. Her use of color is bold, her shading is very interesting, and her attention to detail as far as the model's portrait goes is fabulous. I am quite certain that this artist will go far once she decides upon her style, and as such, her early works will one* day be quite the collector's item. I know I have never recommended any of today's young artists before, but you must consider Sofie O'Neil.

YOUR DEAR FRIEND, MARY CASSATT

Sofie hugged her pillow, knowing she wept like a child. She could tell herself time and again that it was because the baby was due in six weeks, but she was a poor liar, even to herself. She was becoming frightened. She did not want to be alone, not now, and not six weeks from now when she delivered the baby, and not for the rest of her life.

Georges's handsome, unsmiling face came to mind. So did Edward's. Sofie wished she could forget Edward, God, how she wished she could forget him. Because then she would be free to find love with another man. With Georges, or with someone like him.

It was somehow ironic. She had never wanted love. At an early age she had buried any foolish romantic dreams she might have entertained. She had only wanted to be a professional artist. But Edward had entered her life with his dazzling charm, his perfect gallantry, his hot kisses, his manliness. Breathing life into those schoolgirl dreams.

As her tears slowly ceased, Sofie slipped from her bed and found a pen and sheet of paper. She sat down in her bedroom's single chair, an overstuffed, somewhat shabby affair, and found a book to write upon. She wondered how she would find the words to tell Edward that he would soon become a father. She could delay no longer. He must know. And she must keep the letter light and breezy. At all costs, she must not let him see into her heart. Sofie began to write.

May 5, 1902

DEAR EDWARD,

Many months have gone by since last we conversed, and undoubtedly I am at fault for the lack thereof. I apologize. But moving to Paris was a big step for me. I have had to rent a flat, a studio, find a master and a lady's companion. All is going very well. I have many friends, including a wonderful companion, Rachelle, and my old art instructor is also my mentor now, Paul Verault. I am studying with the great Gerard Leon, and he appears satisfied with my work. Even more wonderful, I am being courted by two rival dealers. Paul Durand-Ruel, you know. He has hinted that he might hold a solo exhibition for me—which is every artist's dream. André Vollard has handled such great artists as Van Gogh and Gauguin when no one else would. They are both enthused about my work. And in case you have not heard, your portrait sold in New York some time ago, as did the portraits of my father and Lisa.

Now I must arrive at the real reason for my letter. I hope you will not be too shocked. I am expecting a child towards the end of June. I thought you might want to know.

Hoping that all is well with you, Sincerely,

SOFIE O'NEIL

Quickly, before she might lose her courage, she signed the letter, folded the sheet, and slid it into an envelope. She sealed it with wax, and was relieved to see that no teardrops marred the thick white vellum.

19

*T*he spade dug into the ground. Thump. He ground the blade in deep, tossed up the raw red earth. Then the spade hit again. Thump. He tossed up more dirt, again and yet again. He worked with mindless diligence, his motions automatic, despite the fact that his arms were so tired that every time he lifted the spade, he felt as if he were wrenching them from their sockets. Despite the fact that hours ago the muscles in his back had knotted painfully. Despite the tortured state of his body, he did not stop—as if relishing the self-inflicted agony.

"Why don't you hire some men?"

Edward jerked. An old man stood not far away, watching him. Edward vaguely recognized him. He was a farmer, except he had nothing left to farm—in the continuing hostilities that spring, his farm had been razed to the ground. Edward seemed to recall hearing that his wife and two sons had also died in the blaze.

Edward knew that something had died inside him, because he felt no sadness for the old man's horrendous loss. He felt nothing, nothing at all, just emptiness.

Edward dropped his spade. He had been laboring all day long since sunrise, without a moment of respite, and he would not quit until sundown. Now he moved to the shade of a lonely, misshapen tree where he'd left some equipment and supplies. He picked up the canteen and drank sparingly. The old man watched him, did not seem intent on leaving. Edward ignored him.

But the farmer said, "Why don't you hire help? Got some boys in town who'd be glad for the work."

"I like working alone," Edward said brusquely. Not wanting to talk. Not really. Even though it had been months since he'd had a decent conversation with anyone. The last conversation he'd had had been on Christmas eve, with Sofie's mother. He'd sailed for Africa the next day on a British merchantman.

"Know you can afford it," the old man said, watching him with hawk eyes. "Everyone knows you're rich, even though you don't look it or act it. Except for how you spend those diamonds like they grow in that dirt there."

Edward picked up his shovel without answering. He had been using small diamonds to barter for the goods he subsisted on ever since he first arrived in southern Africa in February. He'd run out of cash long ago, back in New York, the reason he'd returned to this small spot of hell on earth in the first place. That was the reason he was there, working his diamond mine. It had nothing to do with anything—or anyone—else.

Still, a representative from the DeBeers company had been in town last week, trying to buy him out. Edward had refused in an act of sheer insanity. DeBeers would pay him a small fortune, enabling him to go home. But just where, exactly, was that? New York? Was home his unfinished Fifth Avenue mansion? Or was it the extravagant suite he could let yet again at the Savoy Hotel? Surely it was not California. He could not imagine returning to Rancho Miramar, where his father lived with Edward's brother Slade and Slade's wife and child. And home was not San Francisco, where his mother lived alone. Edward had not seen or spoken with her since his parents had separated more than two years ago.

His gut ached. In fact, his entire body ached, and his temples throbbed painfully as well. There was no point in selling. He had nowhere to go. There was nowhere he even wanted to go. It looked like Hopeville, Cape Colony, Africa, was his destiny, his life.

It certainly was not Paris, where *she* was.

Edward could not believe he'd had such a rude and monstrous thought. Furious, he turned his back on the old man and stomped back to the dig.

"You're a strange one," the old man remarked to his back. "Like torturing yourself, do you?"

Edward ignored him until the old man left. He began to shovel, hard and rhythmic. If he wanted to torture himself, it was his right.

He did not stop to rest, urinate, or drink water again—not until dusk had fallen across the bare, rocky land. It was the time of day he hated most. For during the walk into town, despite the physical exhaustion, his mind was free to wander.

Edward packed up his equipment and slung the rucksack over one shoulder, the spade in his other hand. He walked into Hopeville, using all of his willpower not to think. It was very hard for a man to keep his mind blank. Worse, he now hungered for the old man's company. It would be better to listen to the old man's dry comments than to his own burgeoning thoughts.

By the time Edward strode into Hopeville, he was angry. Angry with himself, angry with Sofie, angry with the world.

It was the ultimate irony. He had entered her life to set her free, but he had become enslaved. Because by now she had forgotten all about him, but he could not forget her. Not for a single second of a single minute of a single day. No matter what he did, no matter how he did it.

Edward walked up the main street of town, nodding to an occasional merchant or soldier. Because the train from Kimberley came through Hopeville, the redcoats were a constant presence there. A truce had been signed in May, but there were still sporadic acts of violence and terror committed by radicals on both sides.

The street was wide, quiet, and composed of dirt. It was winter in the Orange River valley, meaning that it was cool but pleasant out. Mud coated everything; rainfall had been heavier than usual. The whitewashed clapboard homes on the outskirts of town were mottled brownish-gray as a result. In the center of town the storekeepers didn't bother to paint anything white or any other color, anticipating both the winter rains and the dust of summer. Drab, somewhat ramshackle false-fronted wooden buildings lined the treeless thoroughfare.

Edward had taken a room in Hopeville's best hotel, a two-story stucco affair. He strode up the brick steps, passed through the dark wood-floored lobby. He received his key from the dozing clerk, determined not to think about Sofie—desperately determined.

Upstairs, Edward inserted the key in his lock. The door was already open and it swung ajar, causing Edward to reach for his gun, which he withdrew from the back waistband of his pants. Flattening himself against the wall, he waited for the intruder in his room to come forward. The fact that he wallowed in diamonds was no secret.

"Edward?"

Surprised but expressionless, Edward came forward, holding the gun down now. A woman sat up from where she had been lying in his bed.

She smiled, her ebony hair unbound and in enticing disarray. Her skirts were up about her knees, revealing long, shapely, coffee-colored calves. "I've brought you something," she said coyly.

Annoyed, he kicked his door closed with one dusty booted foot. "How'd you get in?"

"A pretty smile," she whispered, standing and coming to him. She looped her soft arms around his neck and pressed her voluptuous body against his.

Because he had not buttoned his shirt, his chest was bare and he was instantly aware of her hard nipples through the thin silk of her dress. Edward put the gun on the bureau, then took her wrists in his hands and removed them from his neck, which also removed her breasts from contact with his chest. He did not smile. "This is quite a surprise. I don't believe we've met."

"Not through lack of trying on my part." She stared at him. "I'm Helen, and I've been trying to catch your eye since February, Edward. Don't you like women?"

Edward had seen her around. She was the only pretty young woman left in town. In fact, once upon a time he might have found her stunning. He had also been aware of her advances, which he had ignored. He had lost his desire long ago, on Christmas morning when he'd woken up in bed with two cheap women whose names he didn't remember and didn't care to remember, filled with self-disgust.

Helen pressed against him, her own smile gone. "Don't you like women? Don't you like me?" she whispered.

Even now, despite eight months of sexual abstinence, despite his body's obvious physical reaction to her heated curves, he had no real desire to pull her down on the bed. "No. I don't like women."

She laughed then, and said, "You may not, but your body seems to feel otherwise." Edward's face remained like stone.

She stared, then backed away. "You're strange. You don't smile, you don't laugh. You don't even talk—not if you can avoid it. I know. I've watched you. You work like a man possessed, then gamble in the exact same way. You drink that way, too. You act like you hate everyone."

Edward turned his back on her, tossing his hat on a chair and stripping off his shirt. His words were so low, she could barely hear them. "I don't hate everyone. Just myself."

He did not look at her reflection in the small cracked mirror on the bureau he faced. The floorboards creaked as she crossed the room. He heard her pausing at the door as he unbuckled his belt and unbuttoned his fly.

"Who is she?" Helen whispered. "Who's the woman who broke your heart?"

Edward froze, his jaw tight. Then he regained control and pulled his pants down over his hard hips. He wore thin linen drawers that came to midthigh, revealing as much as they concealed.

"It's a shame." The door opened; she paused. "You can change your mind anytime, Edward."

Edward bent over the washbasin, splashing his face with tepid water.

"You have a letter. From New York City. It's there on the bureau." She walked out, closing the door behind her.

Edward stared at Sofie's bold script, the words blurred and unreadable. His hands were shaking. He was shaking, badly.

I thought you might want to know.
I am expecting a child towards the end of June.
I hope you will not be too shocked.

God! Sofie was expecting a child, and although she hadn't come right out and said it, she had made it clear that it was his child, and in any case, Edward had counted backwards from June—the child had been conceived at the end of the summer. The child—their child.

I hope you will not be too shocked.

Shocked? Shocked was far too mild to even begin to describe his dumb-founded and furious amazement. Jesus Christ! It was August, August, for God's sake. Sofie'd had a child. His child. Jesus Christ!

Edward was on his feet. He glimpsed his wild expression in the mirror. He looked like a lunatic. But then, he felt like one, too. God! Why in hell hadn't she told him sooner? Why in hell hadn't she told him right away?

And there was no question as to what he was going to do now. Suddenly he had a purpose, a destination, a destiny.

His child was in Paris. His child. Edward was catching the next train from Kimberley. By tomorrow evening he would be in Cape Town, and with a little luck, in a month or so he would be in Paris, too.

And very deliberately, he avoided thinking about Sofie, and about what he would do when he saw her again.

Paris—October 1902

There was no answer at the flat.

Edward stood outside the locked door, his heart pumping hard and fast, even though Sofie was not home.

She was not at home. She and the baby were out. He had come so far, as fast as possible, and it hadn't been easy getting out of war-torn southern Africa in one piece. Despite the recent truce, signed in May at Vereeniging,

Boer gunmen had attacked the Kimberley train, derailing it and delaying it for two days. Several passengers had been killed in the attack, and Edward had narrowly escaped being wounded himself. Once in Cape Town, he had been unable to find a vessel not belonging to the British navy. Without hesitation, he had spent a fortune in bribes in order to gain a berth on one of Her Majesty's warships. And that ship had been bound for Dover, not France. All in all, it had taken him six weeks, not four, to arrive in Paris.

And she was not at home. To calm himself, Edward leaned against the wall and searched through the pocket of his suit jacket for a cigarette. Lighting it, he inhaled deeply. His heart rate did not slow.

Dubiously he glanced around. For the first time, he really took in his surroundings. The landing he stood on was made of unpainted, unwaxed, rotting wood. Some of the floorboards were coming up, all were scarred and chipped. The walls were also scarred and peeling and needed painting badly.

The apartment building was old and run-down, and as far as Edward was concerned, it was no different from one of New York's rat-infested tenements. Indeed, all of Montmartre was nothing but crumbling tenements and decrepit cabarets. Its inhabitants seemed to be pimps, prostitutes, beggars, and thieves. Edward could not believe that she lived there, in such a place, with their child. It had to be a mistake.

Not for the first time, Edward wondered desperately if it was a boy or a girl. The image in his mind was the same as it had been ever since that fateful day in August when he had learned that he was a father. He saw Sofie holding a bundled-up baby, her smile soft and serene and joyous, directed not at their child, but at him.

Tension riddled him the way bullets might. She should have told him sooner, she should told him immediately. She must have known, or at least suspected, that she was pregnant when she left for Paris last fall. Edward banged harder on the door this time. There was no excuse. And Sofie was not going to beam at him like a besotted fool. She had never been besotted, not where he was concerned. Thinking so, once long ago, had been a vast mistake on his part. No, she would be composed and dignified when they met now, as if they were polite strangers and nothing more. As if she were not the mother of his child, as if she had not ever been his passionate lover.

And what the hell was she doing living in such a hovel? This was not right. A single lady like Sofie could not possibly live here. His child could not live in such a place. Unwed ladies, even radical ones like Sofie O'Neil, even unwed and with a child, lived in fashionable, proper homes with a chaperon and a full staff. Edward banged harder, furiously, on the door.

He inhaled hard, in an effort to control his trembling and his sudden rage. If she really lived here—and this was the address on the letter she had sent—he would see to it that she moved elsewhere, immediately. His child was not going to be raised in poverty and neglect.

Edward dropped the cigarette and ground out the butt with his heel on the ancient floor. Too late he realized that it was clean, even if in need of repair. He turned abruptly to descend the stairs, to go to the Galerie Durand-Ruel. Surely someone there would know of her whereabouts.

Someone was coming upstairs. Edward paused, wondering if he might gain information about her from the passerby. But the man froze when he saw Edward, staring at him in stunned surprise.

Instantly the hairs on Edward's nape prickled with unease. He was positive that he had never before met this stranger who was staring at him with the wide-eyed shock of recognition. Worse, as they stared at each other, dark anger boiled visibly in the other man's blue eyes. Edward had the feeling that this man not only knew him—but that he hated him as well.

Yet he could not know him. Edward was certain that they had never met.

The man recovered, continuing up the stairs until he stood on the landing with Edward. He was shabbily dressed in patched trousers, black boots, a cotton shirt, and a lightweight jacket, but he was handsome nevertheless. He faced Edward. "Are you looking for Sofie?"

Edward's heart lurched painfully. Dear God. Sofie did live here—and she knew this man. He began to tremble ever so slightly, beginning to fathom the other man's hostility. He was too worldly not to understand. "Does she live here?" Edward asked, lighting up another cigarette, his pulse racing, his hand shaking discernibly.

"Yes." The man's blue eyes blazed. Abruptly he turned his back on Edward and rapped on the door. "Sofie? *Chérie, c'est Georges. Ouvrez la porte.*"

Edward's mouth formed a snarl. He did not speak French, but he understood the word *chérie*, just as he understood Georges's undisguised hostility.

Georges turned. "She is not at home."

"No."

"Does she know you are here?"

"No." Edward's smile was unpleasant. "Not yet."

For a moment Georges said nothing and the two men stared at each other like two bulls in one small ring. Then he said, "She is not in her atelier either, I have just been there—I imagine she might be with Paul at Zut."

"Who is Paul?"

"Her friend. Her best friend."

Edward reassessed. Georges was obviously very interested in Sofie, and Edward was already wondering just what kind of relationship he had with her. Exactly. But who in hell was Paul? Edward thought the name sounded familiar, and he struggled to remember. "Paul Verault?"

"Yes." Georges was not volunteering any information.

"Where is Zut?" Edward asked, grinding down his jaw.

"I'm going there now," Georges said. "Do you wish to come?"

"Yes," Edward said tersely, following the stranger down the stairs and outside, where it was a pleasant fall day, brisk but not cool, all the trees on the streets flaming red. "I don't know you, but you know me. Why?"

"We all know you, monsieur, from Sofie's paintings."

"From Sofie's paintings?" he echoed.

Georges shot him a dark glance. "*Oui.* She has used you as a model several times."

Edward tried to fathom what he had said. He was reeling in surprise. Sofie had painted him—again. Several times. How many times? And why? Excitement crept along his veins, defusing some of his anger. She must have some small *tendresse* for him, she must.

But then he thought about the fact that painters all over the world had been painting various subjects since the beginning of time, and whether it was an apple or a man being portrayed, the artist need not be in love with his subject matter. His initial euphoria died rapidly. His mouth formed a hard, determined line.

They didn't exchange another word, continuing across the narrow streets. They finally turned a corner and the sounds of a piano's lively refrain became discernible, followed by the deep pitch of male laughter, some of it inebriated. Edward thought he also heard the higher sounds of feminine voices, as well.

They entered Zut. It was not a café. It was a saloon.

Edward's eyes widened. This *was* a mistake! Sofie could not be found at a saloon! Ladies did not frequent bars filled with drunken, lecherous men, not even unconventional ladies like Sofie. And she was a mother! But even as he tried to reassure himself, he knew damn well that she lived in that rat-hole a few blocks away—and that this man was her friend and he said she might be here.

Rigid, stunned, rage creeping over him, he scanned the saloon. The bar consisted of a single crowded, smoky room. Edward's glance slid quickly around. Its inhabitants were raucous and animated. Most of the tables, crowded together, were occupied, and another dozen men and two women stood at the bar. He was struck by an awareness that many of the patrons were turning to stare at him, recognizing him as Georges had.

Edward did not give a damn. For Sofie was here, as this fellow had said. His gaze riveted on her, and he was frozen in time, in place.

His heart twisted. A raw aching began in his gut. She sat at a small, crowded table with three men, two her own age, one far older and gray-haired. She had changed. He saw that immediately. She still wore a navy blue skirt and a plain white shirtwaist, but she had a brightly patterned red and gold scarf thrown about her shoulders. Her hair was pulled loosely back in one thick braid, as was often the case for her, but she was not sitting as if in school with a book upon her head. She almost lolled in her chair. She was not so slender now, not as fragile-looking. And her cheeks were flushed, perhaps from the effects of the glass of white wine that sat on the table before her, and she was laughing at something someone had said. Her smile was sunny and bright. She *had* changed.

The Sofie O'Neil Edward knew never would have dreamed of sitting in a smoky bar at a table with boisterous young men, drinking wine and smoking cigarettes.

He felt as if the stick of dynamite that had derailed the Kimberley train in Africa had gone off again—this time inside him.

He looked at her, the shock turning to real anger.

All this time he had been in a living hell—because of her. All this time she had been in gay, carefree Paris, painting and playing with bohemian abandon. Which one was her lover? he wondered in icy rage. And where in hell was their child?

Edward stalked towards her. She sat with her back to him, hadn't seen him yet, but the others had, and they all stopped speaking and stared. Sofie stilled. Edward smiled grimly. Then his heart stopped, for Georges was squatting beside her, whispering rapidly in her ear. Murderous rage engulfed Edward. He knew that he was her lover. He had never been more sure of anything.

Georges stood. Sofie turned slowly, still sitting, her face as white as a freshly laundered sheet. She saw him and cried out. Georges stepped closer to her, putting his hand protectively on her shoulder.

Edward wanted to smash it off, then smash him in the balls.

Sofie was on her feet.

Edward halted in front of her. He did not smash the Frenchman as he longed to do. Instead, he smiled coldly. He made no attempt to hide his rage or to keep his tone low and discreet. "Where the hell is our child, Sofie?" he demanded, fists clenched. "And what in hell are you doing here?"

20

$\mathcal{S}$ofie stared at him, briefly incapable of assimilating the fact that Edward stood there in Zut, somehow larger than life and more devastating than ever. It felt like a dream. But this was no dream—he had finally come. Oh, God!

She was speechless.

"I am not a ghost," Edward said, his blue gaze frigid and piercing. "But you're looking at me as if I am one. What's wrong, Sofie? Aren't you glad to see me? After all, you did write me a letter. Or am I interrupting something?"

She finally caught the anger and mockery in his tone and she stiffened. Almost frantically she tried to gather her composure around her, which she must wear as one would a shield while he remained in Paris. Hadn't she known he would come? Hadn't she prayed he would come?

Yet he had not come in time. Rough, distorted images flashed through her mind. Of Rachelle's and Paul's worried faces as Sofie clawed at their arms, screaming in pain that was beyond any and all imagination. Bitterness rose up fast, like a flood tide. Edward had not been there for the birth of her daughter. It had been a long and difficult delivery. Sofie had labored for almost twenty-four hours, most of the time in intense pain, and only sheer will had enabled her to finally push Edana from her womb when she was so utterly exhausted that she had nothing left to give. By that time, Georges had been there, too, holding her hand. When Sofie had been handed her tiny daughter she had wept, not in joy, but in relief.

But not Edward. He had not even come in July, or August, or September. Sofie trembled with anger, clenching her fists in a fierce attempt to control it. "Of course you are not interrupting. I am startled, that is all."

"Really?" His smile flashed, dimples deep, but it was insincere. It was ugly. "Now, why would you be surprised to find me in a watering hole like this? Men have been coming to places like this since the beginning of time. Of course, I didn't realize that ladies frequent saloons nowadays, too."

Sofie told herself that she need not defend her behavior to him. "Paul Durand-Ruel is holding an exhibition for me in New York, not Paris, where the critics are kinder. It is definitely cause to celebrate, Edward. And my friends insisted."

He leered. "Is that what you were doing here? Celebrating? With your *friends*?"

Her shoulders squared. "Yes."

His blazing eyes raked her not just with insolence, but with contempt. "Where is the baby?" he shot.

She inhaled. "With Rachelle. Rachelle is my dearest friend. They have gone for a walk. Edana goes for a walk every morning and every afternoon."

He stood utterly still. "Edana?"

"Yes. Edana Jacqueline O'Neil."

Their gazes locked. Edward's expression was peculiar, strained. "I want to see her."

"Of course," Sofie said. "They'll be back soon. Perhaps if you come to my flat later—"

"We'll go there together," he interrupted quickly, flatly.

Sofie tensed. Dread consumed her—while her pulse rioted.

Edward's mouth turned up then, not pleasantly—knowingly. "Yeah," he said, low and rough. Reading her mind. "We can do that, too."

Sofie whirled to flee him.

Edward was so fast that it was a blur of movement, nothing more. His hand shot out, gripping her elbow. Sofie cried out, because he was hardly gentle. "Oh, no," he ground out. "You're not running from me now. We're going to talk." And before Sofie could protest, he was propelling her across the room.

Sofie did not want to make a scene. "All right. Just let me go. Before someone decides you are manhandling me and tries to do something about it."

Edward slanted her a cold glance. Then he dropped her arm. Side by side but not touching, they walked out of Zut and into the nip of the autumn afternoon. She could feel the tension coiled up in him, simmering, sizzling, sparking—explosive.

She was trembling, out of breath. Sofie told herself that she must remain in control. She had half expected Edward to appear, after all, but not like this. She had not expected him to be so cold and hostile that he was almost unrecognizable. Now was not the time to dwell on cherished memories. Now was not the time to succumb to anguish and heartache. Nor was it the time to be aware of his overpowering masculinity. Sofie inhaled, blinking back tears. In her most proper, polite voice, she asked, "What is it you wish to discuss?"

He eyed her, then threw back his head and barked with laughter. "What in hell do you think I want to discuss? I want to talk about my daughter—and I want to know what the hell you think you're doing in a goddamn saloon."

Sofie had had enough. "You have no rights over me, Edward. I am not going to explain my behavior."

He caught her arms, hauled her up against his shockingly hard body. "I have lots of rights," he said, soft and dangerous. "Because I'm Edana's father."

Sofie tensed as his gaze slid over her, at once angry and hot, stripping away her clothes, lingering on her milk-swollen breasts. Although Sofie was angry, she was frozen, acutely aware of the power of his thighs against hers.

"How often do you come here?" he shot, shaking her once.

Sofie wanted to fight. Fighting was not as dangerous as succumbing to the desire kindling so fiercely within her. "That is none of your affair."

"I'm making it my affair."

Their gazes met. Edward's expression changed. Suddenly one of his hands was on her buttocks, and he had pressed her forward so that her loins touched his. Sofie cried out incoherently. His manhood was fully enlarged. "I'm making *you* my affair," he said.

"No," she whimpered.

"Yeah," he said roughly. "I still want you, too."

Sofie could not believe that this was happening. She had loved Edward once, and perhaps she still did. It was hard to say. She had been so angry that he had not come to be with her for Edana's birth, or even shortly afterwards. So angry, so disappointed, yet so relieved. And all of her passion had gone to the baby from the very moment she was born. There had not been any room in her life for another love.

But Edward was not in love with her. He had never been in love with her. But at least he had been kind and gallant in the past. No longer. He was rough and crude and shockingly frank. He was making her feel cheap, like some hussy from the streets.

And Sofie was trying very hard not to recall how his hands had played her when he'd taken her to his bed the night of the hurricane. How they had played her then—how they could play her again. Unwillingly she remembered the scorching heat they had shared, a desire so strong, she had cried out repeatedly, shamelessly, in her rapture. She could even remember the expression on his face as he moved over her—inside her. Ecstasy and agony combined, potent, unforgettable, and male.

And afterwards he had held her tenderly, as if he loved her.

This time, if she succumbed to the feverish need building within her, there would not be a single moment of tenderness.

"Aren't you going to invite me to join you in your bed?" Edward asked in a low voice, undulating his pelvis suggestively against her.

Tears filled Sofie's eyes. "No," she said in a choked whisper. "No." If only the desire would go away, but he was stoking it—purposefully, expertly. Her body was quivering against his. It was hard to breathe.

"Whyever not, dear Sofie?" Edward asked, suddenly gripping both of her arms again. His thigh slid between both of hers. Hard, hot. Male. "Surely you are not faithful to dear Georges?"

Sofie stared into his handsome face, eyes wide, determined to ignore the position of their bodies. She stared into his cold blue eyes, as beautiful as ever despite the frost there, and at his firm, mobile, expressive mouth. "How dare you cast stones at me!"

He laughed. "I dare. I dare *everything*."

His innuendo was sexual and she knew it. "You are despicable. You have changed. You are every bit as ugly as your reputation claims!" She tried to push away from him.

His laughter died, but he would not release her.

She ceased wriggling and struggling, for her every movement only made her more aware of him. "Let me go. This moment, before I scream for help."

Edward's grip only tightened. "Damn you! Are you in love with him, Sofie? Are you?"

"You do not understand!" Sofie cried.

"Oh, I understand, darling. I understand perfectly." His smile flashed. His thigh pushed harder and higher so that she was forced to ride him. "Come, sweet, we need not play games, we know each other too well for games—unless they are games of pleasure."

Sofie gasped. With real indignation, she tried to jerk free, to dismount him. He laughed, low and rough, and bent over her, unsmiling. Sofie comprehended that he was going to kiss her—and she froze completely.

"Better," he murmured, "much, much better. Let's see how much you've learned during your stay in gay Paris," he murmured in a bedroom tone. He pressed her closer, so that the size of his erection could not be in any doubt.

Immediately Sofie's hands came up to press him away. She did not want this, she did not. At least, not with her mind. But her body was so hungry, starved, and Sofie had actually forgotten how urgent desire could be. How mind-shattering, how consuming. Images tormented her now, not images of the past—but images of the future. Of her and Edward, naked and entwined and flushed with passion. Straining at each other, clinging, gasping. Edward driving deep and hard and smoothly, so smoothly, inside of her. The ecstasy she had once known. "No, Edward. Not like this."

"Why?" he whispered, his mouth close to hers, his breath feathering her lips. "We're friends. Old friends. Don't you have any fondness for me at all?"

"Old friends?" she gasped, but the rest of her reply was cut off. His mouth touched hers. A moment later she was the subject of a massive invasion, open to him as he thrust his tongue deep inside her, repeatedly. It was not a mating. It was a rape.

Sofie cried out, not because he was hurting her, but because she was becoming afraid. Of him—of herself. She tried to push him away even as her lips yielded and became pliant. He tore his mouth from hers, panting. "God, Sofie! It's so damn good!"

She was panting, too. "You think that because we were . . . we were lovers . . . that gives you a right to treat me like . . . like . . ."

"Like what, Sofie?" he gasped, dangerously. "Like a hussy? Like a harlot? Like a whore?"

She whimpered, turning white.

"Forget your new lover." His eyes blazed. "I'm better than he is. I'll prove it. We'll be better. Come. Come willingly, Sofie . . . This time it won't be rough. I promise."

Sofie stared at him, his seductive tone enveloping her like a warm cocoon.

He stared back. "Sofie. We both know you want me. And I want you. It was good. It can be good again. Better now, in fact, because you have experience. It can be *the best*, Sofie."

"Get away from me," she whispered.

"Why? Do you love him?" he snarled.

"You are mad," she gasped. "I like Georges—I do not love him!"

"Good. I wasn't too fond of the idea of taking a woman to my bed who was in love with another man." His smile flashed eerily. "But if that's the way it was—" he shrugged "—I would."

She stared, for he had become a monster. Someone she did not know—had never known. "You do not understand."

His vivid blue eyes were as hard as sapphires. "I understand. I understand how bohemian you are. I understand you Sofie, and your needs. I was your first, remember? I awoke you to desire. I guess that makes me a lucky man."

"Get away from me," Sofie said, low, desperate. "Please."

"You prefer him to me?" His smile flashed, cruel and cold. "You won't—not after today."

Panting, Sofie lost all control and struggled against his hold. Wild and crazed. Edward released her immediately. Sofie backed away and stumbled, then hit the redbrick wall. She hugged herself, panting, close to tears. "How dare you!"

"No," Edward shouted abruptly, pointing his finger at her. "How dare you! How dare you deny me my daughter, damn you, Sofie O'Neil!"

Sofie met his blindingly furious gaze. "I am not denying you Edana."

"No?" He paced towards her, then halted, raised a hand, fist clenched. It was shaking. "I want to know why you didn't tell me sooner."

Sofie hesitated. She decided he deserved the truth. "I was afraid."

"Afraid! Afraid of what?"

Tears filled her eyes. She hugged herself harder. "I don't know. Of this."

He stared, his mouth twisted and down-turned. She saw he was trying to understand but did not. Sofie was not going to enlighten him. Because it was as she had feared. He had come because he cared too much. About their daughter. Not about her.

They walked in silence back to her flat, careful not to touch one another. Sofie was also careful not to look at Edward. Her spine stiffened when they entered her apartment building, for she expected him to hold her elbow to aid her up the narrow, steep stairs. He did not. For the first time in a long time, Sofie became aware of how awkwardly she still moved as she climbed the stairs ahead of Edward. She was quite certain he saw everything.

Sofie heard Rachelle singing when they reached the top of the landing. "They are home." She inserted her key into the lock and pushed open the door. "Edana, *chérie,* Mama is home!" Sofie cried, rushing to her daughter.

Rachelle and Edana were on the floor on a big blanket. Rachelle was sitting cross-legged, in a black skirt and a stark white shirt and her heavy black boots. She wore a bright blue shawl. Edana was not sitting up yet. She lay on her back, waving her hands in the air, cooing. But at the sound of Sofie's voice, the sweet baby sounds stopped and she smiled instead.

Rachelle's gaze was wide as she got to her feet. Sofie had already scooped up Edana and was hugging her, hard. The baby laughed. Sofie half turned, just enough to glimpse Edward remarking Rachelle, just for an instant. Then his gaze was on the baby—and only on the baby.

"Oh, God," he said harshly.

Tears came to Sofie's eyes. There was no mistaking the fact that Edward loved his child already, utterly and irrevocably. His eyes were shining and suspiciously bright. The tip of his nose had turned red. Sofie held Edana out to her father.

His gaze shot up, startled. "I don't know."

Sofie's heart pumped in painful spurts. Still she offered her daughter to Edward, agonizingly aware of how special the moment was—and that it should have taken place long ago in the hospital, and that it should have been shared by man and wife. "It's all right. Edana is friendly."

"I'm afraid," Edward confessed, staring at the baby girl. "She's so small—so beautiful."

"You won't hurt her," Sofie said, perilously close to shattering.

Edward took Edana and cradled her carefully in his arms. He sat down on the worn sofa, never removing his rapt, besotted gaze from the child. "God, she's blond like you—but blue-eyed like me."

Sofie wiped her eyes with her shirtsleeve. But the tears wouldn't stop. Fortunately, Edward only had eyes for his daughter and was unaware of her upheaval. "M-Most children are blond and blue-eyed. She m-might have black hair as an adult, or brown eyes."

Edward made a sound, half a laugh. Edana was smiling up at him, waving her hands, as if trying to touch his face. "She likes me," Edward said thickly. "Hi. Hi, sweetheart. I'm your daddy."

Sofie could not stand it. Bursting into tears, she hurried from the room before Edward might see. But he was still bent over Edana.

Edana began to cry.

Sofie came to the doorway and saw Edward walking the baby, rocking her in his arms, trying to hush her. He sensed Sofie's presence and turned, alarmed. "What's wrong? Did I upset her? She was fine a minute ago!"

"She's only hungry, Edward," Sofie said softly. "It's time for her to eat."

Edward paused and stared at her, his gaze moving to her breasts.

Sofie had been nursing her child ever since she was born, but she began to blush. Briskly she strode into the room and took Edana from Edward.

"Perhaps this is a good time for you to leave." She would not meet his gaze. Edana had begun to wail. "You can visit her again tomorrow."

"No. I'll wait."

Sofie's gaze flew up at his flat, emphatic tone. Edward's jaw was firm, his eyes dark, determined. She could not bicker now. Edana was becoming red-faced. Sofie turned her back on Edward and rushed her child into the bedroom. Quickly she unbuttoned her blouse as she sat down in a rocking chair Rachelle had bought for her. Within moments Edana was suckling vigorously. Sofie began to relax.

But then she sensed his presence. Her gaze shot up. In her haste, she had not shut the door fully. Edward stood there on the threshold, watching her nurse their child.

Sofie's pulse skyrocketed. Not expecting an audience, she had exposed herself completely. Her breasts were full, pale, and blue-veined. And Edward was staring, but not at his daughter.

It was thoroughly inappropriate, but Sofie was stabbed with lust. She did not need to be a mind reader to know what Edward was thinking, either. Abruptly he turned away, closing the door behind him.

Sofie began to shake, in relief. She moved Edana to her left breast, pulling her chemise up on the other side. She was perspiring. Edana was content and did not notice.

Oh, God, Sofie thought. She had never dreamed it would be like this if he returned. Insanely, she had thought that she could keep her distance, both physically and emotionally, and remain blandly unaffected by him. What a fool she had been.

Sofie dared not think about what would transpire next. She only knew one thing. Once before he had so casually happened into her life. But then, he had almost destroyed it. Every instinct Sofie had told her that this time he would be successful—if she let him.

Sofie closed the bedroom door carefully, leaving it just slightly ajar. Edward's brow lifted. "She is asleep," Sofie said.

He stared at her, far too intensely for Sofie to be comfortable. She recalled how he had looked at her breasts. She recalled how he had felt against her when he had been kissing her with punishing strength. His kiss had been hurtful. But there had been nothing hurtful about the feel of the rest of his hard, aroused body.

"When do you want to get married, Sofie?"

"*What?*"

His jaw flexed. "You heard me. When do you want to get married? Now? Tonight? Tomorrow? There's no point in waiting, the sooner Edana has my name, the better."

Sofie could not breathe. It was exactly as she had feared. He cared too much—about Edana. She fought for calm. It was impossible. "You are very arrogant, Edward, to assume I would marry you because of Edana."

His eyes widened. "Goddammit! You have to marry me, and we both know it! Isn't that why you sent that letter?"

"No! That is exactly why I did not write to you until the very last possible minute!" Sofie shouted, forgetting all about the sleeping baby.

Edward gripped her arms. "I don't understand."

"And I don't care! I am not marrying you, Edward. Not because of Edana."

He was shocked. He had turned a ghostly shade of white. He released her, too dumbfounded to speak. "Jesus," he finally said. "I don't believe you!"

Sofie backed away from him, intent on staying out of his reach.

"You'd rather live like this?"

She knew better than to answer.

But now he was furious. "It's him, is that it?"

She hesitated, then shook her head. "No."

"It's him!" he shouted. Edana began to cry. "Jesus, if that's the way it is . . . I never meant it would be a real marriage, Sofie. Christ! You want your lover, that's fine! Hell, take ten lovers, I don't give a damn! But Edana will have my name. I won't have my daughter a bastard, dammit!"

"You've woken the baby," Sofie cried, shaking with her own anger, her own grief. "It's time for you to leave, Edward. Now!"

He hesitated. Edana wailed. "All right. We'll finish this tomorrow. But we will finish it, Sofie."

Sofie did not answer. She rushed into her bedroom, as much to run from him as to soothe her child. Quickly she picked up Edana, forcing a smile through her tears. "It's all right, darling, it's all right. Hush, now, Mama's not angry, Mama's not upset. Mama loves you. And your daddy loves you, too." She cradled Edana to her chest, crying harder than before.

Eventually the baby stopped crying. Sofie put her down, covering her with a light blanket, crocheted by her neighbor. She wiped her eyes. She hesitated, then saw that Rachelle stood in the salon, unmoving and somber. She took one look at her face and knew that Rachelle realized what was going on. Sofie left the bedroom.

"What are you going to do?" Rachelle asked, putting her arm around Sofie.

Sofie trembled. "You heard?"

"I heard."

"I'm not marrying him. I can't. Not like this." A horrible scenario flashed through Sofie's mind. Herself in a luxurious, canopied bed, nursing Edana in the middle of the black night, alone and knowing Edward was out with someone else and would not return anytime soon, and even then, would not return to her. Never to her.

"Oh, Sofie," Rachelle whispered, seeing her stricken expression. She hugged her again. "I understand. But what will you do?"

"Leave. Now. Tonight." As she spoke, her determination crystalized, fueled by a very real panic that bordered on terror. Very grim, Sofie said, "It's time for me to take Edana home."

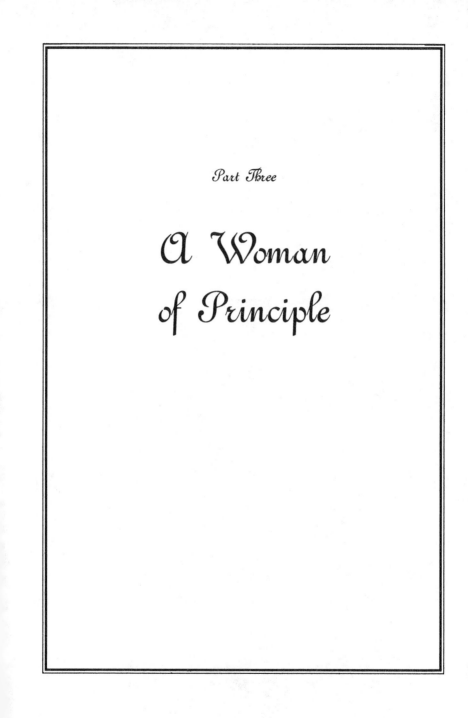

Part Three

A Woman
of Principle

21

When Sofie first glimpsed the great Statue of Liberty and the distant Manhattan skyline, a feeling of joyous relief overwhelmed her. Sofie clung to the ship's railing, almost weak with relief. Never had she needed her family more. She missed them terribly.

And she could not wait to show off Edana. Sofie knew that Suzanne would fall in love with her granddaughter the moment she saw her. Everyone did, for the small baby girl was so pretty and sweet, she was picture-perfect.

Sofie's hands tightened on the rail. Edana had undoubtedly received her good looks from her father. Sofie had tried to imagine Edward's wrath many times since she had fled Paris in the dead of night with Edana and Rachelle. Guilt consumed her every time, for hadn't she said she would never deny him his daughter? And God, she had meant it, and not only out of fairness to Edward. Too well Sofie recalled growing up without her own father. She could not ever wish such a fate upon Edana. She did not want to sever the relationship between Edward and Edana, she did not. But she could not marry Edward. Not even for Edana's sake.

Briefly she thought of that frightening night. The carriage ride to Le Havre had been endless and terrifying, for Sofie had expected Edward to materialize out of the night like a nineteenth-century highwayman, preventing her from escaping with their daughter, perhaps even dragging her before the nearest cleric. It was not until she had boarded an outbound vessel that next morning, and not until that ship had actually slipped free of its moorings and steamed into the harbor, away from the docks, away from French soil, that Sofie's fear had finally diminished. And then she had sagged over Edana, sobbing, torn.

Now the huge French steamer chugged up beside the docks on the East River harbor, the seamen crying out with gusty excitement, planks and gangways crashing down. As they disembarked, gulls wheeled overhead and the waiting throng cheered the arrival of the passengers. Rachelle carried Edana, for she was far stronger than Sofie in any case, but especially now. Sofie had not been able to sleep well on this journey. She had little appetite and she had lost weight. What appetite she had was forced, for she must nourish her daughter—she was afraid she might cease producing milk. Rachelle had hovered over her like a hawk. She had scolded like a mother hen. Sofie did not know what she would have done if Rachelle had not insisted that she come with them.

They had fled with one single bag that contained just a few changes of clothing and necessities for the baby. A porter took that valise and summoned a hansom. Sofie could not relax. She began to point out landmarks to both Edana and Rachelle. At five months old, Edana was alert and happily watching everything.

They passed Tiffany's, Lord & Taylor, F.A.O. Schwarz, the Company Gorham. They left Union Square, turned onto Madison Avenue. Sofie's smile faded. They were not far from Delmonico's.

It felt like yesterday, not more than a year ago. If she closed her eyes, she could transport herself back to that day, to that wondrous moment in time, with Edward sitting across from her, so handsome and elegant and seemingly so sincere, and she could feel how she had loved him. It was insane, but she could feel how she still loved him, despite it all.

"Sofie, *petite?* Are you all right?" Rachelle asked.

Sofie blinked and took a deep breath. "Everywhere I look . . . I see him."

Rachelle reached out and squeezed her hand.

Finally they turned past the two guardian lions and into the circular, graveled drive in front of the imposing Ralston residence. Sofie leaned forward, eager and trembling. The hansom pulled up and Jenson appeared on the wide stone stoop. Sofie handed Edana to Rachelle and stepped from the hansom. Jenson cried out when he saw her.

Sofie smiled then. "Jenson! I'm home!"

He rushed forward to greet her, beaming in a manner thoroughly inappropriate for a butler. "Miss Sofie! That you are! And about time—if you don't mind my saying so!"

Rachelle climbed out of the hansom, holding Edana. Smiling, Sofie pulled her friend forward. And as she did so, an old memory suddenly surfaced and Suzanne's warning words echoed in her mind. *You cannot bring a child home.*

Jarred, feeling slightly uneasy, Sofie gripped Rachelle tighter. "Jenson, this is my dear friend and companion, Rachelle du Fleury. And this is my daughter, Edana Jacqueline O'Neil."

In the foyer, more servants rushed out once Sofie's presence was known. Although she could not shake off her slight uneasiness, the warm welcome of the staff made Sofie terribly glad to be home. She hugged Mrs. Murdock, who had tears in her eyes. "This is my friend and companion, Rachelle," she said, pulling Rachelle forward with the baby. "And this is my daughter, Edana."

Mrs. Murdock's eyes widened and she paled. It took her a moment to recover, unlike Jenson, who had hidden his shock by retreating behind formality almost immediately. "She is beautiful, Sofie." Mrs. Murdock gripped Sofie's hand. "Oh, my dear—I did not know!"

Sofie managed a smile.

Mrs. Murdock became a briskly efficient housekeeper once more. "We shall put you in your old room, of course, and the baby next door with Rachelle. I will have your studio cleaned inside and out today, and it will be ready for you to go to work first thing tomorrow!"

Sofie was moved. "Thank you." She cleared her throat. "Edana sleeps with me, but Rachelle can have the adjoining room."

Mrs. Murdock nodded and sent maids scurrying upstairs.

"Is no one home?" Sofie asked then.

"Mr. Ralston is attending to business downtown. Your mother is out to lunch with the ladies. Lisa is in the garden."

Sofie turned to Rachelle. "Come. Lisa knows, of course, and is eager to meet her niece."

They hurried through the house. Sofie paused on the threshold of the terrace, which overlooked the gardens. She had expected Lisa to be alone. She was not.

She was in a gentleman's embrace. And he was kissing her.

Sofie's eyes widened. From where she stood she had an unobstructed view of the couple—and this was no chaste kiss. The man, who was tall and broad-shouldered, had Lisa bent over one of his arms while he kissed her very deeply. Sofie coughed. Instantly they broke apart. Lisa was flushed, with far more than just guilt. But then she saw Sofie and she cried out and lifted her skirts and came running.

Sofie cried out as well, stretching out her arms. Lisa had never been lovelier. Clad in a green-on-green striped gown with darker gloves and hat, she was stunning. Lisa rushed into her embrace.

When they separated Sofie turned to face the gentleman, who had strolled up to them. Lisa stood proudly beside him, her arm now looped in his. Sofie started, not just at the open display of intimacy. For he was not just tall and powerfully formed, he was very handsome, gray-eyed and darkly golden; in short, he was more Greek Adonis than mere man. Sofie recognized the glitter in his gaze. She was dismayed. She knew firsthand where such desire would lead Lisa.

"This is my fiancé," Lisa said, beaming and clinging. Beside him she appeared dark and small, the perfect foil to his blinding brilliance. "The Marquis of Connaught, Julian St. Clare."

"Lisa, I did not know!" Sofie cried. She was pleased—and relieved. They hugged again. Sofie turned to the marquis. "I am so pleased to meet you. I am Lisa's stepsister, Sofie O'Neil."

He was not smiling. His nod was somewhat curt, but he bowed politely. His words were correct, but that was all. "I am honored to meet you, madam. My betrothed has told me much about you."

Sofie managed a smile, stealing a glance at Lisa, who did not seem to notice her fiancé's dark humor. She could only assume that he was displeased with Sofie's untimely intrusion. And then Edana made a loud burp, distracting everyone.

Lisa froze. Sofie grew rigid, as well. It was one thing to introduce Edana to Jenson, Mrs. Murdock, and Lisa, quite another to a stranger. Despite having lived in Montmartre for more than a year, despite her bravado, Sofie was well aware that society would frown upon her daughter and herself.

But Lisa broke the moment. "Oh, Sofie," she whispered, her eyes glazing, a question there. Sofie nodded, and Lisa slipped free of the marquis and took Edana from Rachelle. "How beautiful she is!"

Sofie stole a glance at the marquis. He was looking at her hands—she wore no rings. Calmly he lifted his gaze to hers. No expression showed in his eyes.

"Might I introduce my daughter?" Sofie said, hoping her voice was steadier than her sudden case of nerves. "Edana Jacqueline O'Neil."

Something flickered in his eyes, surprise, perhaps, at her courage, but certainly not admiration. St. Clare left them shortly afterwards, claiming that he had business to attend to. Apparently he would pick up Lisa that night to escort her to a ball.

"I am so glad you are home," Lisa said eagerly as they retired to a small, cozy parlor used for the family alone. They watched Edana, playing with a rattle on the Persian carpet on the floor. "My engagement ball is next week, when it shall become official, and now you can attend! It would not have been the same, Sofie, if you were not there."

"Of course I will come," Sofie said. "Lisa—how long have you known the marquis?"

"We met last spring." Lisa smiled, her eyes shining. "Sofie—I was enamored right away."

Sofie could guess why. Hadn't she fallen for Edward the moment she had first glimpsed him?

"Isn't he wonderful?" Lisa asked, her eyes shining.

How well Sofie recalled what it was to be in love like that. "He is certainly very handsome. The two of you make a striking couple."

"Yes, I have been told that before." Lisa's smile wavered. "You heard, though, that he was married once before?"

"His wife died?"

"Yes, some time ago. Or so Father has said. The marquis—Julian—refuses to discuss it. I brought it up but once, and, well . . . he was furious." Lisa's gaze, worried now, held Sofie's. "He said the past is dead and that I must never bring it up again."

Sofie was somber, afraid that the marquis had loved his first wife—or that he still did. "Perhaps, after you are wed, when you know one another better, he will be able to talk about her."

"I am counting on it," Lisa said. She smiled again and reached out and took Sofie's hand. "Enough about myself. Tell me about life in Paris—and tell me all about Edana."

Sofie was nursing Edana when Suzanne barged into her bedroom.

It was sometime later. Rachelle had retired to take a nap, fatigued from the journey. Lisa was dressing for her engagement later that evening with the marquis. Sofie and Edana were alone. Sofie was feeling quite overwhelmed, and teetering on the brink of exhaustion herself. Somehow it was disturbing to have her daughter there, in the home she had grown up in, in the bedroom she had had since she was a small child of nine. It seemed wrong. As if something was missing. Which of course, it was. Sofie was not in her own home, but in the home of her parents.

Edward's recent marriage proposal flashed through her mind.

"Sofie!" Suzanne cried.

Sofie stiffened, twisting to face her mother, who stared wide-eyed at her as if she had never seen a woman nursing a baby before. "Mother."

"I cannot believe this! What are you doing?" Suzanne did not move, as if afraid to approach.

"Edana is hungry. I am feeding her. I will put her down for the night in a few more minutes."

"No!" Suzanne cried. "Oh, God! How could you bring the child here! Are you mad?"

Sofie tensed. "Mother, I am not mad. Don't you wish to meet Edana?"

"No!" Suzanne cried shrilly.

Perspiration gathered along Sofie's hairline and between her breasts. It was terribly hard to remain calm. "Mother, please. Come here." Desperation inched its way into her tone. "Come, please, take a look at my daughter. At *your* granddaughter."

But Suzanne refused to budge. "I told you that you could not bring the child here! And if you had to, you should have told the staff it was the maid's! Have you lost your mind?"

Sofie's jaw clamped. She managed to stroke Edana's downy head, managed to keep her tone calm. But her hand was shaking. "I am not going to tell people that Edana is Rachelle's."

"You must!" Now Suzanne paced forward, but halted before she came too close. She kept her eyes averted from Edana. "The staff will remain close-lipped out of loyalty—and fear of instant dismissal without references. Who else knows?"

Sofie began to pant.

"Who else knows?" Suzanne snapped.

"Lisa. And the Marquis of Connaught."

Suzanne turned white. "You fool!" She sucked in her breath, trembling visibly. "Well, he is family now, so I suppose he can be trusted, too. Sofie, we need only pretend until the adoption."

Sofie jumped to her feet, hugging Edana, who had lost her hold on her nipple and began to protest. "No. *No.*"

Suzanne faced her. "You must."

"No!" Sofie screamed, shrill.

"Listen to me!" Suzanne screamed back. "It is your life we are discussing. Your life! You will be cast out of society forever if you claim that child—do you hear me? You will never be accepted, not ever! I am protecting you!"

"But what about Edana!" Sofie cried. Edana was wailing now, but Sofie could not comfort her. "What about my baby? What about her life? *I* am her life!"

"You must try to be sensible," Suzanne cried. "In fact, I have found a wonderful couple in Boston, well-off and highly respectable, who are eager to adopt her. Had you remained in Paris, you would just now be getting my letter. It has been arranged, Sofie. It—"

"Get out!" Sofie screamed. "Get out!" Holding the shrieking baby in one arm, she picked up an ornamental candlestick and threw it at Suzanne. It missed, but it hit the wall behind her with such force that it tore the fabric covering it. "Get out!" Sofie screamed again.

Suzanne was frozen, afraid.

Sofie was weeping, and filled with murderous fury.

Suzanne turned and fled.

"Sofie?"

Sofie cuddled Edana, choking on her sobs. She looked up at Rachelle, who had entered her bedroom from the adjoining door. "We are leaving."

"Surely she would not insist—despite your feelings."

Sofie pursed her lips, broken of heart. "Yes." She began to cry again. "She would not even look at her. Not once. We must leave. Immediately!"

Rachelle nodded. She was as pale as any ethereal spirit. But then, so was Sofie. Only Edana was oblivious, for she had fallen asleep.

Sofie stared out of the hotel window. Dawn had grayed the city. But the streets were far from deserted on the avenue below. Milkmen and green-grocers drove their wagons by. Two homeless vagrants slept in the doorway across the street. A newspaper boy hurried past on a bicycle, and two policemen mounted on splendid bays trotted on down the block. A dog began to bark from somewhere not too far away.

Sofie had not been able to sleep. The horrible argument with her mother replayed again and again in her mind. She had never dreamed that Suzanne still thought she must give up Edana for adoption. Sofie felt the bitter pain of betrayal; worse, she was afraid.

Every instinct she possessed was far more acute now that she was a mother. She would defend her daughter to the death, if need be. She knew it would not come to that, but her senses shrieked at her, warning her that she had just escaped an impossible fate. Sofie knew she could not survive if separated from Edana.

Losing one love had been enough to last her an entire lifetime. She could not lose Edana, too.

Sofie shuddered, pressing her nose to the cold pane of glass. Where was Edward even now? She had little doubt he was on his way to New York.

If only she could marry him—if only he loved her. Then Sofie knew she could withstand the pain of Suzanne's heartless convictions, of her terrible betrayal.

But it was not to be. Sofie felt like some wild animal, caught in a corner, about to be trapped. It was almost incomprehensible, but Suzanne had turned into her enemy, and Edward was the enemy, as well. Sofie knew he would seek her out in New York. And even though her motivations in running from him were honest enough, he had every right. He *was* Edana's father. Sofie knew she must prepare herself for the upcoming battle. She must prepare herself to dissuade him from his intention to marry her and give Edana his name.

And suddenly Sofie wondered if she was doing the right thing, and if so, if she even had the strength to fight him now, too. She had never expected to return to New York and find herself as homeless as an orphan. She had expected to find a haven of love and support. And Edana deserved a father; more important, she did not deserve to be stigmatized for the rest of her life as a bastard. And if Edward were her husband, Suzanne would have to accept Edana.

But, dear God, Sofie knew she would wither up and die inside herself if she married Edward under these circumstances. Every time he returned from time spent with another woman, she would suffer untold, endless agony. Every day spent together masquerading as man and wife would be as painful as the blade of a knife twisting inside her flesh.

Sofie did not know what to do.

How could she fight Edward on the one hand, and Suzanne on the other? As horrible as Suzanne had become, she believed she was doing what was right. Sofie could not remember ever winning a battle with her mother when her mother had been convinced that she was right. This time she must win. But she was already so tired, and the battle had hardly begun. On either front.

Rachelle stirred and sat up. "Sofie? Have you not slept at all?"

Sofie looked over at the room's one big bed, which they were all three sharing. "No."

"I'm so sorry," Rachelle said. Then, "What are we going to do?"

Sofie was grim. "I think I had best talk to Benjamin. Surely he does not agree with my mother. Perhaps he can make her see reason."

Rachelle flushed with anger. "I am surprised you would even go back there."

Sofie regarded Rachelle, careful to keep her voice steady as she revealed yet another cause for worry. "I must. We are very low on funds, Rachelle."

* * *

Benjamin closed the door behind them. Sofie found herself nervous, especially as he had barred Suzanne from joining them. He sat down behind his desk. Sofie sank into a leather chair in front of him, gripping both smooth arms. Suzanne had given her a dark look filled with dire warning. Sofie understood. It meant that Sofie had better come to her senses and give in to her mother, fast.

Some of yesterday's shock and grief was fading. In its place was anger.

"Suzanne told me what happened. I think it was rash of you to leave in the manner which you did."

Sofie nodded stiffly.

"Suzanne wished to be present, but she is so distraught right now that I thought it best we proceed alone. And immediately."

Sofie nodded again.

"I think I understand how difficult this is for you. It cannot be easy to be an unwed mother at your age." His brown eyes were direct, and not unkind. "I thought that, when you left New York last year, you and your mother had agreed that adoption was best."

Sofie inhaled. "We never agreed upon any such thing! I refused then—just as I refuse now!" Sofie was standing, wide-eyed, shaking. She was also feeling faint. She had nursed Edana last night and that morning, but had not eaten a single thing.

He raised a brow. "I did not realize. Sofie, dear, you cannot possibly exist as an unwed mother in New York City. No one will even speak to you when you pass on the street. You will be an outcast. A social pariah."

"I was a social pariah before."

Benjamin also stood. "You were hardly a social pariah, my dear. Had you been interested in a come-out, it would have been arranged and you would have been deluged with offers, I have no doubt. You can still find a husband—you are only twenty-one. I will be glad to help. But you will never marry if word of this gets out."

"I do not want to marry!" Sofie cried, but it was a heartbreaking lie. "I intend to devote myself to my daughter and my profession."

For a moment he stared at her as if she were an alien creature the likes of which he had never seen before. "I am not only thinking of what is in your best interest—but of the child's as well. Can you not see that it would be better for Edana to grow up as the daughter of a married couple? I can assure you that we have met the couple, and that they are eminently suitable. As a matter of fact, the wife is barren and desperate for a child. She is already in love with your baby."

Sofie was rooted to the spot. Horrific images afflicted her. A young woman, incapable of bearing her own child, crying into her pillow, filled with yearning, praying to be able to adopt a baby. A faceless husband, also suffering, sharing his wife's grief. A beautiful home in a beautiful neighborhood. And then she saw Edana there with them. Sofie could not bear it.

She turned and ran.

"Sofie!" Benjamin cried. "Wait, please!"

Sofie stumbled down the corridor. Mrs. Murdock tried to speak with her, but Sofie did not stop. Jenson said something also, his tone frank with concern, but Sofie did not really hear. Suzanne came running after her, screaming at her, at once angry and demanding, hysterical and panicked. The hansom she had hired with the last of her precious pocket money was waiting, and Sofie leapt into it. She banged on the door, signaling the driver. Repeatedly. The carriage rumbled down the driveway. Sofie slumped in her seat.

Sofie could not return to the hotel without having solved their current dilemma. Which was money.

She had saved two thousand francs in France, but they had not been able to wait for the banks to open in order to withdraw the funds before leaving, and they had traveled on the cash they kept in the house. Two thousand francs, in any case, was not enough to get by on for very long—not when the support of three people was involved. Normally Sofie received her allowance from Suzanne quarterly, and it came from the trust left to her by her father. The next installment was due on December first. Sofie was afraid that Suzanne might try to withhold the money in order to bend her to her will.

She must find out immediately. She must also find out what her recourse was should this be the case. Surely, as the trust belonged to her, in this unusual situation Suzanne could be bypassed. Sofie decided that she needed a lawyer—and she needed one who would not charge her for his intervention in advance.

Henry Marten's kind image flashed through her mind.

Hope swelled in Sofie's breast. She knew he would help her. She recalled that his new office had been just off of Union Square. She had never been there, but she remembered noting the fact when she had idly perused the calling card he had left with her the day he had invited her to ride in the park. Sofie instructed the driver to go downtown.

About an hour later, Sofie found his office purely by chance on Twenty-third Street, a few blocks from the square, when she had just about given up. It was on the upper floor of a two-story false-fronted older brick building above a merchandiser of men's clothing. Sofie cried out, the hansom stopped, and she got out. She let the cabbie go, because he made it clear that he was going to charge her extra for the past hour, and she did not have enough to pay him very much more.

Sofie prayed that Henry was in. She hurried up the narrow stairs and paused outside a heavy glass door, catching her breath. She was exhausted. Inside, Henry sat behind a desk, immersed in a folder of some sort. Her heart moved into her throat. Sofie knocked on the rippled glass.

Henry looked up, mouth open to call "enter," but he did not speak. Eyes wide, he rose to his feet. Then he smiled, at first unsurely, but it quickly expanded. He opened the door. "Sofie! I mean—Miss O'Neil! What a surprise—do come in!"

Sofie shook in relief—he was actually pleased to see her. "Hello, Mr. Marten. I hope I am not calling at an inconvenient time."

"Not at all!" He guided her inside and pulled up a chair for her. His gaze was warm as it swept over her face. "I had no idea you were back from France. Are your studies finished, then?"

Sofie sat down, clasping her hands in her lap so he would not see them shake. "I hope that my study of art will never be finished."

He was somewhat chagrined. "May I offer you some coffee? I can make a fresh pot." In the back of the room there was a small sink and an iron stove.

Sofie shook her head "no". Henry regarded her more intently and walked around his desk to sit behind it. He pushed the clutter aside, clearing a space in front of him. "Is this business, Miss O'Neil?"

Sofie wet her lips. "Oh, Mr. Marten, I am afraid so," she cried, losing her firm grip on her composure.

"What is wrong, Sofie? May I call you Sofie?"

She nodded, pulling a handkerchief from her reticule. She dabbed at her eyes. Henry was so kind. She tried to remember why she had not gone riding with him that day in Central Park. Of course. Edward had come to model for her. *Edward. If only* . . . "Henry, I am in some difficulty."

He waited, his mien lawyerly now, listening.

"I am without funds and stranded in the city. I have had a severe falling out with my mother and her husband." Sofie met his gaze. "I receive a quarterly allowance from Suzanne, but it comes from a trust left to me by my father.

I am afraid my next allowance will not be forthcoming. I am afraid Suzanne will not send it."

"When is it due?"

"On December first."

"And how much is due?"

"Five hundred dollars."

"Is your mother the executrix of the trust?"

"Yes," Sofie said.

"When does control of the trust turn to you, Sofie?" He was taking notes.

"When I am twenty-five. Or if I marry."

"How old are you?" He did not blush. "That is a professional question, of course."

"Of course. I am twenty-one. I will be twenty-two in May."

"I see. Is there any chance of a reconciliation between you and your family?"

"I do not think so."

"Perhaps with the intervention of a third party?"

"It is unlikely," Sofie said.

Henry nodded. "Well, I believe I can answer your questions in a day or two."

Sofie leaned forward. "That would be wonderful." She hesitated. "Henry— can you wait for payment of your fee until I receive the monies owed me?" Her voice caught. "I am without funds at the moment."

"Sofie, I am not going to charge you at all for something like this," he said, and now he blushed. "You are my friend."

Sofie wanted to cry. She sniffled a little instead. "Thank you," she said softly.

Henry hesitated. "Sofie, is anything else wrong?"

Sofie swallowed, thinking about Edana, who was hungry by now. Rachelle would feed her cow's milk from a bottle. Edana had yet to become accustomed to the idea. Sofie knew she must get home to nurse her. And for the first time that day, her own stomach clenched with hunger pangs. But she did not have more than a few dollars left, just enough for a meal or two for her and Rachelle. How was she going to survive three weeks like this until the first of December?

"Sofie." Henry was watching her too closely. "Can I lend you some funds? Until you are back on your feet?"

Sofie hesitated. "Perhaps, in another day or two, I might need to borrow something." She was breathing a bit unevenly. He had no idea that she had two other mouths to feed. Would he be this kind if he knew she was providing for her illegitimate daughter?

Henry stood, reaching into his breast pocket. "Here." He came around his desk, shoving the bills into her hand. "Please. Take this. You look very tired. I am afraid you will become ill if you continue to worry as you seem to be doing."

Sofie managed a smile. "You are so kind."

He was frozen. Then, "How can I not be kind to you, Sofie?"

22

"Madam, you have a caller."

Suzanne was not in the mood for callers. She was tired from not having slept at all last night, and her eyes were red and swollen from crying. She knew she did not look very well. "Whoever it is, Jenson, send them away."

Jenson retreated, leaving Suzanne to her hot black coffee and uneaten breakfast toast. But he returned almost at once. "I am afraid the gentleman insists that it is urgent."

Irritably Suzanne snatched the calling card and studied it. "Henry Marten, Esquire. What does he want?"

"He states his business is most personal."

Suzanne was annoyed, but instinct made her instruct Jenson to send him in. A moment later Henry Marten appeared, looking somewhat disheveled in his baggy, ill-fitting suit. Suzanne realized that he had lost weight.

"I am sorry to interrupt your breakfast," he said.

Suzanne shrugged. She did not stand up, nor did she offer him a seat. "What is so urgent, Mr. Marten?"

"I am representing your daughter, Mrs. Ralston."

Suzanne stiffened with shock. "What!"

Henry cleared his throat. "She has monies due on the first of next month. Will they be forthcoming?"

Slowly Suzanne got to her feet, gripping the smooth lacquered tabletop, in a state of disbelief. "Only if Sofie comes home—alone."

"Alone?"

"Yes," Suzanne said harshly. "You may tell her that she will receive her trust payment if and when she comes home—alone."

"I am afraid I do not understand," Henry said.

"If Sofie continues to reside elsewhere, defying me, she will not be supported by me."

"The money is held in trust by you from her father, is it not?"

Her jaw ground down. "Yes."

"I am afraid I must ask to see a copy of the trust agreements, Mrs. Ralston."

Suzanne was incredulous. Then she was furious. "My lawyer is Jonathan Hartford, Mr. Marten. He has those agreements, not I."

Henry smiled briefly. "Then I might tell him you have approved my request for copies?"

"Do I have a choice?"

"It would be silly for me to have to go to the courts merely to be afforded the opportunity to read the documents," Henry said.

"Yes, you have my approval," Suzanne snapped. "But let me save you some time. The agreements are ironclad. Unless Sofie marries, she will not take possession of her father's estate until she is twenty-five. There are no ifs, ands, or buts about *that*."

Henry only bowed. "Thank you for your cooperation, Mrs. Ralston."

Suzanne watched him leave. Then she cried out, in fury, in distress.

A lawyer! Sofie had gone to a lawyer! It was unbelievable. God, didn't she know that Suzanne was only trying to protect her? To protect her from the very same kind of anguish Suzanne comprehended firsthand from having lived through it once, a long time ago? Suzanne did not want Sofie to make the same horrible mistakes that she had made. Yet she had already made some of them, and if she continued on her present course, she was going to repeat more of them.

Shaking, Suzanne sank down in her chair. She did not recognize her own daughter, not anymore. Once Sofie had been complacent, obedient, malleable. If she had her art and the seclusion with which to work, she was happy. But it had all changed when Edward Delanza had walked into her life. Yes, that was when it had changed. In every way, this was all his fault.

Suzanne hated him. God, how she hated him!

Two summers ago Sofie had become brave, defiant. She had ignored all of Suzanne's warnings and plunged recklessly into an affair with him. Suzanne shuddered. In doing so, Sofie was repeating the past mistakes of her mother *exactly*.

Suzanne remembered being fifteen and heated with lust for Jake, so much so that she could think about nothing or no one else. So much so that she had purposefully given her virginity to him. So much so that she had been in love and she had married him in complete defiance of her family. They had cut her off without a cent. To this day, Suzanne was not on speaking terms with her parents. The day she had married Jake was the day they had buried her alive.

Like mother, like daughter. A worldly, virile man, an innocent virgin. Lust. Defiance. Loss of innocence. The similarities were frightening.

But the similarities ended there. Suzanne had married Jake before having her baby. Sofie had run away to Paris to have her child—and now refused to give the baby up for adoption.

Suzanne's face lowered to her arms and she began to cry. All she had ever wanted to do was protect Sofie from hurt and suffering. The day she had realized that Sofie had broken her ankle in her fall down the stairs, Suzanne had been shaken free of her selfish grief over Jake's loss. Sofie had looked so small and helpless, lying in her bed, numb with pain, and Suzanne had been consumed with guilt.

A guilt that had never quite disappeared. For when Sofie's broken ankle had healed, it became apparent that she would be a cripple for the rest of her life. Suzanne had felt that she was responsible. To make up for what she had done, she would protect Sofie from any further hurt—for the rest of her life.

Suzanne had risen to the role of motherhood with a vengeance. It was as if she had been waiting for this role of mother of a wounded cub her entire life. And once she had lost Jake, all of her passion was transferred to her daughter. Sofie might be crippled, but she had her art and she had Suzanne. Suzanne, who would protect her from society's scorn by encouraging her to hide behind her eccentric penchant for art.

But Sofie no longer wanted to be protected. Yet Suzanne knew her daughter did not understand. No one could ever understand what it was to be a social misfit until she was firmly cast out and stoned.

Suzanne could not let her daughter do this to herself. To take on the burden of an illegitimate child that would surely destroy her. Suzanne knew what it was like to give up respectability in exchange for love. Love was not enough. Nothing was enough to make up for the pain of social ostracism.

But she had had Jake. Sofie did not even have Edward Delanza. And even if she could have him, the suffering that was only beginning now would be multiplied a thousand times. Suzanne thought of the heartbreak and suffering she had endured during her marriage. She thought about the vicious, violent fights. She thought about the nights Jake did not come home, or when he did, how he had reeked of cheap perfume. Even now, so many years later, remembering brought forth such hatred, and such regret. For what made it worse was the fact that it was mingled with a love that would never, ever die.

Suzanne knew that Sofie had no choice. She could not become an unwed mother. Nor could she marry Edward Delanza—who was exactly the bastard her father had been. No, there was no choice. She must give up the child and move forward with her life. In time, the pain of loss would be tolerable. It was best for everyone—for Sofie, for the child, and even for Suzanne.

Suzanne ordered her carriage brought around. She hurried upstairs to change into a better dress, to dab a touch of rouge onto her pale cheeks and pinched lips. She pinned a black hat with a half veil onto her head, hoping to shadow her red-rimmed eyes. Her pulse began to race.

She needed Jake now, she did. But she doubted he was in the city, much less at home.

Suzanne hurried downstairs, enveloped in a mink coat. She ordered Billings to drive uptown on Riverside Drive. Then she settled back against the seat, clutching herself.

If only Jake had returned. He would help. Somehow, he would help. Jake was the only man she knew who could move mountains, and Sofie had become a mountain.

She did not see Central Park as they drove through it. Her stomach hurt. She had not seen Jake in almost a year, not since that one single time. But not through lack of trying on her part.

After she had learned that Jake was alive again, and with little difficulty, what name he was going under, Suzanne had immediately hired a private investigator to find out where he lived. Within a few days the agent had located Jake Ryan's residence at 101 Riverside Drive. Suzanne had gone there immediately.

And she had been stunned. The mansion occupied five acres, from Ninety-first to Ninety-third streets. Tall wrought-iron gates enclosed the entire property. A small brick cottage guarded the closed front gates. Tall oaks and pines lined the perimeter of the property, but the house set at the other end of the emerald green lawns was so large and so imposing that it could be seen quite clearly nonetheless. It resembled a medieval manor, complete with side towers and arched entryway, boasting steep roofs and parapets, more than it did a home.

Suzanne had been in shock. Jake lived here? In this mansion that could swallow the Ralston residence whole—and then some? How had he done it? How had he made such a fortune for himself? When she had met him he had been nothing but an Irish immigrant laborer!

And she had been stabbed with fury, too. She was his wife! She should be there, with him! She had spent the first years of their marriage living in a small house that was little more than a shack, dressed in couture gowns that quickly became threadbare. She had not been able to afford a servant, and she had had to care for Sofie all by herself—with only Jake to help her at nights. She'd had to cook, too, or they would not eat. Suzanne had been reduced to being little more than a peasant. It wasn't fair!

Suzanne had gone to seek Jake out because she loved him, but now she was furious at being denied her place at his side. However, Jake was not in residence. When they had tried to enter, they had found the wrought-iron gates padlocked. Someone had finally been roused from the cottage. The custodian told them that Mr. Ryan had left New York several days ago. But he did not know where he had gone or when he would return. However, upon being pressed, he had finally given them the name of the man he reported to. That turned out to be Jake's solicitor.

Suzanne had confronted the lawyer, without success. He was not about to reveal Jake's whereabouts to her or anyone else. He had finally agreed, however, to pass along a letter. Suzanne had sent him a ten-page missive in which she had proclaimed her undying love for him, her anger at being deceived and duped by him, and her desire to be reunited with him as his wife. It had never been answered, but the lawyer had assured her that Jake received all of his mail. Just before the end of the year, Suzanne had sent another letter. She had yet to receive any reply.

And every few days Suzanne returned to the astounding manorlike mansion on the West side, hoping he had come back. But he did not. Her private agent finally learned that he kept a residence in London, another in Belfast, and a country estate in Ireland. Suzanne had never been more shocked. And he maintained such a low profile that it was impossible to discern in which location he currently lived. Suzanne was forced to give up.

Now Billings was driving the Ralston coach past the tall barred and padlocked front gates. Suzanne wanted to cry, she wanted to scream. Damn you, Jake! I need you—where are you? Sofie needs you!

She closed her eyes, sinking back on her seat. If only she had not lost her temper the last time she had seen him. If only she could relive—and change—the past. Worse, she did not know when she would see him again—or if she ever would. Goddamn him to hell.

Suzanne's temples were throbbing when Billings helped her down from the coach. She was too absorbed in her thoughts to thank him and she hurried into the house. She should not have gone back there, to his Gothic West Side manor. But she could not stay away. Damn Jake for hiding. Damn him for not being there when she needed him so much.

She thought about Henry Marten's visit, and the pounding of her head increased while her stomach pitched and sank like lead. She must send for Hartford, her lawyer. She was almost certain the trust was controlled by her absolutely, but she must make sure there were no loopholes. If not, perhaps the agreement could be doctored. She should not have told Henry Marten he could have a copy—not yet. But copies took time, so perhaps no damage had been done.

Suzanne was counting on the fact that she controlled the trust and that Sofie would have to come home if she was kept impoverished. Come home—and give up the child.

Massaging her temples, Suzanne strode down the hall. Someone moved inside the salon as she passed the open doors. One foot on the stairs, Suzanne paused, filled with unease. Had she glimpsed a man? She turned as Edward Delanza sauntered into view.

Her eyes widened, her heart stopped. "You are not welcome here!"

He did not smile. "So I've been told repeatedly. Where is Sofie?"

Suzanne faced him fully, gripping the banister with white-knuckled tension. Her mind sped. "She is not here."

"I know. Where is she?"

Suzanne tried to control her uneven breathing. She sensed danger. She saw the furious determination in his eyes. Was he after Sofie—or his child? Did he even know about the child? Why else would he want Sofie—and be so angry as well? Instinct told her the child might bring Edward and her daughter together. A vision swept her. Sofie and Edana in a lavish home that belonged to Edward Delanza. But Sofie was weeping as she tended her child. Weeping and heartbroken and alone.

An alternate vision swept her, as quickly, as thoroughly. Sofie and Edana in the same home, but Edward was there with them. Father and mother were aglow with laughter, alight with love, the baby cooing contentedly.

Suzanne shook off her thoughts. She knew that she must keep them apart. "Sofie is in Boston."

"In Boston!" He stared. "What in hell is she doing there?"

"She is visiting relatives," Suzanne lied smoothly. "Now, get out."

Edward studied her coldly. "I will find her," he said. "With or without your help. Even if it takes me the rest of my life."

Suzanne inhaled hard as he stormed from the house.

He was trembling. He had come so far, so fast, but she had eluded him. It was unbelievable. When he had found her in Montmartre, she had told

him she would never deny him his child. But that very same night she had
fled with Edana, doing just that. When Edward had realized that she had run
away with the child, he had been enraged.

He was still enraged, but it was cold now, silent and still and deep.

He swung open the door of the Daimler. Damn her. Damn Sofie O'Neil for
doing this. For taking his child away from him. For running away from him.
Well, the whole world wasn't far enough. Not for her. She couldn't escape
him. Not anymore, not now. He was going after her, no matter how long it
took, and in the end she would be his wife, and Edana would bear his name.
Edward was going to do what was right—for everybody.

But he didn't buy Suzanne's story that Sofie was in Boston with relatives,
not for a minute. He had only arrived in the city that morning, but his next
stop would be the Gallery Durand-Ruel. She damn well would have been in
touch with them.

"Mr. Delanza, sir!"

He paused, about to slide his long body into the motorcar. The housekeeper,
Mrs. Murdock, came running out of the house. Edward straightened, very
alert. "Mrs. Murdock?"

"Yes, sir," she panted, pausing before him. "If she finds out I'm talking
to you, she might very well fire me without references—and I've been with
her since Sofie was four years old."

He gripped the elderly lady's plump arms. "Mrs. Murdock, if Suzanne
dismisses you, you can come work for me."

Her eyes widened. "Thank you, sir."

"Now, tell me about Sofie."

Tears filled her eyes. "It's a lie, it is! There are no relatives in Boston,
none at all. You should have been here, sir. Oh, Lord, they were screaming
at one another enough to bring the house down. It's lucky Mr. Ralston wasn't
home."

"Who was screaming? Suzanne?"

"Suzanne and Sofie! I never heard Sofie scream and shout, she was so
angry, not ever, sir!" Mrs. Murdock was crying.

He was grim, but he kept his tone matter-of-fact. "What were they fighting
about?"

"They were fighting about the child. It was so horrid! So horrid, sir!"

He sucked in his breath, his heart turning over in a very sickening manner.
"What about Edana? Is she all right?"

"The babe is fine, sir. But Mrs. Ralston wants Sofie to give her up to
another couple for adoption—and Mrs. Ralston always does as she wants.

She and Mr. Ralston have already arranged it. Sofie refused. That was why she was screaming so. She left with the babe and the Frenchwoman right after that, in the night, it was, without hardly a stitch except the clothes on their backs! And I don't think they have any money—because they were a ragged lot, they were, when they arrived."

Adrenaline flooded his body, tension quivered within him, but his tone was calm, flat. "Where did they go?" Edward asked, fighting down a horrible image of Sofie clutching Edana on a street corner, like any common vagrant.

"I don't know!" Mrs. Murdock wailed. "If only I knew!"

Edward patted her. "It will be all right. I will find her, you can be sure of that."

Mrs. Murdock gazed up at him, both beseeching and eager. "Yes, sir, I know you will. But please, do it fast. Before something awful happens!"

"If you hear from her, you can reach me at the Savoy."

Mrs. Murdock nodded.

Edward thanked her and hurried to the Daimler, the composed facade he had struggled to maintain vanishing instantly. His heart felt like it was wedged in his throat. He was trembling, out of breath. God! He wanted to kill Suzanne with his own bare hands for chasing Sofie out into the street with Edana. Mrs. Murdock was afraid that something awful would happen. Edward was afraid, too. There were dozens of gruesome possibilities. The city was no place for a young woman to be alone with a small baby, especially without means. Edward knew that he must find Sofie and end this madness once and for all. Find Sofie and rescue her. Apparently he would play the champion one more time—but this time, her future was also his.

23

$\mathcal{S}$ ofie was nervous and had been that way all day, in anticipation of her meeting with Henry Marten. Henry saw her standing outside the thick glass door of his office and he came forward before she could knock. He smiled at her. "Right on time, I see. Why don't we walk in the square? It's a beautiful afternoon."

Sofie nodded, trying to guess whether he was bearing good or bad tidings, but it was impossible to tell from his benign expression. He held her elbow as they went back downstairs. Outside, the sun was bright, the trees mostly bare, red and gold leaves swirling across the sidewalk. The air felt cool and crisp.

Henry did not release her arm as they strolled down the street. "I spoke with Suzanne, and I am in agreement with you. A reconciliation is unlikely unless you compromise with her."

Sofie shot a worried glance at Henry. "What did she say?"

He hesitated. "She said she is withholding your money until you come home . . . alone."

Sofie flinched. A pink color had suffused Henry's face. Dismay filled her. She knew he did not understand. But what did he comprehend from Suzanne's words? And should she tell him the truth about why she was so desperate for funds? It would be a relief to share her predicament—and all of her worries— with him. But he might very well be appalled. Sofie was afraid to risk losing his friendship. "Can she do that? Withhold my money from me?"

Henry sighed. "I attained copies of the trust contracts from her lawyer. And the answer is yes. It is not proper, nor is it ethical, but technically she can withhold the funds. We do have a recourse. But it is not timely. We can sue her personally, or we can appeal to the courts to have a new trustee appointed in her stead."

Sofie halted and faced Henry, aghast. "I cannot believe this! I must sue my own mother? Or go to court to have her removed as trustee? This is horrible. A nightmare!"

"It is not pleasant," Henry agreed, regarding her closely.

Sofie felt hysteria rising up in her. And anger. Some of the hurt over her mother's betrayal had been diminishing these past few days. In its place was a seeping rage at the callous cruelty and injustice of her behavior. "I have savings in France. Unfortunately I left in such haste that I did not receive any letters from my bank. I am having those savings transferred here, but without those letters, it will take four to six weeks." Her voice trembled. She was so worried about the future that she could barely sleep at night. She had never been more tired. She needed someone to lean on other than Rachelle.

Especially because, as every day passed, the probability of Edward's arriving in the city increased.

Sofie fought for control, aware of Henry's probing gaze. "In another few weeks Durand-Ruel is holding an exhibition for me. If I am lucky, it will be a success. Much of the work he is showing, he already owns, but several new works will be sold on commission. I think Paul will agree to advance me funds in any case against future work and future sales. I will ask him immediately." The gallery was only some dozen blocks away, and she was ready to run there on foot right now.

Henry plucked her sleeve. "Sofie, wait. You are distressed. Are you sure you cannot go home? Perhaps if I intervene—"

"No!" she cried vehemently, startling them both.

Henry dropped his hand from her arm.

She squared her shoulders, trembling. "Henry, you do not understand why I cannot go home alone."

"No. I do not understand."

Sofie swallowed, feeling shaky and faint. "I cannot go home because Suzanne wants me to give up my daughter for adoption."

Henry gasped.

Sofie dared to meet his shocked gaze. "Yes, I have a child. An illegitimate child—a little girl named Edana Jacqueline O'Neil whom I love with all my heart."

"Dear God," Henry said. And then his face flushed with anger. His gaze became wide with comprehension. "Delanza? Is he the father? The bastard!"

Sofie cried out, gripping his wrist. "Please. I cannot tell you who Edana's father is, I cannot!" But she knew he knew that it could not have been anybody else. And she realized that his reaction would be typical of the rest of society once Edana's existence became public knowledge.

Henry nodded, mouth tight, shoulders stiff and rigid. "I understand."

"How can you? When I am not sure that I do?" Sofie asked, almost in a whisper. She had not thought it out yet. There was too much on her mind for her to consider the ramifications of revealing who Edana's father was to the world at large. It would be for the best, she knew, to reach an agreement with Edward first on whether they would make public the fact of his paternity. Yet such a discussion could not take place when she was hiding from him. Sofie faced Henry, feeling lost, alone, overwhelmed. "Henry, I love her. I am not going to give her up. No compromise is possible on my part. I am furious with my mother—I am not going back."

"Now I finally understand," Henry said slowly.

She looked at him, searching for signs of revulsion and condemnation, but she only saw sorrow. "You are shocked, and rightfully so. But . . . you will still represent me?"

"Sofie, I am your friend. Of course I will continue to represent you—and help you in any way that I can."

Sofie stared at him in mute gratitude.

Henry handed her a handkerchief.

Sofie wiped her eyes. "Thank you. Thank you so very much."

He took her arm and they walked again, this time in silence. After another block they entered Union Square. Henry led her to a deserted park bench, where they both sat down, scattering pigeons. He shifted to face her, their knees touching. He coughed.

Sofie clenched the wadded-up handkerchief. "I am sure Paul will advance me funds," she said, as desperate as she was hopeful.

"I will not let you starve, Sofie. Don't you know that?"

"You are so kind," she whispered.

"It is more than kindness." He appeared ill at ease. "Don't you know that by now?"

She became utterly still.

He was red of face. "I am very fond of you, Sofie."

Sofie stared, shocked.

He seemed to feel that he owed her an explanation. "You know, two summers ago, I came to Newport Beach to meet you—for all the wrong reasons. But now I am motivated by the right reasons.

"I hoped to marry you then. I was encouraged by my aunt because of your inheritance. But when I met you I found you both fetching and fascinating. Even though your mother did succeed in putting me off, at first."

Sofie stared. "She . . . did?"

"She did. She was very discouraging. Still, you are one of the most sincere, kindest women I have ever known—and the bravest, too. I would like to marry you, Sofie. Not for the wrong reasons—but for the right reasons." He was beet red. "I have been fond of you for a long time. More than fond, actually. You should not be so surprised."

"Henry . . . I did not know."

"I know. You only had eyes for him."

Sofie said nothing, for he was right. She thought about Edward, filled with anguish. She wondered if this would be her only chance for love.

Henry said, low, "I have never said such things to a woman before. I cannot bear to see you suffer like this. You should not be alone. You need a husband, and your daughter needs a father."

Sofie shook herself free of Edward's image with vast effort. She took his hands in hers. "I don't know what to say. I am moved beyond words."

"Say yes. Would you become my wife, Sofie? I know I have not met Edana, but I would be a good father. I would never hold the past against her—or against you."

Instinctively Sofie knew that Henry would be a good father—and that he would be a good husband, too. He would be loyal, kind, affectionate, and faithful. She closed her eyes, stabbed with both grief and longing. How could she marry him when she loved another? Yet she yearned for a home of her own, for a man to love, for a man to love her. "I am overwhelmed by your offer. Henry, please, I need some time."

Gravely he nodded.

Sofie could not miss Lisa's engagement party. She had not returned to the house since the day she had seen Benjamin and fled when she realized he also approved of Suzanne's plans. She had been so immersed in her own problems and in taking care of Edana this past week that she had hardly spared her sister a thought. Lisa must be on pins and needles, Sofie thought.

The afternoon before the ball, Sofie dared to go home, leaving Edana with Rachelle at the hotel. She chose her time carefully. Suzanne dined out every afternoon with other ladies, and Sofie was counting on that fact. She had no wish to even see her mother, much less engage in another heated battle.

Sofie found Lisa in her bathtub covered with Saratoga mud. "Hello, Lisa. I have come to borrow a gown for the ball tomorrow."

"Sofie!"

Sofie had to smile at the sight her sister made. Only her eyes and mouth were visible. The mud was black and it was a sight both comical and gruesome. She sat down on a footstool. "Does that mud really improve one's skin?"

Lisa was sitting up. "Where have you been? Oh, God! I have been so worried about you and the baby!" She began to cry.

Sofie sank down on her knees beside Lisa, and gingerly patted her muddy back. "I am fine. Really."

Lisa gulped down her sobs. "Your mother is a witch—and so is my father. How could they be so cruel to you?"

"They are only doing what they believe to be best," Sofie said.

"You are defending them?"

"No." Sofie sighed.

"Are you both all right?" Lisa asked, gripping the sides of the claw-footed tub.

"Yes. We are making do. Suzanne has cut off my funds, but Henry Marten has lent me money—and so did Paul Durand-Ruel." Sofie had seen him immediately after receiving Henry Marten's shocking offer of matrimony. He had been sympathetic to her plight and more than willing to help.

"I know," Lisa said. "Sofie, you are almost all they talk about."

Sofie did not like the sound of that.

"When I get my next allowance, you can have that, too," Lisa said firmly. "So you plan to come tonight after all?"

"I would not miss your engagement ball for anything, Lisa, and thank you," Sofie said, smiling ruefully. "I guess I am not quite as alone as I feared. Everyone has rallied to my side in this small crisis."

"Sofie—you are not alone!" Lisa was fierce. "When Julian and I wed in May, you and Edana can come live with us."

Sofie was stunned by the magnitude of the offer. "Lisa, surely you do not want your sister and niece underfoot as you begin your married life."

"Yes, I do." She was stubborn.

"And the marquis?"

"He will be as eager as I am, I am sure of it."

Sofie doubted it. If there was one thing she was sure of, it was the passion that could be had between lovers on a honeymoon. The marquis would not appreciate company. "And how is your illustrious bridegroom?"

Lisa's smile faded.

"Lisa? Is something wrong?"

"Oh, Sofie," Lisa cried, "I am in love with him and have been since we first met, but I have finally faced the truth! I do not think he is enamored of me!"

Sofie had only met Julian St. Clare that one single time the day she had arrived. But she remembered how stiffly courteous he had been—and how quick he had been to note her ringless hands. She remembered now that she had not seen him smile, not even once. Had she not seen the burning glitter in his eyes, had she not seen his kiss, she would have thought the man as cold as his facade.

And Lisa was more than just a pretty young woman. She was intelligent, kind, and terribly generous. A man would be a fool not to fall in love with her. But on the other hand . . . St. Clare reminded Sofie so much of Edward.

He reminded her of Edward, despite his being golden-haired, because he was another version of virile male perfection. Such a man would always have his choice of women, even without charm, and it would be idiotic to think that St. Clare had lived his life as a saint. Clearly he was attracted to Lisa. But Sofie knew firsthand that lust was not love. "What makes you think that, Lisa?"

She hesitated. "He doesn't smile, Sofie. He is perfectly polite, but he doesn't smile—not with me." She hesitated. "And his conversation is perfunctory."

"I hope he does not smile with other women?"

"No. I wonder . . . Perhaps he doesn't really like women," Lisa said uncertainly. "Could that be possible? When his kisses are so passionate? When he is so—" Lisa paused, blushing "—virile?"

"Anything is possible," Sofie said, worried now and thinking about his first wife. "What else do you know about him?"

"I know that he is the only son of the Earl of Keith, and that his mother also died many years ago."

"Lisa, perhaps you are rushing this," Sofie said gently. But she wondered at the void of information about the marquis.

Tears filled Lisa's eyes. "But I do love him—to distraction! If I could, I would marry him tonight. I pray his reserve is just stiff British cordiality, and that after we are wed, I will be privy to his real personality—and to his love."

Sofie did not like the sound of things. "I think you should have a long talk with the marquis as soon as possible. Be direct and honest and voice all the concerns you have shared with me. I think you must learn more about his past—and about his first wife."

Lisa's eyes widened. "I am not seeing him until the ball tomorrow."

"Then that will have to do." Sofie forced a cheery tone into her voice.

Lisa was aghast.

"I must leave." Sofie stood. "Edana will be hungry soon, and I do not wish to see Suzanne."

"Wait," Lisa cried, standing and wrapping a towel around her muddy body. "Sofie—where are you staying? How can I reach you?"

"I am staying at the Lexington Inn on Thirteenth Street," Sofie said.

Lisa stepped from the tub. "He was here, last week."

Sofie froze, certain she had misunderstood. "I beg your pardon?"

"Edward Delanza came to the house, looking for you. I was not home. Suzanne sent him away. Mrs. Murdock told me that she told him you have gone to Boston to stay with relatives."

Sofie knew she should be relieved that Suzanne had put Edward on the wrong track. Crazily, she was dismayed instead. "What did he want?"

"Just to see you. Does he know about Edana?" Lisa asked.

Sofie nodded.

Lisa stared. "Sofie—you must see him. Immediately."

"I cannot."

"Whyever not?" Lisa cried. "He is the father of your child. Dammit, Sofie, he should marry you!"

Sofie had never heard Lisa curse before. "He has already asked me," she said hoarsely. "But I refused."

Lisa gaped. "You refused! Why?"

"Because I love him. Because he does not want me. Because he only wants Edana. Because I cannot tolerate the thought of being married to him while he consorts with other women."

"Sofie, if he comes back—"

"No! Don't you dare tell him where to find me!" Sofie cried.

Lisa did not answer. And because Sofie did not like the gleam in her eyes, later that afternoon she, Rachelle, and Edana moved from the Lexington Inn to a boardinghouse down by the river.

As Sofie dressed for Lisa's engagement party, she developed a plan of hiding behind stiff-backed formality when she next saw her mother and stepfather later that night. After all, it worked so well for servants—why should it not work for her?

She assured herself that no fiasco would occur at the ball. Suzanne would have her hands full with her five hundred guests. So would Benjamin. There would be no opportunity for them to drag her aside and badger her with their ludicrous scheme to give up Edana for adoption. If Sofie was adept, she might very well avoid them entirely—and she might even enjoy herself.

It had been a very long time since she had gone to a good party. She grew wistful, thinking of her birthday last May. Although she had not danced with Georges, it had been fun to watch the revelers. It occurred to her that she had never attended a society ball before.

Undoubtedly this would be her last and only time, as well.

"Sofie, how lovely you are," Rachelle cried.

Sofie turned, brows raised.

"Edana is asleep—and you *are* beautiful," Rachelle said.

Sofie had not even tried to view herself in the hand mirror she shared with Rachelle. The boardinghouse was run-down and they had let two rooms, not one, quite cheaply—but each room contained nothing but a single bed with a thin mattress, threadbare sheets, and ancient blankets, a small bureau with a washstand, and a single light.

Sofie had borrowed a gown from Lisa in a soft coral, a color that, Lisa had remarked, did wonderful things for Sofie's golden hair, amber eyes, and tawny complexion. Sofie had loved the gown the moment she had spotted it in Lisa's armoire. It was far brighter than anything she had ever worn before, but Lisa had insisted she take it—almost wickedly. "Bright colors are cheerful, unlike your navy blue and gray clothing, which is mournful and depressing," she had stated, shoving the gown into Sofie's arms. "I do not even own a gray gown. Of course, I do have something very straight, *very* low-cut, and silver."

Sofie had taken the coral gown.

Now she faced Rachelle. "This gown did not seem as daring on the hanger as it does on me," she remarked, not particularly liking the display of cleavage she was faced with when she happened to look down at herself.

"You are nursing. You cannot possibly hide your bosom in this circumstance." Rachelle smiled. "You look very sexy, *mon amie*. Monsieur Marten will be troubled not to goggle you."

Despite feeling half-naked, Sofie smiled. "Ogle. The word is ogle."

Rachelle shrugged gracefully. "Ogle, goggle, who cares? I am ogling you. I have never seen you look like such a siren, *petite amie*."

"Please, Rachelle! We both know I am no siren." Sofie walked hesitantly to the bed and sat down. "Thank God this dress is not tight everywhere."

"You have lost too much weight," Rachelle said disapprovingly. "Otherwise you could not wear Lisa's clothes. Henry is downstairs."

Sofie jumped to her feet, her heart slamming with real nervousness now. "Why didn't you say so!" She grabbed the beaded satin reticule she had borrowed with the gown, and the black velvet wrap. "How is my hair?"

"Considering you pinned it up without a mirror—excellent, *chère*."

"Is it even?"

Rachelle laughed, kissing her on both cheeks. "It is perfect. *Allez*. Amuse yourself tonight."

Sofie darted into the other room to kiss her sleeping daughter good-bye. "I will not stay late," she promised.

"If you come home before two in the morning, I will not let you in," Rachelle called after her.

Sofie had to smile, hurrying down the stairs. Henry was pacing there, looking quite handsome in his black tails and patent leather shoes. He looked up. Sofie slowed. His gaze widened with frank appreciation. Sofie almost felt beautiful. And despite herself, for just a moment, she imagined it was Edward waiting to escort her to the ball.

Sofie's steps slowed as they approached the house. She realized that she was clinging to Henry's arm.

"Are you all right?" he asked her with concern.

She gazed up at him. "I am nervous. I have this feeling—a bad one—about tonight."

"We do not have to go in," Henry said.

Sofie forced a smile. "This is the greatest moment of Lisa's life—second only to the day of her wedding. I promised her I am coming."

"I admire you, Sofie," Henry said.

Uncomfortably flattered and somewhat amazed, Sofie loosened her hold on his arm as they entered the house. Jenson was delighted to see her as he took her wrap.

"How is Lisa?" Sofie asked him.

"She has been sick all day, poor thing."

"And my mother?"

"She is in the kitchens, somewhat hysterical."

Sofie nodded tersely. "Let's go," she said to Henry, wanting to escape into the ballroom and disappear among the other guests before Suzanne saw her.

"I am not in the kitchens," Suzanne cried loudly, her heels clicking on the marble floors. "Sofie—stop right there!"

But Sofie was already frozen. Slowly she turned to face her mother.

They stared at each other. "We must talk, right now," Suzanne said.

"No," Sofie said.

Suzanne shot a glance at Henry. "Sir, would you excuse us? I wish a private word with my daughter."

But Sofie did not allow Henry to answer. Rage engulfed her and she began to shake. "No! We have nothing to say to one another, nothing, do you hear me? You are cruel and selfish and think of no one other than yourself!" Once the words began to flow, they would not stop, and it was almost as if someone else lived inside Sofie and was speaking for her. "For years I did as you wished—always as you wished! You wanted me to hide from the world because I am crippled, and I hid! Of course I would not embarrass you. You wanted me to remain unwed, and I agreed, for it was easier to agree than to be brave and daring and take a chance on finding love. I listened to you—I trusted you! I even trusted you enough to think you would love Edana when you saw her and I came home, needing you! But you have betrayed me— *betrayed* me for the very last time—and I do not think I can ever forgive you for what you have done."

Suzanne had turned ashen. "Sofie—I love you. Everything I have done, I have done for you."

"Everything you have done," Sofie said tersely, wishing she could stop but unable to, "you have done because it was best for you, not because it was best for me."

Suzanne whimpered. "I love you."

Sofie choked back a sob. "And I love Edana."

Suzanne's regard darted to Henry.

"He knows, Mother, he knows everything," Sofie said.

"You fool," Suzanne whispered.

"No—you are the fool for trying to tear me and my daughter apart." Sofie whirled and rushed away, Henry hurrying after her.

She could not stop shaking. She could hear the vibrant strains of the band, which played in the ballroom on the ground floor, as well as the growing tenor of the animated conversation of the guests. She could not remember ever being this angry. She told herself that, if she held her head high and kept her smile in place, no one was going to know how upset she was tonight or that she had just said such horrible—but truthful—things to her mother.

And despite having gotten that confrontation over with, she could not relax. She felt even worse. No matter how hurt and angry she was, Suzanne was her mother. A part of Sofie was ashamed for all that she had said, and another part of her ached for Suzanne, knowing how severely she had wounded her.

And she was sad. Would she ever be able to go to her mother as a daughter again?

The slightly nauseating feeling of dread that had afflicted Sofie all evening increased. Henry caught up to her as they descended the three white marble steps into the ballroom, a vast room with gleaming parquet floors, white pillars, and high, canary yellow ceilings with elaborate mahogany moldings. It could accommodate five hundred guests with ease, and undoubtedly did so now.

Sofie told herself that the dreadful feeling she carried was because of the past few minutes, not because of anything that might occur next.

"Is there anything I can do?" Henry asked.

"Your very presence is a comfort, Henry," Sofie said, meaning it. "I am sorry you had to witness that."

Before he could respond, the band stopped playing and the crowd suddenly hushed. "There she is," someone whispered.

Sofie turned and inhaled as Lisa appeared on the top of the stairs in a cloud of white lace and chiffon. Lisa was so very beautiful. Suzanne was smiling, and Benjamin was beaming in parental pride. The marquis's expression was grim and set in stone. Sofie was swept with disbelief. Did he hate the fact of his upcoming marriage to Lisa? Was this a forced marriage on his part?

Worse, Lisa stared blindly ahead, and Sofie realized that she, too, was upset. Her smile was forced. By the time Benjamin cleared his throat to speak, tears glinted in her eyes.

Benjamin began to introduce the marquis, after which he would announce the engagement and make it official.

Sofie did not listen. She tried to catch Lisa's eye, hoping to comfort her somehow across the distance separating them, but Lisa did not look at anyone. Sofie ached now for her sister, instead of herself, and silently she encouraged Lisa to bear up. Eventually Sofie turned and glanced around the room. She was faced with a glittering sea of the ladies in their red, yellow, blue, and green gowns, interspersed with the stark black and white of the gentlemen in their tuxedos. The dozens of huge crystal chandeliers overhead seemed to make the air shimmer and sparkle.

Sudddenly her gaze shot back to a man standing on the fringes of the crowd, but in the front lines, near the terrace doors across from where Sofie stood with Henry. Sofie could not help staring, perplexed. He was her mother's age or a bit older, with tawny hair that was too thick and too long to be fashionable. He was darkly bronzed, tall and fit, and he was superbly elegant in his black tuxedo and snowy white shirtfront. And he was staring at her intensely.

Sofie gazed back, confused. He seemed familiar, but she could not recall who he was, nor could she recollect ever meeting him. He must be a friend of Suzanne's, or of Benjamin's. But why was he staring at her so relentlessly?

Suddenly he looked away. Sofie watched him melt into the crowd. She glanced back at the landing where Lisa stood with the marquis, her father, and Suzanne. The crowd was applauding. To Sofie's surprise, Suzanne was also staring after the man—and she was white with shock.

The marquis withdrew a small jeweler's box from his pocket, casually flicking it open. Briefly he held it up; the crowd gasped and Sofie's eyes widened. The ring was incredible, obviously a priceless heirloom belonging to his family, a huge ruby set in diamonds that was sparking like fire in the ballroom's bright lights. As the marquis placed it on Lisa's third finger, the crowd began to applaud another time.

Sofie clapped, too, praying that Lisa would come to her senses and call off the wedding before it was too late. She knew that Lisa was right. St. Clare did not love her—in fact, he seemed exceedingly unhappy with the engagement.

The band began to play. The marquis led Lisa onto the dance floor, his face expressionless, took her in his arms, and effortlessly they began to whirl around the dance floor.

They were a stunning couple. He so tall and powerful, so blond and male, she so pale and delicate, so dark and so utterly dainty. More applause filled the room, until it was thunderous. Only Sofie knew, from Lisa's tight, ravaged expression, that she was vehemently fighting tears.

More couples began to dance. Benjamin took Suzanne onto the dance floor as well, but Sofie shook her head when Henry asked her to dance. Briefly she succumbed to an intense yearning and an intense, aching loneliness. It seemed as if everyone was on that dance floor, waltzing with the natural, profound grace of butterflies—it seemed as if everyone had someone with whom to feel complete, except her.

Sofie straightened her spine. To feel sorry for herself now, when she had borne so much already, was sheer nonsense.

And then Sofie's nape prickled. Her heart stopped. A feeling of horror engulfed her. And with it, an intense, shattering feeling that could almost be described as joy.

Sofie knew that Edward had appeared. In the next instant, she saw him.

Edward was coming down the hallway, devastatingly handsome in his black tails, his stride long but casual, and he was staring unwaveringly at her.

"Oh, God," Sofie whispered. She clutched Henry's arm. His eyes were brilliant with fury—and he was coming directly to her.

24

Sofie could not move, no matter how her mind told her to turn and run, to flee.

And a traitorous part of herself looked at the man she loved and felt a fierce exultation. For hadn't it become clear that she could not really live without him?

Edward halted in front of her, unsmiling, eyes blazing. Sofie's unease crystalized into fear. His lips turned down and he darted a glance at Henry, who held her arm. His regard moved back to her. "We are going to talk."

Sofie drew in a deep breath, but could not find any sense of calm. "E-Edward. We c-can talk later—"

His hand whipped out. Before Sofie knew it, he had gripped her arm and jerked her forward to his side. Sofie cried out.

"Later?" he asked, both incredulous and furious. "I have spent four weeks chasing you across the Atlantic and you tell me we will settle this later?" His expression was thunderous. "No. We are going to talk, now. We are settling this, now."

Sofie was helpless to refuse and she nodded, restraining a whimper. What did he wish to settle? The fact that she had fled with Edana—or the marriage he insisted upon?

"Sofie." Henry came forward, pale. He turned to Edward. "Unhand her, Delanza," he said thickly.

Sofie's eyes widened at Henry's display of courage.

And Edward faced Henry, a snarl marring his perfect features. *"Get lost."*

Henry stiffened. "Unhand her. Before I am forced to make a scene."

Edward released Sofie abruptly, visibly seething with rage. His fists curled closed at his sides. "Go right ahead," he said softly, dangerously. "Come on, Marten. I'm going to enjoy taking you to pieces."

Henry blanched.

Sofie cried out. "Stop it!" She was in a state of abject disbelief. These two men were fighting over her? Over her? It seemed impossible—but it was not, it was real. "Henry, I am fine. Really." She tried to smile and failed.

"You don't have to go with him, Sofie," Henry said.

"No," Edward snapped, his fist close to Henry's nose. It shook. "She has to go with me, Marten—she has no choice in this. None. When she left France in the dead of night, *with my daughter, denying me my rights,* she forfeited all of *her* rights."

Sofie swallowed, wet her lips. Guilt made her flush. He made it sound terrible—running away with his daughter. Taking his daughter from him. God—it was terrible. But if only he had been more understanding and less demanding! If only she did not love him so.

"Every human being has inalienable rights," Henry shot, but he was sweating, his brow beaded with moisture.

Edward laughed rudely. "Spoken like a damned lawyer! So you know? Then you know that you have *no* rights where Sofie is concerned, and that I have *every* right as the father of her child!"

Sofie looked from Edward to Henry, dumbfounded that they were still fighting over her. Then she realized that they were drawing a small crowd. For the men's adversarial stances were unmistakable—as was her own frightened posture.

Had people overheard their conversation, as well? Despite her determination to survive as an unwed mother, her stomach curdled with more anxiety. She dared not look around her now.

"I have rights," Henry said with great dignity, keeping his voice low. "Because I wish to marry her."

Edward turned stark white. He stared. A dozen seconds must have ticked by. He said grimly, "Then that makes two of us."

Sofie looked at Henry, who still appeared as tenacious as any bulldog. She looked at Edward, who was itching for a physical battle.

"Henry, it is all right, I assure you," Sofie said quickly. "Edward only wishes to talk. We will be gone a few minutes, no more. Edward—let's go outside and continue this discussion privately."

Edward swept his arm out, the gesture mocking and angry. As Sofie walked past him, leaving Henry appearing both doubtful and anxious, the hairs on her nape prickled with unease yet again. Her stomach roiled with the same dread she had been afflicted with all night.

Only now did she recognize that it had been a premonition of doom.

*   *   *

The night was black and cold. A thousand stars glittered like diamonds over their heads in the cloudless purple sky. Sofie flinched when Edward took her elbow in a viselike grip. She had to hurry to keep up with his long strides. She was afraid to start any conversation, afraid of where any words would lead, so she did not ask him where they were going.

The pale stones of the circular driveway glistened like pearls in the glow of the bright gaslights. Dozens of carriages and several automobiles lined it, and many more conveyances were double and triple-parked on Fifth Avenue outside the front gates. Edward paused before a long, round-nosed, gleaming black motorcar with a stark white leather interior. Before Sofie knew it, he had opened the door and shoved her inside and had climbed in beside her. He leaned over her and locked her door, then turned to stare at her.

Panic rose up in her. "You can't lock me in this car!"

"No?" One brow rose. "I just did."

Sofie trembled and hugged herself. "Where are we going?"

"We're not going anywhere. Not until we've resolved things between us."

Sofie's teeth chattered, not as much from the cold as from his dire words. *Not until we've resolved things between us.* Edward's gaze dropped to her mostly bare shoulders. Sofie tensed. It dropped lower, to the voluptuous curve of her very bare bosom, swelling above the neckline of her dress. His jaw tightened. His eyes flicked away.

And he shrugged off his tuxedo jacket and settled it on her shoulders.

Sofie turned her face away from him, gazing blindly at the Ralston lawns, fighting the sudden urge to cry.

"How could you?" he said harshly, bitterly, staring at her again. "How could you have been so selfish and so cruel?"

Sofie's gaze flew to his. "Edward, I'm sorry." She was, more sorry than he could ever know.

"Why?"

"Because I was afraid. Of you."

"I don't understand."

Sofie flung precaution to the wind. "I cannot marry you without love, Edward."

Time stood still. Her heart beat so hard and so loudly, she was sure he could hear it, too. His face grew stark and the myriad muscles there all tightened.

He stared out over the steering wheel, bound in braided black leather, at Fifth Avenue. "I see."

Sofie was swamped with dismay. For if he had any feelings for her at all, he would have told her, giving her a chance to compromise her position and accept his proposal. For perhaps she could live with his affection, perhaps it would be enough.

But he only wanted Edana. Sofie hugged his jacket to her. His profile was bold and beautiful, but his eyes were bleak, frightening. She lowered her face, buried it against the warm, black wool. She could smell him. Faintly spicy, faintly musky, terribly male.

Edward faced her again, expressionlessly. "I want to see Edana."

Sofie could hardly believe that they had settled the issue of their marriage so easily, and she almost sagged, but whether it was in relief or disappointment, she refused to consider. "Of course."

"Is she all right?"

Sofie nodded, forced herself to speak. "Rachelle came with us. She is with Edana now."

"Rachelle? The woman with the red hair?"

"Yes."

He studied her, his emotions buried so deeply that they were impossible to read. "Where are you staying?"

"A boardinghouse. I'll take you there. You can visit Edana anytime." Sofie forced a bright smile to her face. All the while thinking, *He was not going to force me into marriage after all.* How happy she should be—how thrilled.

He stared at her. His gaze dropped. Sofie had let the jacket fall open, exposing her lush cleavage, and she pulled it closed abruptly. Now that the crisis was past, desire kindled between her thighs, forbidden but too powerful to pretend it did not exist.

"Do you wish to marry Marten?" he asked as one might ask a stranger for a weather forecast.

Sofie tensed. "I . . . I am thinking about it."

His nostrils flared. "I see." Fury sparked in his eyes. "Should I take that to mean you love him?"

Sofie drew back against her door. She wondered if he was afraid of losing Edana to another man. "Edward, you don't have to worry," she began quickly.

He gripped her shoulders and pulled her across the seat and into his arms.

Sofie cried out, too late. He pushed her backwards so that her head fell against the plush leather headrest while his hands slid around her waist. And then his mouth was on hers and he was kissing her with all of his explosive rage.

His embrace was steel, and Sofie could not move a single muscle. Edward tore his mouth from hers, ending the punishing kiss. He leaned his forehead against hers. Sofie was afraid to move, afraid to speak. She was afraid to trigger his anger again. He was panting, but so was she.

And then she felt his hands on her waist, caressing her through the taffeta of her gown.

Strong, lean fingers moved high, then low, leaving a trail of fire in their wake.

He moved against her again. His chest crushed her breasts, his mouth brushed her lips. A moment later he was pulling her lower lip very gently between his teeth. It was a request. Sofie reached for his shoulders and whimpered and opened and he covered her mouth completely.

She had forgotten what it was to be kissed like this. Edward sucked her lips, mated with her tongue. Sofie entwined with him helplessly, eagerly. His hands slid down her hips, kneading greedily. As greedily, Sofie clasped and unclasped his shoulders. She strained against him, on fire now, wishing desperately that he would trail his kisses down her throat and to her achingly sensitive breasts.

Instead, his mouth locked voraciously with hers, his hands slid up her rib cage, thumbs splayed, and then over her breasts. An exhilarating pleasure swept over Sofie. She arched into him. Edward molded her, thrusting his tongue deeper still into her mouth, and suddenly Sofie found herself lying on her back, with Edward on top of her.

She cried out at the feel of his loins, massive and hard, her hands sliding down his back. Any coherent protest she might have wanted to make died deep in her throat.

Edward lifted his face from hers, his big body shuddering. Their gazes met. Something wild and fierce filled Sofie at the sight of his eyes, filled with hot male lust. She had never felt more wanton, more womanly, or more beautiful than in that moment. Tenderly she touched his cheek.

He said, "Does Marten make you moan and thrash the way I do?"

Sofie gasped.

"Does he?" he demanded.

His words were as hurtful as the lash of a whip. "No." She writhed to push him off of her. "Please, let me up."

Edward sat up immediately, staring at her.

Sofie struggled to rise. She saw where he was looking, and hot color, some of it shame, flooded her features. She pulled up the bodice of her dress, then slid as far away from him as possible. "Why? Why would you say such a thing?"

His smile lacked any humor. "Curiosity."

She bristled. "The answer is no."

He appeared indifferent and he shrugged.

Tears came to Sofie's eyes and she blinked them back furiously. "Why did you do that, Edward?"

"You have to ask?" He was incredulous, bitter, and mocking.

"Why would you try to seduce me?"

He said nothing, staring, eyes hard and bright—reminding Sofie of the diamonds he was notorious for smuggling.

"Do you deny that you were trying to seduce me?" she cried, her voice pitched far too high.

"Yes. Seduction was not my intent."

She regarded him, trying to penetrate past the anger and into his mind. It was impossible. "I do not understand."

"Oh, Christ! I'm a man, Sofie, and you're a woman, and that's one helluva sexy gown." He leaned over her and unlocked her door. His arm brushed her breasts. Sofie forced herself to ignore it.

And she fought to keep from crying. His words could have been a compliment, if said differently, in a different circumstance. But they were an insult, and he knew it just as she did. He was making it very clear that she had kindled his animal-like lust with her dress, nothing more.

Sofie turned, groping blindly for the handle to the door. Edward appeared on the other side of the motorcar and opened her door for her. He reached for her arm and helped her out, but once standing, Sofie shook him off. She started up the drive, realized that he was following. She whirled. "Haven't you done enough? What do you want now? Go away!"

"We're not through, lady," he said. "I want to see Edana, remember? And I don't trust you worth a damn. You're going to say good-bye to your hosts and to Marten, and then I'm taking you home."

Sofie was frozen and furious and filled with indignation and fear.

Suzanne attended to her guests, feigning calm and forcing gaiety. But Lisa's engagement party, which she had planned with such enthusiasm, had turned into her worst nightmare.

Outwardly Suzanne was smiling. Inwardly she was bleeding. *Oh, Sofie. You hate me—but I love you, I do!*

Suzanne had not thought that Sofie would attend Lisa's engagement party. And when she had first seen her, she had been as thrilled as she was relieved. Her worry for her daughter knew no bounds. As more time passed, as Sofie failed to come home in capitulation to Suzanne's demands, Suzanne began to fear that she had seriously miscalculated—that her daughter was far stronger than anyone would have ever dreamed.

But not only had Sofie come to the party, she had lashed out at Suzanne with a fury Suzanne had never known her capable of.

Remembering made Suzanne sick. Had she lost her daughter? Had she meant those things? Didn't Sofie know how much she loved her?

Suzanne greeted yet another couple, for she was working her way through the crowd, performing her duty as hostess. Her social pleasantries were automatic and she hardly heard a word anyone said to her. If only she could find Sofie and talk to her, yet instinct told her that she could not break through to Sofie now. Her daughter was far too furious.

Her pulse skittered and her palms were wet. What had happened with Sofie was bad enough, but Jake was here, too. *When she found him, she would kill him.* Jake had nerve, *utter nerve,* coming here like this! She had sent him two more letters, which he had not answered, and this time she had apologized for her loss of temper in her first letters, while insisting that she had changed for the better. This time she had even confessed that she still loved him—and that she always would.

But the son of a bitch had ignored her yet another time.

And now he was here. He had dared to attend a party in Benjamin's house. What was he trying to do? Destroy her marriage, destroy her publicly?

Shaking, a smile plastered on her face, Suzanne nodded to a friend of Benjamin's and paused behind a pillar, gulping air. She could not relax, could not shake Sofie's vicious, hurtful words from her mind, could not free herself of the terror that someone was going to recognize Jake at any moment and destroy her once and for all. At that moment, she hated him far more than she loved him—but she had never needed him more.

She froze, spotting him out of the corner of her eye. Jake lounged against a pillar, sipping a glass of champagne, the picture of male beauty, male dissipation, and arrogant male indifference. Their gazes locked. Jake lifted his flute to her in a mock salute.

Fury swept through her. Suzanne itched to claw that smug expression right off his face. But she must rein in her outrage. If anyone could help her, it was Jake. Because in the end, Jake was her Rock of Gibraltar, her half-ton anchor in stormy seas.

Trying to control her trembling, she started towards Jake—but in the next instant she was frozen in shock.

The Marquis of Connaught had paused at Jake's side. For the first time in ages, Suzanne saw Jake smile with genuine goodwill. The two men shook hands, Suzanne watching in disbelief and horror. They knew each other? Then the marquis pulled Lisa forward, clearly introducing her. Suzanne actually felt the floor tilt beneath her feet.

How much worse could this evening get?

For she expected Lisa to reveal the truth. Lisa had seen not just the portrait that Sofie had done of Jake, but the photograph from which Sofie had painted him. Jake had hardly changed.

Time stood still. Suzanne could not breathe. She knew her life was about to be destroyed—and that this time, she would never be able to recover.

But Lisa did not scream or faint. She nodded politely at Jake, appearing quite pale and strained, and a moment later the marquis moved on, Lisa in tow. Suzanne sagged, gasping for breath.

But the evening had only just begun. What if the marquis inadvertently introduced Jake to Benjamin?! The possibility was terrifying. Surely he would recognize Jake even though Lisa had failed to.

Suzanne marched to him.

He saw her coming and settled more comfortably against the pillar, watching her in an insolent, thoroughly male manner that never failed to elicit a dark, heated response within Suzanne. No matter how afraid and furious she was, no matter how desperate for his aid, he was the man of all her dreams, he was the only man she wanted. She wanted him back, and she had from the moment she had learned that he was still alive.

And she would get him back, or die trying.

Suzanne forced her mind back to the issue at hand, no easy task with her blood running so hot now through her veins. "What are you doing here?" she snarled. "You are mad! What if you are recognized?"

His white teeth flashed. "Julian invited me."

"Julian?" The word came out strangled with hysteria. "How in God's name do you know him?"

"We're friends." Jake grinned at her. "Good friends."

"What if he introduces you to Benjamin?" Suzanne cried, much too loudly. She froze when she realized that several guests had turned to look at them, but then they all resumed their own conversations. Flushing, Suzanne squared off against Jake. "Damn you for putting me in this predicament! Maybe you should have stayed dead!"

"But I thought you wanted to be my wife," Jake mocked. "Surely you wouldn't be content with a ghost for a husband?"

"As far as I'm concerned, I am your wife," Suzanne whispered tersely. "You're hardly a ghost, and we both know it."

"Then just what is Benjamin?"

Suzanne's cheeks were mottled red. She had done some very discreet checking into the legality of the situation. "He is my husband."

Jake sputtered with laughter. "Are you telling me that you're a bigamist, darling?"

"It wasn't intentional and you know it," she cried, fists clenched. "What if St. Clare introduces you to Benjamin?"

"He won't."

"How can you be sure?"

"Because he knows the real story. Because he knows who I really am." Suzanne cried out.

Jake smiled, but it wasn't friendly. "I wasn't lying when I said he was my good friend, Suzanne."

Suzanne forced the hysteria down. "You are a miserable bastard and I hate you."

"That's not what you said in your letters."

"Why do you bring out the worst in me?"

"I hate to tell you this, Suzanne, but nobody forces you to act the way that you do."

She could not win, not with him, never with him. "Jake—we need to talk privately."

His gaze drifted over her nearly naked breasts. "Talk?"

Despite her very acute worries, various scenarios flashed through her mind. In bed, Jake was insatiable, selfishly demanding but also selflessly giving. In bed, Jake would use her until she begged for mercy; but she would use him until he begged for surcease, too. "Damn you, you are teasing me," she said low, unable to prevent herself from licking her lips.

"Can't take what you're so good at giving out?"

Suzanne stiffened. "I'll meet you in the library at the end of the hall," she said. She turned and hurried away.

Jake watched her through heavy, lidded eyes. Phrases from her letters echoed in his mind. *I miss you, I always have—I always will. You are the only man I've ever wanted, really. I will leave Benjamin—I will destroy myself—for you, if you only say the word. I am your wife, Jake, and you know it. Take me back.*

I love you so much, darling.

Every time Jake had received one of her letters, he knew he should burn it, unopened. But he had read every one, more than once.

I love you so much, darling.

Once he had loved her. He wondered if somewhere inside himself, he still did.

Still watching her, his pulse too fast, his breathing not quite steady, he pushed himself off the pillar and followed her.

The only reason Jake had stayed at the ball so long was to annoy Suzanne and anger her. Even though he had asked her for a divorce once long ago, even though, shortly after, he had been forced to flee New York, leaving her and their daughter behind, even though he was legally dead, the truth of the matter was that she was still his wife because he was very much alive.

Like any man, no matter what his feelings really were for her, every time he thought about her with Benjamin, he felt a surge of rage.

She claimed that she loved him. Did she love him when her current husband made love to her? Did she? Jake could tell himself that he did not give a damn, could hope fervently that it was true, but he knew damn well that she did not cry out his name when she slept with Benjamin Ralston.

He paused outside a pair of heavy walnut doors, which she had left ajar. He hesitated, his instincts telling him to turn and go back, then shoved through them. Suzanne stood inside the room, her back to the door, as still as a classical Greek statue. And, despite it all, despite the past, as lovely.

Once, Jake had worshiped her beauty. Once, he had loved her completely. She had been everything he was not, everything a man like him dreamed of having in a woman. She had been beautiful, elegant, aristocratic, and wealthy. Because he was a common Irishman and she was high society, she should have been unattainable—yet he'd married her, and she had given him his precious child.

Since then, there had been so many betrayals and so much anger, so much disillusionment and so much sorrow. For both of them. He could not forgive her her many lovers when they were wed, but perhaps most of all, he could not forgive her marrying Benjamin Ralston within weeks of learning that he was dead.

Sometimes in the dead of night, alone with a bottle of Irish whiskey, Jake wondered what would have happened if she had not remarried, if he had succeeded in contacting her, if she had met him in Australia with Sofie as he had planned while in prison before escaping. He dreamed of a simple life, one in which he worked hard with his hands in order to provide the basic necessities for his family. He dreamed of love and laughter and undying passion.

It was nonsense. When sober, he knew that for a fact. Suzanne had hated him when they were newlyweds for taking her away from high society. How could he have ever dreamed that she would be happy as a farmer's wife in the Australian outback?

Now she had what she'd wanted to begin with, a place in high society, a wealthy, blue-blooded husband, riches and respectability. Jake stared. He only half believed her claims of undying love. He only half believed she would throw it all away for a common Irishman like himself.

Purposefully, yet with some regret, he kept his distance from her. "What is it you want to discuss? What is so important?"

Suzanne wet her lips. "Sofie."

Jake stared. "What's wrong?"

Suzanne swallowed. "Jake—everything's wrong. Sofie is ruining her life, and I cannot make her see reason! I am so afraid. To make matters worse—" and suddenly genuine tears spilled down her cheeks "—she has left home. I thought she would come back—but she hates me. Jake!"

He strode forward and gripped her arms, shaking her. "What the hell do you mean, she has left home?"

"Exactly that!" Suzanne cried. "She rushed out of the house—I don't even know where she is living!"

He shook her again. "Why? What did you do? I know that this is your fault!"

Suzanne stiffened. "Damn you! It is not my fault! I only want the best for her, and I have encouraged her to do what's right." She jerked free of his hold. Their gazes locked. "I want her to give up her illegitimate daughter to a wonderful couple for adoption."

All the color left Jake's face. "*What?!*"

"Sofie had a baby. In France. She thinks to remain unwed and to keep the child. Of course, she can do no such thing and we both know it. Already the entire household has learned the truth—but no one will spread any gossip, I can assure you of that, because I will destroy *anyone* who dares to besmirch my daughter."

Jake clung to the back of a chair to remain upright. His face was a mask of shock. "I didn't know. I didn't know."

"How could you? You cannot expect to keep abreast of our lives while living in seclusion and anonymity in the Irish countryside!"

Jake lifted his head, some of the shock fading. "The father. Who is he?" he snarled.

Suzanne hesitated.

"Tell me, damn you!" he roared. He reached Suzanne in two strides and lifted her off the floor. Then his eyes widened. "It's Delanza, isn't it? Isn't it?" he shouted, shaking her again.

Suzanne nodded, her eyes filling with tears.

"Goddamn it," Jake shouted. He set her down abruptly. "Forget adoption, Suzanne. That bastard is going to marry Sofie, and there's no two ways about it."

Suzanne was white, shaking her head. "No."

Jake's smile was ugly. "Yes," he said. "Yes."

25

Sofie finally regained some of her composure and moved away from where she had been hiding behind one of the pillars beside the terrace doors. She knew that Edward was watching her from across the room. It had not been easy to convince him that she must take her leave of Henry alone.

And now she must find Henry. Sofie walked rapidly along the edge of the ballroom, the terrace on her right, hoping to avoid any and all social encounters, still more shaken than she would like to admit from all that had transpired outside. Edward's open animosity and his angry yet thoroughly arousing kiss were more than enough to distress her, but his question about her relationship with Henry was unforgivable.

Sofie scanned the festive crowd, but did not see Henry anywhere. She was afraid that his feelings were wounded by Edward's abrupt appearance and by the way Edward had proprietarily dragged her from Henry's side. And Henry would be wounded yet again when she told him that Edward insisted on being taken to Edana right now.

Tense, Sofie glanced towards the entrance to the ballroom, where she had last seen Edward, but he was gone. Starting, she glanced uneasily around her, expecting him to be lurking behind her in the shadows of tall, potted ferns. He was not.

She had no time to wonder at his disappearance. She espied her mother entering the ballroom on the other side of the room. Sofie turned abruptly and fled outside onto the terrace. Her heart was pounding much too hard, her fists were clenched. Edward had instructed her to say all of her good-byes, but she had no intention of speaking with Suzanne again tonight. Perhaps not even ever.

She swallowed back the hard lump of anguish that had risen suddenly. Glowing lanterns illuminated the center of the sprawling, tiled terrace, which was empty and deserted, but the fringes were lit only by the full moon. Sofie hesitated, her pulse beginning to slow, inhaling the scent of evergreen, which was pungent and thick. She realized that she was shivering, and rightly so.

It was too cold to be standing outside without a cloak or a wrap. And soon Edward would come looking for her if she did not meet him in the foyer as she had promised that she would. She must go on about her business.

Sofie turned back towards the interior of the house. Her eyes widened. Not far from where she stood was Julian St. Clare. Undoubtedly he also thought this spot ideally secluded. For he was bent over a woman, kissing her passionately—a woman who had to be Lisa.

But recalling Lisa's anxiety, Sofie remained very still, watching the heated embrace.

The marquis straightened and said something, low and matter-of-fact. There was a blur of movement and the sound of a palm cracking over flesh. Then Lisa raced away from him and past Sofie, without ever noticing that she stood there.

But Sofie had seen Lisa well enough to know that she was in tears. Lifting her gown, forgetting all about Henry and Edward, Sofie raced after her.

Lisa ran through the ballroom, turning heads. Oblivious or too upset to care, she raced on up the stairs and into the central foyer. Sofie followed. "Lisa! Wait! It's me—Sofie!"

Lisa did not stop. Gown lifted high, exposing calf and ankle, she pounded up the stairs.

Sofie paused on the bottom of the stairs to catch her breath, gulping air, her ankle hurting from the mad race across the ballroom, determined to help her sister. Edward appeared at her side. "What's going on?"

"I don't know," she said, still panting. "Lisa is very upset. I must go to her." Her eyes flashed in a challenge that dared him to try to stop her.

Edward's jaw firmed. "I'm waiting right here. If you're not down in fifteen minutes, I'm coming up to get you."

Sofie lifted her chin. "I meant it when I said I was sorry for taking Edana from you. I have no intention of running away again."

His smile was bitter and full of mistrust. It wrenched at Sofie. Abruptly she turned and hurried up the stairs, wishing that she could undo the past— change it and make it perfect.

Outside Lisa's door, she paused, hearing a loud thump. There was another noise, an uneven bumping, as if an object were being dragged across the room. She could not imagine what Lisa was doing. Sofie tried the door even as she called out Lisa's name. But the door was locked. "Lisa?" She knocked sharply. "Please, it's Sofie; I want to help you."

And the door flew open abruptly. Lisa faced her, disheveled in appearance and clearly distraught. "Lisa! What's wrong?"

Lisa's hand shot out and she jerked Sofie into her room, shutting the door behind them and locking it.

And Sofie saw the valise on the bed—and the dresses and underclothes apparently just ripped from their hangers and drawers, strewn across the floor. "What happened?!"

Lisa gripped Sofie's shoulders. "Don't you dare stop me!" She cried, her face streaked with tears.

An inkling made Sofie freeze. "Lisa," she said unevenly, "do not do anything rash."

"I am running away!" Lisa cried, and then burst into tears again. Immediately she turned her back on Sofie and began wadding up clothing and shoving it into the valise.

Sofie took her arm, halting her and turning her so they faced each other. "Dear—what has happened?" she asked softly.

"I hate him," Lisa said, her bosom heaving. "I will *never* marry him—I am running away—and Sofie—you must help me!"

Sofie froze again. Then, carefully, she said, "Let's sit down and we can decide what you should do together."

"I already know what I must do. And I do not have time to chat!" Lisa cried hysterically. "I *refuse* to be sacrificed at the altar to the likes of him!"

"What makes you speak like that?" Sofie asked.

Lisa turned and buckled the valise. "Tonight I learned the truth. He *hates* women; it's well known in London. He hates *all* women. He is only marrying me because . . ." She looked at Sofie, her eyes welling with tears. "Because he is penniless, worse than penniless, absolutely destitute!"

Sofie patted Lisa's shoulders as she wept, then pulled her into her arms. "Who told you this?"

"I overheard Carmine and Hilary. In fact, the marquis overheard them, too. *He is so cold!* He did not bat an eye at hearing their ugly words, did not offer a single explanation; indeed, he appeared to be waiting for me to say something!"

"And did you?"

"I asked him if it was true."

Sofie waited.

Lisa wiped more tears with the back of her hand. "He said, 'Yes,' just like that, one word, 'yes,' not an explanation, no words of love, just 'yes,' cold and hateful—and then he dragged me outside and kissed me and told me I would not mind being married to him and we both knew it. How I hate him!"

Sofie embraced Lisa again, almost as angry as her stepsister. Although it was a fact of life that Lisa was an heiress and that a part of her allure was her dowry, no woman deserved such cold, callous, disrespectful treatment. Especially not Lisa.

"I am a fool," Lisa said. "For some reason, because so many men like me, I expected Julian to like me too—at the very least." Her face crumpled and she sobbed into her hands.

Too well Sofie knew what Lisa was feeling. But she felt obliged to be the voice of reason. "You should talk to your father in the morning. It would be better if Benjamin called it off, Lisa. Running away will ruin your other prospects."

"Father is enamored of the marquis!" Lisa cried. "He arranged this—he is thrilled to marry me off to a blue-blooded aristocrat. He will be calm and reasonable and he will do his best to convince me that I am being irrational." Lisa swallowed. "You know I have never disobeyed my father. I cannot go to him now, Sofie. I am afraid he will convince me to marry that brute." Lisa wiped her eyes. "Please help me get this horrid gown off!"

Torn with wanting to help Lisa and knowing that running away was not proper or correct, yet fully aware that she herself had run away from her own problems, not once but twice, Sofie unbuttoned the gown and helped Lisa step out of it. "I am afraid of what will happen when your disappearance is remarked."

Lisa stepped into a navy blue silk skirt boldly striped with red, and laughed wildly. "I will humiliate the marquis so thoroughly that he will never even consider trying to wed me afterwards." She shrugged on the matching waist-length jacket, buttoning it up swiftly.

Sofie watched her stepsister. Even with swollen eyes and a red nose, prepared to run away from her fiancé, she was stunning and elegant, dainty and perfect. The marquis must hate women, Sofie thought. What other explanation could there be for his dislike of Lisa, who was not only beautiful, but sweet and generous of nature? Lisa, who had never hurt anyone or anything purposefully, who should have been thoroughly spoiled, yet somehow was not. Yet Sofie sensed that hatred was no simple thing, that it was connected to his dark past—and to his dead first wife. "He will be humiliated, have no fear. Unless ice runs in his veins," Sofie said quietly. "Where will you go?"

Lisa laughed, exultant. "To Newport! No one is there in the fall, no one, and I will break a window to get into the house. The pantry is always full of food—I will not starve. I will stay there until he has engaged himself to someone else or has returned to London. Oh, Sofie! It is the perfect hiding place, is it not? No one will think to look for me there."

Sofie had to agree. Yet she could not shake her unease. What if Julian St. Clare did have ice in his veins? She did not like the thought.

Lisa bent and retrieved her bag. "Now my only problem is to escape the house unseen."

"How are you going to do that?" Sofie asked.

Lisa smiled grimly. "I am going to climb out the window and down the tree."

Sofie froze. "Lisa! It's far too dangerous! You've never climbed a tree in your life!"

"I have no choice, Sofie. This is the only way. I cannot possibly leave through the front door—or even the back door, not tonight."

Both girls walked to the window and peered outside. They were on the third story. Sofie could not imagine how Lisa would manage. Sofie was very afraid that Lisa would break her neck. "Please be careful," she pleaded.

"I will," Lisa said, a quaver giving away her fear. She sat on the windowsill and cautiously swung her legs over. She looked at Sofie. "You are my dearest friend," she said softly. "And I love you as if you were my real sister. And one day you will forgive me for interfering in *your* life." With that enigmatic statement, Lisa smiled briefly, and then she disappeared.

Sofie screamed, then clapped a hand over her mouth when she saw that Lisa had managed to pull herself onto the nearest branch of the oak tree. Lisa's smile flashed bravely, and then she shifted slowly around, muttering "blast it" a few times, and finally began to inch her way down the tree. Sofie watched her progress with her heart in her mouth. Finally Lisa was hanging onto the lowest limb with both hands, suspended in the air. Sofie gripped the sill as she jumped. She landed on her feet and collapsed.

"Lisa!" Sofie whispered urgently. "Lisa! Are you all right?"

Lisa sat up slowly, rubbing her hip. Finally she looked up and waved. "Yes! I think I'm intact!" Slowly she stood, then retrieved her valise. She glanced up one last time and blew a kiss. Then she turned and ran across the lawn, down the end of the driveway, slipped through the front gates and onto Fifth Avenue, and was gone.

Sofie leaned against the window, trembling with relief. Dear God, she had done it, Lisa had run away. She stood there for a full five minutes, recovering her composure. Then she hurried across the room, locked the door from the inside, and slipped out. As the door shut, she heard the lock click loudly.

She could not smile, she could not feel any satisfaction with the many twists and turns the evening had taken. Lisa was giving back as good as she had gotten. The marquis was about to suffer a serious let-down, one he richly deserved. But Sofie had the disturbing feeling that he would not slink back to England with his tail between his legs.

Then she thought of her own ill-fated love, and her lips tightened. Edward was waiting for her downstairs. In fact, if she delayed any longer, in another moment he would be coming up to find her.

As Sofie traversed the corridor, she recalled Lisa's parting words. What had Lisa done to interfere in her life? How obvious the answer suddenly was! It was Lisa who had summoned Edward to the ball, who had alerted him to the fact that Sofie would be attending. No one else had known she intended to come except for Lisa—there was no other explanation for his timely appearance. Sofie did not know whether to laugh or cry.

"You are staying here?"

Sofie was regretting the fact that she had agreed to take Edward to see Edana tonight. In another hour or so it would be midnight. They had left the engagement party some time ago; it had been a long drive from the upper East Side to the docks downtown. Sofie had never said good-bye to Henry, whom she had been unable to find.

Now she sat in his Daimler, wrapped in her borrowed black velvet cloak, acutely conscious of the man beside her. Not only did she love him, she desired him in the most shocking, thorough manner. Little bits and pieces of the past they had shared taunted and teased her. Glorious moments, like that day at Delmonico's, or like his so very recent kiss. And most of all, she did not trust him—she was afraid of what he might do next.

"Christ," Edward cursed. "This is no place for a lady; dammit, Sofie, all sorts of riffraff loiter on the wharves."

As if to prove the veracity of his comment, the silent night was broken by the drunken singing of a group of men. Sofie tensed as several sailors, arm in arm, came into view stumbling down the dirt street towards them. "I am short of funds," she said huskily. "What would you have me do, Edward?"

He turned to face her. "Did Suzanne cut you off, Sofie?"

She blinked.

"Because you refused to give Edana up for adoption?"

She gasped. "You know!"

"I know."

Tears filled her eyes. It was hard not to reach out and grab his hands and cling to them like a lifeline. "Yes."

His jaw flexed. "You don't have to worry anymore. Not about that—not about anything."

Sofie closed her eyes, sinking back against the seat. How stupid she had been. Edward loved his child—he would support Edana, and undoubtedly Sofie as well. She should have realized that he was her salvation in this instance. It was very hard not to be overwhelmed with gratitude. It was very hard to want to resist this man. "Thank you."

Edward said nothing, sliding out of the car and helping Sofie out, too. He held her arm firmly, guiding her over the rutted road and then across the uneven planking of the boardinghouse's dilapidated front porch. Sofie extracted the key she had been given. Edward took it from her and opened the front door. Unfortunately, Sofie felt that they were acting very much as any married couple would. Except that married couples did not reside in rotting boardinghouses on the docks of the East River. If they were a married couple, he would be opening the door for her to a very different kind of house.

And Sofie knew that there would not be the stiff tension that simmered palpably between them. A tension born of mistrust, betrayal, and hurt, on both their parts. A tension that was also hungry and sexual.

He had said that his rough desire was due to her dress, but her dress wasn't visible now, and Sofie knew he was still as aware of her as she was of him. She derived some small amount of satisfaction from the thought. Somehow, in the past year and a half, a transformation had taken place. Very much like an ugly duckling turning into a swan, the crippled child had become a seductive woman.

And not only for Edward. It was somewhat amazing, but Sofie was jolted by the realization that Georges Fraggard had also found her desirable, as did Henry Marten. Two years ago Sofie would have ridiculed the very notion of any man—much less three men—finding her enticing. And perhaps even more important, two of those three men had confessed to loving her, as well.

Sofie knew it was dangerous to dwell on these kinds of thoughts, for already angry sorrow was trying to root in her heart. She focused on seeing through the house's dimly lit shadows. The stairs creaked as they went up. She opened the door to her room and slipped inside. Edana slept in her makeshift cradle, made from a milkman's crate. Sofie bent over her to fix the small bedcovering. It was horrid that Edward should see his daughter this way, in a wretched, shabby room, asleep in a wooden box, covered with Rachelle's red wool shawl.

She tensed when he came to stand beside her. Unable to restrain herself, Sofie glanced up at him. Edward stared down at his daughter, his expression close to tears, the tip of his nose red. "I thought I had lost her," he said harshly. "I was afraid you had taken her away and I would never be able to find either one of you again."

Sofie hated herself for what she had done. "Oh, Edward, what I did was wrong, terribly wrong—please forgive me!"

His gaze met hers, somber and searching. Sofie held her hands to stop herself from touching him. He had been anguished because of what she had done, and her instinct was to comfort him. But to touch him invited disaster. Sofie knew she could not resist the temptation he offered as a man.

They stood staring at each other for a timeless interval. Something passed between them, something strong and potent. Some kind of timeless bond, already forged, became recognizable. In that instant, Sofie knew that Edana would bind Edward to her in one way or another forever. She was glad— fiercely so.

Edward's mouth tensed. His body shifted towards her.

"*Chèrie*, you are home too early!" Rachelle said. "Oh!"

Sofie inhaled, trembling, almost certain that, had Rachelle not appeared in the doorway between their adjoining rooms, Edward would have kissed her. She stepped away from him, hugging herself, telling herself that this was for the best. She must not get involved with him, she must not. She must not let her heart lead her astray. She could not withstand the hurt a second time around.

"*Pardonnez-moi*," Rachel murmured, her gaze flying between the two of them.

"You have interrupted nothing," Sofie declared, a bit too loudly and much too emphatically. "Rachelle, you remember Edward."

Rachelle nodded. Edward's glance flicked over her, and Sofie realized with a start that he did not like her dear friend. In Paris she had assumed that he found her attractive, as all men did. "*Bien sûr*," Rachelle murmured. "*Enchantée, monsieur.*"

Edward nodded curtly, and he turned to Sofie. "You can't stay here."

She started. "What?"

"You cannot possibly stay here. I cannot allow Edana to be raised in this kind of environment. Don't tell me that you *wish* to stay here, Sofie?"

She was frightened, wary—hopeful. "What are you suggesting?"

"We will let you a suite at the Savoy until a more suitable arrangement is found," Edward said flatly.

Sofie nodded slowly. "All right."

"Pack up whatever you have now. There's no point in waiting until tomorrow to get all of you out of this rat infested hellhole."

Sofie had only been at the Savoy once before, when she had deliberately thrown herself at Edward in the hope of becoming his paramour. She had not paid any attention to her surroundings then. But now she, Rachelle, and Edana, who slept in Sofie's arms, stood in the wide-open lobby of the hotel, watching Edward as he checked them in at the front desk.

It was after midnight, and the lobby was shockingly quiet. No one else was present except for the hotel staff, which relieved Sofie. Coming here like this was making her feel uneasy, and very much like a fallen woman. At any moment she expected the hotel staff to lift their heads and stare and point accusingly at her.

Edward turned and strode to them. Sofie's heart danced a little as he approached. It was impossible not to be affected by such a man. And clad as he was in his black tuxedo, he was stunningly elegant. But especially now, when he had rescued her so heroically and when she was exhausted beyond words from the strain of the past week and at her most vulnerable, did she find him almost larger than life. "I am afraid that there are no more suites available," Edward announced.

Sofie tried to hide her dismay. "We can manage with a room, Edward."

"Forget it. You can have my suite. I've already taken a single room for myself."

"Edward."

"Shh. You will not change my mind, it is made up." And for the first time that evening, his mouth quirked, revealing his dimples ever so slightly. His eyes, holding hers, were suddenly warm. It was the man she had known and loved so thoroughly almost two years ago.

Sofie ducked her head, cuddling Edana. The four of them piled into the brass-doored elevator. A few minutes later they alighted on the fifth floor. Edward threw open the door to the suite that had previously been his. "Fortunately there are two bedrooms. I was using the smaller one as an office, but tomorrow I will come and remove all of my things. Sofie, the master bedroom is directly ahead."

Although Sofie had come to this hotel in search of him once before, he had not allowed her inside his suite. She was quite certain that this was the same set of rooms. Very curious, and very awed, she glanced around.

She stood in a circular foyer. The floors were beige marble, the walls painted in a trompe l'oeil, and it appeared as if one were looking into a huge and sumptuous salon. But the real salon was directly ahead. Blue Oriental rugs covered more beige and white marble floors. There were two seating areas, one with chintz sofas, another with a red damask love seat and a pair of red and beige striped bergères. A floor-to-ceiling mahogany breakfront covered one wall. Opposite it was a marble-manteled fireplace. Red damask draperies covered the windows overlooking Central Park, and some very nice eighteenth- and nineteenth-century French and English works of art hung on the walls.

There was a dining area to the left which could seat eight, a small kitchen just behind it. Also on the left was the second bedroom Edward used as his office. Sofie could see that he had already been working at the small escritoire there, where papers cluttered the leather writing surface.

He took her arm, guiding her across the salon. Sofie ignored the heat of his hand, and when his thigh brushed against her taffeta skirts, she vowed that she did not care.

They paused on the threshold of the master bedroom. His room. Sofie looked at the oversize, canopied bed and realized that he had slept there last night, and the night before that as well. The bed had been made up since then, of course, and now the yellow silk covers were turned down, revealing darker gold sheets beneath. It was shameless, but Sofie wondered if he had slept there with another woman. She despised the very thought.

He had released her arm. The moment was too intimate for Sofie. It was difficult enough to be taking over his suite, his bedroom, his bed. He should have known better than to escort her within. Sofie looked for a place for Edana to sleep. She knew her cheeks were heated.

He said, "I have asked that a cradle be sent up. It should arrive immediately."

How had he guessed her thoughts? Sofie was afraid to meet his eyes. She moved to the bed and laid Edana down in the center of it, but did not dare sit down beside her, afraid he might think it an invitation of sorts. She stroked the silk counterpane, her back to him. "Perhaps you had better leave before the cradle arrives," she said, trying not to think about all the ramifications of being in a public hotel with her daughter—and taking over Edward's suite. Trying not to think about the ramifications of Edward having entered her life once again.

She was too tired. Tomorrow she would unscramble her thoughts—and her feelings.

"All right." Edward nodded, hesitant. Then he moved swiftly forward. Sofie froze, but he bent over Edana, not her, and brushed his mouth to the baby's temple. He straightened, locked gazes with her. Sofie could not move.

"Good night." He bowed slightly, politely, formally. Then he spun on his heel and crossed the room. Sofie clutched the silk bedcovering, watching him cross the salon. A moment later he had entered the foyer and was lost from view. She heard the front door open, and close. With a ragged sigh, she lay down beside her daughter.

"What am I going to do now?" she whispered to herself.

Rachelle had taken Edana after her dawn feeding, as was customary. Sofie had fallen back to sleep immediately. Never had she slept as deeply, as dreamlessly, as she did in those few hours after sunrise. Now she awoke gradually. She became aware of the sunlight streaming through the bedroom's windows. Briefly she was confused, certain that the drapes had been drawn when she went to sleep last night.

Then Sofie realized where she was. She was not at the waterfront rooming house. She was at the luxurious Savoy Hotel—in Edward's suite—in his luxurious bed. She snuggled more deeply under the plush down-quilted covers. For the first time in a long time she felt safe, secure, almost free of worry. It was a tremendous relief not to awake to fear.

Sofie turned over. The sheets beneath her bare cheek, her bare arms and legs, were smooth satin and faintly erotic. Sofie sighed. Last night Edward had charged into her life the way a knight in shining armor might in a fairy tale, rescuing her the way beautiful damsels were rescued, in a moment of great distress. Something fluttered more insistently low in Sofie's abdomen, muscles knotted more tightly in her thighs. Desire. Fierce and burning bright.

She turned again, this time onto her back, shoving the covers down to her waist. This was not the first time that she had awakened to throbbing need and fanciful thoughts of Edward. But it was the first time she had awakened to such thoughts while in satin sheets in his bed, and she was more undressed than dressed, having been too tired last night to exchange her worn shift for a full-length flannel nightgown. Fully awake now, she wondered why she was not ashamed of what her body was feeling, why she had never been ashamed of the desire he had taught her once so long ago. Perhaps it was because when they had made love that one single time, it had seemed exactly like that, like making love. It had been wonderful, not dirty or lewd or unclean. But it *had* been so very long ago. She wondered how she would resist temptation, how she would resist him.

Shivering slightly, Sofie sat up. Her hair was loose instead of in its usual nightly braid, and she shoved the wild mass back and off her shoulders. She flung the covers off her legs and slipped to the floor. Two paces later, her steps slowed.

Suddenly she froze. Afraid that she was being watched.

Her heart skidding, Sofie turned slowly, and froze yet again.

Edward stood in the doorway, regarding her intently.

She could not move. Sofie became utterly still, except for the fierce, wild beating of her heart.

His gaze was blue smoke. His eyes were as piercing as a hunting hawk's.

Sofie felt panic bubble up in her breast. For the dark gleam in his gaze left her in no doubt as to the nature of his thoughts.

And she realized exactly how she looked. Her hair was loose but as tangled as a bird's nest. She wore only a thin, threadbare, thigh-length chemise. She was naked beneath it. She looked as wanton as her body was feeling—she was sure of it.

She told herself to move, to run. He had the look of a predator about him. But her legs refused to obey her mind—which was functioning only halfheartedly.

She met his gaze. As she had feared, he was looking through her undergarment—and down her slim white legs and at her breasts, which were hardly contained by the chemise. His hungry blue eyes moved to her mouth.

Sofie came to life. She jerked the entire yellow silk bedspread off the bed and wrapped herself in it. "What are you doing in here?" she asked hoarsely.

"Enjoying the best view in Manhattan." Without another word he whirled and stalked from the room.

Sofie stared after him, shaking with hot, liquid desire, and with a curious mixture of both disappointment and relief. And she was furious. Furious with him—furious with herself—and most of all, furious with Life.

She rushed into the master bath, throwing the bedspread down. She snatched the long paisley robe from the hook where it hung on the door, pulled it on. Too late, she realized it was a man's robe—that it was his. His scent was unmistakable. Gritting her teeth, acutely aware of the silk teasing her mostly bare skin, she ran out of the bedroom. In the salon she skidded to a stop.

Edward stood staring out the window at Central Park, his back to her. Behind him, the oval dining room table was set with a breakfast that could feed a king. No—four kings. Tantalizing smells came from several covered platters that undoubtedly hid bacon, eggs, sausages, and steaks. Cold platters of smoked salmon and whitefish, of hams and cheeses, of various fruits and baskets of pastries, covered every other available inch of space. Except for the two china and silver place settings. And Edana and Rachelle were nowhere in sight.

Sofie found her voice. "Where is Edana?"

"I told Rachelle to take her to the park."

She bristled. "You what?"

He turned to face her and repeated what he had said.

"And Rachelle left me here alone, asleep, with you?!"

He stared at her. "It's my suite."

She inhaled. "Is that the way it's going to be?"

His gaze was unfathomable now. "My room is barely big enough to hold a bed, and I certainly did not feel like having my breakfast there. I thought you'd be hungry, too. I've been waiting for over an hour for you to wake up. I finally decided to see if you were even alive. It's not my fault you were sleeping in a wisp of cotton that hides absolutely nothing."

She folded her arms across her breasts, quite certain he was remembering how she had looked in her ancient, threadbare chemise. "I can assure you," she said acidly, "if I had known you would come into my bedroom, I would have worn a monk's robes."

His eyes narrowed. "Really?"

She did not like the interest she saw there, for somehow, she had kindled it anew. Or it had never died, and he failed to hide it now. She stepped backwards. "Yes."

"How quickly we forget last night," he murmured. "You still have that scrap of cotton on?"

Sofie began to move steadily backwards. "Edward, it was very thoughtful of you to order breakfast, and of course, I understand that you would rather eat here than in your room. You have every right to take your meals here! I will go and get dressed. You may start without me."

His smile flashed. It was one hundred percent wicked, the dimples deep and damnably attractive. "Somehow what I ordered just doesn't seem appetizing anymore."

Sofie turned to flee, but Edward's hand clamped on her shoulder and he spun her back around. Sofie found herself an inch away from being in his arms. "You look good enough to eat," he said softly as he pulled her slowly forward.

Sofie stiffened, finding it difficult to breathe, to think. She whimpered as his hands slid over her back and down her backside. "I have no intention of being your breakfast," she whispered.

"Why not?" he whispered, his mouth very close to hers. Sofie whimpered again as he pressed forward until their loins touched. He was erect, hot and huge and quiveringly erect. "Why the hell not?" he whispered against her mouth.

Sofie tried to find words, tried to think of why she should not make love with him. Her heart, she finally remembered. She was trying to protect her heart. "Don't, Edward. Please."

But he ignored her. "I'm going to kiss you," he murmured, leaning over her, "and we *both* know you're going to like it."

26

S ofie shook her head in denial. Their gazes fused. She heard herself
whimper when he slowly slid his arm around her, pulling her up even
more firmly against his body. She pressed her hands against his chest, but it
was only a feeble gesture—she could not make herself push away from him
with any real effort.

If only she did not love this man. Then maybe she would not want to melt
into his body so badly. Then maybe there would not be the burning red-hot
urgency, the sheer, insane desire.

Edward's mouth brushed hers. It was a deliberately teasing action, and
Sofie gasped. "You feel the way I do," he said, the sound undisguised, raw
in both lust and triumph. His eyes blazed. "I can see it in your eyes—feel it
in your body."

"No!" Sofie managed to lie, frantic now, for she knew he was going to
kiss her, just as she knew he was expertly seducing her, and that wounded
part of her was terrified. He would hurt her again—and she could not possibly
survive another blow from him.

"Yes," he whispered, smiling slightly and slowly rubbing his hardened
loins against her. His hands moved up her rib cage, over the silk robe,
cupping her aching, swollen breasts. "Oh, God, Sofie."

And Sofie knew that he was thinking, as she was, about what it would be
like when he pushed his way deep inside her. She felt faint, even dizzy. She
was acutely aware of the hot, rigid muscle pulsing against her moist, clefted
flesh. Acutely aware of his fingers plucking her enlarged nipples through both
cotton and silk, and of his warm, uneven breath feathering her lips.

Sofie moaned.

Edward made a harsh sound and bent her over backwards. His mouth
covered hers.

And then there was nothing in existence except for his mouth on hers and
his hard body shuddering against her. Sofie gave up. She opened, she clung.
Instantly the kiss changed, became a greedy, devouring monster.

Sofie kissed him back, licking his lips. She nipped him, he sucked her. Her hands slid down and gripped his high, hard buttocks. She fought with and conquered his tongue. He massaged and molded her breasts with increasing urgency until her warm milk began to flow.

Sofie cried out, aware of her need for him growing into something insatiable and overpowering. Her hands slid to his hips, holding him firmly against her throbbing sex. Edward ripped open robe and chemise, the worn shift tearing with hardly a sound. Sofie gasped in exultant pleasure when his lips claimed one of her taut, aching nipples. Sobbing, she threw back her head as he suckled.

And then she could stand it no more. Desire exploded inside Sofie and became madness. Her hands slid over the massive bulge behind the fly of his trousers. Shaking, frantic, determined, she followed his shape and molded his form. Edward gasped, tearing his mouth from her breast. An instant later she was in his arms and he was running into the master bedroom. He kicked the door closed. Still carrying her, he moved onto the bed, coming down on top of her.

And nothing mattered except this. Sofie spread her knees and hooked her ankles around his hips. Edward ripped open his fly. For one shocking instant they looked into each other's eyes. Then he was on her, impaling her fully.

Sofie clung to his shoulders, rocking her hips wildly, crying, "Yes, Edward, yes!" Her nails dug into his back. For a moment he had frozen, but now he responded to her frantic urging and began to move hard and fast. Sofie had one coherent thought—she loved this man, she always would. An instant later she was swept upwards into a spiraling, red-hot, maniacal vortex, and she shattered in mindless ecstasy.

When she opened her eyes, panting uncontrollably, she met Edward's wide, wild gaze. He was not moving, but he was still full and hard inside her. When their gazes met, something fierce flared in his. Instantly Edward's mouth came down on hers for a long, intimate kiss. His raised his head, looked her piercingly in the eye. "Sofie."

And then he began to stroke her, harder and faster now than before. Despite having just reached a stunning peak, Sofie's blood surged yet again. Edward wrapped his arms around her, sinking deep one last time. He cried out, shuddering, his face buried in the hollow of her neck and shoulder.

Sofie slid her hand down his back, closing her eyes, exulting in the feel of him. Her heart still beat like a wild, trapped bird, and his pounded even more forcefully against her breast. Sofie did not want to think. She pressed her cheek to his. Being with him like this was bittersweet.

Edward stirred. Sofie dared not move, afraid of what might happen next. Dear God, they were strangers now. What had happened should have never been—yet it had been so right. What would they say to each other now? Hello? Good-bye? That was very nice, thank you?

She blinked back hot tears.

Edward shifted onto his side, keeping one strong arm around her, so that she was nestled against his side. Sofie was afraid to look at him, but was relieved he had not pushed her away. She tensed when his hand stroked over her shoulder and down her arm. A moment later she felt him exploring her waist, her abdomen.

She could not avoid him for much longer and she opened her eyes, looking up at his face. She did not know what she expected to see, perhaps insolent male arrogance, but he was very solemn, almost grim. She was stricken. Did he regret their encounter?

She could handle almost anything, the past two years had proved that— but not his regret for such splendid, abandoned passion.

"I didn't come here for this," Edward said.

Sofie choked. Before, she wouldn't have believed him, but now, looking into his eyes, she did.

"It just happened," Edward said, his hand lying still and motionless on her stomach. "I won't apologize."

Sofie stared at his large, tanned hand, sprawled on her white, flat belly just below her navel, only inches from the nest of hair that shielded her femininity. Sofie extricated herself from his arm and sat up, pulling his robe closed around her. "I d-didn't ask for an apology."

A muscle in Edward's cheek flexed. He also sat up, shoving his shirt into his trousers and buttoning his fly. "It's very good between us, Sofie."

She averted her gaze, trying not to be hurt by his words, certain he did not mean to hurt her now. But she would have never categorized their lovemaking as "very good." Superb, glorious, unforgettable, yes, but not "very good." He seemed to expect a response, so she murmured, "Yes."

"Why are you so skinny?"

She blinked. "What?"

"You've had a child. But you're thinner than you were when we met. You don't eat, do you?"

She was stiff with wariness. She chose her words with care. "It is not easy, right now. I never get a full night's sleep—a child is a lot of work, even with Rachelle's help. And . . . I have been worried. I have not had an appetite."

His gaze darkened. "But you're nursing Edana."

She flushed, thinking not about Edana, but about how Edward had suckled her breasts. "Of course."

Edward slid from the bed, hands in his pockets, his back to her. He stared out the window. Outside, it had started to snow. "There's no need for you to worry anymore, you know that."

Sofie wished that she could see his face. "What are you saying, Edward?"

He turned, fierce. "Edana is my daughter. You are her mother. That gives me certain rights. Supporting her—and you—is one of them."

She swallowed, aching for his love. "And is using my body another one of them?"

He jerked. "Honey, you used me as much as I used you!"

Sofie folded her arms, incapable of responding.

But Edward was angry now, and not to be stopped. "I don't think I've ever been with such a hot, eager woman."

Sofie pursed her mouth. What could she say? That the lust she felt for him was fueled by the love she felt for him? That she would probably grow old and gray still aching for him?

Edward's gaze lurched down to her heaving breasts. "No—I know I've never been with such a hot woman before."

"Stop it."

"You've had good teachers, Sofie."

"You were my teacher."

He laughed. "That was a long time ago. You were a virgin then, not a seductress."

"Stop it. Please."

"Why? Because the truth is ugly? Because you can't reconcile it with your proper facade?" His eyes blazed. "Does Henry know how hot you are? Does he know firsthand?"

"Stop it!" Sofie screamed.

"No!" Edward shouted back. Sofie froze. "No!" He shouted again, and his hand lashed out, sweeping every single item on the bureau beside him to the floor. Glass bottles and porcelain bowls broke and shattered.

Sofie gripped the bedding, beginning to shake with fear.

Edward paced towards her, explosive rage in his every stride, then halted. "Are you going to see him tonight?" he snarled.

She stared at him, too frightened to respond.

"Are you?" he shouted, livid.

"No," Sofie whispered. "I mean, I don't know."

"You don't know!" He turned and sent his fist into a beautiful blue and white Oriental lamp and sent it crashing to the floor.

Sofie inched back against the headboard of the bed.

"Are you going to marry him?" he roared.

Sofie knew better than to answer him. Tears streamed down her face.

Edward cursed. He slammed to the bureau and pulled out one of the drawers so hard that it crashed to the floor. He straightened, holding a square blue velvet box, then kicked the drawer out of his way. He approached Sofie, throwing the box at her. It hit her knees. "Open it!"

She looked at the box, lying by her feet, afraid to touch it, afraid of what she would see.

"Open it, damn you!" he roared.

Whimpering, Sofie knelt and reached for the box. Her heart turned over hard. Inside was a pair of magnificent chandelier earrings, the stones diamonds, worth a fortune by itself. But also inside was a triple-tiered matching necklace, and a diamond solitaire ring. The ring alone boasted a stone that was at least eight carats. It was an engagement ring.

"That's what I can give you," Edward said harshly.

Sofie blinked at him, helplessly holding the open box in her hands, not knowing what to do with it—or him.

"Isn't that enough for you?" His tone shot up again. "Isn't that what you want? Isn't that what all women want?" Edward shouted. "Or do you still want to marry Henry Marten?"

His face was flushed red with his rage. "I never said I wanted to marry Henry," she whispered, her voice almost inaudible.

But Edward was too furious to hear her. He strode to the wall, jerked a small painting—a beautiful David—from its hook, revealing a safe. His fingers twirled the lock. The iron door slammed open. He faced her, one hand fisted. "Still thinking about marrying Henry?" he asked. He flung the contents of his hand at her.

Sofie cried out in fear as she was bombarded with small, sharp objects. Then she realized that he had thrown diamonds at her—diamonds in all shapes and sizes, all cut and polished and afire—and now they lay scattered about the bed and in the folds of her robe, winking up at her.

"What's wrong, Sofie?" Edward shouted. "Damn you! Damn you! I'm not good enough—is that it? But doesn't this make me good enough?" He gestured at the sparkling bed. He gripped her robe and thrust a handful of silk and diamonds in her face, revealing the length of her naked thighs as he did so.

Sofie covered her face with her hands and sobbed.

Edward cursed. Sofie cried out when he dropped her robe, only to grip her shoulders far too hard, jerking her upright on the bed. They were nose to nose, eye to eye. Sofie had never seen anyone as angry as Edward.

"You are not marrying Henry Marten," he rasped. He released her abruptly and she fell back against the pillows in a boneless heap.

"Damn you," he said, and he left the room.

The front door of the suite slammed closed.

Sofie choked, curling up on her side, Edward's diamonds digging painfully into her hip and thigh. With a bitter, angry cry, she flung out her arm, sending more of the bright, hard stones flying to the floor. "Damn you," she whispered back hoarsely. "Damn you."

Edward stood waiting for the elevator, hands in his pockets, his jaws clamped hard together. Some of his rage was settling very much the way dust does after a windstorm, but it was by no means gone. It fluttered in his veins very much like dust motes riding a breeze.

Although he did regret his terrible loss of temper, he could not regret their lovemaking. Despite her bohemian past, Sofie could not have the experience that he had, so she would not know how extraordinary their union was. But he understood. He understood exactly why the passion they shared was unlike any other. For he had never made love to a woman whom he was head over heels in love with before—a woman he had missed body and soul for nearly two years.

Edward trembled again, this time less with anger than with anguish, hurt, and steel-edged determination. How could she be considering marriage to Henry Marten—while having unequivocally rejected his own suit? It was incomprehensible. It made him want to turn on his heel, stride down the corridor, bash her door in, and rip that suite apart before her very eyes— and then drag her by her hair to the nearest city judge.

Edward closed his eyes, fighting the new wave of red-hot rage that swept over him. He had never been this angry before. He was sane enough to know that his earlier display had been far more than childish—it had been unforgivable. But he had never been in love before, either. In fact, if he were not this angry, he might find the situation so ironic that it was amusing.

For the woman he loved had rejected his proposal not once but twice, and if that morning counted, three times. Not only that, she had carried and borne his baby girl without attempting to tell him until it was too late—so that he had not found out he had a daughter until many months after the fact. And now she was considering marriage to another man.

No, there was nothing to laugh about, nothing at all. It was too heartbreaking—this was a matter for tears. How could she have deceived him about Edana—and how could she have run away with her? How could she have refused him without even thinking about his offer? God—over the years he'd had hundreds of women hint to him that they would dearly love to become his wife! Glancing up at the dial, Edward saw that the elevator was only on the third floor. He cursed the elevator; he cursed her.

Perhaps he really did not know Sofie O'Neil. He would have never in his life dreamed that such behavior was possible from her. He had thought her to be honest and incapable of deceit or treachery. But he had never thought her capable of living like a bohemian, either, and he had witnessed that with his own two eyes. Edward trembled with jealousy, thinking about the Frenchman Georges, so clearly infatuated with her. Had he been the one to teach her to be so free with her passion? The elevator door finally opened and Edward stalked inside the wood-paneled box.

He told himself that the past no longer mattered. What mattered was that Sofie was the mother of his child, that he loved her, that he could make her love him—he was certain of it—and he was going to get her to the altar, one way or another. A few more days in his suite at the Savoy and she would be so thoroughly compromised that she would have no choice. And this time he was not about to trust her. Although he believed she regretted her deception about Edana and having run away from him in Paris, this time he would not take any chances. The stakes were too high. Emotions were running too hot, too wild. He knew he could not survive if he lost them both, forever. He would keep a close eye on her—to make sure she did not try to run away again, or worse, elope with Henry Marten.

Edward moved up the hall on the second floor, suddenly drained and tired. He had hardly slept last night. He had been so elated with having finally found Sofie and his daughter, and he had been so angry whenever he had thought about all that she had done or about her relationship with Henry Marten. And whenever he had remembered how she had looked in that sexy dress, or how her lips and body had felt beneath his, he had become wound up with a lust that threatened to derail his self-control. After all, he was acutely aware of the fact that she slept just a few floors above him in his suite, in his bed.

Now, his anger finally evaporating, a weariness as emotional as it was physical settled over him like a shroud.

Edward retrieved his key, then froze, instantly aware that the door of his hotel room was unlocked. He glanced at the floor. Sure enough, the thin matchstick that he had left inserted between door and jamb lay on the rug. Someone had been in his room—or was still inside.

In Africa Edward had always carried a concealed knife and a small gun. In New York he rarely did, and never during the day. Tensing, he pushed the door open, but did not walk inside. The single bed and two nightstands greeted his view.

Edward took one more step forward, not quite on the threshold. While doing so, he swung the door open even more. Now he could see the brocade wing chair by the window with the red-striped draperies, and the bureau and armoire on the other side of the room just opposite. Whoever was inside— if someone was indeed inside—was standing behind the open door or flat on the wall on its other side.

Edward chose to believe there was an intruder and that he stood behind the door. He kicked the door open as hard as he could, charging inside, expecting the intruder to scream in pain, expecting to hear bone cracking from impact with the heavy maple wood.

Instead, someone gripped him from behind from the other side of the doorway, spinning him powerfully around. Edward was ready to attack, but too late, he was the one being attacked. A shattering blow landed on his jaw, followed quickly by one to his abdomen. Edward grunted in pain and fell backwards against the bureau. Something crashed to the floor and shattered.

The next blow stunned Edward and white lights danced before his eyes.

"Fight back, you lousy prick, I want to enjoy this!"

Edward was being dragged upright. He was dazed, but he gripped the man's wrists in an effort to dislodge him. Unfortunately, his attacker was as tall as he, perhaps taller, and muscular and fit. But Edward was a very powerful man, and as they struggled, he finally managed to fling the assailant off him.

Instantly Edward crouched to attack. His vision was clearing. Edward saw that his attacker was the man who had hustled him in the hotel lobby those many months ago. As his attacker lurched to his feet, Edward had no time to think. He drew back his arm and landed a solid blow to the man's abdomen, which was as hard as a washboard. He hardly flinched.

"I'm going to take you apart and enjoy every minute of it," the man growled.

Edward blocked the man's next blow. He launched himself forward, pushing the older man back against the wall. They began to wrestle, each one relying on superior strength and weight to overcome the other. They were face-to-face, eye to eye. As Edward finally looked into the man's golden eyes, he said, "Who the hell are you?" But he knew.

The man relaxed ever so slightly, the two men locked in each other's grips, braced against one another, pound for pound and panting. "I am Sofie's father," he said, soft and dangerous. Savage satisfaction glittered in his eyes. "I'm finally getting my chance to make amends," he said. "And I am going to enjoy taking you apart, bone by bone and hair by hair. And *then* you're going to marry her."

Edward stared into his enraged eyes. "Jesus," he whispered. Jake O'Neil wasn't dead. He had suspected as much before and he had been right.

But relaxing was a mistake.

"Fight me!" Jake O'Neil roared, breaking free of Edward's loose grip. His fist shot out. Edward's head snapped back so hard that he heard a crack and he was propelled backwards across the room.

Jake grunted in satisfaction, diving after him.

Edward hit the floor, beginning to realize that the other man did not understand and that he had motivation to kill him. When Jake landed on top of him, Edward rolled. And Edward wound up on his feet, as quick as a jungle cat, poised now to defend himself from the other man—from Sofie's father.

"I'm not going to fight you," he gasped.

Slowly Jake got to his feet. The two men danced warily around each other like bareknuckle boxers. "I'm not giving you a choice."

Edward decided to get right to the point. "I love your daughter—I always have."

Jake barked with laughter.

"I've asked her to marry me two times—three times if you include this morning."

Jake paused. "I don't believe you."

Edward came down from the balls of his feet, although he remained ready to leap aside should Jake go after him yet again. "Obviously you know that she's the mother of my child."

"Yes."

"Did you know that she never told me about the child until a month ago? Did you know that I proposed to her two summers ago when I first took her innocence? Did you know that I proposed to her again when next we met— last month in Paris? Did you know that she not only refused, but that she ran away—taking my daughter with her?" By now Edward was unable to contain his own anger, his own anguish, or the bitterness in his heart. His fists fell to his sides, but they were clenched and they shook. "She's the one who should be turned upside down over your knee, O'Neil, and spanked like a bad child. She's the one who has denied me my rights as a father—denied me my child. She's the one considering marrying *another man*."

Jake's fists lowered, too. "You really are in love with her," he said, amazed.

"I'm going to marry her," Edward said, eyes blazing. "Even if it's against her will."

Jake studied him intently, wiping perspiration from his brow with one sleeve. "Why has she refused you? What did you do to make her run away?"

"Nothing!" Edward shouted. He struggled for calm. "Your daughter says she will not marry me because she does not love me. She prefers to live like a bohemian in Montmartre—taking lovers as she chooses, while studying art."

Jake stared. "I don't believe you."

"Then maybe you should go and ask her," Edward said tightly. His smile was dangerous now. Their roles of attacker and defender had been reversed. "But you can't do that, can you? Because you're dead."

Jake's shoulders squared. "That's right."

Edward stepped forward, his face contorted with new anger. "And just how right is that, Mr. O'Neil? Your daughter needs you—she always has. But you've never been there for her, you son of a bitch."

Jake stared, shadows flitting across his eyes. He said nothing, making no attempt to defend himself.

"Your disappearance from her life is inexcusable," Edward said harshly.

Jake's jaw flexed. "Who gave you the goddamn right to be judge and jury?"

"Loving Sofie gave me the right," Edward said fiercely.

Jake suddenly reached out and grabbed Edward's arm. "Maybe you're right." His eyes looked suspiciously moist. "Let's go and have a drink. I'm buying, and we're talking."

Edward looked into his haunted eyes and saw too many ghosts—and regrets—to count. "All right," he said more evenly. Then he smiled ever so slightly. "But I'll do the buying, Jake."

27

Sofie checked to make sure that Edana was sleeping peacefully. Then she moved to the window of the master bedroom, which overlooked Grand Army Plaza and Central Park. She stared out at the snow-carpeted square, at the oversize statue of the soldiers, at the horse-drawn carriages and heavily cloaked pedestrians on the snowy street below. Her heart was beating unsteadily and each stroke was painful.

Her eyes were red and swollen and she closed them, pierced with anguish. How could she continue to stay like this, in Edward's rooms? How could she function, living apart from him, yet having him enter her life at will—and perhaps even her bed? And his anger was so frightening. She could not blame him for being angry with her for running away from him with Edana. And she understood his jealousy of Henry, too—for it was coupled with fear. He was afraid to lose Edana to the other man. Sofie knew she must work hard to reassure him that she would never deny him Edana again. How sorry she was for doing so the first time.

The question burned. Had he made love to her in anger—or in real, honest, uncontrollable desire?

Sofie was afraid of the answer. She was afraid that only his anger had brought him to her. And she was afraid of herself. How could she yearn for more under the circumstances? She was so close to succumbing to his demands. If desire was a genuine bond between them, could she not marry him after all? For Edana, who needed a father? Forgoing love for Edana's sake? Accepting his body and his passion in its stead?

Sofie turned slightly at the sound of a knock on her door. Rachelle came into the bedroom, looking anxious and worried. "Sofie, your mother is here."

Sofie froze, then darted a wild glance at Edana's cradle. The baby slept blissfully. "Send her away," she hissed.

"She said she must speak with you. Sofie, she has been crying. Perhaps—"

Sofie stiffened her resolve. "I do not care."

And then Suzanne appeared in the doorway, behind Rachelle. Mother and daughter stared at each other, Sofie with frozen rage, Suzanne pale and distraught. "Please, Sofie," Suzanne said. "Please."

"Get out."

"Sofie! You are my child and—"

Sofie said, "If you do not leave, Mother, I will be forced to call for the hotel staff and ask them to escort you out."

Suzanne blanched.

Sofie refused to feel guilt, or anguish. But she was choking on painful emotions nonetheless.

Abruptly Suzanne whirled and ran out. She was sobbing.

Sofie collapsed on the gold floral love seat in front of the bed. Rachelle instantly came to her, taking her hands. "*Ma pauvre*. What can I do?"

Sofie shook her head. "Nothing. You cannot help, no one can." She felt the crush of heartbreak. It was undeniable.

Less than an hour later, Sofie found herself faced with more visitors. But this time it was Benjamin Ralston and the Marquis of Connaught.

The instant Sofie learned of their presence in the salon, her pulse rioted. She fought to take a deep breath. In the trauma engendered by all that had transpired since she had gone to the ball and seen Edward again, she had forgotten all about Lisa's flight from Julian St. Clare. Clearly Benjamin had learned her whereabouts from her mother—and Sofie had already guessed that more than a few people had seen her leaving last night with Edward. It was no secret that Edward resided at the Savoy. Sofie could not help wondering if Suzanne had had a confrontation with Edward before coming up to her suite.

Now Sofie checked her appearance in the mirror, knowing she must speak with Benjamin and St. Clare. Indeed, she must prepare herself to lie for Lisa's sake. She had never been a good liar, but this time she must excel at deceit.

Sofie winced, because her eyes were red and swollen and it was obvious that she had been crying. In fact, she looked singularly bad. There were circles underneath her eyes and brackets around her mouth. She did not have time to fix her hair, either, which was in a loose braid. Sighing, Sofie splashed water on her face and toweled dry, then smoothed down her worn navy blue skirt. She left the bathroom and walked into the salon.

Benjamin stood in its center, ashen and grim, the marquis beside him. St. Clare was furious. Sofie took one look in his stormy gray eyes and realized that he was not about to let this matter pass without some kind of resolution. And she wondered if she had been wrong. She wondered if, despite his grim expression on the night of his engagement—and his even grimmer confession—he felt something for Lisa after all.

"Lisa is gone," Benjamin cried.

Sofie steeled herself to appear surprised. "Lisa has gone where?"

"She disappeared last night," Benjamin said. "We all thought that she had retired early. But this morning Lisa did not come downstairs. At noon I grew concerned and I sent Suzanne up to wake her. Not only was her door still locked, there was no answer. We managed to find a key to her room—thank God for Mrs. Murdock—and we discovered it was a shambles. There were clothes everywhere! The armoire was open, drawers askew! The window was open! At first we were afraid she had been abducted by burglars!"

Sofie's eyes widened. She had never thought that Suzanne and Benjamin might suspect the worst—falsely. How could she let her mother and Benjamin believe that Lisa had been abducted? Then she felt the marquis's eyes on her, and despite herself, she flushed. Their gazes met. Sofie knew then that he comprehended without a doubt that Lisa had run away from him. "Surely she was not abducted," Sofie said slowly, uncertain. Did the marquis suspect her role in aiding Lisa in her escape?

Benjamin waved a note in his hand. "No—she was not abducted," he said grimly. "I found this shortly afterwards on her nightstand."

Sofie's heart leapt when she realized that Lisa must have written a note before Sofie had found her packing her bag in her bedroom.

For the first time the marquis spoke, quite calmly, in spite of his stormy eyes, looking only at Sofie. "She claims that she is never going to marry me and that she will not return home until the engagement has been broken off, or until, preferably, I have returned to Great Britain."

Sofie felt the blood drain from her face. Why had Benjamin let St. Clare read such an incriminating letter?

"I insisted Ralston let me read the missive," he said coolly, as if aware of Sofie's thoughts. He was sardonic. "Apparently my bride has a severe case of prenuptial jitters."

Sofie stared at him. His tone was ice, but the light in his eyes was not. "I am sure this is just a small misunderstanding," Sofie began lamely.

His mouth twisted. "Are you sure of that, really, Miss O'Neil?"

Sofie shivered.

"This is not like Lisa," Benjamin said harshly. "I am very sorry—no apology can make up for this. I do not blame you for ending this engagement immediately. But I can assure you, Julian, that Lisa will be very sorry for this hysterical prank of hers."

The marquis's smile was chilling. "*You* may rest assured, Benjamin, for I have no intention of breaking it off with the little chit. I am sure that, once I find her, she can be convinced of the merits that will accrue to both of us from this marriage."

Sofie stared, afraid for Lisa. She knew, then and there, that Lisa had made a terrible mistake—and that the marquis would find her, force her to the altar, and make sure she paid the price for running away. He was not going to seek resolution for this matter, but retribution. His winter gray regard met hers again. "Perhaps Miss O'Neil has an idea of where we might begin our search," he said.

Sofie stiffened. "M-Me?"

He inclined his head, his gaze piercing.

"Sofie!" Benjamin barked. "Did Lisa tell you where she was going?"

Sofie managed to shake her head, but her cheeks were burning.

"Can you think of anything she might have said that would give us a clue of where to look?"

Wondering if her guilt was written all over her face, Sofie shook her head again.

Benjamin hesitated, grim and tense and unsure. "We shall have to turn to the police."

"No," the marquis said. "Not yet. We can still avoid scandal. I will hire Pinkertons, and I will search for her myself."

"A good idea. Sofie, is there a telephone in this suite?"

Sofie nodded.

Benjamin walked to where the telephone was posted on the wall, picked up the receiver and waited for an operator. The marquis faced Sofie.

"Come, Miss O'Neil," he said, not quite pleasantly, "we both know that you know where Lisa has gone. Why don't you tell me? Before the situation gets worse?"

Sofie hoped her trembling was not apparent. "I d-do not know where my sister is," she lied through her teeth. "A-And if I did, I would not tell you!"

He studied her. "And what have I done to you to set you against me?"

"You have done nothing to me," Sofie blurted, "but you do not deserve a woman like Lisa, I can assure you of that!"

"Ahh—you are not impressed with my ancient lineage, my noble title, and the very idea that my wife will one day be a countess?" He was mocking.

She stood her ground. "No. Not at all."

"How unalike you and your stepsister are. Lisa was so very impressed by it all."

"You make it sound as if you would rather your bride be disdainful."

"I would," he said bluntly, startling her. His gaze pinned her. "You would probably stand up to the rigors of being my bride far better than your delicate stepsister," he said.

Sofie's eyes widened.

He lifted a large hand. It was as tanned as his face, and Sofie saw that it was heavily callused. The marquis might have a title and ancestral estates, but he labored like a farmer. "Have no fear. While I admire your courage and daring, I am in need of a very well-heeled heiress, and you do not fit the bill."

Sofie drew herself together. "I am relieved!" she snapped.

"Where is she?"

She did not hesitate. "At this exact moment, I do not know!" That, at least, was not a lie.

His smile was cold. "Very well, Miss O'Neil. Your loyalty is admirable. But you may be confident that I will find my bride, and I will marry her—even if I have to truss her up like a sheep for shearing." He turned and stalked away. But Sofie had seen his fury again.

Sofie covered her mouth with her hand, to cut off her cry of relief that he was leaving. Poor Lisa! She was doomed.

Suzanne's pulse raced far too wildly as she waited for a servant to answer the doorbell. Her heart felt as if it were lodged somewhere in the vicinity of her throat. God! She had to see Jake, talk to him, tell him what had happened, she just had to!

Suzanne tensed as the door was finally opened. It was the middle of the afternoon and she was expecting to see a servant. To her shock, Jake stood there—clad only in a strange wide-sleeved red silk robe that somehow made Suzanne think of the Orient.

Jake's expression did not flicker when he remarked her standing there in her finest, most elegant, most flattering day dress, one striped in shades of teal. Suzanne's heart leapt in glad joy at the sight of him. He had obviously just gotten up; he was rumpled, sleepy-eyed, and very naked beneath the robe—she was sure of it. Her blood filled her veins and capillaries in a rush.

"Jake," she said much too huskily, "please let me come inside."

"How come I'm not surprised to find you standing at my front door?" he asked, sighing.

Suzanne started, realizing that he had been drinking quite recently. She heard it in his husky tone, and moving past him as she entered, she smelled fine French brandy on his breath. It crossed her mind that, unlike most men, Jake had always performed best when slightly drunk.

But that was not why she had come to him today. Not the first reason, anyway. She had come because her heart was broken, because she needed his advice.

The foyer was more ostentatious than the front stoop. Not only was it the size of her own morning room, but the carved ceiling was many stories above her and was completely round; looking up, the effect was dizzying. There was a small glass dome at the top, through which sunlight strayed.

Four very high arched entrances opened onto other rooms and corridors. The arches were black marble, shot with gold, and the floor she stood on was glaringly white marble, as were the walls.

She turned to face him, duly impressed. "I've always wondered how you came into the kind of fortune necessary to build this kind of home."

Jake leaned against the wall, arms folded, watching her through slitted eyes.

A tremor swept through her—one of anticipation. Jake was looking at her the way a man looks at a woman he wants to bed—for the first time since she had learned that he was alive. Crazily, she was nervous. "Not to mention your other three homes."

"I already told you," he said. "In building."

She raised a brow. "I don't believe you."

"And shipping." One corner of his mouth lifted in a lopsided and tantalizing grin.

"I'm afraid to ask what you were shipping."

"Then don't."

She wet her lips. Despite her better intentions, her gaze strayed to his large feet and his strong, curved calves, and the hemline of his red silk robe. "Where are your servants, Jake?"

"I only have a housekeeper and a valet. They are both somewhere doing whatever it is that housekeepers and valets do."

"You need a wife," Suzanne said, then regretted her candor, for hadn't she begged him to take her back in one letter after the other? Letters he disdained to answer? But then, Jake always knew how to annoy her more than anyone else.

Yet this time Jake neither laughed nor mocked her. He stared at her, shadows in his eyes. Then he shoved himself off the wall. "Why are you here?"

Suzanne could not help notice how his robe parted when he moved. Revealing a swath of hard, dark thigh. She shook herself free of unwanted thoughts. Seduction—his or hers—was not her intent. "Sofie hates me."

"So you said last night."

Tears filled her eyes. "Jake, I tried to see her—she ordered me out. She was prepared to have the hotel staff throw me out." She told herself that she was not going to reveal the depth of her anguish to him, not now, not after he had abandoned her for so many years. But the tears trickled down her cheeks.

"She'll come around," Jake said, staring at her.

Suzanne shuddered and bent over double and sobbed. "N-No! I-I d-don't think s-so! Y-You d-don't understand! You c-can't understand! I'm her mother! I love her! I can't lose her! Oh, God! F-First you—n-now h-her!" The only time she had ever felt this kind of pain was when she had learned that Jake had died, so many years before, but even then, she had been younger and less wise, not really understanding life or mortality, certainly not as she did now.

"Don't cry," Jake said roughly. "Sofie loves you, and she will come around."

Suzanne straightened and sucked down the sobs, but the tears still gushed. She met Jake's gaze, and saw that he was sorry for her—more than sorry, stricken. "She h-hates me. I w-was only trying to spare her more p-pain."

Jake stood very still, his mouth turned down, stark sympathy in his eyes. A moment later he moved towards her. But Suzanne had been waiting, torn between the hurting and the joy. For she had sensed almost immediately after arriving that they would finally come together as they should have long before. His arms moved around her. "Don't cry," he said again, pulling her against his hard, muscular body. "Please, Suzanne."

Suzanne wept harder now, for everything. For losing Sofie, for having once lost Jake—and for having him back again.

Jake's hands moved over her back, tender strokes meant to soothe, not inflame. Yet as he caressed her, Suzanne's pulse rioted. Blood surged almost instantly to her sex. Dizzying desire assaulted her.

Her tears died as she clung to his broad, strong shoulders. His hands lingered on her hips. She shifted, pressing closer to him, whimpering his name. His hands slid down her buttocks. Suzanne shuddered, her wet face pressed against his neck. It was the most natural thing in the world to press one kiss after another there. Then she felt his mouth brush her temple, slowly, just below the brim of her hat. As his lips touched her skin, lingering there, his hands slid over both of her buttocks where they formed a sensual seam. Suzanne shifted again and came into contact with the full length of his erection, covered only in a wisp of red silk robe.

She gripped his shoulders, looking up at him. "Oh, Jake."

He met her gaze for an instant, revealing his soul-deep hunger. And then his mouth was on hers, engulfing her, tearing at her, as if he were a starving man. Suzanne cried out. She thrust her pelvis up against his swollen loins. His heated hardness burned her. This was no fantasy. This was Jake.

Without removing his mouth from hers—and now his tongue plumbed her depths—he lifted her into his arms and strode swiftly through one pair of black arches into a black and white marble-floored salon. Suzanne heard a door slam closed. Jake settled her onto a sofa, coming down on top of her, finally breaking the kiss.

He cupped her face in his hands and stared searchingly into her eyes.

"I love you," Suzanne said hoarsely. "I do, Jake, I really do."

His jaw flexed and he covered her mouth again. When he lifted his mouth from hers, many minutes later, he said, "Show me."

There was a challenge there. Suzanne smiled, her eyes glowing, easily slipping into the role of seductress. She ripped open his robe. Still smiling, she let her gaze slide down the swath of hard, flat chest she had revealed, down his lean, tense belly, finally coming to rest on his distended phallus. She had forgotten how large and strong he was. For a moment, she could not breathe.

Then she ducked her head and teased the plumlike tip with her tongue. Jake cried out.

Suzanne encouraged him to fall backwards on the couch, following him and coming down on top of him. Instantly she took him in her mouth. Jake threw back his head and allowed her to minister to him. She was experienced, she knew exactly what she was doing, and she had not enjoyed doing this in a very long time.

"Enough!" Jake flung her onto her back, his hands behind her, expertly unbuttoning her dress. "It's been so long," he said roughly. "I want to see every inch of you, Suzanne. Every single bare inch."

She laughed in excitement and irrepressible triumph. She knew she was in her prime, that she had never looked better. She wanted Jake to see her naked. She wanted to excite him with her lush, ripe beauty.

Her clothing rapidly formed a pile on the floor. Jake gripped her breasts, his eyes black now with passion, then bent to lave the long tips. Suzanne cried out. He sucked hard and harder still until Suzanne began to beg him for release. Ignoring her, he spread her thighs wide. He bent lower, inserted his tongue between the throbbing folds of her sex. Suzanne wept when he touched the most sensitive, aroused bud of flesh there. Jake used his tongue on her the way a butterfly uses its wings to fly.

Suzanne shouted and sobbed in pleasure. Jake moved over her, impaling her immediately. Their bodies pumped, frantic and wild. Suzanne peaked again. Jake rolled onto his back, taking her with him. He slid one finger against her cleft, still driving into her, watching her face.

"Oh, you bastard," Suzanne cried, eyes closed, head back, long white neck exposed. Another wave of almost painful pleasure washed over her and crashed around her. Pleasure drummed through her, again and again.

When her senses returned, she was still astride him, and he was very still, regarding her with his gleaming golden eyes. His gaze alone told her that he was far from finished, as did the fact that he was still hard and long inside her, pulsing there like an idling motor. Her eyes widened when their gazes met.

Jake's smile was wicked. "It's been a long time, Suzanne. I'm not a boy anymore."

Her pulse elevated. "I never thought you were."

He laughed once, harshly, and pulled her down, turning her beneath him in one very smooth movement. His mouth found the sensitive skin on the underside of her throat. He began to move inside her again, but this time very, very slowly.

The long silk draperies were surprisingly pale, the color of moonlight, and they pooled on the marble floor. No one had closed them, of course, and they formed a stark contrast to the black night outside the windows of the salon. Suzanne lay entwined with Jake on the sofa, in his arms. His red silk robe lay on top of the pile of her clothing on the pale cream and rose-hued Aubusson carpet on the floor.

She appeared to be asleep, but Jake knew she was awake, for her fingers stroked his wrist very lightly, and from time to time, she sighed.

Jake did not have to glance down at her face to know that she smiled like a well-fed cat. But he did. Without expression, and without very much feeling, either.

It hadn't gone away. The emptiness was still there.

He had thought—even hoped—that he still loved her. Secretly and deep inside himself. But he felt as empty and alone as he always did after sleeping with a woman. Although he had known Suzanne for more than twenty years, although she had been his wife for ten of those years, although she had borne his daughter, there was nothing there, nothing at all, except for carnal lust.

And had he not been drinking with Delanza earlier that afternoon, shedding all of his secrets, unburdening himself in a way he had never before unburdened himself to anyone, not even St. Clare, he might have never caved in to the desire he still felt for Suzanne. He had been avoiding her siren call for years.

But in a way, their sexual reunion had been inevitable. He suspected now that he had needed to be with her again, to see if there was any love left at all.

But there wasn't. Not a shred of it. He told himself that he was relieved, and the sane part of him was, but even more than that, he was so goddamned sad. Achingly sad.

How could a man have both wife and daughter, yet be barred in every substantive way from their lives? Suzanne was his wife, yet she would go home now to another man. Sofie was his daughter, but she did not even know that he was alive, and if she did, she would be shocked, and certainly she would be repulsed as well. He was a traitor, a murderer—and a liar. Jake closed his eyes, recalling how Edward had tried for hours on end to convince him that Sofie would be overjoyed to learn that he was alive—that she would not run away from him, but into his embrace. If only it were true.

Suzanne sighed again and languidly sat up. Jake looked at her, almost glad at having his morbid thoughts interrupted. She smiled, having no inkling as to his feelings—or lack thereof. Although she had hurt him so many times in the past, and he had likewise hurt her, he didn't want to hurt her now. It was time to let go of the past—if he somehow could. "You have become a truly beautiful woman, Suzanne," he said somberly. It was true. She was like a Venus, with her oval face and classic features, with her cloud of mahogany hair, with her full breasts, her ripe hips, and her lush thighs.

Suzanne laughed, pleased, tossing her head. "And you are devastating, Jake. You are more beautiful, too." She bent and kissed his mouth lightly.

Jake did not smile.

Her smile faded, too. "Jake?"

He wondered what he should say. He wondered what he could say. Slowly he sat up, swinging his long, hard legs over the pale, cream-on-white striped damask sofa, reaching for his robe. He slipped it on. Suzanne gripped his wrist. "Jake? What are we going to do?"

He tensed. "It's late. You've missed supper. You're going to have to go home, Suzanne."

She did not move. "I realize that. But . . ."

He had no choice. "There are no buts. Benjamin is your husband now, not I." He hesitated. "This was my fault. I'm sorry. It shouldn't have happened."

She was on her feet, pale, aghast. *"This shouldn't have happened?!* This was the best thing that has ever happened to either one of us. Jake! I love you! And you love me—I am sure of it!"

He stood up, closing his robe and tying the sash. She was very beautiful in her absolute nakedness, but he did not feel the slightest stirring of desire. He was struck by the realization that it was truly over for them. He wasn't ever going to feel desire for her again. Somehow, he knew that. "No, Suzanne, you're wrong."

She stared, frozen. "What are you saying?"

"You're married to Benjamin now, remember?"

"I said I'd leave him for you, and I meant it."

"You can't do that," he said softly. "You would destroy yourself and you know it. You hated me once for taking you away from all of this. You'd hate me again if you could not hold your head up with your friends."

"No. This time is different. This time you're not a dirt-poor immigrant!"

He winced. "That hurts. For a minute there I thought you did love me in your own inimitable manner—not my money."

"I do!" Suzanne wept. "You're twisting my words around."

But he knew that he hadn't twisted her meaning. Just as he also knew that Suzanne did love him, in her own selfish, self-absorbed way. Just as he knew that he had once loved her—completely—and that he didn't love her at all anymore. "Go back to Benjamin," he said gently. "That's where you belong."

Suzanne gasped. "I belong with you. You know it, you bastard! What happened here today proves it. My God, we made love like animals for hours and hours!"

He felt sad for her. "Suzanne, you just hit the nail on the head. We were like animals. It wasn't love. It was sex. Great sex, but sex. Nothing more. Go home."

She whimpered, close to tears, her hand against her mouth. "I can't live without you."

"Yes you can," he said. "You've been living without me for years." He was still bitter, thinking about how easily she had adapted to his death, how quickly she had remarried.

She bent and grabbed her chemise and pulled it on before facing him again. Clutching her dress, she said, "I am your wife. I've checked. Discreetly, of course. But legally we are still wed."

"Then you're also a bigamist."

"That's not my fault!"

"I'll see if my lawyer can arrange a secret divorce somehow." He had toyed with the idea before, but had always dismissed it, telling himself that a secret divorce was impossible. And he had every reason to be afraid of being discovered alive, both then and now. But now he wanted that divorce, if there was any way of gaining it in complete secrecy.

"No!" Suzanne cried. "Even if it could be done, I won't sign!"

He shrugged. "Give up, Suzanne. It's over." He went to her and touched her cheek. "I'm sorry. I'm sorry about everything."

She hissed and smacked his hand away. "It is not over. I'm your wife. I'm always going to be your wife. You're not going to win in this, Jake! There won't be any divorce!"

He stared at her for a long time.

Suzanne wet her lips. "I'm not ever going to give up. Do you understand me?"

He did not answer.

"Never!" she cried hysterically.

Jake turned and walked across the vast room, his red silk kimono ebbing and flowing around him, pausing at the door. "Good-bye, Suzanne."

"Don't! I love you! You bastard!"

He closed his eyes briefly. "It's too late. Fifteen years too late, to be exact."

Suzanne gazed after him, tearful and furious and frightened as he left the room. The black lacquer door closed behind him and he was gone.

Suzanne stood alone in the huge, high-ceilinged, black and white marble salon with its eerily pale furnishings, absolutely alone. Jake was gone, Sofie was gone. She was overwhelmed with anguish.

Abruptly she brushed away a tear. Crying was not going to win him back. Once, long ago, tears had been an effective weapon against Jake, but this man was far too wise for such ploys now.

But she would win him back. She had waited all these years, thinking him dead; she could wait even longer if she had to. Suzanne would do whatever she had to in order to get him back. It was a promise she made to them both. She was his wife. Nothing was going to change that, nothing short of an act of God.

28

Sofie pretended absolute indifference as she walked through the lobby of the Savoy, carrying Edana. The baby was awake and she was regarding everything and everyone with innocent fascination. Sofie paused beside an older couple waiting for the elevator. She wore gloves, which hid the fact that her hands were ringless—which hid the fact that she was unwed and that Edana did not have a father.

Until an hour ago, Sofie had not ventured out of the hotel since arriving there late last night. She had not realized until she was preparing Edana for a walk in the park just how difficult going out in public would be. She knew very well that the hotel staff remarked her, and was certain they gossiped about her being in Edward's suite, as well. As for the other guests, she refused to look at anyone, but she felt that they were all staring at her. It felt as if everyone knew the sordid details of her life.

The elevator came. The gentleman ushered his wife and Sofie in first. The elevator operator turned to her. "Which floor, miss?"

Sofie did not look at him for more than a half second. "Five, thank you." Her cheeks burned. How could he have guessed she was not married?

They rode up in silence, and then the well-dressed matron said, "What a pretty baby. Is she a girl?"

Sofie nodded, very briefly meeting the woman's friendly eyes.

"Who do you work for, do you mind my asking?" the matron continued. "Perhaps I know this beautiful baby's mother."

Sofie realized with utter mortification that this lady thought her to be Edana's nurse. But then, she was dressed like a nurse, was she not? Her clothes were plain and shabby—she had needed a new wardrobe ever since returning from Paris. Sofie did not know what to say. It was insulting—but not as horrible as being labeled a scarlet woman. "I don't think so."

Fortunately the elevator lurched to a stop and the couple alighted. When the doors closed again, Sofie hugged Edana, trembling slightly.

On the fifth floor she hurried to her suite. She put Edana down in order to unlock the door. Rachelle had taken the afternoon to herself to browse The Ladies' Mile and would not be back until dark. Sofie picked up Edana and pushed into the foyer, nudging the door closed with her toe.

She came up short. There was a light on in the salon—and she distinctly recalled turning off all the lights when she had gone out. Then she realized it must be Rachelle. She must have returned early. "Rachelle?" She walked towards the salon, pausing on the threshold.

A man rose from where he sat on one of the sofas. He nodded curtly at her.

Sofie gaped. "Edward! What are you doing here! How did you get in?"

He did not move, staring at her and Edana. "I let myself in."

She tensed. "You have a key?"

"This is my suite, remember?"

She was furious—frightened. "You cannot walk in here whenever you damn well choose!"

"No? Edana's my daughter. I wanted to see her before I go out for the evening."

Sofie couldn't help flinching at the thought of him going out—undoubtedly to carouse as bachelors did. Undoubtedly the night would end with him in some promiscuous woman's arms. "You cannot let yourself in here whenever you feel like it."

"You're upsetting the baby. She's going to cry."

Sofie shifted Edana. "She's hungry. Why don't you come back another time." Very rudely, she hurried into the master bedroom, not just closing the door, but locking it as well. Then, beginning to shake, she set about nursing Edana. But all the while she listened for the sound of Edward leaving. She heard nothing. She was quite certain that he waited in the salon.

But waited for what?

She could not help thinking about the wild passion they had shared just that morning. God, it did not seem like eight hours ago. It seemed like days or even weeks had passed since she had been in his powerful arms.

Desperately Sofie wondered what she was going to do. There was no question that the current arrangement was unsatisfactory—more than unsatisfactory. It was heartbreaking.

Edana had fallen asleep. Sofie changed her and put her down in her cradle. She debated remaining in the bedroom until Rachelle returned. Then she marched to the door. They must resolve something.

Edward turned to face her as she entered the salon. He gestured to the sofa. "Please, sit down, Sofie." He was grim.

She stood on the other side of the pale blue rug, not moving. "What do you want from me?" Her voice was unnaturally high. She was hugging herself.

Edward said quietly, "I didn't come here to seduce you, if that's what's bothering you."

"Everything's bothering me."

His gaze flicked over her features. "I'm not going to apologize for this morning."

"I didn't think you would."

"We have to talk."

"Yes," Sofie said as grimly, "we have to talk."

"Please, sit down."

Sofie gave in and sat stiffly on the edge of one sofa, her knees together, her spine erect, her hands clasped in her lap. Fortunately Edward could not know how hard and fast her heart beat, or that she perspired. Edward sat down, too. Not on the facing sofa, which was some ten feet distant, but on an ottoman he quickly pulled over. Had he sat any closer, their knees would have touched. Sofie stared at him, afraid to move, afraid that their knees would touch.

"Why are you so afraid of me?"

"After this morning, you have to ask?"

"That's not fair and you know it. This morning you were as eager as I. I am sorry for saying such rude things to you afterwards."

She looked into his blue, long-lashed eyes and thought she saw sincerity shining there. But she had thought him sincere long ago, too, and she had been wrong. "What are we going to do, Edward?"

He held her gaze. "I'm sorry for being abusive afterwards, but I meant it when I said I was not going to let you marry Henry Marten."

She wet her lips, which were dry. "I realized that."

"Do you love him, Sofie?"

She shook her head, dropping her gaze. "No," she said miserably, wanting to tell Edward that it was him she loved, wanting to beg him for his love— wanting to scream and shout at him, why! Why couldn't he love her back?

"Sofie, you're living here in my suite, with my child. I have no intention of hiding the fact."

Her head shot up. "Are you advertising it?"

"Not yet."

"But you will?"

"Yes."

She was bitter—she was relieved. "You are going to force me into marriage, are you not?"

"Yes."

She lifted her hand. "You don't have to resort to such foul tactics. I find I cannot live like this anyway. I will marry you, Edward."

He started, eyes wide.

"Are you really surprised?" she asked, being brisk to hide her grief.

"Yes, I am. You are a very surprising woman, Sofie. It's been one surprise after another since we first met."

She looked away. He spoke as if it were a compliment, as if he found her desirable because of her eccentricities.

"Sofie?" He lifted her chin in his large, warm hand.

Sofie stopped breathing, forced to stare into his eyes.

"I will be a good husband. I swear it." His eyes blazed with the force of his vow.

She inhaled. She wanted to ask him if he would be faithful—she did not dare. Once, long ago, that day at Delmonico's, he had told her he could never be faithful to any woman for very long. Unable to speak, she merely nodded.

Edward finally dropped his hand, but his gaze moved over her in a liquid caress.

Sofie's heart began to pound. Did he expect to take her to bed whenever it suited him, once she became his wife? Or would this be a marriage of convenience? The way he was looking at her left her in little doubt. Yet she could not bear to share his bed from time to time and then suffer his extramarital liaisons. Sofie turned her head away. This was a subject that must be discussed, but it was too painful. Perhaps later—after they were wed.

"When do you want to get married?" he asked.

Sofie blinked a few times determinedly. She shrugged.

Edward picked up her hand. She jerked when she realized that he was sliding the solitaire diamond onto her finger. "What are you doing?" she cried.

"We are engaged, are we not?" His eyes were as hard and bright as the diamond he had just placed on her finger.

Sofie looked from his piercing gaze to the cold, sparkling gem. "You don't have to do this, Edward," she managed.

He stood, hands in his pockets. "How about tomorrow?"

She felt sheer panic then. She also stood. "No!"

His smile was twisted. "Then when? The day after? Another week? There is no sense waiting." His gaze pinned her, daring her to commit treachery—daring her to even try to back out now.

She gulped air, filling both lungs. "H-How about after my solo exhibition?"

"When the hell is that?"

"It's only another two weeks," she whispered, her voice unrecognizable.

He nodded abruptly.

Sofie could not hold back another moment, and she burst into tears.

Edward stared.

"I'm s-sorry," she choked, covering her face with her hands. Wasn't a marriage, any kind of marriage, as impossible as their current living arrangement? "I don't know how we will manage."

Suddenly Edward was standing before her and he pulled her hands from her face. "We will manage," he gritted, his eyes blazing.

Sofie recoiled.

Edward turned and stalked from the room. A moment later the front door slammed, sounding like thunder before the onslaught of the storm.

Rachelle had not come back yet. Sofie picked up a pen she often used when she did ink and washes. Her hand moved of its own volition. She sketched Edward quickly, his head, his neck and shoulders, just hinting at the power in his broad frame, then she began to detail his face. When his bold gaze looked up at her from the page, she dropped the pen and covered her face with her hands.

Oh, God, she was more in love with him than ever—and it hurt more than ever before, too.

Sofie stared at the rough sketch. She had done some sketches during the transatlantic crossing, but they had not been very good and she had torn them up. In truth, she had not worked since the day Edward had found her in Zut with her friends celebrating the fact that Paul Durand-Ruel intended a solo exhibition for her in New York.

But what did it matter if she drew him now? Soon they would be married. Soon she might even be able to ask him to model for her. Despite her distress, Sofie's heart fluttered a little at the thought.

It had been so long. How she needed to work, losing herself to her passion and love of work.

Abruptly Sofie picked up the pen and gave in. She began to sketch Edward in earnest as she had seen him last night. Her strokes were bolder than usual, and hard and fast and long. As she could not resist temptation, as he had always been her favorite subject, once again she would do him in oils. Perhaps if she concentrated on the professional aspects of portraying him, it would help her distress. Both Vollard and Durand-Ruel liked her canvases of Edward best. Her exhibition was in ten days. Perhaps she would have this canvas done by then. As her works of Edward so far had all been exemplary, and as she had completed each and every one in a matter of a few frenzied, and therefore exhausting, days, it was probable. If this work was up to par, Jacques Durand-Ruel was going to be thrilled.

With a few more tense strokes, she added the impression of power to his body. Edward lounged against the wall, but he appeared tense and explosive. As tense and explosive as she herself was feeling. How was she going to go through with this? How could she not?

Sighing, Sofie laid down the pen. She stared at the sketch of Edward as he had been last night at Lisa's ball. Superbly elegant, superbly male. Last night. It hardly seemed possible that after all the time that had elapsed since she had run away from New York to Paris, Edward had found her only last night. Not only had he found her last night, but within the space of twenty-four hours he had put an engagement ring on her finger.

Sofie told herself that it was for the best. It was best for Edana; there was no question about that. Edana was going to grow up loved and cherished by her father. Sofie could recall how much her own father had loved her before circumstance had forced him to flee New York, and vividly she remembered all the years growing up wishing Jake were still alive, wishing that she had a father to love her as the other little girls did. It had been selfish of Sofie to run away from Edward after his second proposal, even though it had been an act of sheer self-preservation. Edana deserved a father, and now she was going to have one.

And if her own panic over the impending marriage threatened to get out of control, Sofie was going to think about Edana's relationship with Edward, not her own.

Sofie had been so caught up in her own turmoil that she had not spared Henry Marten a single thought. Dismay filled her. Henry was in love with her. Henry was waiting for her answer regarding his proposal. Oh, God. Sofie did not want to hurt him, but there was not going to be any avoiding it.

Sofie realized that she must not delay. First thing tomorrow, she must go and tell him of her engagement to Edward Delanza.

Sofie hid her hands in her lap, so he would not see the eight-carat diamond ring. Henry held her arms, peering into her face. They stood just inside the door of his office. "God, Sofie, are you all right? Has he hurt you?"

Sofie swallowed. "No."

"I heard that you left the ball with him. I told myself that you had no choice. You didn't have a choice, did you?"

"No. Edward insisted upon seeing Edana immediately."

Henry's jaw was tight. "And did he also insist upon giving you his suite at the Savoy?"

Sofie lost some of her rosy color. "News travels fast, I see."

"Yes."

Sofie inhaled. "He insisted that I take his suite as none other were available." She squared her shoulders, met Henry's eyes. "I have agreed to marry him, Henry."

"Oh, God, I knew it!" Henry cried in open anguish.

Sofie touched his arm. "Oh, please, I am so sorry."

He turned to stare at her, looking as close to tears as possible for a man who was determined not to cry. "You love him, don't you? And you always have. From the moment he began pursuing you at your parents' home in Newport Beach that summer."

"Yes."

Henry ducked his head. "I think he loves you, too."

Sofie started. She knew better, knew it wasn't true, but hope crashed over her. Oh, God—if only it were true!

The day before the exhibition, Sofie was sick. She had always been scared by the thought of facing the critics and public alone, but when the exhibition date had been far in the future, it had been easy not to dwell on her fear. Now that very justifiable fear was compounded by the fact that the day after tomorrow, she and Edward were going before a judge to get married. She was so ill that she retched up the single piece of toast she had for breakfast, and remained queasy throughout the day.

Their relationship had not improved. Henry was wrong. Edward did not love her and he never had—the very idea was absurd.

Edward used his key to enter the suite at will to visit Edana several times a day. He was unfailingly polite to Sofie as he would be to any stranger. The explosive tension riddling him, which she had captured in the new oil she was doing, somewhat secretively, remained very visible. In fact, the moment

Edward entered the suite, the air between them changed. It became thick and hot, a seething foglike monster, ready to strike flames.

Sofie tried to pretend she was indifferent to his presence, just as she pretended that she did not notice the way he looked at her as if she were some piece of candy he craved. But when his back was turned, she looked at him in the exact same manner, and she knew it. She had never been ashamed of her lust before and could not be ashamed of it now. But at all costs, she would hide it.

Sofie walked the few blocks downtown on Fifth Avenue so she might review the exhibition with Jacques Durand-Ruel privately before the public would on the morrow. She was sorry for setting such a foolish date for their wedding. The solo exhibition should have been the most important event of her life. But it was taking a backseat now to a loveless marriage to a man who felt obliged to give her daughter his name. But Sofie knew she did not dare even speak of postponing the nuptials.

Jacques was expecting her, and he saw her the moment she entered the gallery's front door. "Dearest Sofie," he cried, hurrying to her. He embraced her, then kissed her on both cheeks. "*Ma chère*, you are pale. I suspect you are afraid?"

"Terrified," Sofie said, honestly.

Jacques guided her into the gallery, his arm around her. "Do not be afraid. As a rule, the critics in America are far more friendly than those in Paris. Too, we have played up the fact that you live abroad, which the Americans, both critic and buyer, just adore. I have a feeling, dear Sofie, a feeling that tomorrow will exceed all of our expectations."

"I hope you are right," Sofie said as they walked into the huge room where all of her work was displayed.

At a glance, she knew it was right. She had thirty-three works in all: twelve oils, twelve studies in charcoal or ink upon which the oils had been based, a half dozen pastels, and three watercolors. There were two still lives, but all the rest of her canvases were figural subjects, and eight of them were of Edward. Seeing him everywhere she turned, even if only on canvas or paper, so masculine and beautiful, took her breath away. As always, she was afflicted with the odd combination of joy and pain.

Then Sofie froze. Two workers were lifting a large canvas onto the last remaining empty spot on the far wall at the other end of the gallery. It was the nude she had done of him in Montmartre.

Jacques saw where she gazed, and smiled. "*La pièce de résistance.*"

"No!" Sofie cried, mortified.

"Ma chère?"

Sofie rushed forward to face the canvas, which measured four feet by
five and was now hanging on the wall, dominating all of the art around it.
Edward stared at her and Jacques, unsmiling. One of his shoulders rested
against a wall with peeling paint; behind him was a window, and through
it the windmills of Montmartre were just visible. His near leg was bent at
the knee, all of his weight on his far leg, so the posture was as modest as
possible considering the fact that he was nude. No shocking part of male
anatomy was revealed.

In the lower right corner of the canvas, the rumpled edge of a bed was
clearly visible. The room was drenched in sunlight, yet Sofie had used a very
blue palette, and had kept the background airy and unfocused. For Edward
she had used strong, warm, vibrant tones, and the corner of the bed boasted
a crimson blanket. As Edward had been portrayed with almost classical
attention to detail, he dominated the canvas, appeared larger than life.

His eyes were gleaming. It was obvious what he was thinking about. Sofie
had forgotten just how good this work was.

Jacques ambled up behind her. "Your finest work. Stunning, powerful. This
will make your career, Sofie."

Sofie turned to Jacques. "We cannot show it."

"We must!"

Sofie's heart beat hard and fast. "Jacques, I did not have Mr. Delanza's
permission to do this—much less to show it."

Jacques's eyes widened. "He did not model for you?"

"No. He modeled for the first canvas, which you sold long ago, and he
modeled for *Delmonico's*."

"Yes, I remember *A Gentleman at Newport Beach*. And Mademoiselle
Cassatt has so kindly lent us *Delmonico's* for the showing."

"That is wonderful," Sofie said. "But, Jacques, really, we cannot show the
nude."

"Sofie, why do you not simply ask your fiancé if he minds if you show
this work?"

Sofie could not tell Jacques that she and Edward were hardly on speaking
terms—unless it was to discuss the weather. She was aware that most of
New York knew she lived at the Savoy in Edward's suite with a child—and
surely the gossips were having a field day with that—and that they were now
engaged. Benjamin had come to offer his congratulations and best wishes. As
Lisa was still missing, he had been gaunt and weary. Suzanne had tried to
see Sofie as well, but Sofie had refused to admit her. As far as Sofie was

concerned, the day her mother had tried to separate her from Edana was the day Suzanne had stopped being her mother.

"Can you not ask him?" Jacques smiled. "*Chérie*, it is so romantic, *la bohème* and Monsieur Delanza, the diamond king! The critics already love your story—and they will love this. Ask Monsieur if he minds showing the nude. How could he? He has modeled for you before. He knows the business. And he is shrewd. He will understand what a coup this work will be for you."

Sofie could not imagine approaching Edward and asking him if he had an objection to her showing a nude portrait of him, not under the current circumstances. In fact, Sofie did not want Edward to come to the exhibition at all, and if he knew she had a nude of him there, she was quite certain that he would come. She did not want him to see how often she had returned to him as an inspiration. If he did, he would immediately discern that she loved him.

"I cannot ask him," Sofie finally said. "And please, do not ask me why."

"You must show the nude, Sofie," Jacques argued. "This work will make you, *chérie*! Nudes are controversial anyway, but this one! *C'est vraiment intime*! A nude of your lover—and you a woman—*oh là là*! It could not be better! You desperately need the publicity!"

Sofie knew she could not show it without Edward's permission, no matter how beneficial it might be to her career. "No. I am sorry. Please, Jacques, have it taken down."

Jacques stared at her in dismay.

And Sofie could not help feeling regret. She glanced up at the nude. It was magnificent, stunning and powerful, and disturbingly intimate, as if the public were being allowed a glimpse into Edward's bedroom. Undoubtedly it was her best work. Edward was magnificent. He was everything a man should be. She knew that her dearest friends, Braque, Picasso, Georges Fraggard, and Paul Verault, would have urged her to change her mind and show it. But she could not. "I will see you tomorrow," she said.

Sighing, Jacques nodded. "But I may show it privately?"

"Yes," Sofie said. "But only to a serious buyer, Jacques."

Jacques smiled. "That is better than nothing, then. One last thing, *chérie*. You have not titled the canvas."

Sofie did not hesitate, looking into Edward's brilliant blue eyes. "*After Innocence*," she said softly.

29

$\mathcal{E}$ dward was tense. He drove his Daimler more aggressively than usual down Fifth Avenue, angry with Sofie yet again. But this time he was angry with her for going without him to her exhibition. He had intended to escort her. He was her fiancé. It was his obligation to be by her side at this event. But most of all, he wanted to be beside her to support her and to share in her triumph.

It was almost incredible to think about her having such an exhibition now at the foremost gallery in the city in juxtaposition to the past. It didn't seem like very long ago that Edward had first met Sofie, a small, frightened girl afraid of life, hiding behind her limp and her art. Very much the way a butterfly emerges from its cocoon, in less than two years Sofie had blossomed into an extraordinary woman. An extraordinary woman who would soon be his wife.

And who was damn unhappy about it.

Every time Edward walked into the same room with her, he saw her unhappiness, her grief.

But he was determined. Determined not just to marry her and give Edana his name. One day, dammit, Sofie would be happy with her choice. He had vowed it to both of them, even if she did not know it. Tomorrow they would be married in Judge Heller's chambers in the municipal courthouse downtown. And Edward would begin to show her that marriage to him was not so bad—that it had more than a few fine moments.

Edward shoved the thought of their marriage aside. He slowed the Daimler. The tricolored flag of France had come into view, waving beside the red, white, and blue stars and stripes of the American flag. Both sides of Fifth Avenue in front of the Gallery Durand-Ruel were lined in quadruple rows with vehicles, mostly carriages and curricles, grooms and coachmen in white breeches clustered on the sidewalk, but also a few motorcars. Edward had to drive another block in order to double-park. But he was fiercely glad. Obviously there was a huge turnout for Sofie's very first exhibition in New York.

His heart was lodged in his throat as he swung out of the Daimler. He knew how important this show must be for her. He remembered as if it were only yesterday how afraid she had been to let Jacques Durand-Ruel view her art in the seclusion of her own studio. Today she must be close to hysteria and stricken with nerves.

As Edward walked up the block, he watched a well-dressed couple leave the gallery, the woman speaking fast and low, the man nodding. As he passed them he heard the matron say, "Shocking! Shocking! To be portraying that man so openly . . . I will never, ever view Sofie O'Neil's art again!"

Edward's heart seemed to stop. And he was very glad he had come now. Sofie needed him. He only hoped that this woman's reaction to the showing was not a universal one.

He entered the two large front doors and walked towards the showroom where the crowd had gathered, searching for Sofie but failing to find her. It was crowded but not noisy; people were speaking in hushed voices. His heart beat double time. He paused just outside the exhibit, his way blocked by a distinguished lady in gray stripes and a gentleman in a three-piece suit. They were in the midst of an intense conversation and did not realize they barred his way. Edward was about to shove past them when he heard the woman, flushed with excitement, say, "Harry, we *must* buy it! Thank God Jacques showed it to us! We must buy it even if only to hang it in our closet! We cannot let that magnificent work leave the country—we cannot—and you know it as well as I do!"

"Louisine," the gentleman said, "we already have that equally magnificent and equally shocking Courbet in our closet."

"Please," the lady begged, clinging to his arm. "We must have that painting even if we dare not display it in our home!"

"I will think about it," Harry promised.

They moved out of earshot, back into the exhibit.

Edward stared after them, wondering which work they had been speaking of, thrilled the lady had wanted to purchase it so badly. Women usually ruled the roost, and he imagined that Sofie was going to make at least one sale that day.

Edward moved past several gentlemen, entering the exhibit. The first thing he saw was several canvases hanging on the wall—and two were of him.

His heart stopped. He gaped.

He recognized Delmonico's restaurant before he moved closer to stare at the small brass plate on the wall beside the boldly colored oil. Sure enough, the work was titled *Delmonico's*, and it was on loan and not for sale. Edward's pulse began to riot. He stared for an instant at himself, at the way Sofie had portrayed him. Once again she had romanticized him, making him appear far more attractive and far more elegant than he actually was, although this time he appeared carelessly indolent, too.

Stunned, Edward scanned the entire room. Eight of the thirty-odd canvases featured him as the subject matter. *Delmonico's* was the only work that was based on reality. In the other works she portrayed him in places he had never been, frequently in a café or in some other social setting. Sometimes other figures were in the background, more often not. In each portrait she appeared to have captured his expression at a precise moment in time. But these moments had never happened. Sofie had fantasized them. Or had she recalled his changes of mood and his facial expressions from memory— merely fantasizing the setting?

In the next instant, as Edward stared around the room and at his images there, he comprehended it all. Sofie had done all this work in the past year and a half, since rejecting his first proposal in order to study in Paris. While he had been slaving in his diamond mine in southern Africa, thinking of her night and day, she had *not* been casually whiling away the time with her male friends in bars and cabarets. There were too many works here—she had been far too prolific. Not to mention the fact that she had also been pregnant and had given birth to their daughter. She must have worked every spare moment available to her, both night and day, in order to accomplish so much. He had never been more amazed, or more overwhelmed, than he was at that moment with the woman who was to become his wife.

But one fact was astoundingly clear. In the time they had been apart, she had been as consumed with him as he had been with her. As obsessed.

Sofie had arrived at the gallery early and alone. Briefly she had thought about asking Edward to come with her. Terrified now of rejection by both critics and buyers alike, it would be so easy to succumb to Edward's strength and to go to the exhibition with his arm around her. But she must be stronger than that. She must not forget that she did not want him to see her collection of work at all.

Sofie arrived half an hour before the showing opened with her heart lodged in her chest like an ungainly, undigestible lump. She could not converse with Jacques, who was too busy anyway seeing to last-minute details, frantically rearranging several of the oils. The minutes ticked by like years. And suddenly the doors were thrown open and the first public spectators filtered in.

The gallery was quickly becoming crowded when Sofie espied Suzanne and Benjamin. Her heart flopped—she had not expected either one of them. She had nothing to say to Suzanne, but she must thank Benjamin for supporting her both with his presence today and with the generous check he had sent her as a wedding present. Too late, as she came forward, she realized that the Marquis of Connaught was with them.

"Sofie, dear," Suzanne cried.

Sofie nodded curtly at her, then strained on tiptoe to kiss Benjamin's cheek. He looked horrible. His face was ravaged—he had lost at least a stone of weight. Tears filled Sofie's eyes. She wanted to tell him that Lisa was fine. He was suffering so. But then she felt the marquis's cold gaze on her, knew he waited for her to come forward and reveal Lisa's whereabouts. She gripped Benjamin's hands. "Thank you for coming—and thank you for your generous gift."

He managed a smile. "I am so pleased that you are finally marrying, Sofie. And—" he glanced around the room "—now I begin to see that Delanza is the right man for you. I wish you much happiness, dear."

Sofie wanted to cry. She nodded and thanked him again instead. If Benjamin realized that she loved Edward from looking at her work, would everyone else realize as well? Tomorrow they were getting married. Perhaps it was a natural assumption. Perhaps if everyone thought they were marrying for love, the scandal of her having had his child out of wedlock would quickly fade away and die. Either that or everyone would realize the truth—that poor Sofie O'Neil was hopelessly in love with a scoundrel and a rake.

Suzanne tried to gain her attention again. "Sofie, dear, please."

Sofie glimpsed her white face and anguished eyes before turning her back on her. She thought about Edana and let her anger at Suzanne carry her a safe distance away. Trying not to feel mean and cruel for rejecting her own mother—reminding herself that Suzanne had wanted to do far more than reject her own granddaughter.

Sofie fought for her composure. How could she have failed to consider that Suzanne would show up today? Sofie could not help wondering if her mother still disliked and misunderstood her art. She told herself that Suzanne's opinion no longer mattered the way it once had.

"Sofie, *chérie*, I think this is going to be a big success," Jacques cried in her ear, having come up behind her.

Sofie turned and smiled somewhat wanly. "I don't know. I think some of the ladies here are disgusted because of who I am and how I've lived and that I've portrayed Edward so frequently when he is the father of my child.

I think they have come to gawk so tomorrow they might have more gossip to spread around town."

"Ahh, maybe so, but the press and the critics love the romance of your story! For it is *la grande passion, n'est-ce pas?*"

Sofie looked away. *La grande passion?* It was hardly that, and she could not help feeling more than sad, but bitter and cheated as well.

Then she felt herself being stared at. Sofie started when she met the intense golden gaze of the same man who had watched her during Lisa's engagement party. She gripped Jacques's arm. Something was bothering her now, very much so. "Jacques, who is that? Do you know that man?"

Jacques followed her gaze. Seeing that he was the object of their attention, the stranger turned and faded into the growing crowd. "Ahh—he bought two of your works anonymously just after you left for Paris last year."

Sofie was shaken and very disturbed. "Who is he? I must know!"

"*Chérie*—you know that if a buyer wishes to remain anonymous, I cannot—"

"I must know!" Sofie cried.

"His name is Jake Ryan."

"Jake!"

Jake froze, then ever so slowly, he turned.

Suzanne gripped his sleeve. Her eyes glittered wildly. They stood by the front door of the gallery, but they were hardly alone, because the exhibition was packed. "You would dare to come here!" she accused.

He had not seen her since they had spent the afternoon making love in the salon of his mansion, almost two weeks ago. But Jake was well aware that Suzanne had tried to see him on several occasions. He had said all there was to say, and he had left orders that she was not to be admitted into his house— that he was not home should she come calling. Now he looked at her and saw a somewhat maniacal woman, one who might have been attractive if her eyes were not so wild. But he felt nothing for her at all. It was hard to understand the fierce desire he had felt for her that day, a desire he could so easily blame on drinking but would not, knowing better. "I had to come. I could not miss Sofie's greatest day."

"And will tomorrow be a great day, too, when she marries that bastard who seduced her and gave her his child?" Suzanne spat.

"I think it will be an even better day," Jake said quietly. "Delanza is head over heels in love with her. He'll make her happy."

Suzanne blanched. "Don't tell me he is your friend, too!"

Jake nodded.

"You are mad!" Tears filled her eyes. "You have told that horrid valet of yours that you will not see me, haven't you?"

"Suzanne—what is the point?"

"You cannot turn away from me like that—you cannot! Jake—God—I can't stop thinking about you—about us!"

Heavily he said, "There is no 'us.' It's over, Suzanne. Over."

"No!"

He turned his back on her.

She lashed out, gripping him so hard that he stumbled backwards. Her strength had been unnatural. Warily he faced her. "Suzanne?"

"Do you know that sometimes I hate you more than I love you?"

He watched her uneasily.

"I want you back, Jake."

"No."

She hissed. Her expression was at once livid and sly. "I did it once—I'll do it again!"

The hairs on his nape prickled. His whole body tensed. "I don't know what you're talking about."

She laughed, triumphant. "You don't, do you? You never did. You never knew!"

"I never knew what?"

"That there was no visiting British dignitary!"

Jake stared at her. He was filled with a horrible, impossible inkling—and sick dread. "What?"

"Fifteen years ago. There was no visiting British dignitary!"

His mind began to spin. Fifteen years ago. The winter of 1887. There had been a blizzard that year—it had been one of the worst winters of recent memory. Eighteen eighty-seven. The year he had been recognized at a public gala by a visiting British dignitary. Lord Carrington. Sheer coincidence. Mad Fate. Recognized, identified, and forced to flee the country—his wife—his child. His eyes wide with horror, Jake stared at his wife.

Suzanne laughed. "It was me! It was me! I turned you in! Me!"

Jake felt the floor tilting beneath his feet. It was hard to breathe—even harder to believe what she was saying. "Why? Dear God, *why?*"

Tears filled her eyes and she glared at him. "I hated you for that dance-hall girl."

Jake stared at her, barely comprehending what she said. A dancer? Had there been another woman? He could not remember. He had been faithful to her for so many years despite her infidelities, but he seemed to vaguely remember that he had finally sought solace with another woman. Dear God. Jake closed his eyes, sick to the very bottom of his soul.

It hadn't been sheer coincidence. It hadn't been fate. It had been Suzanne, the woman he loved—his malicious, vengeful wife.

"You stupid fool!" Suzanne screamed. "It was me! I turned you in then— and I'll turn you in again! I will! Take me back, Jake!"

Jake opened his eyes and stared. Then he turned and ran out the door. Running—once again.

"Sofie, *chère!*" Jacques cried, rushing to her. "Look at the crowd! This is already a great success!"

"Is it?"

"It is!" he assured her excitedly, pulling her close. "Everyone is most admiring of your work, and several big buyers have expressed interest in acquiring some of the canvases. More importantly, Louisine Havemeyer is enamored of *After Innocence*. She told me if I sell it to anyone else, she will never buy from my gallery again."

Sofie inhaled, shocked. Louisine Havemeyer and her husband were two of the greatest, most influential collectors in New York, if not the world. If the Havemeyers bought one of her works, soon other collectors would look at her with interest, too. And rarely did the Havemeyers buy a single work from an artist—usually they collected that artist with a frenzy. "Oh, Lord," Sofie whispered, crossing her fingers behind her back.

"She must convince her husband. They feel that they can not hang such a work in their salon. Come. The press is here. And several clients wish to speak with you!"

Sofie followed Jacques in a daze as he rushed her across the room.

"First we will meet some of my best clients," Jacques told her. Immediately he introduced her to a German baron who resided in New York.

"I am enthralled with your work," the baron said, bowing over her hand, several oversize gems glittering on his fingers.

"And I just love your oils which feature that handsome young man," a well-dressed young lady put in eagerly.

"Your colors are so bright and bold and always surprising," a gentleman chimed in. He smiled at Sofie. "I have bought the pastel, *Man at a Café.*"

"Thank you," Sofie whispered, dazed now with success.

"Miss O'Neil?"

Sofie turned, smiling.

The lean gentleman extended his hand. "I am Rob Green, with *Harper's*. Can we set up a time for an interview? I'm going to do a feature on you." He smiled at her.

Sofie blinked at him, nodding. A feature news story in *Harper's*. It was too good to be true, all of it. Sofie felt as if she had just become Cinderella. And then she glimpsed Edward striding towards her through the crowd, which was parting for him like the Red Sea for the Jews. She forgot the reporter, forgot the three admiring fans, forgot Jacques. Reality reclaimed her. She was not Cinderella—and Edward was not a prince coming to claim her with his love.

He paused in front of her, taking her arm proprietarily in his. He gave her a look so warm, it was blinding. Sofie froze. Edward was smiling at her, not only with his mouth, but with his eyes—with his heart. "Hello, darling," he said. "Sorry I'm late."

Sofie was very dazed when, a few hours later, Edward guided her up the red-carpeted steps of the Savoy and into the spacious lobby. She was so exhausted that it was hard not to lean against him as he moved her across it and to the elevator. She made no protest as he ushered her inside without relinquishing his hold on her arm.

But she was not in a complete stupor from the fantastic day. She was aware of the way he was looking at her now, with smoldering warmth—which was the exact same way he had been regarding her all afternoon. In effect, he was acting as if he truly were her admiring bridegroom. Where was his anger? His hostility? What was going on?

Worse, how could she defend herself from him in this kind of circumstance? Her bones felt as if they had turned into a molten mass long ago. Her heart fluttered unsteadily in her chest. He was up to something—she was certain of it. But was seduction the first or the last of his intentions?

He propelled her down the hall and finally released her in order to unlock the door to the suite with his key. Sofie quickly walked inside ahead of him, hoping to bar his entrance. Her heart beat harder now and her mouth was cotton-dry. But he sidestepped her and said to Rachelle, who was playing with Edana on the blue rug on the floor, "Why don't you take Edana out for an hour or two?"

Sofie cried out in a very feeble protest—because her racing pulse and sensitized body were giving her quite contrary instructions.

Rachelle jumped up, looking at both of them, smiling. A moment later she was gathering up Edana. Becoming more weak-kneed with every moment,

Sofie held on to a beautiful Chippendale table in order to support herself. He could not do this, she told herself. He could not prance into her suite and take her to bed just because he felt like it.

But oh, how glorious it would be to make love with him now after such a magnificent day.

Sofie lifted her gaze to his, her cheeks heated, and was incapable of any further resistance. For his gaze was promising her every single one of her wildest dreams—and the moon and the stars, too. She gripped the table harder. Her blood seemed to roar in her veins. Lust had taken over her lower body the way a devil takes over saints. She was mesmerized by what was about to come.

"We will be gone for a while, *chérie*," Rachelle said, a bundled-up Edana in her arms. Her expression was bland, but her eyes sparked with sly delight. A moment later she had brushed past Sofie and was gone.

Sofie could not move. She was afraid to look at Edward again. But she did.

"Come here, love," he said.

Her eyes widened.

His smile was gentle. "You can't run from me anymore, Sofie."

Sofie felt very close to collapse.

He smiled again. "Besides, we're getting married tomorrow, remember?" He moved towards her.

She found her voice. "To—Tomorrow. A-And we n-never did discuss the ex—exact nature of our m-marriage."

He laughed softly, eyes dancing and gleaming at once, his hands closing on her arms. Sofie did not stiffen as he pulled her up against his body, which was firmly aroused. In fact, she turned boneless and pliant, melting against him. "There is nothing to discuss," he whispered, his gaze searching hers. He smiled again and brushed a kiss on the tip of her nose. Sofie shuddered. "You're going to be my wife," he murmured, and his mouth brushed her eyes, one by one. Sofie bit back a whimper. "A very beloved wife," he added huskily, this time kissing her mouth.

Sofie jerked. "Wh-What?" Her hands pressed against his chest as he now feathered kisses to her cheeks, her chin, and lips.

"You heard," Edward said, his tone deepening to a growl. "I love you, enchantress. And I'm going to show you—right now."

Sofie gaped at him, clutching the lapels of his jacket, incredulous. "I . . . I don't understand."

"No?" He grinned very wickedly, anchored her hips, and shifted his loins against her. "Then let me explain."

Sofie gasped when he swung her up into his arms. "Edward—what are you doing?!"

He laughed, carrying her towards the master bedroom. "How can you even ask?"

Sofie looked up into his handsome face, a face of strong, beautiful planes and high, precise angles, a face dominated by vivid blue eyes and a strong, classical nose, a face that would always mesmerize her, haunt her, enthrall her. "Please don't lie to me," she cried.

He tossed her onto the bed. "The one thing I'm not," he stated, slipping off his tie and tossing it to the floor, "is a liar. Darling." He smiled and his jacket followed his tie.

Sofie scrambled up into a sitting position, watching him unbutton his shirt a bit too slowly. He continued to smile, watching her, revealing his magnificent physique inch by inch. She pressed her thighs together, trying not to hyperventilate, a prisoner of extraordinary lust—a prisoner of love. "What are you saying?" she croaked, all the muscles in her body knotted tight.

"I love you, dammit." He threw the shirt behind him and pushed his wool trousers down over his lean hips, his gaze on hers. His thigh-length drawers were pale blue silk, finely woven and hardly concealing Edward's very visible and very large erection. "I've loved you since the day I first saw you—and I'm going to love you until the day I die, dammit. And maybe even afterwards, too." His gaze was lancing. "If there are such things as ghosts."

Sofie stared at him, her heart thundering in her ears, stupefied.

He stepped out of his drawers. He was six feet four inches of superbly sculpted muscle, firm flesh and hard bone. "And you love me, don't you?"

She inhaled. No sight was as superb as Edward nude and ready to love her—no sight. And no moment was as glorious as this moment of confession. Sofie realized that she was crying.

Edward came onto the bed, pulling her forward and into a tender embrace. "Why are you crying? And why, dear God, have you been fighting me for so very long?"

Sofie shook her head, unable to speak, sobbing and clinging. Finally she whispered, "I was afraid. Because I've loved you so much for so long."

He wasn't smiling and their gazes locked.

She opened her mouth to tell him again that she loved him, that she always had and always would. But she was cut off by his deep, urgent, openmouthed kiss. His tongue entered her as if he was striving to plumb the very depths of her soul.

Edward pushed her backwards onto the bed, coming down on top of her, holding her tight, devouring her mouth. Sometime later he lifted his head, smiling slightly, eyes smoking and hot. "Later," he said harshly, his fingers in her hair, pulling out the pins, "later we'll talk."

Sofie did not move—could not move—as Edward freed her tresses and allowed her hair to cascade around them. A dimple flashed, dug deep, his mouth in a wicked curve. His eyes were bright with carnal promise; his hand slid up her thigh, under her skirts. "Now, get rid of these damn clothes, Sofie," he ordered.

Sofie obeyed.

She lay naked and unmoving, not yet sated. She wondered if she would ever be sated.

Edward smiled at her, sitting on the bed by her side. He took the triple-tiered diamond necklace from the velvet box and leaned forward to place it on her neck. Sofie did not blush. She met Edward's admiring gaze, watching his eyes turn black with desire as he clasped the dazzling strands of gems around her pale white throat.

He reached out and rubbed one of her nipples, already rosy and erect from their lovemaking, then pushed her hair behind her shoulders. He fastened each of the sparkling chandelier earrings to her lobes. "God, you are so beautiful."

Sofie slanted a look at him, moving restlessly against the pillows, arching slightly beneath his questing gaze, feeling every inch a seductress. Edward's eyes smoked. His hand dropped to her neck, curving over the diamond necklace, then lower, curving over her full, aching breast.

"Every single one of those diamonds," he whispered, "I dug up with my own two hands."

Sofie looked at him, hips shifting, thighs parted. "Y-You're not a smuggler of stolen gems?" she whispered breathlessly.

He laughed, too harshly for the sound to be mirth alone. "No. Hell no. That's a myth."

"I'm glad," Sofie said, taking his hand and sliding it down her breast and to her abdomen. She was shameless, she did not care. "Even though there is something incredibly attractive about a man who dares to smuggle diamonds." Their gazes fastened on each other.

Unsmiling, he slid his hand lower, palming her the way she wanted to be palmed. Sofie inhaled. "I'll smuggle diamonds if you want me to, Sofie." His eyes gleamed. "Tell me what you want."

She shifted and moved restlessly beneath him. Thighs widened more. "Yes," she whispered. "Yes."

His thumb stroked the heavy seaming of her lips. "There?"

She nodded, arching slightly again, her full breasts glistening with a fine sheen of sweat, nipples pointed and painfully hard. The diamonds at her throat and ears caught the overhead lights and sparked with fire. Edward's thumb slid inward, over slick, screamingly sensitive flesh. Sofie gasped, arching again—this time coming up off the bed.

He laughed, low and deep in his throat. "You are the most beautiful woman I have ever known," he said harshly.

Sofie met his gaze, ripples of agonizing pleasure washing over her, threatening to crest to another crescendo, and quickly, and she knew it was true. "Edward, please."

His hand had become still. His gaze was brilliant. "When I first met you, I wanted to do this. Dress you only in diamonds—my diamonds."

She met his smoldering glance. "Yes."

He lifted his other hand. It was fisted. Sofie did not understand, then she whimpered a little as the first small shower began. Opening his fist ever so slightly, he allowed dozens of diamonds of every imaginable size to trickle down onto her breasts. Sofie gasped, arching, nipples tightening. Some of the dazzling stones spilled lower, onto her torso, a few scattered onto the bed. His hand waved like a wand over her. More diamonds sifted down onto her abdomen, and then lower still, perilously low. Sofie stared at her breasts, where one very small stone glittered close to her engorged nipple, then at her belly, where sparkling gems were clustered around her navel. And lower still. The tawny thatch of hair at the apex of her thighs glistened with moisture, glittered with fire.

"I even imagined doing this," Edward whispered, his gaze following the path of diamonds. So did his hand. Another fiery shower followed, and the last few tiny stones rained down on the swollen, throbbing folds of her sex.

Their gazes met.

"Everything I have is yours," Edward said.

Sofie shifted to sit, shudders of desire wracking her body, reaching out. Edward came into her arms, his mouth taking hers, pushing her down and kneeing her thighs apart. As he moved on top of her, he thrust deep. Sofie cried out instantly as wave after wave of incredible, shattering, almost painful ecstasy crashed upon her. Edward drove hot and hard and huge, deeper still, gasping, arching, convulsing. "Everything," he cried.

30

ofie smiled at Edward, and Edward smiled at her. They had re-dressed and were sitting snuggled up on the sofa in the salon, with Edana in Edward's lap. Rachelle had claimed to have made a rendezvous and had long since gone. Sofie watched Edward playing with Edana, talking to her and making the kinds of funny faces babies so loved, her heart so swollen with love that it almost hurt.

Edward had not wanted to re-dress. He had ordered them a large supper and had wanted to eat it in bed. Sofie had refused. She had reminded him that their household consisted of four, not two. She could not imagine partaking of supper while nude in bed with Rachelle and Edana elsewhere in the suite. Edward had succumbed to her sensibility, but his look had promised her that one day they would do as he preferred. It was hard for Sofie to pretend to herself that she was unaffected by the notion.

Several knocks sounded on the door. Sofie restrained Edward from getting up. "Stay with Edana," she said, smiling, her gaze drinking in the sight of him. It was so incredible that he was there with her and their daughter like this. Their sudden domesticity was amazing, a near miracle. "Undoubtedly it is our supper."

But it was not. Sofie opened the door to admit Jacques Durand-Ruel, who was beaming. "Jacques!" she said, bemused. "*Qu'est-ce que c'est que ça?* Is something wrong?"

He laughed. "You have sold four oils, two sketches, and a pastel. And one of the oils was bought by the Havemeyers."

Sofie cried out. Edward had risen and come to stand beside her, Edana squirming in his arms. He freed one arm to hug Sofie, who gaped at Jacques, pulse pounding.

Jacques gripped her hand. "It wasn't *After Innocence*. But a work like that never sells quickly. It was *A Gentleman At Ease*."

"Oh, Edward, can you believe it?!" Sofie cried, trembling with elation.

Edward pulled her close. "I knew it. I knew the moment I first saw your work last year that you were destined for great things."

Sofie turned in to his embrace, then saw how Edana was beaming, too, and she kissed her daughter's cheek fiercely before kissing Edward. "It hasn't happened yet," she said, trying to restrain the urge to shout with abandon, to jump with glee. "They bought one work. One. Just one."

"They will buy more," Jacques said confidently. "I knew you would not want to wait to hear such news."

Edward smiled at him. "Thank you, Jacques. We are expecting supper at any moment. Would you like to join us?"

Sofie glanced at Edward, a surge of intense emotion riding through her veins. She had never loved him more than she did in that moment. She knew Edward wanted nothing more than to spend the evening alone with her and Edana, now that they were reunited as a family again after so long a time apart But he was smiling at Jacques as if he wanted the art dealer to stay with them.

But Jacques was a Frenchman and he comprehended them too well. *"Non, mes amies,* I think tonight you should celebrate *en famille.* I have ordered a bottle of fine champagne for you. Drink it in good health!"

Sofie kissed Jacques on both cheeks. "Thank you for coming tonight."

"Ce n'est pas de problème, chérie. But we must sit down and talk tomorrow about your future."

Sofie grinned and promised him that she would be at the gallery as soon as it opened. But when Edward coughed, she glanced at him and amended, "Rather, I will be there by noon."

Jacques laughed and left.

Edward put Edana down in the salon on the rug, where she could not hurt herself, and went to Sofie and caught her up in his embrace. He spun her around and around as if in a frenetic dance. Sofie laughed and laughed. When he stopped she was dizzy, as he undoubtedly was, too. But his kiss was hardly chaste.

"Edward." Sofie broke away. "I want a real wedding."

He studied her, suddenly as serious as she. "No civil ceremony in a courthouse in front of a judge?"

Sofie bit her lip. Visions of herself clad in a sumptuous white gown, floating down the aisle of a church, assailed her. "Oh, Edward," she whispered.

He cradled her face. "We've been apart for a year and a half. Now that I've found you, I'm almost afraid to let you out of my sight. I want nothing more—*nothing more*—than to be your husband, Sofie. But I understand."

"You do?"

"Yes." He hesitated, his gaze drifting far away. "I have family in California. My father, Rick, my brother, Slade, and his wife, Regina. If we delayed a month, they could attend. I have another brother, James, but no one knows where he is."

"Oh, Edward, I did not know you have family! You've never talked about them!" Sofie was surprised. Somehow he had presented himself as a man without a home, a man without roots, without a past. But everyone came from somewhere.

"Once I was very close to them all."

"Did something happen?"

"It's a long story." He was troubled, his mouth tense. "I'm going to invite my mother, too."

Sofie started.

Edward smiled and kissed her nose. "One day I'll tell you everything, but not tonight."

She understood, but felt a sudden, intense pang of longing herself. Yes, she wanted a real wedding, and Edward was going to allow her to have one, even though it meant waiting another few weeks to marry. But the people she cared most about would not be there. Lisa had run away; Suzanne and she were not speaking. Oh, God. Sofie thought about her mother and tried to imagine her wedding without her there. It was a painful thought.

And as if reading her mind exactly, Edward said, "What will you do about Suzanne, Sofie?"

Sofie looked at him, frozen. "I don't know."

The next day Sofie left the Savoy before ten, after all. She had not been able to sleep well the night before. After Edward had finally left the suite, unable to stay the night with her for appearance's sake, she had lain awake, agonizing over Suzanne.

And in the end the answer was simple. Forgiveness. Although Suzanne had tried to do something unforgivable, her motivation had been to protect Sofie, not to hurt her. And although Sofie had been both furious and devastated, she knew she could not turn her back on her mother forever. The bond was there between them, inseparable, that of mother and daughter; it had been there for too many years, would remain forever. Sofie loved Suzanne. If she had hated her briefly once, perhaps it was because hatred could only spring from love.

And now the hatred was gone. Somehow being reunited with Edward had changed all that. There was only sorrow for a past that could not be changed, and a determination to go forward into a future that promised to be glorious. And Sofie was determined that Suzanne be a part of that future, as she had every right to be.

When Sofie climbed out of the hired hansom, the door of the Ralston residence opened immediately. Jenson stood there, grinning at her. "Miss Sofie!"

Sofie smiled and went to him and kissed him on his whiskery cheek. She had never trespassed across the boundaries between them quite so thoroughly before, and he blushed. "I am getting married, Jenson."

"I am delighted, miss!"

"Edward is at *Delmonico's* engaging the ballroom, and by tonight I will know the exact date. I insist you attend," Sofie said earnestly. "I shall insist that Mrs. Murdock attend, too."

Jenson gaped. "I most certainly will, Miss Sofie—even if your mother dismisses me for it!"

"If she does, you can come to work for me." Sofie hesitated by the stairs. "Is she in her room?"

"Yes."

Uneasy now, Sofie started up the stairs. Outside her mother's rooms, she paused. Then she walked in.

Suzanne was sitting at her dressing table, a maid putting up her hair. Instantly she saw Sofie in the mirror and froze. Then she was on her feet, facing Sofie, eyes wide. "Lucy, leave us, please."

The maid hurried out.

"Hello, Mother," Sofie whispered.

"Sofie." Suzanne blinked back tears.

"Mother, I have come waving a white flag."

"Thank God," Suzanne cried, rushing forward. And suddenly they were in each other's arms, clinging and rocking.

Sofie fought her own tears and looked up at Suzanne, who was wiping her eyes with a kerchief. "Mother, I am getting married, so the issue of giving up Edana is no longer relevant."

"I know. I made a mistake, Sofie. I thought I was doing the right thing, but now I realize I have made a terrible mistake. I am sorry."

"It's all right," Sofie said.

"Can you ever forgive me?"

"Yes. I already have." Sofie went to Suzanne, who began weeping again. She stroked her back. "Now, will you come this afternoon to meet your granddaughter—finally?"

Suzanne sniffed and smiled, nodding slowly.

* * *

"This is a surprise," Jake said.

Edward walked past him into the huge foyer. "I saw you there yesterday. At the exhibition. What in hell are you doing, Jake? Why are you torturing yourself like this?" He faced the older man, hands on his hips. "Come forward, Jake. I'll prepare Sofie for your sudden emergence from the dead if you like. Please. She loves you. Come forward."

Jake stared, eyes glowing, mouth grim and down-turned. "I'm a murderer. She'll run away from me, screaming."

"She thinks you're a hero, not a murderer!" Edward snapped. "She'll be thrilled that you're alive!"

"I'll brand her mother a bigamist. She'll suffer from the scandal, too."

Edward was furious. "Sofie has already suffered from the scandal of having my daughter out of wedlock. But if you want, you know damn well that we can keep this secret. No one needs to know you're alive except for me and Sofie."

Jake wet his lips. "I love her more than I love anyone or anything. I think she would be repulsed, and hurt, and shocked. She has everything now, wealth, respectability, marriage. She doesn't need her father to rise up from the dead to haunt her life now, to jeopardize it all." Jake stared, agonized. "If she runs away from me, I couldn't bear it."

"You don't know your own daughter at all—but whose fault is that?" Edward stormed to the door, then turned. "You're a big fat coward, Jake! Fine! Lurk in the shadows. Do I give a damn?" Edward jerked open the front door. "You missed out on your own daughter growing up—I don't give a damn if you miss out on your granddaughter, too."

Jake stared, expressionless and unmoving.

But Edward wasn't through. "Oh, and by the way, Sofie and I have decided to have a real wedding after all. January first, one o'clock, St. Paul's Church." Edward's smile was hardly pleasant. "But I forgot. A ghost can't attend a wedding—he can only lurk about, hiding in corners!" He turned and slammed out.

Jake sank down into a chair, then covered his face with his hands and sobbed.

"Are you all right?"

Edward glanced at his older brother, Slade, who stood beside him near the front doors of the church, grinning from ear to ear despite the fact that neither one of them wore a coat and it was frigidly cold outside. Ahead of them their father, Rick, and Benjamin stood, greeting the last of the five dozen odd guests invited to attend Sofie and Edward's wedding. Security guards had been hired to keep out the curious public and greedy press. Sofie's exhibition had fueled the gossip surrounding their scandalous love, as had the feature story in *Harper's*, in which Sofie had admitted to falling in love with Edward the moment she had first seen him. They had decided not to use their wedding as a vehicle for more publicity, and newsmen were not allowed to attend the small event, although many members of the press had made it clear that they wished to attend. Still, Edward thought he'd spotted several reporters in the crowd so far, but how they had gotten their hands on invitations, he could not imagine.

"Well?" Slade jabbed him in the ribs. He was naturally swarthy, and just a hair shorter and leaner than Edward. His blue eyes twinkled and teased. Beside him a small, dark-haired boy of almost three gripped his hand, heavily bundled up, watching the milling crowd with wide eyes, and especially the many vehicles, which included several motorcars. "Car," he said. "Go car park?"

Edward and Slade laughed. Edward had taken Nick for a drive in his Daimler the day he had arrived—and he had demanded another drive every day since. "Not today, Nick," Slade said, rubbing his hands. His breath made vapor in the air.

"Go car!" Nick cried.

"Your uncle Edward is getting married," Slade said, then grinned wickedly at Edward. "What's wrong, Ed?"

"You know I could not eat breakfast this morning," Edward growled, in no mood to be teased now, just minutes before actually getting married.

"Got a case of nerves?" Slade laughed.

"You are shameless, teasing him on his wedding day," his wife, Regina, chastised, coming up behind the brothers and linking her arm with Slade's. But she was smiling, a lovely golden-haired woman who was quite clearly pregnant with their second child beneath her fur-lined cloak.

"Thank you," Edward said stiffly. "Of course I am nervous. I never thought I'd actually do this!"

Slade sobered. "You're marrying a wonderful woman, Ed."

Edward gave him a look of utter exasperation. "I am not afraid of marriage—not to Sofie. Not anymore. But I really would have preferred eloping!"

Slade and Regina chuckled. Slade said dryly, "You won't think that way when you see your pretty bride come floating up the aisle with her eyes all shiny with love for you."

"Is that how I looked?" Regina asked, pressing close.

Slade bent his head, kissed her small nose. "Actually, you were terrified."
Regina smiled. "I had better get back to the bride. Nick, Mama's going
back inside."

But Nick was too busy watching the cars to pay his mama attention, and
Regina slipped away after squeezing Edward's arm.

Edward turned away from her; his heart was racing far too fast, and
although it was not hot out, he was sweating. He could imagine Sofie just
as Slade had described, and he was so excited—and nervous—he could not
quite stand it.

Then he stiffened. "Christ!"

Slade came to attention, followed his gaze. "Who is it? A reporter?"

Edward stared at the tall, tanned, golden-eyed man strolling casually past
both Rick and Benjamin—with utterly cool nerve. "Son of a bitch," he
muttered. Then, "I'm not going to let him get away with it!"

And Edward rushed into the church after Jake O'Neil.

Sofie went to the door of her dressing room and pressed her ear against
it, listening to the organ music. It was New Year's Day, nineteen hundred
and three—her wedding day—and her heart beat wildly.

Edward's family had arrived three days ago, just in time for all of the
wedding festivities. Since they had begun planning their wedding, Sofie
had learned that her groom had been born and raised on a California ranch
which had belonged to his family for two generations. She had been thrilled
to finally meet his family, and had been warmly welcomed into their midst.
Everyone had come—his father, Rick, his mother, Victoria, his brother Slade
and Slade's wife, Regina—everyone except for his oldest brother, James,
whose whereabouts were not known. James had been wandering the world
for several years now.

It had been a wonderful reunion for Edward and his family; Sofie had seen
that at once. The two brothers were clearly very close, and father and son
obviously cared deeply for each other. Sofie knew a little bit about Edward's
relationship with his mother before his family had arrived. His parents were
separated and lived apart, and Sofie knew that Edward had not spoken to his
mother in three years. Somehow he seemed to blame her for the separation.
Sofie was very glad that he had ended that nonsense once and for all. She
had seen at once that Victoria missed Edward desperately, that she loved
him as only a mother can love her son. She had sobbed when Edward had
walked into her arms.

Sofie's wedding was almost perfect. Almost.

For Lisa was not there. Lisa was still hiding in Newport Beach. She had telephoned Sofie once to reassure her of her welfare and to learn what was happening with the marquis. Sofie had told Lisa that with every passing day, St. Clare grew more determined to find her and wed her. Sofie had tried to convince Lisa to come home and face him and cry off herself, but Lisa refused. She was certain his pride would finally take the beating she intended it to take, that he would ultimately turn tail and run home to his run-down ancestral estates. Sofie had seen him periodically, and she doubted it. He was more furious than ever as time crept by without his locating his errant bride. More furious and more determined.

Sofie had persuaded Lisa to pen a short note to her father to relieve his tremendous anxiety, and that note had arrived two weeks ago. Benjamin had gone from being severely distraught to furious, and had put his detectives on the new clue to his daughter's whereabouts immediately. Sofie had a bad feeling that Lisa's days of freedom were numbered.

Sofie knew she should not think about Lisa now. Today was a day for joyous thoughts. She had asked Rachelle, Regina, and Victoria to give her and her mother a moment alone, and now she cracked open the door to call them back. It was then that she realized that the music had stopped, and her own heart seemed to stop as well.

"Well, being as the music has stopped, I can only assume that all the guests have arrived and been seated," Suzanne said. "Come, Sofie, we must put on your veil. It is only a matter of minutes until you walk down the aisle."

Sofie began to tremble, assailed with real bridal nerves. In her mind's eye she saw Edward standing at the end of the aisle in his black tuxedo, waiting for her—and then she saw herself gliding towards him in a cloud of white. Excitement, joy, and love washed over her with stunning force, making her feel faint. But now was not the time to succumb to nerves. In a few more minutes the ceremony would begin—and she would finally become Edward Delanza's wife. It seemed that she had waited a lifetime for this moment, for this stunning gift of fate.

"What in hell do you think you're doing?" Edward demanded.

Jake froze. He had just taken his seat in the rear pew and they were alone, the rest of the wedding guests taking up the six front rows. "You know why I'm here. Now, get lost, Delanza."

Edward reached out and gripped Jake's suit by its narrow lapels. "No! The time for games is over!"

Jake paled.

Edward leaned close, furious. "I'm going to drag you in to meet her, Jake, whether you want to or not. If you want to fight and make a scene, hey, that's fine with me. I'm not the one who's going to be sent back to prison if I'm recognized."

Jake slowly got to his feet. "You bastard."

"Sofie needs to know that you're alive."

"Edward—you can't imagine what prison is like. I can't go back there."

"And you won't. Not if you come with me willingly."

"Why are you doing this!?" Jake cried.

"Because I can't stand to see you suffering needlessly like this—you fool." Edward looped his arm in his. "Because Sofie loves you—because I love her."

The two men's gazes met. And finally, finally, Jake nodded.

"Oh, Sofie," Regina cried. "You are stunning—I can't wait for Edward to see you like this."

Sofie smiled at her sister-in-law, a woman Sofie had liked and respected enormously the moment they had met. Regina was not just utterly lovely and elegant and ladylike, but warm and kind and generous. "Thank you," she whispered, her heart pounding at a dangerous rate. "But I fear I may never make it down the aisle—I feel quite faint."

"Come, sit down," Victoria said, helping Sofie sit without wrinkling her full skirts. Rachelle brought her a cup of water, Suzanne gripped her shoulder, and Regina cheerfully slipped smelling salts out of her reticule. "Just in case," she said, smiling.

There was a knock on the door.

"That must be Benjamin," Suzanne said tensely, looking very pale now and on the verge of tears all over again. "Sofie, do you want a whiff of the salts?"

Sofie shook her head no while Regina ran to the door. They both glimpsed Edward standing there with another man at the same instant. Regina immediately tried to slam the door closed on Edward. "You can't see the bride now!" she cried, panicked.

Sofie was standing. "Edward!?" Her initial reaction of gladness at seeing him changed to fear. And she saw the man standing beside him—and it was the golden-eyed stranger she had remarked at her exhibition and at Lisa's engagement party.

"This is important," Edward said, stepping past Regina and into the room. Sofie saw that he held the other man tightly by the arm. Very white, Regina closed the door behind them—and Sofie heard Suzanne cry out.

Sofie turned as her mother crumpled into the chair she had just vacated, tears pouring down her cheeks. "No, no," she moaned.

Stunned, she felt a sudden, dark inkling stab her, one too incredible for Sofie to truly comprehend. She glanced at Edward and the stranger, then sank down beside her mother. "Mother? What is it? What's wrong?"

"Oh, God," Suzanne moaned, covering her face with her hands and weeping.

Slowly Sofie turned. Edward stood before her and he gripped her hands tightly. "Sofie, darling, you're going to be shocked."

Sofie glanced numbly past Edward, whom she trusted with her very life, and at the stranger—who stared at her with heartbreakingly familiar eyes.

"Your father, Jake, is not dead," Edward said. "He never died in that fire. His partner died—he escaped. And he's been hiding from the law ever since." Edward's eyes held hers, intense and urgent, but his tone was soothing and calm.

Sofie jerked her hands free, staring at the golden-eyed man who had always appeared so familiar to her. "No!" she cried, too shocked to think. "My father is dead!"

The man stepped forward, into the center of the room. He was haggard, pale, his eyes glistening. "Sofie, darling, forgive me," he whispered.

And Sofie froze. Because Jake had a distinct voice, a tone she would never forget, one both as rough as sandpaper and as smooth as silk. Their eyes locked. Recognition leapt from deep in her soul, and Sofie gave a small and glad cry.

Jake went rigid as Sofie rushed into his arms.

"Father!" she gasped, hugging him, her cheek pressed against his chest. And as she embraced him, his arms went around her and he leaned over her and crushed her to him, tears pouring down his face.

"Daughter," he whispered. "Oh, God, I never thought I'd see this day."

And behind them, Suzanne had stopped crying, watching fearfully, while Edward smiled, his heart expanding impossibly with joy. The tip of his nose had turned red.

A mad discussion ensued. Sofie wanted details, wanted to know how her father had escaped death and how he had eluded capture by the British authorities these past fifteen years, how long he had been in New York and what his plans were now. She also wanted him to participate in her wedding. Suzanne was speechless, but Victoria, Regina, Rachelle, and Edward immediately voted down that last idea.

"Darling," Edward said to Sofie, "we cannot risk his being recognized even if close to fifteen years has gone by since he fled the country."

Sofie held Jake's hand, squeezed it once, saw that he was in complete agreement with Edward just as she sensed how much he wished he could lead her down the aisle. She nodded slowly, unfortunately just beginning to understand what Jake's presence really meant—and what it might portend. She turned to Edward, wringing her hands. "After the ceremony—Edward—please. Can we delay our honeymoon for a few days?"

He slipped his arm around her shoulders. "Of course we can."

Suddenly Sofie's eyes filled with tears. "This is the greatest gift I could ever be given, Edward. To return my father to me—alive. Thank you."

Edward took her shoulders, pulled her close, and kissed her on the mouth.

A brisk rapping sounded on the door and Slade slipped into the room. "Edward! You'd better get down the aisle, fast, before Reverend Harper comes in here looking for you and sees this little circus and starts asking questions. I've held up Ralston the best I can, but he's getting impatient and he's going to be heading this way himself in another minute, if I don't miss my guess!"

The brothers' gazes held and Edward nodded. "One more minute," he said. Slade nodded and slipped out of the room. Edward looked at Sofie, smiled briefly, then glanced at Suzanne. "Are you all right?"

Suzanne nodded, but she was shaking.

Sofie realized then that Suzanne was seeing Jake for the very first time too. "Mother," she whispered. But then she saw the way that Suzanne stared at Jake, and she wondered if it was their first reunion in fifteen years. But it had to be. The idea that Suzanne had known of Jake's existence for all these years was just too horrible to contemplate.

And Suzanne met her gaze, but only barely. "I'm fine." She lifted her chin, refused to look at Jake. Did not say a single word to him. "Perhaps he had better leave."

Sofie was unmoving, her heart lurching. It occurred to her that many problems lay ahead for her family now, with Jake's sudden reappearance in their lives, but come what may, his being alive and with them was more important than any dilemma they might have to face. Sofie resolved to stand by both Jake and Suzanne, no matter the differences that might arise between them, no matter what scandal might occur.

Jake hugged Sofie again. "This is the greatest day of my life," he told her quietly, "not just to be at your wedding, but to have held you in my arms, to have talked to you as a father does to a daughter. I love you, Sofie. You're the force that's kept me alive these many years when another man might have given up."

Sofie embraced him, too. "I love you too, Father. I always have. I've missed you terribly. We will speak tomorrow at leisure. I am so excited—thinking of all the time we can spend together now."

Jake flashed a grin. "After all these years, I can wait a half day for our reunion." Giving her another kiss, he shook Edward's hand with real respect. "I owe you thanks, Edward."

"They're accepted," Edward said. Then, softly, "Welcome home, Jake."

And humor sparked in Jake's amber eyes. "Welcome to the O'Neil family, Edward," he said, and then he strode from the room.

"My turn to go, before Harper or your stepfather comes searching for you," Edward said. Then his eyes lit up with admiration. "God, Sofie, you are beautiful."

Sofie beamed, her eyes still wet with tears. "I thought you'd never notice."

Sofie listened to the organs rendering Wagner's classic and stately bridal march. Benjamin smiled at her, extending his arm. Sofie took it, tears misting her vision.

Benjamin guided her down the lily-strewn, red-carpeted aisle. Sofie smiled through her tears, and Edward turned to face her from where he stood beside the reverend, as resplendent as she'd always imagined him being on this day. Beside him stood his brother and father, and on the other side of the altar stood Suzanne, Rachelle, his mother, and his sister-in-law. Her glance found Jake, sitting halfway down the church, smiling at her. Sofie looked at Edward again, her heart bursting with joy. As she floated towards him in her cloud of white lace and chiffon, their gazes met and held. Unquestionably this was the finest moment of her life. Fate had blessed her with the greatest gift of all—the gift of love.

Part Four

After

Innocence

Epilogue

*H*er strides were long and brisk as she hurried down Park Avenue, weaving through the throng of noonday pedestrians. She was six feet tall in her two-inch platforms and she wore sleek black leather jeans, a classic white shirt with a black cardigan draped over her shoulders, and a big Donna Karan belt with a triple tier of gold chains. Her hair was thick, black, and cut very short. Everyone she passed, man and woman alike, did a double take, wondering who she was. She was extraordinarily beautiful, and it was said that she took after her grandfather.

Mara Delanza passed under the cream-colored canopy of Delmonico's and paused to allow the doorman of Christie's to open the door and stand back as she entered. Her heart was beating from more than the exertion engendered by her rapid walk downtown. By her careful estimation, Lot number 1502 would come up around twelve forty-five. But if the bidding on the prior lots was very swift, it could come up as early as noon. It was eleven forty-five now.

Mara ignored the several discreetly garbed gentlemen who were security guards and hurried into the auctioning room. Most of the seats were taken. Her heart rate accelerated when she realized that *After Innocence* was to come up for auction next.

Mara slid into an aisle seat in the back row, tall enough that she had no trouble seeing the Vlaminck now being auctioned. The bidding was already up to a hundred thousand dollars. Her mouth had become cotton-dry. She opened her catalog and quickly found the entry for her grandmother's work—the one she had talked about so much—the one she had regretted ever selling.

Lot #1502. After Innocence, by Sofie O'Neil, 1902–1903, oil on canvas. Provenance—Anonymous. Estimated purchase price, $500,000.

Mara shut her book, wishing her grandparents were still alive. How pleased they would be that *After Innocence* was finally reappearing in the public eye after disappearing for ninety-one years. But they had both died in 1972 within six months of each other, well into their nineties but spry and mentally alert and still enamored of each other. Mara had often heard her grandmother lament the fact that *After Innocence* had been sold immediately after her first exhibition in New York City in 1902. The work had been bought by a Russian aristocrat and had been taken out of the country to hang in seclusion with the rest of his extensive collection in one of his palaces near St. Petersburg. That palace had been destroyed in the First World War, or during the revolutions, and everyone had thought the work to have been destroyed as well.

But it had not been destroyed. Somehow it had traveled from a palace in Russia to Argentina, but no one knew how long the work had been in South America, only that it had come to Christie's from Buenos Aires. Gossip had been running rampant in the New York art world ever since Christie's had made its acquisition of the work public. Rumor held that the owner, who insisted upon anonymity, was one of Hitler's last living Nazis, and that he had fled Germany after the fall of the Third Reich with *Innocence* and several other fabulous works of art that he had also looted. As the work had not been seen since its acquisition by the Russian nobleman in 1902, not even in textbook representations, most of New York's art world had been to Christie's all week to view the painting.

Mara had come as well. She had been astounded and overwhelmed by her grandfather's portrait—and never had she been more proud of her grandmother, for her talent, yes, but even more, for her courage and her love.

And the critics were saying that it was the most important work of her grandmother's "early period" and one of the most important in her entire career as well, not as much for its beauty and power as for the subject matter. Mara had often wondered about her grandmother's daring. She had admired her so. How hard it must have been to be a woman artist at the time—and how brave it had been to break taboos long held to by female artists and to risk scandal and censure by portraying a male nude in such an intimate manner.

"Lot number 1502," the auctioneer boomed as the circular stage turned. The Vlaminck disappeared and *After Innocence* rotated into view. Mara made a small cry, tears filling her eyes, as the auctioneer said, "We have an offer of one hundred thousand dollars. Do I hear two?"

It felt as if her heart had stopped beating. Mara gazed at her grandmother's portrait of her grandfather as a young man and was overwhelmed yet again. He was so rakish and so handsome, and she felt as if he might walk out of the canvas and into the room at any moment. Tingles swept up and then down her spine. How beautiful it was. How powerful, how strong. And this was how her grandfather had looked at—and felt about—her grandmother once upon a time.

The bidding had become fast and furious. Mara realized that there were three serious bidders, two men and a woman. One of the men was a young Saudi prince renowned ever since he had paid two million for a Monet four years past. The other man was an agent for a very avid and ferocious Japanese collector. Mara wondered who the woman was. She was in her thirties and looked to be wearing a dark Armani pantsuit, a pair of oversize tortoiseshell glasses hardly concealing a lovely and classic face. Dark blond hair was pulled back into an elegant chignon.

The woman raised her hand, five fingers spread.

Mara sat up straighter, shooting the woman a glance, instantly recognizing her determination.

"Five hundred thousand dollars!" the auctioneer cried. "I have five—do I have six?"

The prince raised his hand. The auctioneer rattled, "Six!"

The Japanese agent nodded. The auctioneer cried, "Seven," and looked at the woman.

She smiled. The auctioneer shouted, "Eight! Do I have nine?"

The prince nodded. The auctioneer looked at the agent. He nodded. The woman raised her finger; her nail was red. The auctioneer was sweating as he turned back to the prince. "I have one million dollars. Do I have one five?"

A sharp nod—but the prince was drawn and tense now, looking worried. The agent had been listening to a cordless phone, undoubtedly receiving his instructions from the Tokyo collector, and his arm shot into the air.

"Two!" the auctioneer cried, turning to the blond woman.

She was cool, unruffled. "Three million dollars," she said in a precise and silken English accent.

The auctioneer's face lit up as he turned to the Saudi prince. Mara tore her gaze away from the woman with an effort, and saw the prince shake his head negatively. She looked at the agent of the Tokyo tycoon. He had gone pale beneath his natural coloring and he was speaking frantically now into the wireless receiver. He looked up and nodded.

"Four million dollars!" the auctioneer cried.

"Five," the woman said.

The agent was on his cordless phone again. The auctioneer stared at him. "Five? I have five!" he cried. The agent was now listening, sweat dripping from his temples. "I have five once, five twice . . ." His gaze was inquisitive.

Mara held her breath. The agent removed the phone from his ear and shook his head. No. The Japanese tycoon would not make another bid.

"*Sold!*" the auctioneer boomed. "*After Innocence* is sold for five million dollars!" His gavel banged down hard on the wood podium where he stood.

Mara sank back in her seat, trembling with sheer disbelief. God—*After Innocence* had sold for five million dollars—beyond the gallery's estimates, beyond anyone's estimates—in a recession year. Sudden elation—euphoria—rose up in Mara, swelled in her veins. How thrilled Sofie and Edward would be if only they knew! If only they knew!

And then she caught a fluid movement of black wool crepe out of the corner of her eye. Mara swiveled to see the woman leaving the room, her strides long and sure. Mara tapped the man in front of her on the shoulder. She knew him vaguely—he had an elitist gallery uptown on Madison Avenue. "Who bought the Sofie O'Neil?" she cried. "Who was that woman?"

The man turned to face her. "I have no idea. I've never seen her before this week—but she was here every day to view the canvas, Mara. Clearly she is an agent."

Mara was frozen. She had to know who had bought *After Innocence*. She had to know—because the oil could not possibly disappear again after so brief an appearance into the art world. It could not. It must not. It was so unfair.

Mara leapt up and dashed down the aisle and through the two swinging doors of the auditorium. She rushed down the green marble stairs. In the lobby she saw the woman exiting through the front door. Mara cried out. "Wait! Wait!"

The woman looked over her shoulder. Their gazes met. Then the woman lengthened her stride, crossing the sidewalk and stepping out into the street, raising her hand for a cab.

Mara ran across the lobby and through the front door. "Wait . . . please!"

But it was too late. The woman slid into a yellow cab and the taxi peeled away before Mara could reach the door to bang on it and stop her. She stood on Park Avenue staring after the disappearing taxi, dismayed.

"*It doesn't matter, Mara.*"

Mara stiffened at the sound of her grandfather's voice, knew she was hallucinating at the very least, but turned anyway, almost expecting him to be standing behind her, smiling in his warm, inimitable way. But no one was there except Christie's doorman, and he raised a brow at her.

Mara turned abruptly, head down, and she began to walk slowly up Park Avenue. She told herself that it didn't matter. They were dead, but their souls lingered; Mara could almost feel them with her, and she knew they were happy and proud. But . . . the painting belonged to the public. Mara knew she could not rest until she had learned who had bought *After Innocence.*

"*And who did buy it, Edward?*"

"*Do you think I know? Come, Sofie, let's leave the mystery to Mara—for I can see that she's dying to solve it.*"

A laugh sounded, soft and feminine. His voice rumbled again, but this time low and intimate, impossible to clearly hear.

But even had a passerby heard the ghostly exchange, no one would have cared. After all, this was New York City in 1993, and stranger things happened all the time.

Dear Reader,

I hope that you have enjoyed Edward and Sofie's story. I'm aware that this may be a departure from my past novels, but these two lovers demanded that I tell their story. I simply couldn't refuse them. I'm currently finishing an epic Elizabethan featuring a powerful pirate hero who finally meets his match in the courageous daughter of an Irish earl. It's a wonderful, lusty adventure that I look forward to sharing with you.

I so love to hear from my readers. Please write to me at P.O. Box 1208, Wainscott, New York 11975.

Happy Reading!